Loukas looked at her unhelpfully. 'For what, Jess?'

'For you sitting here and behaving as if—'

That half-smile again. 'As if I own the place?'

She swallowed, thinking how arrogant he sounded. 'Well, yes.'

'Because I do own it,' he said, suddenly impatient. 'I've bought the company, Jess. I now own every one of the Lulu outlets, in cities and airports and on cruise ships all over the world.'

Shock rippled over her skin. *Stay focused*, she told herself. She kept her voice casual. 'I didn't realise—'

'That I was rich enough?

'Well, there's that, of course.' Her smile felt as if it was slicing her face in two. 'Or that you had an interest in jewellery and watches.'

Loukas touched the tips of his fingers together and stared into eyes which were the exact colour of aquamarines. Jessica Cartwright. The one woman he'd never been able to forget. The woman who had unravelled him and then tied him up in knots. His pale and unexpected nemesis. He expelled a slow breath and let his gaze travel over her at a leisurely pace— because surely he had earned the right to study her as he would any other thing of beauty which he'd just purchased.

'There's plenty you don't know about me.' His mouth hardened and he felt the delicious rush of blood to his groin. *And plenty she was about to find out.*

Sharon Kendrick once won a national writing competition by describing her ideal date: being flown to an exotic island by a gorgeous and powerful man. Little did she realise that she'd just wandered into her dream job! Today she writes for Mills & Boon®, featuring often stubborn but always *to-die-for* heroes and the women who bring them to their knees. She believes that the best books are those you never want to end. Just like life…

Books by Sharon Kendrick

Mills & Boon® Modern™ Romance

Christmas in Da Conti's Bed
The Greek's Marriage Bargain
A Scandal, a Secret, a Baby
The Sheikh's Undoing
Monarch of the Sands
Too Proud to be Bought

One Night With Consequences

Carrying the Greek's Heir

At His Service

The Housekeeper's Awakening

Desert Men of Qurhah

Defiant in the Desert
Shamed in the Sands
Seduced by the Sultan

Scandal in the Spotlight

Back in the Headlines

Visit the author profile page at millsandboon.co.uk for more titles

THE RUTHLESS GREEK'S RETURN

BY
SHARON KENDRICK

First published in Great Britain 2015
by Mills & Boon, an imprint of Harlequin (UK) Limited,
Eton House, 18-24 Paradise Road, Richmond, Surrey, TW9 1SR

© 2015 Sharon Kendrick

ISBN: 978-0-263-25828-8

Printed and bound in Great Britain
by CPI Antony Rowe, Chippenham, Wiltshire

THE RUTHLESS
GREEK'S RETURN

This book acknowledges with grateful thanks the help and inspiration given to me by Piero Campomarte, patron of the Citera Hotel in Venice.

Thanks also to one of the Citera's most famous and favoured guests—Dennis Riddiford.

CHAPTER ONE

SOMETHING WAS DIFFERENT. Jessica felt it the moment she walked into the building. An unmistakable air of excitement and expectation. A rippling sense of change. She felt her throat constrict with something which felt like fear. Because people didn't like change. Even though it was about the only thing in life you could guarantee, nobody really welcomed it—and she was right up there with all those change-haters, wasn't she?

Outwardly the headquarters of the upmarket chain of jewellery stores was the same. Same plush sofas and scented candles and twinkling chandeliers. Same posters of glittering jewels spilled casually onto folds of dark velvet. There were glossy shots of women gazing dreamily at engagement rings, while their impossibly handsome fiancés looked on. There was even a poster of *her*, leaning reflectively against a sea wall and gazing into the distance, with a chunky platinum watch gleaming against her wrist. Briefly, Jessica's gaze flicked over it. Anyone looking at that poster would think the woman in the crisp shirt and sleek ponytail inhabited a life which was all neat and sorted. She gave a wry smile. Whoever said the camera never lied had been very misguided.

Glancing down at her pale leather boots, which had somehow survived the journey from Cornwall without being splashed, she walked over to the desk where the receptionist was wearing a new blouse which displayed her ample cleavage. Jessica blinked. She was *sure* she could smell furniture polish mingling with the scent of gardenia from the flickering candles. Even the extralarge display of roses sitting on the fancy glass desk looked as if they'd been given a makeover.

'Hi, Suzy,' said Jessica, bending her head to sniff at one of the roses and finding it completely without fragrance. 'I have a three o'clock appointment.'

Suzy glanced down at her computer screen and smiled. 'So you do. Nice to see you, Jessica.'

'Nice to be here,' said Jessica, although that bit wasn't *quite* true. Her life in the country had claimed her wholesale and she only came to London when she had to. And today it seemed she had to—summoned by an enigmatic email, which had provoked more questions than it had answered and left her feeling slightly confused. Which was why she had abandoned her jeans and sweater and was standing in reception in her city clothes, with the cool smile expected of her. And if inside her heart was aching because Hannah had gone…well, she would soon learn to deal with that. She had dealt with plenty worse.

Brushing fine droplets of water from her raincoat, she lowered her voice. 'You don't happen to know what's going on?' she said. 'Why I received a mystery summons out of the blue, when I'm not due to start shooting the new catalogue until early summer?'

Suzy started looking from side to side, like someone who had been watching too many spy films. 'Actually, I do.' She paused. 'We have a new boss.'

Jessica's smile didn't slip. 'Really? First I've heard about it.'

'Oh, you wouldn't have heard anything. Big take-over deal—very hush-hush. The new owner's Greek. Very Greek. A playboy by all accounts,' said Suzy succinctly, her eyes suddenly darkening. 'And *very* dangerous.'

Jessica felt the hairs on the back of her neck prickle, as if someone had just stroked an icy finger over her skin. Hearing someone say *Greek* shouldn't produce a reaction, but the stupid thing was that it did, every time. It wasn't as bad as it used to be, but she could never hear the mention of anything Hellenic without the sudden rush of blood to her heart. She was like one of Pavlov's dogs, who used to salivate whenever a bell was rung. One of those dumb dogs who expected to be fed and instead were presented with nothing but an empty bowl. And how sad was that? She stared at Suzy and injected a light-hearted note into her voice.

'Really?' she questioned. 'You mean dangerous as in swashbuckling?'

Suzy shook her mop of red curls. 'I mean dangerous as in oozing sex appeal, and knows it.' A light flashed on her desk and she clicked the button with a perfectly manicured fingernail. 'Something which you're just about to find out for yourself.'

Jessica thought about Suzy's words as she rode in the elevator towards the penthouse offices, wishing they could have swopped places. Because the new boss would be completely wasted on her—no matter how hunky he was. She'd met men who'd oozed testosterone and she'd had her fingers burnt. She stared at her reflection in the smoky elevator mirrors. Actually, it had only been one man and she'd had her whole body burnt—her heart and soul completely fried—and as a consequence she steered clear of *dangerous* men and all the stuff which came with them.

The elevator stopped and the first thing Jessica noticed was that things were different up here, too. More flowers, but the place was deserted and oddly quiet. She'd expected a small delegation of executives or some sort of fanfare, but even the usual rather scary-looking assistant who guarded the inner sanctum was missing. She looked around. The doors to the executive suite were open. She glanced down at her watch. Dead on three. So did she just walk in and announce herself? Or hang around here and wait until someone came out to find her? For a moment she stood there feeling slightly uncertain, when a richly accented voice brushed over her skin like gravel which had been steeped in honey.

'Don't just stand there, Jess. Come right in. I've been waiting for you.'

Her heart clenched and at first she thought her mind was playing tricks. She told herself that all Mediterranean voices sounded similar and that it couldn't possibly be him. Because how could she instantly recognise a voice she hadn't heard for years?

But she was wrong. *Wrong, wrong, wrong.*

She walked into the office in the direction of the voice and stopped dead in the centre of the vast room. And even though her brain was sending out frantic and confused messages to her suddenly tightening body, there was no denying the identity of the man behind the desk.

It *was* him.

Loukas Sarantos, framed by the backdrop of a London skyline—looking like the king of all he surveyed. Big, and brooding and in total command. A mocking half-smile curved his lips. His long legs were spread out beneath the desk while his hands were spread-eagled on the expansive surface, as if emphasising that it all belonged to him. With a shock she noted the expensive charcoal suit which hugged his powerful frame and more confusion washed over her. Because Loukas was a bodyguard. A top-notch bodyguard with clothes which made him blend in, not stand out. What was he doing *here*, dressed like that?

He had been forbidden to her from the start and it was easy to see why. He could intimidate people with a single glance from those searing black eyes. He was like no one else she'd ever met, nor was ever likely to. He made her want things she hadn't even realised she wanted—and when he'd given them to her, he'd made her want even more. He was trouble. He was the night to her day. She knew that.

The room seemed to shift in and out of focus, blurring at the edges before reappearing with a clarity so sharp that it almost hurt her eyes. She wanted the sight of him to leave her cold. For him to be nothing but a distant reminder of another time and another life.

Some hope.

He was leaning back in a black leather chair, which gleamed like the thick hair that curled against his neck. But his half-smile held no trace of humour—it was nothing but an icy assessment which seemed to hit her like a chill wind. His eyes bored through her and for a moment Jessica felt as if she was going to faint, and part of her wondered if that might not be a good thing. Because if she crumpled to the floor, wouldn't that give her a let-out clause? Wouldn't it force him to ring for medical assistance, so that his potency would be diluted by the presence of other people?

But the feeling quickly passed and a lifetime of hiding her emotions meant she was able to look around the room with nothing but curiosity on her face and say almost casually, 'Where's the assistant who's usually here?'

A flicker of irritation passed across his face as he leaned forward. 'Eight years,' he said softly. 'Eight long years since we've seen each other—and all you can do is ask me some banal question about a member of staff?'

His confidence unnerved her almost as much as his appearance, because the brashness of yesteryear seemed to have disappeared—along with the beaten-up leather jacket and faded jeans. Yet even in his made-to-measure suit, he still exuded a carnal sexuality which nothing could disguise. Was that why the almost forgotten aching had started deep inside her? Why she suddenly found herself remembering the burn of his lips pressing down on hers and the impatience of his fingers as he pushed up her little tennis skirt and…and…

'What are you doing here?' she questioned, only suddenly she didn't sound quite so calm and she wondered if he'd picked up on that.

'Why don't you take off your coat and sit down,

Jess?' he suggested silkily. 'Your face has gone very white.'

She wanted to tell him that she'd stay standing, but the shock of seeing him again really *had* affected her equilibrium. And maybe fainting wasn't such a good idea after all. She would only find herself horizontal—and imagine just how disconcerting it would be to find Loukas bending over her. Bending over her as if he wanted to kiss her...when the reality was that he was looking at her as if she'd recently crawled out from beneath a stone.

She walked over to the chair he'd indicated and sank down, letting her leather bag slide noiselessly to the ground as she lifted her gaze towards the empty blackness of his. 'This is a...surprise,' she said lightly.

'I imagine it must be. Tell me...' his eyes gleamed '...how it felt to walk into the room and realise it was me?'

She lifted her shoulders as if there were no words to answer that particular question, and even if there were she wasn't sure she'd want him to hear them. 'I suppose there must be some sort of...explanation?'

He looked at her unhelpfully. 'To what, Jess? Perhaps you could be a little more specific.'

'To you sitting here and behaving as if—'

That half-smile again. 'As if I own the place?'

She swallowed, thinking how arrogant he sounded. 'Well, yes.'

'Because I do own it,' he said, suddenly impatient. 'I've bought the company, Jess—I should have thought that much was obvious. I now own every one of the Lulu outlets, in cities and airports and cruise ships all over the world.'

Shock rippled over her skin. Stay focused, she told herself. You can do it. You were trained in the art of staying focused.

She kept her voice casual. 'I didn't realise—'

'That I was rich enough?'

'Well, there's that, of course.' Her smile felt as if it were slicing her face in two. 'Or that you had an interest in jewellery and watches.'

Loukas touched the tips of his fingers together and stared into eyes which were the exact colour of aquamarines. As always, not a single strand of her blonde hair was out of place and he remembered that even after the most strenuous sex, it always seemed to fall back into a neat and shiny curtain. He looked at the pink gleam of her lips and something dark and nebulous whispered over his skin. Jessica Cartwright. The one woman he'd never been able to forget. The woman who had unravelled him and then tied him up in knots. His pale and unexpected nemesis. He expelled a slow breath and let his gaze travel over her at a leisurely pace—because surely he had earned the right to study her as he would any other thing of beauty which he'd just purchased.

As usual, her style was understated. Classy and cool. A streamlined body, which left the observer in no doubt about her athletic background. She'd never been into revealing clothes or heavy make-up—her look had always been scrubbed and fairly natural and that hadn't changed. He had been attracted to her in a way which had taken him by surprise and he'd never been able to work out why. He noticed how her white shirt hugged those neat little breasts and the subtle gleam of pearls at her ears. With her pale hair pulled back in a ponytail, which emphasised her high cheek-bones, he thought how remote she seemed. How *un-touchable*. And it was all a lie. Because behind the false ice-maiden image, wasn't there a woman as shallow and as grasping as all the others? Someone who would take what they wanted from you and then just leave you—gasping like a fish which had been tossed from the water.

'There's plenty you don't know about me.' His mouth hardened and he felt the delicious rush of blood to his groin. *And plenty she was about to find out.*

'I don't understand…' She shrugged her shoulders and now her aquamarine eyes were wide with question. 'The last time I saw you, you were a bodyguard. You worked for that Russian oligarch.' She frowned as if she was trying to remember. 'Dimitri Makarov. That was his name, wasn't it?'

'*Neh.* That was his name.' Loukas nodded. 'I was the guy with the gun inside his jacket. The guy who knew no fear. The wall of muscle who could smash through a plank with a single blow.' He paused and flicked her a look because he remembered the way she used to run those long fingers over the hard bulge of his muscles, cooing her satisfaction as she touched his iron-hard flesh. 'But one day I decided to start using my brains instead of just my brawn. I realised that a life spent protecting others has a very limited time-scale and that I needed to look towards the future. And, of course, some women consider such men to be little more than *savages*—don't they, Jess?'

She flinched. He could see the whitening of her knuckles in her lap and her reaction gave him a rush of pleasure. Because he wanted to see her react. He wanted to see her coolness melt and to watch her squirm.

'You know I never said that.' Her voice was trembling.

'No,' he agreed grimly. 'But your father said it and you just stood there and agreed with every damned word, didn't you, Jess? You were complicit in your silence. The little princess, agreeing with Daddy. Shall I remind you of some of the other things he said?'

'No!' Her hand had flown to her neck, as if her fingers could disguise the little pulse which was working frantically there.

'He called me a thug. He said I would drag you down to the gutter where I came from, if you stayed with me. Do you remember that, Jess?'

She shook her head. 'Wh—why are we sitting here talking about the past?' she questioned and suddenly her voice didn't sound so cool. 'I dated you when I was a teenager and, yes, my father reacted badly when he found out we were...'

'Lovers,' he put in silkily.

She swallowed. 'Lovers,' she repeated, as if it hurt her to say it. 'But it all happened such a long time ago and none of it matters any more. I've...well, I've moved on and I expect you have, too.'

Loukas might have laughed if he hadn't felt the cold twist of rage. She had humiliated him as no woman had ever dared try. She had trampled on his foolish dreams—and she thought that none of it mattered? Well, he was about to show her that it did. That if you betrayed someone then sooner or later it would come back to haunt you.

He picked up a gold pen which was lying on his

desk and began to twirl it between his thumb and fore-finger, his eyes never leaving her face.

'Maybe you're right,' he said. 'It isn't the past we should be concentrating on, but the present. And, of course, the future. Or rather more importantly—your future.'

He saw her shoulders stiffen. Did she guess what was coming? Surely she realised that anyone in his position would set about terminating her contract with as little fallout as possible.

'What about it?'

He heard the defensiveness in her voice as he twirled the pen in the opposite direction. 'You've been working for the company for—how long is it now, Jess?'

'I'm sure you know exactly how long it is.'

'You're right. I do. I have your contract here in front of me.' He glanced down at it before looking up again. 'You joined Lulu right after you gave up your tennis career, yes?'

Jessica didn't answer straight away because she was afraid of giving herself away. She didn't want to show anything which might make her vulnerable to this very intimidating Loukas. Given up her tennis career? He made it sound as if she'd given up taking sugar in her coffee! As if the thing she'd devoted her entire life to—the sport she'd lived and breathed since she was barely out of nappies—hadn't suddenly been snatched away from her. It had left a great, gaping hole in her life and, coming straight after her break-up with him, it had been a double whammy she'd found difficult to claw her way back from. But she'd done it because it had been either sink or swim, and very soon after that she'd had Hannah to care for. So sinking had never really been an option. 'That's right,' she said.

'So why don't you tell me how you got the job, which I understand surprised a lot of people in the industry, since you had zero modelling experience?' He raised his eyebrows. 'Did you sleep with the boss?'

'Don't be stupid,' she snapped, before she could stop herself. 'He was a man in his sixties.'

'Otherwise you might have been tempted?' He leaned back in his chair and smiled, as if he was pleased to have got some kind of reaction from her at last. 'I know from my own experience that sportswomen have particularly *voracious* sexual appetites. You in particular were pretty spectacular in bed, Jess. And out of it. You could never get enough of me, could you?'

Jessica willed herself not to respond to the taunt, even though it was true. She felt as if he was toying with her, the way a cat sometimes toyed with a dragonfly just before its sheathed paw finally stilled the chattering wings. But for the time being she would play along. What choice did she have when the balance of power was so unevenly divided? Flouncing out of here wasn't an option, because this wasn't just about survival—it was about pride. She might have got the job by chance, but she'd grown into the unexpected career which fate had provided by way of compensation for her shattered dreams. She was *proud* of what she'd achieved and she wasn't going to toss it all away in a heated moment of retaliation, just because the man asking the questions was the man she'd never been able to forget.

'Do you want an answer to your question?' she

asked quietly. 'Or are you just going to sit there insulting me?'

A hint of a smile tugged at the edges of his lips, but just as quickly it was gone. 'Carry on,' he said.

She drew in a deep breath, like one which used to fire her up just before she began a service game. 'You know I tore a ligament, which effectively ended my career?' She stared into his face, but any sympathy she might have been hoping for was absent. His cursory nod was an acknowledgment, not a condolence. There was no understanding in the cold gleam of his eyes. She wondered if he knew that her father had died.

'I heard you pulled out on the eve of a big tournament,' he said.

'I did.' She nodded. 'Obviously, there was a lot of publicity. I was...'

'You were poised on the brink of international success,' he interjected softly. 'Expected to win at least one Grand Slam, despite your precocious age.'

'That's right,' she said, and this time no amount of training could keep the faint crack of emotion from her voice. Didn't matter how many times she told herself that worse things had happened to people than having to pull out of a career before it had really begun—it still hurt. She thought of all the pain and practice. Of the friends and relationships she'd lost along the way. Of the disapproving silences at home and the way her father had pushed her and pushed her until she'd felt she couldn't be pushed any more. The endless sacrifices and the sense that she was never quite good enough. All ended with the sickening snap of her ligament as she ran across the court for a ball she was never going to reach.

She swallowed. 'The papers ran a photo of me leaving the press conference after I'd been discharged from hospital.' It had become an iconic image, which had been splashed all over the tabloids. Her face had been pale and edged with strain. Her trademark blonde plait falling over the narrow shoulders on which a nation's hopes had been resting.

'And?

His bullet-like interjection snapped Jessica back to the present and she looked into the rugged beauty of his olive-skinned face. And wasn't it a mark of her own weakness that she found herself aching to touch it again? To whisper her fingertips all over its hard angles and hollows and feel the shadowed roughness of his jaw. Couldn't he blot out the uncomfortable way she was feeling with the power of one of his incredible kisses and make everything seem all right? She swallowed as she met the answering gleam in his eyes. As if he had guessed what she was thinking. And that was a mistake. It was the most important lesson drummed into her since childhood, that she could never afford to show weakness, not to anyone—but especially not to Loukas. Because hadn't he been trained to leap on any such weakness, and exploit it?

'Lulu noticed in the photo that I was wearing a plastic wristwatch,' she continued. 'And it just so happened that they were launching a sporty new watch aimed at teenagers and thought I had the ideal image to front their advertising campaign.'

'Yet you are not conventionally beautiful,' he observed.

She met the dark ice of his gaze, determined not to show her hurt, but you couldn't really blame someone for telling the truth, could you? 'I know I'm not. But I'm photogenic. I have that curious alchemy of high cheekbones and widely spaced eyes, which makes the camera like me—at least, that's what the photographer told me. I realised a long time ago that I look better in photos than in real life. That's why they took me on. I think they were just capitalising on all the publicity of my stalled career to begin with, but the campaign was a surprise success. And then when my father and stepmother were killed in the avalanche, I think they felt sorry for me—and of course, there was more publicity, which was good for the brand.'

'I'm sorry about your father and stepmother,' he said, almost as an afterthought. 'But these things happen.'

'Yes, I know they do.' She looked into his hard eyes and it was difficult not to feel defensive. 'But they wouldn't have kept me on all these years unless I was helping the watches to sell. That's why they keep renewing my contract.'

'But they aren't selling any more, because you are no longer a teenager,' he said slowly. 'And you no longer represent that age group.'

She felt a beat of disquiet. She told herself to forget they'd been lovers and to forget that it had ended so badly. She needed to treat him the way she would any other executive—male *or* female. Be nice to him. He's your sponsor. *Charm him.* 'I'm twenty-six, Loukas. That's hardly over the hill,' she said, managing to produce a smile from somewhere. The kind of smile a woman might use on a passing car mechanic, if she discovered her car had developed a puncture on a badly lit road. 'Even in these youth-obsessed times.'

She saw the flicker of a nerve at his temple—as if he was aware of her charm offensive. As if he didn't approve of it very much. She wondered if she came over as manipulative but suddenly she didn't care, because she was fighting for her livelihood. And Hannah's, too.

'I don't think you understand what I'm saying, Jess.'

Jessica felt her future flash before her as it suddenly occurred to her why she was here. Why she'd received that terse email demanding her presence. Of *course* he had her contract on his desk. He now owned the company and could do anything he pleased. He was about to tell her that her contract wouldn't be renewed—that it only operated on a year-to-year basis. And then what would she do—a burnt-out tennis player with no real qualifications? She thought about Hannah and her college fees. About the little house she'd bought after she'd paid off all her father's debts. The house that had become their only security. About all the difficulties and heartbreak along the way, and the slow breaking down of barriers to arrive at the workable and loving relationship she had with her half-sister today.

A shiver whispered its way down her spine and she prayed Loukas wouldn't notice—even though he'd been trained to notice every little thing about other people. Especially their weaknesses.

'How can I understand what you're saying when you've been nothing but enigmatic?' she said. 'When you've sat there for the entire time with that judgemental look on your face?'

'Then perhaps I should be a little clearer.' He drummed his fingertips on the contract. 'If you want your contract extended, you might want to rethink your attitude. Being a little nicer to the boss might be a good place to start.'

'Be nice to you?' she questioned. 'That's rich. You're the one who has been hostile from the moment I walked into this office—and you still haven't told me anything.' There was a pause. 'What are you planning to do?'

Loukas swivelled his chair round, removing the distraction of her fine-boned face from his line of vision and replacing it with the gleam of the London skyline. It was a view which carried an eye-watering price tag. The view which reinforced just how far he had come. The space-age circle of the Eye framing the pewter ribbon of the river. Jostling for position among all the centuries-old monuments were all the new kids on the block—the skyscrapers aimed at the stars. A bit like him, really. He stared at the Walkie-Talkie building with its fabled sky garden. Whoever would have thought that the boy who'd once had to ferret for food at the back of restaurants would have ended up sitting here, with such unbelievable wealth at his fingertips?

It had been his burning ambition to crawl out of the poverty and despair which had defined his childhood. To make right a life steeped in bitterness and betrayal. And he had done as he had set out to, ticking off every ambition along the way. He'd done his best for his mother, even though... Painfully, he closed his eyes and refocused his thoughts. He'd made the fortune he'd always lusted after when he'd worked as a bodyguard for oligarchs and billionaires and seen their lavish displays of wealth. He'd always wondered what it would be like to carelessly lose a million dollars at a casino table and not even notice the loss. And he'd discovered that he used to get more pleasure from the food he'd been forced to steal from the restaurant bins when his belly was empty. Because that was the thing about money. The pleasure it was supposed to give you was a myth, peddled by those who were in possession of it. It brought nothing but problems and expectations. It made people behave in ways which sickened him.

Even when he'd been poor he'd never had a problem finding women, but he'd often wondered whether it would make a difference if you were rich. His mouth hardened. And it did. Oh, it did. He felt the acrid taste of old-fashioned disapproval in his mouth as he recalled the variety of *extras* women had offered him since he'd become a billionaire in his own right. Did he like to watch? Did he want threesomes? Foursomes? Was he interested in dressing up and role play? It had been made clear to him that anything he wanted was his for the taking and all he had to do was ask. And he had tried it all. He would have tried anything to fill the dark emptiness inside him, but nothing ever did. He'd cavorted with women with plastic bodies and gorgeous, vacuous faces. Models and princesses were his for the taking. So many things had been dangled in front of him in order to entice him, but he had been like a child let loose in a candy store who, after a few days of indulging himself, had felt completely jaded.

And that was when he had decided that you couldn't move on until your life was straightened out. Until you'd tied up all the loose ends which had threatened to trip you up over the years. His mother was dead. His brother was found. Briefly, he closed his eyes as he thought about the rest of that story and felt a painful beat of his heart. Which left only Jessica Cartwright.

His mouth hardened. And she was a loose end he was going to take particular pleasure tying up.

He turned his chair back around. She was still sitting there, trying to hide her natural anxiety, and he allowed himself a moment of pure, sadistic pleasure. Because he wouldn't have been human if he hadn't appreciated the exquisite irony of seeing how much the tables had turned. How the snooty tennis prodigy who'd kept him hidden away like a guilty secret— while he *serviced her physical needs*—was now waiting for an answer on which her whole future would be decided.

How far would she go to keep her job? he wondered idly. If he ordered her to crawl under the desk and unzip him and take him in her mouth—would she oblige? He felt the hard throb at his groin as he imagined his seed spilling inside her mouth, before changing his mind. No. He didn't want Jess behaving like a hooker. What he wanted—what he *really* wanted— was for her to be compliant and willing and giving. He wanted her beneath him, preferably naked. He wanted to see her eyes darken and hear her gasp of disbelieving pleasure as he entered her. He wanted to feed her hunger for him, until she was dependent on him. Until she couldn't draw a breath without thinking of him.

And then he would walk away, just as she'd done.

The tables would be turned.

They would be equals.

He looked into her aquamarine eyes.

'You're going to have to change,' he said.

CHAPTER TWO

JESSICA'S HEART WAS pounding loudly as she looked across the desk at Loukas, who in that moment seemed to symbolise everything which was darkness…and power. As if he held her future in the palm of his hand and was just about to crush it.

He had begun removing the jacket of his beautiful suit. Sliding it from his shoulders and looping it over the back of his chair and that was making her feel even more disorientated. He looked so…intimidating. Yet the instant he started rolling up his sleeves to display his hair-roughened arms, it seemed much more like the Loukas of old. Sexy and sleek and completely compelling. Her thoughts were skittering all over the place and suddenly she was having to try very hard to keep the anxiety from her voice. 'What do you mean—I have to change? Change what, exactly?'

His smile didn't meet his eyes. In fact, it barely touched his lips. He was enjoying this, she realised. He was enjoying it a lot.

'Everything,' he said. 'But mostly, your image.'

Jessica looked at him in confusion. 'My image?'

Again, he did that thing of joining the tips of his fingers together and she was reminded of a head teacher who'd sent for an unruly pupil and was just about to give them a stern telling-off.

'I can't believe that nobody has looked at your particular advertising campaign before,' he continued. 'Or why it has been allowed to continue.' His black eyes glittered. 'A variation of the same old thing—year in and year out. The agency the company have been using have become complacent, which is why the first thing I did when I took over was to sack them.'

'You've sacked them?' Jessica echoed, her heart sinking—because she liked the agency they used and the photographer they employed. She only saw them once a year when they shot the Lulu catalogue but she'd got to know them and they felt *comfortable*.

'Profits have been sliding for the past two years,' he continued remorselessly. 'Which isn't necessarily a bad thing—because it meant I was able to hammer out an excellent price for my buyout. But it does mean that things are going to be very different from now on.'

She heard the dark note in his voice and told herself to stay calm and find the strength to face her fears. Like when you were playing tennis against a tough opponent—it was no good holding back and being defensive and allowing them to dominate and control. You had to take your courage in your hands and rush the net. Face them head-on. She met his cold, black eyes.

'Is this your way of telling me that you're firing me?'

He gave a soft laugh. 'Oh, believe me, Jess—if I was planning on firing you, you would have known about it by now. For a start, we wouldn't be having this conversation, because it would be a waste of my time and my time is very precious. Do you understand what I'm saying?'

Yes, she understood. She thought how *forbidding* he seemed. From the way he was behaving, nobody would ever have guessed they'd once been lovers. She had seen his ruthless streak before—it had been essential in his role as bodyguard to one of Russia's richest men. But around her he had always been playful—the way she'd sometimes imagined a lion might be if it ever allowed you to get close enough to pet it. Until their affair had finished, and then he had acted as if she was dead to him.

Was that why he was doing this—to pay her back for having turned down his proposal of marriage, even though at the time she had known it was the only thing she *could* do?

She must not let him intimidate her, nor allow him to see how terrified she was of losing her livelihood. Because Loukas was the ultimate predator…he saw a weakness and then moved in for the kill. That was what he had been trained to do. She clasped her hands together and looked at him. 'So why are we having this conversation?'

'Because I have a reputation for turning around failing companies, which is what I intend to do with this one.'

'How?'

He was looking at her calculatingly, like a butcher weighing a piece of meat on a set of scales. 'You are no longer a teenager, Jess,' he said softly. 'And neither are the girls who first bought the watch. You are no longer a tennis star, either—you are what's known in the business as a has-been. And there's no point glowering at me like that. I am simply stating a fact. You were taken on because of who you were—a shining talent whose dreams were shattered. You were the tragic heroine. The sporty blonde who kept on smiling through the pain. Young girls wanted to be you.'

'But not any more?' she said slowly.

'I'm afraid not. You're trading on something which has gone. The world has moved on, but you've stayed exactly the same. Same old shots of you with the ponytail and the pearls and the Capri pants and the neat blouses.' His eyes glittered. 'I get bored just thinking about them.'

She nodded, her heart beating very hard, because it hurt to have him talk to her this way. To have her life condensed into a sad little story which left him feeling 'bored'. She met his black eyes and tried to keep the pain from her face. 'So what are you planning to do about it?'

'I am giving you the opportunity to breathe some life back into your career—and to boost Lulu's flagging sales.'

She wished she'd taken her raincoat off, because her body was beginning to grow hot beneath that scorching stare. She tried to keep her voice calm. To forget that this was Loukas. To try to imagine that it was the previous CEO sitting there, a man with a cut-glass accent who used to ask her for tennis tips for his young daughter. 'How?'

He leaned back in his chair, his outward air of relaxation mocking the churned-up way she was feeling inside.

'By giving you a new look—one which reflects the woman you are now and not the girl you used to be.

We make you over. New hairstyle. New clothes. We do the whole Cinderella thing and then reveal you to the public. The nation's sweetheart all grown up. Just imagine the resulting publicity that would generate.' His eyes glittered. 'Priceless.'

She shifted uncomfortably in her chair. 'You make me sound like a commodity, Loukas,' she said, in a low voice.

He laughed. 'But that's exactly what you are. Why would you think any differently? You sell images of yourself to promote a product—of course you're a commodity. You just happen to be one which has reached its sell-by date, I'm afraid—unless you're pre-pared to mix it up a bit.'

She met the hard gleam of his eyes and a real sense of sadness washed over her. Because despite the way their affair had ended, there had still been a portion of her heart which made her think of him with…

With what?

Affection?

No. Affection was too mild a description for the feelings she'd had for Loukas Sarantos. She had *loved* him despite knowing that they were completely wrong for each other. She had loved him more than he'd ever known because she'd been trained to keep her feelings locked away, and she had taken all her training seri-ously. The way they'd parted had filled her with regret and she'd be lying if she tried to deny that sometimes she thought about him with a deep ache in her heart and a very different kind of ache in her body. Who didn't lie in bed at night sometimes, wondering how different life might have been if you'd taken a differ-ent path?

But now? Now he was making her feel angry, frustrated and stretched to breaking point. He made her want to pummel her fists against him, but most of all he made her want to kiss him. That was the most shameful thing of all—that she was still in some kind of physical thrall to him. She wanted him to cover her mouth with one of his hot kisses. To make her melt. To feel that first sharp and piercing wave of pleasure as he entered her and have it blot out the rest of the world.

She stared into his mocking eyes, telling herself that her desire was irrelevant. More than that, it was dangerous, because it unsettled her and made her want things she knew were wrong. No good was ever going to come of their continued association. He wanted to change her. To make her into someone she wasn't. And all the while making her aware of her own failures, while he showcased his own spectacular success.

Was that what *she* wanted?

'Why are you doing this, Loukas?'

'Because I can.' He smiled. 'Why else?'

And suddenly she saw the Loukas of old. The man who could become as still as a piece of dark and forbidding rock. Foreboding whispered over her skin as she rose to her feet. 'This isn't going to work,' she said. 'I just can't imagine having any kind of working association with you. I'm sorry.'

'You should be.' His voice was silky. 'I've had my lawyers take a good look at your contract. Refuse this job and you aren't in line for any compensation. You leave here empty-handed. Have you thought about that?'

Briefly, Jessica imagined Hannah, happily backpacking in Thailand. Hannah who had defied all expectations to land herself a place at Cambridge University. Her teenage half-sister on the other side of the world, blissfully oblivious to what was going on back home. What would she say if she knew that her future security was about to be cut from under her, by a black-eyed man with a heart of stone?

But as she bent to pick up her handbag she told herself that she would think of something. There were opportunities for employment in her native Cornwall—admittedly not many, but she would look at whatever was going. She could turn her hand to plenty of other things. She could cook and clean or even work in a shop. Her embroidery was selling locally and craftwork was becoming more popular, so couldn't she do more of that? Better that than to stay for a second longer in a room where the air seemed to be suffocating her. Where the man she had once loved seemed to be taking real pleasure from watching her squirm.

Her fingers curled around the strap of her handbag. 'You might want to think about changing your own image rather than concentrating on mine,' she said quietly. 'That macho attitude of yours is so passé.'

'You think so?' he drawled, leaning back in his chair and surveying her from between narrowed eyes. 'I've always found it particularly effective. Especially with women. Most of them seem to get turned on by the caveman approach. You certainly did.'

With his middle finger, he began to draw a tiny circle on the contract and Jessica found herself remembering when he used to touch her skin that way. The way he used to drift his fingertip over her body with such light and exquisite precision. She'd been unable to resist him and she wondered whether any woman would be capable of resistance if Loukas Sarantos had them in his sights.

And suddenly he looked up and smiled—a cruel, cold smile—as if he knew exactly what was running through her mind.

'Yes,' he said softly. 'I still want you, Jessica. I didn't realise quite how much until I saw you today. And you'd better understand that these days I get everything I want. So I'll give you time to reconsider your decision, but I'm warning you that my patience is not infinite. And I won't wait long.'

'Don't hold your breath,' she said, meeting his eyes with a defiant look which lasted only as long as it took her to walk out of his office, her heart pounding as she headed for the elevator.

He didn't follow her. Had she really thought he would? Had there been a trace of the old Jessica who thought he might rise to his feet and cover the distance between them with a few purposeful strides, just like in the old days? *Yes, there had.* And wasn't part of her still craving that kind of masterful behaviour? Of course it was. What woman could remain immune to all that brooding power, coupled with the steely new patina which his wealth had given him?

She shook her head as she left the building, realising that Suzy had been right. He *was* dangerous and the way he made her feel was more dangerous still. Far better that she walked away now and left him in the past, where he belonged.

Hurrying through the emerging rush hour, she caught the train to Cornwall with seconds to spare, but the usually breathtaking journey was shrouded in darkness. The January evening was cold and rain lashed against the carriage windows, seeming to echo her gloomy mood.

She leant her head back against the seat, wondering if she was crazy to have turned her back on a job which had been her security for so long. Yet surely she'd be crazier still to put herself in a situation where Loukas held all the power.

Her love for him might have been replaced by a mixture of anger and frustration—but she was far from immune to him. She couldn't deny the sharp kick of desire when she looked at him, or her squirming sense of frustration. And if that frustration had been unexpectedly powerful, was that really so surprising? Because there had been nobody else since Loukas. No other lover in eight long years. He had been her first man and the only man. Wasn't that ridiculous? And unfashionable? He'd accused her of being stuck in a rut, but he didn't know the half of it.

Because nobody had come close to making her feel the way Loukas had done. She'd *tried* to have relationships with other men but they had left her feeling cold. She stared out of the window as the train pulled into the darkness of a rain-lashed Bodmin station. Other men had made her feel nothing, while her Greek lover had made her feel everything.

Just under an hour later and she was home. But the sight of the little Atlantic-facing house which usually filled her with feelings of sanctuary tonight did no such thing. Rods of rain hit her like icy arrows as she got out of the taxi. The crash of the ocean was deafening but for once she took no pleasure from it. Tonight the sound seemed lonely and haunting and full of foreboding.

And of course, the house was empty. She seemed to rattle around in it without the noisy presence of her half-sister. Jessica listened to the unusual sound of silence as the front door slammed closed behind her. She missed Hannah. Missed her a lot. Yet who would have thought it? It certainly hadn't been sunshine and laughter when Jessica's father had split from her mother, to marry his long-term mistress who was already pregnant with his daughter, Hannah.

Jessica had been badly hurt by her parents' bitter divorce and the news that she was going to have a stepmother and a brand-new baby sister had filled her with jealousy and dread. There had been plenty of tensions in their 'blended' family, but somehow they had survived—even when Jessica's mum had died soon after and the villagers had whispered that she'd never got over her broken heart. Jessica had tried to form a good relationship with her stepmother and to improve the one she had with her perfectionist father. Until that terrible day when an avalanche had left both girls orphaned and alone.

After that, it had been a case of sink, or swim. They'd *had* to get along, because there had been no alternative. Jessica had been eighteen and Hannah just ten when the policeman had knocked on the door with that terrible expression on his face. The authorities had wanted to take Hannah into care but Jessica had fought hard to adopt her. But worse was to come when Jessica realised that her father had been living a lie—spending money on the back of her future earnings, which were never going to materialise. The lawyers had sat her down and told her that their affluent lifestyle had been nothing but an illusion, funded by money they didn't have.

She'd been at her wits' end, wondering how she could support herself and Hannah, because there was precious little left after the big house had been sold. That was why the Lulu job had been such a lifesaver. It had given her money to pay the bills, yes, but, more preciously, it had given her the time to try to mother her heartbroken half-sister in a way that a regular job could never have done.

She had learnt to cook and had planted vegetables. And even though the plants hadn't done very well in the salty and wind-lashed Cornish garden, just the act of nurturing something had brought the two sisters closer together. She had attended every single school open evening and had always been there for Hannah, no matter what. She'd tried not to freak out when the young teenager was discovered smoking dope at a party, telling her that everyone was allowed one mistake. She'd stayed calm the year Hannah had flunked all her exams because of some school bad-boy who'd been giving her the runaround. Instead, she had quietly emphasised the importance of learning and told her how much she regretted her own patchy education—all sacrificed in the name of tennis. And somehow love had grown out of a relationship which had begun so badly.

Jessica had cried when she'd seen Hannah off at Heathrow Airport just before Christmas, with that ridiculously bulky rucksack dwarfing her slender frame, but she had waited until the plane had taken off before she had allowed the tears to fall. Not just because she kept her emotions hidden as a matter of habit, but because she knew this was how it was supposed to be. She knew that saying goodbye was part of life.

And today she'd said goodbye to a part-time modelling career which had never been intended to last. She'd had a good run for her money but now it was time to try something new.

Jessica bit her lip as the rain beat down against the window and tried to block out the memories of Loukas's mocking face. She would think of something.

She had to.

CHAPTER THREE

BUT FATE HAD a habit of screwing things up when you least expected it and three things happened in rapid succession which made Jessica regret her decision to walk away from Loukas Sarantos and his job offer. Her washing machine packed up, her car died, and then Hannah had her wallet stolen while swimming off a beach in Thailand.

Jessica's first thought had been sheer panic when she'd heard the teenager's choking tears on the other end of the line, until she started thinking how much worse it could have been. And once her fears had calmed down to a manageable level, she felt nothing but frustration. But it was a wake-up call and the series of unexpected expenses forced her to take a cold, hard look at her finances and to face up to them with a sinking feeling of inevitability. Was she really deluded enough to think she could manage to live by selling a few framed pieces of *embroidery*? Why, that would barely cover the electricity bill.

She stood at the window, watching the white plume of the waves crashing down over the rocky beach. There *were* alternatives, she knew that. She could sell this house and move somewhere without a lusted-after sea view, which added so much money to the property's value. But this was her security. Her rock. When they'd had to sell their childhood home, this had become a place of safety to retreat to when chaos threatened and she hadn't planned on leaving it any time soon. Especially now. She'd read somewhere that young people were left feeling rootless and insecure if the family home was sold when they went off to college. How could she possibly do that to Hannah, who had already lost so much in her short life?

She thought about what Loukas had said to her, his words both a threat and a promise.

I won't wait long.

She picked up the phone and dialled the number before she had a chance to change her mind and asked to speak him. He's probably no longer interested, she thought, her heart pounding loudly. I've probably offended his macho pride by making him wait.

'Jess.' His deep voice fired into her thoughts and sent them scattering.

'Loukas?' she questioned stupidly, because who else could make her shiver with erotic recall, just by saying her name?

'I'd like to say that this is a surprise,' he said softly. 'But it isn't. I've been waiting for your call, although it hasn't come as quickly as I would have expected.' There was a pause. 'What do you want?'

Jessica closed her eyes. He knew exactly what she wanted—was he going to make her crawl in order to get it? She opened them again and saw another wave crash down onto the rocks. Maybe she *was* going to have to swallow her pride—but that didn't mean she needed to fall to the ground and lick his boots.

'I've been thinking about what you said and on re-flection...' She drew in a deep breath. 'On reflection, it does seem too good an opportunity to turn down. So I've decided to accept the offer—if it's still on the table.'

At the other end of the line Loukas clenched and unclenched his free hand, because her cool response frustrated him far more than her opposition had done. He liked her when she was fighting and fiery, because fire he could easily extinguish. Making ice melt was different—that took much longer—and he had neither the time nor the inclination to make his seduction of Jessica Cartwright into a long-term project. She was just another tick on the list he was working his way down. His heart clenched with bitterness even while his body clenched with lust. She was something unfin-ished he needed to file away in the box marked 'over'. He wanted her body. To sate himself until he'd had his fill. And then he wanted to walk away and forget her.

'Loukas,' she was saying, her voice reminding him of all the erotic little things she used to whisper. She had been an incredibly quick learner, he remembered, his groin hardening uncomfortably. His innocent vir-gin had quickly become the most sensual lover he'd ever known.

'Loukas, are you still there?'

'Yes, I'm still here,' he said unevenly. 'And we need to talk.'

'We're talking now.'

'Not like this. Face to face.'

'But I thought...'

Her voice tailed off and Loukas realised that he *liked* the heady kick of power which her uncertainty gave him. Suddenly he wanted her submissive. He wanted to be the one calling all the shots, as once she had called them. 'What did you think, Jess?' he questioned softly. 'That you wouldn't need to see me again?'

He could hear her clearing her throat.

'Well, yes,' she said. 'I always deal with the advertising agency and the stylist—and the photographer, of course. That's what usually happens.'

'Well, you're wrong. None of this is *usual*, because I am in charge now. I like a hands-on approach—and if the previous CEO had possessed any sense, he would have done the same. You need to meet with our new advertising agency and for that you need to be in London. I'll have someone at Lulu book you into a hotel.'

'Okay.' She cleared her throat again. 'When did you have in mind?'

'As soon as possible. A car will be sent to pick you up this afternoon.'

'That soon?' Her voice sounded breathless. 'You're expecting me to be ready in a couple of hours?'

'Are you saying you can't? That you have other commitments?'

'I might have,' she stalled and something made her say it, though she wasn't quite sure what. 'I might have a date.'

There was a pause. 'Then cancel it, *koukla mou.*'

As his words filtered down the line, Jessica froze, because even though it had been a long time since she'd heard it, the Greek term sounded thrillingly familiar. My doll. That was what it meant. Jessica bit her lip. He used to say it to her a lot, but never with quite such contempt. Once she had trembled with pleasure when he had whispered it into her ear but now the words seemed to mean different things. They seemed tinged with foreboding rather than affection.

'And if I don't?' she questioned defiantly.

'Why not take a little advice, mmm? Let's not get this relationship off on a bad footing,' he said. 'Your initial refusal to cooperate irritated me but your game-playing is starting to irritate me even more. Don't make the mistake of overestimating your own appeal, Jess—and don't push me too far.'

'And is that...' she drew in a deep breath '...supposed to intimidate me?'

'It's supposed to make you aware of where we both stand.'

There was a pause and his voice suddenly changed gear. It became sultry and velvety. It sounded *irresistible.*

'Do you really have a date tonight, Jess?'

She wanted to say yes—to tell him that some gorgeous man was coming round to take her out. A man who was carrying a big bunch of flowers and wearing a soppy grin on his face. And that after champagne and oysters, he would bring her back here and make mad, passionate love to her.

But the vision disintegrated before her eyes, because the thought of any man other than Loukas touching her left her cold. And how sad was that?

'No,' she said flatly. 'I don't.'

'Thavmassios.' His voice dipped with satisfaction. 'Then I will see you later. Oh, and make sure you bring your passport.'

'What for?'

'What do you think? The new team want to use an

exotic location for the shoot,' he said impatiently. 'Just *do* it, will you, Jess? I don't intend to run everything past you for your approval—that's not how it works. It's certainly not how *I* work.'

He terminated the connection and Jessica found herself listening frustratedly to a hollow silence. But there was nothing she could do about it. She was going to have to change her image, if that was what it took. She would accept the makeover and smile for the camera and do her best to hold onto her contract for as long as she could. But that was all she would do. She knew what else he wanted and that certainly wasn't written into the deal.

She didn't have to sleep with him.

She closed all the windows, turned off the heating and emptied the fridge and two hours later a sleek black limousine arrived to collect her, slowly negotiating its way along the narrow, unmade road which led to her house.

It felt disorientating to hand her bags to the uniformed driver and slide onto the back seat as the powerful vehicle pulled away. During the journey she tried to read but it was impossible to concentrate. Her mind kept taking her back to places she didn't want to go— and the past was her biggest no-go destination. She stared out of the window and watched as the Cornish countryside gave way to Devon and found herself thinking about Loukas and the way he used to come and watch her practising, way before they'd got to know each other.

The public footpath used to cross right by their tennis court when she lived at the big house, and she would look up with a fast-beating heart to find a dark and brooding figure standing there. It used to drive her father potty, but it was a public space and he could hardly order the Greek bodyguard away. Not that he would have dared try. Loukas Sarantos wasn't the kind of man you would order to do anything. She'd been a bit scared of him herself. He had been so dark and effortlessly powerful, and the way she'd caught him looking at her legs had made her feel... It was difficult to put into words the way he'd made her feel. She had tried very hard to steer her thoughts away from him and to concentrate on the fact that she double-faulted every time he watched her.

'He will destroy your career!' her father had roared and Jessica had promised that she wouldn't see him— though at that point he hadn't even asked her out.

And then she'd run into him in the village when her father had taken his wife and Hannah up to London and Jessica had been given a rare day to herself. She hadn't gone near a tennis ball all day and that had felt like a liberation in itself. She'd been feeling restless and rebellious and had wandered to the nearby shop to buy herself chocolate. Her hand had been hovering over the purple-wrapped bar when a deeply accented voice had said,

'Do you really think you should?'

She had looked up into a pair of mocking black eyes and something had happened. It had felt like being touched by magic. As if her heart had caught fire. She didn't remember what they'd said, only that he'd flirted with her and she'd flirted back in a way which had seemed to come as easily as breathing—because how could you not flirt with a man like Loukas? He had been exotic, different, edgy and enigmatic, but that hadn't mattered. Nothing had mattered other than the urgent need to be near him.

She'd offered to show him the famous borehole which was set in the surrounding cliffs like the imprint of a giant cannonball. His stride had been longer than hers and she remembered the wind whipping her ponytail as they'd stared down into the dark hollow. He'd told her that it reminded him of the diamond mine owned by his Russian boss, but she hadn't been particularly interested in hearing about diamonds. All she'd wanted was for him to kiss her, and he must have known that, because mid-sentence he'd stopped and and said, 'Oh, so *that's* what you want, is it, little Miss Tennis?' And he had caught her in his arms and his dark head had moved slowly towards hers and she had been lost.

The kiss had sealed a deal she hadn't realised they were making. Jessica had wanted to have sex with him instantly, but something had made her pull back. Because even though she'd wanted him very badly, instinct had told her that he was a man used to women falling at his feet and she should take it slowly. And somehow she had.

Two weeks had felt like an eternity before she'd let him take her virginity, and if part of her had wondered if all that sensual promise could possibly be met, she'd discovered that it could. Oh, it had. For someone who'd spent her life relying on her body to help her win, who had worked through all the pain and injuries, she had now discovered a completely different use for it. An intense pleasure which had made the rest of the world fade away. He had made her gasp. He had made her heart want to burst with joy. She had been hooked on sex and hooked on him.

They had snatched what moments they could and maybe the subterfuge had only added to the excitement. He'd told her his boss wouldn't approve of their relationship and Jessica had known her father would have hit the roof if he'd known. But that hadn't stopped her falling in love with Loukas, even though she would sooner have flown to the moon than showed it. Until the night when she'd blurted it out to him. She could remember even now the slow way he had smiled at her...

And then her father had found her contraceptive pills. Even now she cringed at the humiliating scene which had followed. She should have told him it was none of his business, but she had been barely eighteen and had spent her life being told what to do by someone for whom ambition had been everything. He had confronted Loukas. Told him he had *taken advantage* of his daughter, and had threatened to go to his boss. And what had Loukas done? She bit her lip, because even now it hurt to remember him squaring up his shoulders, as if he'd been just about to step into the fray. In a gruff and unfamiliar voice he had offered to marry her.

And her response? She had said no, because what else could she have said? She'd known he had only been asking her because he'd felt it was the right thing to do and she couldn't bear to trap this proud man in a relationship he'd never intended. Had she been able to see the two of them together—even ten years down the line? No, she hadn't. And if she was being honest, her career had been too important for her to want to risk it on the random throw of an emotional dice. She'd been working towards being a champion since she'd been four years old. Had she really been prepared to throw all that away because Loukas had been offering something out of a misplaced sense of duty?

But her heart had been breaking as she'd ended their affair, even though she'd known it was the right thing to do. She remembered the way he had looked at her, an expression of slowly dawning comprehension hardening his black eyes, before he had laughed. A low, bitter laugh—as if she had just confirmed something he'd already known.

She remembered the way she'd felt as he had turned his back on her and walked away—a clear bright pain which had seemed to consume her. That was the last time she'd seen him, until the moment she'd walked into the penthouse office at Lulu's—a bodyguard no longer but an international tycoon. Jessica shook her head in slight disbelief. How on earth had he managed that?

The slowing pace of the traffic made her realise that they'd hit central London and that the limousine was drawing up outside the Vinoly Hotel, a place she'd never stayed in before. The company usually put her up in the infinitely larger Granchester whenever she was in London and she wondered why they'd sent her here.

The driver opened the door. 'Mr Sarantos says to inform you that a suite has been booked in your name and that you are to order anything you need.'

Jessica nodded and walked into the interior of the plush hotel, whose foyer was dominated by a red velvet sofa in the shape of a giant pair of lips. A Perspex chair on a gilt chain was suspended from the ceiling and impossibly cool-looking young people in jeans and expensive jackets were sprawled around, drinking coffee and tapping away furiously on their laptops.

The receptionist smiled as she handed her a key card and an envelope. 'This was delivered for you earlier,' she said. 'We hope you have a pleasant stay with us, Miss Cartwright. The valet will show you to your suite.'

Jessica didn't have to look at the envelope to know who it was from. Her heart was racing as she recognised Loukas's handwriting—bold and flowing and unlike any other she'd ever seen. She knew his education had been patchy. He'd taught himself to read and write, but had ended up at the age of seventeen without a single qualification, other than a driving licence. But that was pretty much all she knew because he had been notoriously tight-lipped about his childhood. A sombre look used to darken his face whenever she dared ask, so that in the end she gave up trying—because wasn't it easier to grab at rainbows rather than chase after storms?

She waited until she was in her suite before opening the envelope, so intent on reading it that she barely noticed the stark decor of the room. Loukas's message was fairly stark, too.

I trust you had a good journey. Meet me in the dining room downstairs at eight. In the wardrobe you will find a black dress. Wear it.

Jessica's mouth dried. It was an explicit request which sounded almost sexual. Had that been his intention? Did he plan to make her skin prickle with excitement the moment she read it, or to make her feel the molten pull of desire? Walking over to the line of wardrobe doors, she pulled open the first to find a dress hanging there—noting without any sense of surprise that it was made by a renowned designer. It was deceptively simple—a masterpiece fashioned from heavy silk and Jessica could instantly see how exquisitely it was cut. She thought how beautifully it would hang, and wasn't there a tiny part of her which longed to wear it? Because it was a sexy dress. A woman's dress. The kind of garment which would be worn in the knowledge that later a man would remove it.

Heart pounding, she turned away from the temptation it presented and everything else it symbolised and stared defiantly at her own belongings. She resented his peremptory tone and much else besides. He had no right to order her what to wear. The job hadn't even started and already he was acting as if he owned her. Being summoned here within the space of a few hours was one thing, but no way was Loukas going to decide on her wardrobe.

By eight she had showered and changed and was heading down towards the restaurant. Outwardly composed, she announced her arrival to the maître d' but her fingers were trembling as she was shown across the candlelit room to where Loukas was already seated.

This time she was prepared for his impact, but it made little difference to her reaction. Illuminated by the soft glow of candlelight, he was occupying the best table in the room and looking completely at home—as if he owned the space and all that surrounded him. She saw the unmistakable darkening of his eyes as she approached, but the flicker of a nerve at his temple indicated a flash of anger, rather than lust.

And suddenly she began to regret the determination with which she had pulled on a cream-coloured dress which fell demurely to just below the knee. She knew she must appear faintly colourless among the exotically clothed women in the room, but surely maintaining her independence was more important than blending in with the slick, city crowd. More importantly, it would send out a subliminal message to her former lover, telling him that she was still very much her own woman, no matter how much she needed the job.

He said nothing until she had been seated and presented with a menu, but he waved the waiter away with an impatient hand, and when he spoke his voice felt like the brushing of dark velvet all the way down her spine.

'I thought I told you to wear the black dress?'

She met his gaze with the imperturbable stare which had once served her so well on the tennis court. 'No woman likes to be told what dress to put on, Loukas.'

'I beg to differ.' His voice was soft. Dangerously soft. 'Why would you object to wearing a costly gown which would make you look amazing?'

'Because I don't want or need your costly gowns.'

'I see.' Reflectively, his finger moved across his lips. 'And presumably you chose that bland-looking outfit to ensure I wouldn't be attracted to you?'

Jessica felt her cheeks grow hot. She might not have dressed to impress but she knew she looked neat and smart, and it hurt to hear him say something unnecessarily cruel like that. Was that the reason she started defending herself—why she was foolish enough to try? 'You didn't used to complain about the colour of my clothes.'

'That's because I was young and I didn't care what you wore. Actually, I was more concerned about getting you naked.' He paused to slant her a flinty smile. 'Something which was never a problem after your initial reluctance.'

'Well, at least that side of things need no longer concern you.'

'*"That side of things"?*' he mimicked in amusement. 'Don't be coy, Jess. If you're talking about sex, why not just come out and say it?'

'Okay, I will.' Jessica waved her menu in front of him, pleased that the candlelight camouflaged her sudden blush. 'And sex isn't on the menu, I'm afraid.'

He leaned back in his chair and smiled. 'Your defiance excites me,' he said. 'Mainly because I wasn't expecting it.'

'No?'

'No.' He shook his head. 'I thought you might be happy to put on a dress which your average female would lust after.'

'Maybe I'm not your average female.'

'No, maybe you're not.' His lashes came down to half shield the ebony gleam of his eyes. 'I was also wondering whether or not you would be *compliant* and it gives me a perverse kind of pleasure that you weren't.'

'Really?' She raised her eyebrows. 'And why's that?'

He smiled. 'Because if you present a man with a woman who is disobedient, then he is conditioned to want to *tame* her. To sublimate her unruly temperament. And that is something which fills me with anticipation and excitement.'

His words washed over her—edged with an eroticism she couldn't ignore. And suddenly Jessica felt out of her depth. As if she'd underestimated him. As if she'd unwittingly signed up for something more than a change of image and a brand-new advertising campaign. He looked so powerful as he sat there. As if he was playing a game, only she didn't know what that game was. Because although this man looked like Loukas—a very polished Loukas—she realised that he was a stranger to her.

He had always been a stranger to her, she realised with a sinking heart. Hadn't he always kept a side of himself locked away?

But her face betrayed nothing, her smile as polite as if they were discussing nothing more controversial than the January weather. 'Do you really think it's acceptable to invite a woman for dinner and then to talk about taming her?'

This time his smile was edged with definite danger. 'Doesn't that turn you on—a masterful man taking control of a stubborn woman? I must say, it has always been one of my enduring fantasies, my little Ice Queen.'

Ice Queen. Jessica didn't react to that either. It was a long time since she'd heard the term which had dogged her junior years as a player and followed her onto the senior circuit. She had hated it, although her father had approved. He'd said it meant she'd achieved what she'd set out to achieve—a cold unflappability. Or rather, what *he* had set out to achieve. All Jessica knew was that being cold didn't make you popular with the other players, even if the ability to keep your feelings hidden made you a formidable opponent. Not showing when you were angry, or sad, or rattled had distinct advantages when you were playing tennis—just not in real life. It made people think you had no real feelings. It made them call you Ice Queen. And it made men like Loukas Sarantos interested in you because they thought you presented the ultimate challenge.

'I'm not interested in your sexual fantasies,' she said quietly.

'Honestly?'

'No. What I'm interested in,' she said, dragging her thoughts away with an effort, 'is how you've become so incredibly rich.'

'Not right now,' he said, with silky resignation—as if he'd been expecting the question a whole lot sooner. 'Here comes the waiter. Let's deal with him first. Do you know what you want to eat? Perhaps you would like me to order for you?'

Jessica bristled. He was doing it again, just as he'd tried to do with the dress. That whole command *thing* which was teetering on the brink of domination. She was perfectly capable of ordering her own food and she ought to tell him that, but, faced with the prospect of deciphering a long menu beneath a gaze which was making her feel so *conflicted*, Jessica shrugged her acceptance.

She listened while he quizzed the sommelier and the waiter with a knowledge he clearly hadn't acquired overnight. It was strange seeing him like this in public—giving orders where in the past he had taken them. As strange as seeing him in his expensive suit. She was left feeling dazed when they were alone once more and two glasses of white wine had been poured for them. All she knew was that she mustn't let him dominate her. That she needed to start asserting herself, just as she had done so often on the tennis court.

'So are you going to tell me?' she persisted, with a determination which seemed to well up from somewhere deep inside her. From the far end of the room a jazz pianist began playing something haunting and sultry and the music seemed to invade her senses as Jessica stared at him. 'What has happened to you to make you the man you are today, Loukas?'

CHAPTER FOUR

LOUKAS STARED INTO Jessica's aquamarine eyes—as cool as any swimming pool he'd ever dived into—and wondered how to answer her question. His instinct was to tell her that his past and his career trajectory were none of her business. Was her sudden interest sparked because she was turned on by his obvious wealth like most of her sex?

Yet in a way she had been partly responsible for the dramatic turnaround in his fortunes, though not in a way which either of them could have predicted. Her rejection of him had cut deep. Deeper than he could ever have anticipated. Her cool dismissal of his proposal had kicked like a horse at his pride and his heart, leaving him angry and empty. And bewildered. Because hadn't he once vowed to himself that never again would he give a woman the opportunity to hurt him?

'I stopped working for Dimitri Makarov,' he said.

She frowned. 'You mean, you got tired of being a bodyguard?'

Loukas gave a hard smile in response to her question. Yes, he had grown tired of living life through someone else. Of standing on the sidelines. Of always having to abide by someone else's rules and someone else's timetable. And waiting—always waiting.

'It was time for a change,' he said, watching the way her hair gleamed in the candlelight. 'I didn't want to carry on indefinitely and at that stage Dimitri's personal life was so out of control that the two of us were living like vampires. He never went to bed before dawn and, as a consequence, neither did I. We spent our life in casinos and then we'd take a plane to another country and another casino, grabbing sleep where we could.'

His Russian boss had been out of control—and so had he. Each of them running from their particular demons and seeking refuge in the bottom of a whisky glass. On the rebound from Jessica, Loukas had gone from woman to woman, despising them all no matter how much they professed to love him, because hadn't he proved once and for all that you could never believe a woman when she said she loved you?

And then one morning he had woken up and looked in the mirror, barely able to recognise the ravaged face staring back, and had known that something needed to change. Or rather, that *he* needed to change. 'It was time for something new,' he finished flatly. 'A new direction.'

He watched while she took a sip of her wine—a wine as cool and as pale as she was.

'So what did you do?' she questioned. 'Go to college?'

Loukas couldn't hold back the bitterness of his answering laugh, but he waited while their food was placed before them—fish and vegetables stacked into intricate towers standing in puddles of shiny orange sauce. Why the hell could you never get simple food these days? he wondered fleetingly. 'No, Jess—I didn't go to *college*,' he said sarcastically. 'Those kinds of opportunities aren't really a good fit with someone like me. I started working as a bouncer at a big night-club in New York.'

She narrowed her eyes. He thought she looked dis-appointed. Was that still too *thuggish* an occupation for someone of her delicate sensibilities to accept?

'And what was that like?' she asked politely, like someone making small talk at a cocktail party.

'It was like every man's fantasy,' he said softly and now he could see the surprise in her eyes, and yes, the hurt—and suddenly he found that he was enjoy-ing himself and that he wanted to hurt her some more. To hurt her as she had hurt him. 'It's a power trip to be in a position like that,' he drawled softly. 'It gives you a kick to turn away people with overstuffed wal-lets who ask if you know who they are. Not a particu-larly admirable admission—but true. And women love bouncers. *Really* love them,' he finished deliberately. 'It's one of the perks of the job.'

She had been sawing at a piece of pumpkin on her plate, but suddenly she put her fork down and he no-ticed that her hand was trembling. And that was un-usual, he thought with satisfaction, because Jess had always had the steadiest hands of anyone he'd ever known. Hands that could throw a tennis ball up to a certain height with pinpoint accuracy. Hands that could smash a ball into kingdom come. He could see the faint uncertainty in her eyes as she asked the in-evitable question.

'And I suppose there must have been, well...*lots* of women?'

He shrugged, because if a female asked you a question as dumb as that, then they deserved to hear the answer. He thought about the pieces of paper slipped into his hand or stuffed into the pockets of his jacket. About waking up in vast bedrooms on the Upper East Side with some sinewy heiress riding him until he cried out. The tiny thong he'd found stuffed in his jacket pocket when he'd been going through airport security and the knowing wink of the uniformed official when he'd seen it. He smiled. 'Enough,' he said succinctly.

'But bouncers don't get to be big bosses,' she said, her words sounding forced and rushed, as if she suddenly wanted to change the subject. 'They don't get to own companies the size of Lulu.'

'No, they don't.' He picked up his wine and swirled it round in the glass, thinking that at one time he could have lived for a month on the money this bottle had cost.

'So, how...' she waved her hand through the air, as if he owned the expensive restaurant too '...did you get all this?'

He drank some wine. 'I started to hear rumours that Dimitri's new protection was not to be trusted. And then one day his secretary contacted me and begged me to help. I'd left months before and didn't want to get involved, but she was worried sick—crying down the phone and telling me she thought he was in danger. So I travelled to Paris to talk to him but by that time he had become so big that he thought he was invincible. He agreed to see me, but he wouldn't believe any of the things I'd discovered about the people he was associating with.' His mouth hardened into a grim line. 'Dimitri only ever listened when it was something he wanted to hear. So I gave up trying and planned to take a flight out of the city that same night.'

'But something...stopped you?' she said, breaking into the sudden silence as his words tailed away. And suddenly her eyes were very wide, as if she'd seen something in his face which she wasn't supposed to see.

'Yes, something stopped me,' he agreed grimly. 'It transpired that his new bodyguard was connected to a gang who were on the brink of stealing from my ex Russian boss, and my presence in the city was seen as a bonus, because I knew more about Dimitri's affairs than anyone else. And that pretty much sealed my fate. They captured me on the way to Charles de Gaulle airport.'

'They *captured* you?' she said, only now her voice had a break in it, as if she didn't quite believe the words she was saying. 'What...what happened?'

For a moment the only sound was the tinkly little flourish which came at the end of the jazz player's song and the smattering of applause which followed.

He shrugged. 'They beat me and threatened me. Said I would die unless I told them what they wanted to know.'

'They said you would *die*?' Her face had gone completely pale.

'It's the underworld's way of suggesting you hand over the information they want,' he said sardonically.

And...did you?'

'Are you crazy?' He picked up his glass but this time he didn't drink from it. 'I was expecting to die anyway, so I was damned if I was going to tell them anything first.'

She was blinking at him as if she'd never really seen him before. 'You thought you were going to *die*?'

He heard the frightened squeak of her voice and thought how protected she'd always been. But then, most people had been protected from the kind of worlds he had inhabited. 'Yeah,' he agreed with soft sarcasm. 'Just like something out of a film isn't it, Jess?'

She shook her head, as if his flippancy was inappropriate. 'So what saved you?'

He shrugged. Tonight the wine tasted good, just as everything had tasted good when he'd first been released. He remembered falling to his knees on the dank concrete of that underground car park with drops of blood dripping darkly from his nose, telling himself that never again would he take anything for granted. But he had, of course. He'd discovered that gratitude didn't last very long.

'Dimitri started to believe that maybe I had been speaking the truth and some hunch made him have me followed to the airport. They got to me in the nick of time, and when I was brought back to his place and he saw the state I was in, I think it made him realise he couldn't carry on the way he was—something his secretary had been telling him for a long time. And he gave me diamonds as a reward for what I'd done.'

'Diamonds?' she questioned blankly.

'He owns one of Russia's biggest mines. He gave me jewels which were priceless and he told me to learn to love them.' He saw her flinch at the word, as if he had just sworn. And maybe he had. Maybe it was easier to think of love as a profanity than as something which was real. He remembered Dimitri's words as he had run his fingers through the glittering cascade. *Learn to love these cold stones, my friend, for they are easier to love than women.*

'And did you?' Jess's cool voice broke into his thoughts. 'Learn to love them?'

He smiled. 'I did. It's easy to love something which is so valuable, but I developed a genuine interest in them. They began to fascinate me. I liked their beauty and perfection and the way all that value could be hidden in the pocket of a man's jacket. I liked the fact that they only ever increase in value and I cannot deny that it gave me pleasure to realise their power over people. Women will do pretty much anything for diamonds,' he said deliberately.

'Will they?' came her light answer, as if she didn't care.

'Some I sold and others I kept,' he continued. 'I'm planning to use some of them as the centrepiece of the new launch. No more wristwatches for you from now on, my blue-eyed doll. You will wear my diamonds, Jess.'

She moved the palm of her hand so that it lay on her breastbone, like someone who had grown suddenly short of breath, but the movement only drew attention to the little pulse which was hammering at the base of her throat.

'So was...' she seemed to pick her words carefully '...was the fact that you bought Lulu just a coincidence?'

'In what way?'

She opened her lips slowly, like someone afraid of setting off a verbal landmine.

'You didn't just buy Lulu because I was working there?'

He gave a soft laugh. 'What do you think?'

'I'm not…I'm not sure.'

But Loukas knew she was lying. Would the Lulu takeover have been *quite* so enticing if she hadn't been involved? Of course not. Plenty of business opportunities came his way and his emotions were never involved. But this was different and it was because of Jess. He felt the sudden hardening of his groin. Because didn't her involvement guarantee the kind of satisfaction which went way beyond mere profit and loss?

'I heard the company was struggling because the management had become lazy, and I realised that I could turn it around. Take a famous brand and bring it bang up to date and you can't fail.' He smiled. 'And you know what they say…buy weak, sell strong.'

She was looking at him in faint surprise, as if she hadn't expected the slick soundbites of the professional negotiator to come from his lips. He felt the flicker of anger. *Because deep down she still thinks of you as a thug. A wall of muscle, without a life of your own or a brain you might be capable of using.*

'But of course your connection to the company made the prospect irresistible,' he said softly. 'Because I wanted to see you again.'

To see whether his desire for her had diminished. Whether the sight of her cool face would leave him cold. He glanced at her untouched plate and his gaze moved upwards. He saw the way the candlelight flickered over her neat breasts and suddenly he was overcome by a wave of lust so powerful that if he had been standing up, it might have knocked him off his feet. Because surprise, surprise, he thought bitterly, it hadn't left him—his desire hadn't left him at all. If anything, it had only increased—as if the years in between had only sharpened his sensual hunger. Right now it was consuming him like a newly lit fire and when he looked at those cool, parted lips he wanted to lean across the table and crush them beneath his. To slide his hand beneath her dull little dress. To move his fingers against her heated flesh. To bring her to a disbelieving orgasm and then have her suck him sweetly to his own.

His mouth hardened.

So what was he planning to do about it?

'You're not eating, Jess,' he said and he could hear how husky his voice sounded. He wondered if she was aware how heavy his groin felt, hidden by the snowy drapery of the tablecloth.

'Neither are you.' She pushed her plate away and nodded her head, as if she'd come to some kind of decision. 'And I'm not surprised. This meal was a bad idea. Just because we're going to work together doesn't mean we have to eat together. I'm going back to my room. I'll order something from Room Service.'

'I'll get the check and come with you.'

'No, honestly. You don't have to.' She licked her lips and gave a forced kind of smile. 'In fact, I'd much rather you didn't.'

'I insist.'

His silky determination silenced her and Jessica watched as he summoned the waiter and signed the check. She wondered if he cared how their behaviour must look to other people. Did the waiter consider it odd? Two people barely touching the amazing food or spectacular wine which had been placed before them. Two people sitting opposite one another, their bodies stiff and tense, looking as if they were engaged in some silent battle when in reality they were trying to ignore the sexual hunger still burning between them. She was aware of people watching as they weaved their way through the tables. The velvet-lined doors swung softly closed behind them, blotting out the faint chatter and low strains of music—and Jessica psyched herself up to say a dignified goodnight.

'Thanks, Loukas.'

'There's nothing to thank me for. I'll see you to your room.'

'But—'

He cut across her objection before she'd had a chance to voice it. 'Again, I insist.'

What else would he try to insist on? she wondered desperately as the elevator doors slid together, shutting out the rest of the world.

She tried to drag her gaze away from the chiselled perfection of his face. The elevator felt claustrophobic. Worse than that—it felt dangerous. There was no giant desk or restaurant table between them now, only a limited space so that he felt much too close, yet much too far. She could practically feel the heat radiating from his powerful body and the air seemed full of the scent which was so uniquely Loukas. She closed her eyes and breathed it in. A hint of citrus cut with spice, and underpinned with a raw and potent masculinity which took her straight back to the past. It filled her lungs, reminding her of all the pleasure he'd brought her. Reminding her of his hard kisses and soft kisses and all the in-between kisses. Of how he used to thrust so deep inside her. The first time, when it had hurt. And the second time, when it had felt as if she'd gone to heaven.

Could he hear the increased breathing, no matter how hard she tried to control it? Probably. His sense of hearing was acute—just like all his other senses. It was one of the things which had made him such a good bodyguard, as well as being such an amazing lover.

And suddenly Jessica found herself resenting the fact that he hadn't so much as touched her. He hadn't even done what anyone else in his position would have done—given her a cool kiss on either cheek when she'd walked into his office. No matter what he was feeling inside, that would have been the civilised thing to do.

But Loukas wasn't civilised, was he? Beneath the exquisite suit and unmistakable veneer of wealth, he was still the same man he'd always been. Basic and primeval and oozing testosterone. But he wasn't acting on it. He wasn't acting out her vivid fantasy of playing the primitive male and pinning her up against the wall and just *taking* her, as he'd done so often in the past.

Did he guess what she was feeling—or wanting? Was that why he was looking at her with that infuriating half-smile on his lips, which was completely at odds with the hunger which had begun to spark like dark fire in the depths of that burning gaze?

She found herself praying they would reach her floor soon, yet part of her never wanted to get there. She wanted to stay here, trapped in this small moving box with him—just the two of them—until one of them cracked.

Did she give herself away?

Was there some small movement which indicated

the struggle she was having with herself? She wondered if she'd wriggled slightly or whether something about her posture had indicated that her breath felt as if it were trapped in the upper part of her throat.

'Oh,' he said slowly, his words suddenly shattering the fraught silence, as if she had just said something which required an answer. 'It's like that, is it?'

And he reached out to cup her chin with his hand, drawing his thumb almost lazily over lips which had begun to tremble uncontrollably. The mere touch of him was electrifying, the effect of it so profound that her head jerked, like a puppet on a string. Jessica's heart began to pound as he slipped the thumb inside her mouth and she couldn't seem to stop him from doing it, even if she'd wanted to. Pavlov's dog, she thought helplessly, aware that he was watching her, still with that infuriating half-smile on his face.

Her eyes had fluttered to a close as her lips closed round the thumb, and she wondered if that was to avoid the mockery in his eyes or because it meant she could pretend. Pretend that this was a normal interaction between a man and a woman, instead of one tainted with bitterness and regret. She felt him move the thumb very slightly—in and out, in and out—demonstrating a provocative mimicry of sex. *Kiss me,* she prayed silently as she sucked. Take some of this aching away and *just kiss me*.

'Open your eyes, Jess.'

Reluctantly, her lashes fluttered open and she found herself meeting the hardness of his piercing black gaze.

'Do you want me to kiss you?' he questioned softly as he withdrew the thumb so slowly that she almost groaned.

Had he read her mind, or had she said the words out loud without realising? Reluctantly, she nodded her head in silent acquiescence.

'Then ask me. Ask me nicely and I'll consider it.'

The corresponding rush of resentment gave her a last-minute reprieve and she glared at him. You don't have to do this, she told herself. You don't have to do what he says. 'Don't play games with me, Loukas.'

'I thought games were your speciality.'

'Go to hell.'

And then he *did* kiss her, laughing a little as he pulled her against him—his hard body driving every objection clean from her mind. All she could think about was how strong he was, and how good it felt to be back in his arms. Within the circle of his powerful embrace she felt warm, like an ice cube which had started to melt. She felt *safe*. But that didn't last long... And maybe that was the wrong description, because how could she possibly feel safe when his hands were sliding down over her breasts like that and making her moan with pleasure? It felt the opposite of safe when her nipples were thrusting against her dress and aching for him to bare them.

The lift pinged to a halt and Jessica felt the punch of frustration as Loukas dragged his mouth away from hers. His gaze was smoky, his expression suggesting he'd been as blown away by that kiss as she had. But his look of sensual surrender quickly cleared and was replaced by a cold-eyed assessment. For a minute she thought he was about to hit the button to send them back down the way they'd come—as if their evening would be spent riding an elevator which represented a private and no-threat world where none of the normal rules applied.

But she was wrong. He kept his finger firmly on the *doors open* button as his black gaze sizzled over her.

'So,' he said.

'So,' she repeated, more to gain time than anything else.

'Aren't you going to invite me inside?' he questioned.

Every fibre of her being was screaming at her to say yes. To open the door and do what she wanted to do more than she could remember wanting anything. She knew exactly what would happen. The look on his face told her that it would be quick. He would rip at her clothing. Push aside the damp panel of her panties with impatient fingers. She could almost *hear* the rasp of his zip as she pictured him freeing himself. Her fingers were itching to reacquaint themselves with that silken, steely shaft—to rub it up and down until he began to groan...

Blood rushed through her veins as she thought of that first intimate touch just before he entered her—the moist tip of him pressing against her—and she could have wept with longing and frustration. Would he be able to tell that there had been no lover since him? That he had been the one and only man she'd ever been intimate with? Would he laugh in disbelief if he knew, or would it simply make him gloat with insufferable pride? That he was still able to make her—the cool and contained Jessica Cartwright—into someone she barely recognised.

He had offered her the job and was now making it very clear that he wanted her. For a man with Loukas's reasoning, one would automatically follow the other. Payback time. And would that be such a terrible thing? If she had sex with him again it might make her look at things more rationally. Reassure herself that she'd built him up in her mind because she'd been young and impressionable. And this was a modern world, wasn't it? She should be able to sleep with whom she pleased.

She opened her mouth to say yes, but something stopped her—and that something was the look in his eyes. Was that *triumph* she could read there?

Some of the heat left her blood. She thought about how she'd feel in the morning if she woke up and found him beside her. Would she be able to deal with the aftermath of such a rash act? She doubted it. Because intimacy terrified her. It brought with it hurt, and pain. And surely only a fool would do something in the knowledge that it was going to bring them pain.

She shook her head. 'No, Loukas,' she said. 'I'm not.'

He bent his head forward, as if he didn't believe her, as if he could change her mind by shortening the physical distance between them. His breath was warm against her face.

'Are you sure?' he whispered.

It took every bit of will power she possessed to step back and shake her head, but will power was something she was good at. It was will power which had made her stand outside in all weathers, smashing ball after ball over the net while her father shouted at her. Will power which had dragged her out of bed on those cold winter mornings while the rest of her school-friends had snuggled beneath the duvet while their mothers made toast.

'Quite sure,' she answered. 'I'm going to bed. Alone. Goodnight.'

The faint flare of surprise she saw in his eyes gave her no real pleasure. It didn't cancel out the ache in her body or the yearning in her heart. Stepping inside her suite, she shut the door on his hard and beautiful face and resisted the desire to smash her fist against the wall.

CHAPTER FIVE

FRUSTRATION WAS NEVER a good feeling to wake up to, but Jessica supposed it was preferable to regret.

Standing beneath the pounding jets of the shower, she scrubbed furiously at her skin, as if doing that would wash the Greek from her memory, but nothing could shift the annoying thoughts going round and round inside her head. Had she been crazy not to invite Loukas into her suite, to kill the fantasy of her ex-lover once and for all? To make her realise that she'd been building him up into some kind of god for all these years, when in reality he was a mere mortal?

She reminded herself of the evening they'd shared. He had shown her no real affection, had he? He had taken her to dinner, then made a cold-blooded move on her afterwards. He had made her feel more like a potential conquest than an object of desire. Was she so desperate for sex that she was regretting not having settled for *that*? No, she was not. She needed to keep her wits about her and she needed to stay in control.

Pulling on a pair of linen trousers, she buttoned up her shirt and twisted her hair into a bun and was just clipping pearl studs into her ears when the phone beside the bed shattered the silence. She hesitated for a moment before picking up the handset. 'Yes?'

'Sleep well?'

The deep voice washed over her like dark honey. It made staying in control seem like the hardest thing in the world.

'Like a log,' she lied. 'Did you?'

'No, not really.' His voice dipped. 'I kept being woken up by the most erotic dreams imaginable and they all seemed to involve you. I blame you for my disturbed night, Jess.'

'Because you didn't get what you wanted?'

Loukas didn't answer. If only it were as simple as that. If only his frustration could be put down to the fact that she'd stopped him making love to her—but it wasn't that simple. It was starting to feel *complicated* and he didn't do complicated. Why had it become so important to possess her again, and why was she so determined to fight him?

He knew she wanted him—she'd made that very clear—and yet she had resisted. He wondered if she revelled in the power it gave her—to tap into that icy self-control which she pulled out just when you were least expecting it. She had fallen apart in his arms the moment he'd touched her, and yet still she had said no.

His mouth hardened. He was aware that he had the double standards of many men to whom sex had always come easily, but his attitudes had been reinforced by the unhappiness of his childhood and the things he had witnessed. Those things had soured him towards the opposite sex and the women he had met subsequently had done little to help modify his prejudices.

But Jess was different. She had always been different. Not just because she was streamlined and blonde, when his taste had always tended towards fleshy brunettes. She was the one woman who had walked away from him. The one he had never been able to work out. She had that indefinable something called *class*, which no amount of money could ever buy. It had been her aloofness which had first drawn him to her—something he'd never come into contact with before. That sense of physical and emotional distance had fascinated him and so had she. She was the first woman he'd ever had to woo. The first—and only—woman he'd ever bought flowers for. Had she secretly laughed at his cheap little offering—when sophisticated bouquets had awaited her when she walked off the tennis court? He'd often wondered whether it had been her secret fantasy to take someone like him as her first lover. Someone as unlike her as possible. Someone who knew what it was all about, but who could safely be discarded afterwards. Her *piece of rough*. Had he served his purpose by deflowering her and introducing her to pleasure?

He considered the options which lay open to him. He could walk away now. Leave the new advertising campaign in the hands of the experts, and keep his own input to the bare minimum. Or he could pay her off with an overinflated sum, since money was the reason she was here. He could find a fresher, newer model, with none of the baggage which Jessica Cartwright carried. And he could easily find himself another lover. One who would not cold-bloodedly shut the door in his face, but who would welcome him with open arms and open legs.

But he had not finished with her. Not yet. His list

was not yet completed. He had met his brother. He had dealt with his mother's betrayal and uncovered all the dark secrets she had left behind. He had built up a fortune beyond his wildest dreams. He had made some of his peace with the world, so that only Jessica remained—and he needed her. He needed to take his fill of her, because only then would he be free of her and able to walk away.

'Maybe I didn't get what I wanted last night, *koukla mou*,' he said softly, 'but I always get there in the end.'

He heard her suck in a deep breath.

'What happened between us last night. You must realise that it changes everything.'

He affected innocence. 'How?'

There was a moment of silence. He could hear her searching for words. He wondered if she would try to hide behind those polite little platitudes which didn't mean a thing.

'I can't possibly work alongside you now!'

'Don't make such a big deal out of it, Jess,' he said. 'Our bodies are programmed to react towards each other that way. You want me and I want you. We've always had chemistry. Big deal. We're both grown-ups and neither of us are in relationships—at least, I'm not and I'm assuming you aren't either.'

'Isn't that something you should have asked me before you leapt on me in the elevator?'

'I don't know if I would describe it as *leaping*,' he commented drily. 'And I was assuming you might have put up some kind of objection had that been the case.'

'How do you manage to twist everything I say?'

'Is that what I am doing, *koukla mou*?' he questioned innocently.

'You know you are.'

'So why don't we put down what happened to curiosity and leave it at that? The advertising team want to meet you at their offices,' he added. 'My car will be outside your hotel at eleven.'

Jessica was left staring at the phone as he did that frustrating thing of ringing off before she felt the conversation was finished. Though really, what was there left to say? She ordered breakfast from Room Service, nibbling half-heartedly on a piece of wholemeal toast, and drank two cups of coffee strong enough to revive her. But when she went down to the front of the hotel just after eleven, it was to find Loukas sitting in the back of a car parked directly outside, reading through a large sheaf of documents.

'Oh, it's you,' she said as he glanced up, and was caught in his ebony gaze. Her heart gave a punch of excitement she didn't *want* to feel, but was it really so surprising that she was reacting to him? Last time she'd seen him he'd had his tongue down her throat and she had been in danger of dissolving beneath his touch. Was he remembering that, too? Was that why his eyes were gleaming with inky provocation and his lips had curved into a mocking smile?

'Yes, Jess. It's me.'

She swallowed as the driver shut the door behind her. 'I wasn't expecting to find you here.'

'But hoping you might?'

'You're…'

'I'm what, Jess?'

She shook her head. 'It doesn't matter.'

'Oh, come on,' he taunted softly. 'Why hide behind that frozen expression you're so fond of—why not come out and say just what you're thinking for once?'

She stared at him, her heart beating very fast, and suddenly she thought, What the heck? Why *shouldn't* he know how she felt about him? She wasn't on a tennis court now and he wasn't her opponent. Well, he *was*, but not in the traditional sense. What did it matter if she was honest with him—the world wouldn't stop turning if she told him the truth, would it? But it wasn't easy to voice her emotions, when she'd been drilled to keep them hidden away ever since she could remember. Wasn't that why sex with him had been so wonderful—and so scary—because it had knocked all those barriers down, and for a little while had made her feel free? 'Actually, you're the last person I wanted to see.'

'Liar,' he said softly. 'Stop pretending—most of all to yourself. Your body language gave you away the moment you saw me again. Even you can't disguise the darkening of your eyes or the unmistakable tightening of those delicious breasts.'

'How come you're even *here*?' she said crossly as the car pulled away from the kerb.

He laughed. 'I live here.'

'You live in a hotel?'

'Why not?'

'Because…because a hotel is somewhere you stay. It's not a real home.'

'For some people it is.'

Loukas stared out of the window as the streets of London passed them by. Would it shock her to discover that he'd never really had a home of his own, just a series of places in which to stay? He remembered the too-thin curtain at one end of the room, and the saving grace of the cotton-wool plugs which he'd crammed into his ears and which had blotted out most of the sounds. 'Actually, it's ideal for all my needs,' he said. 'It's big, it's central and there are several award-winning restaurants just minutes away from my suite. I send out for what I want. My car gets valet parked and there is effective security on the door. What's not to like?'

'But don't you like having all your own things around you?'

He turned back to look at her. 'What things?'

She shrugged. 'Oh, you know. Pictures. Ornaments. Photos.'

'The clutter of the past?' He smiled. 'No. I'm not a big fan of possessions. I try to live by the maxim that you should always be able to walk away, with a single suitcase and your passport.'

She frowned. 'But what about the future? Do you plan to live in a hotel for ever—is that what you want?'

'There is no future,' he said softly. 'There is only what we have right now and right now all I want to do is kiss you, but unfortunately there isn't time.' He reached for his jacket. 'We're here.'

Heart pounding, Jessica stared out of the car window. 'Here?'

'Zeitgeist. The best advertising agency in London.'

She looked up at the cathedral-high dimensions as they entered the modern building, forcing herself to concentrate on her surroundings instead of focusing on how much she had *wanted* him to kiss her back then. 'Tell me why we're here?'

'Gabe and his team would like to show you a mock-up for the new campaign. They've been in pre-production for weeks and want to present you with your brief.'

They were ushered into a huge room filled with a confusing amount of people. She was introduced to Patti, the stylist—a spiky-haired blonde in a bright green mini-dress and a pair of chunky boots who was swishing through a rail of clothes. The long-haired art director was peering at photos of a woman standing on a gondola—a gondola!—who looked suspiciously like her. And when she looked a bit closer she could see that it was indeed her—with her head superimposed onto the body of some sleek model wearing a series of revealing evening dresses, set off with dazzling displays of diamonds.

There was a dynamism in the air which was almost palpable and nothing like the rather slow pace of the advertising agency Lulu had employed before. In fact, it was all a bit of a whirlwind experience, made all the more intense by Loukas at her side—warm and vibrant, and impossible to ignore. He took her over to the far side of the studio to meet Gabe Steel, the agency's owner—a striking man with dark golden hair and steely grey eyes.

'When Loukas explained that he wanted a complete change of image for the Lulu brand,' Gabe was saying, 'I could see it was a change which was long overdue. So we're ditching the Grace Kelly look and going for something more modern. We've had a lot of fun putting these new ideas together, Jessica—and I think you're going to like them. I showed them to my wife last night and she certainly did.' He smiled. 'So why don't you sit down and you can see what we have in mind?'

Jessica sat down on a chair which had clearly been chosen more for style than comfort and watched as the art director and Patti whipped through a series of photos, showcasing different pieces of jewellery.

'We're taking out a two-page spread in one of the broadsheets just in time for Valentine's Day,' explained Gabe, 'which only gives us a few weeks to play with.'

'Valentine's Day?' repeated Jessica, thinking that no other date could have rubbed in her single status quite so effectively.

'Sure. It's one of the jewellery business's most profitable times of the year—and Lulu needs to capitalise on that in a way it has failed to do before. The young girls who used to buy the wristwatch are all grown up now, and we want to show the world that you've grown up, too. We want to show that the new Jessica is definitely not a girl any more. And she won't be wearing a waterproof wristwatch, she'll be wearing jewels—preferably some which have been bought for her by a man.'

'My jewels,' interjected Loukas softly.

Jessica thought how weird it was to hear herself being spoken about in the third person. She stared nervously at the photos. Surely they weren't expecting her to wear clothes like *those*—with half her breasts on show, or a long dress slashed all the way up the way up her thigh?

'The shoot is booked to take place in Venice, as you can see from the mock-ups,' Gabe continued. 'It's the most romantic city in the world and a perfect setting for the kind of look we're aiming for. In winter it's moody and atmospheric, which is why we'll be shooting in black and white with the iconic Lulu pink as the only colour.' He smiled at her. 'The team are going out first to set up the locations and I gather you and Loukas are flying out separately.'

Every face in the room turned to look at her, but all Jessica could see was the gleam of Loukas's black eyes and the faint curve of his mocking smile. Since when had they been travelling out *separately* and why hadn't anyone bothered to tell her about it? She didn't think she'd ever shouted at anyone in her life but right then Jessica wanted to stand up and yell that she didn't want to go *anywhere* with the arrogant Greek—least of all to a city famed for romance, to advertise a campaign which was *all* about romance.

She wanted to be back in Cornwall, far away from him and the uncomfortable way he was making her feel. She had been fine before he'd come back into her life. Things might have been predictable, but at least they had felt *safe*. She hadn't been racked with longing, or regret. She hadn't started thinking about the fact that they'd never even spent a whole night together.

Did she *really* have to take this job—with all the complications which accompanied it? Again, she thought about selling up and buying a cheaper apartment away from the sea.

But then her half-sister's face drifted into her mind and she felt the sharp stab of her conscience. She thought of Hannah sobbing in her arms following the terrible avalanche which had killed her parents. Things had been bad enough when they'd been forced to sell the big house, but they had chosen the new one *together*, and Hannah loved her current home. It was her home, too, and what right did Jessica have to deprive her of that security, just because being around Loukas bothered her more than it should have done?

She didn't have to sleep with him, no matter how much she wanted him. And there was nothing to stop her making it clear to him that it wasn't going to happen. A new sense of determination filled her, because hadn't she come through far worse than having to resist a man like him?

So she gave Gabe a smile—the same smile she always used when people asked if she missed playing tennis. A very useful smile to have in her repertoire. It was bright and convincing.

And it didn't mean a thing.

'I can't wait,' she said.

CHAPTER SIX

LOUKAS WATCHED AS Jessica stood in the gondola, her new, shorter hair being ruffled by the wind. Her face was pale, her eyes looked huge, and the tension surrounding her was almost palpable. Not for the first time that day, he clenched his fists with frustration, because this had been his idea and on paper it had seemed like an outstanding one. All the boxes had been ticked. She wore a tight-fitting, corseted black ballgown which hugged her slender body and emphasised her neat little breasts. Long black satin gloves came up to her elbow and a waterfall of diamonds glittered against her breasts.

It should have been perfect. Jessica Cartwright looking exactly as the team at Zeitgeist had wanted her to look. Sleek and grown-up and very, very sexy.

Yet she stood there like a waxwork. Her eyes seemed empty and her expression blank. Even her smile looked as if it had been plastered on.

He shook his head in disbelief as he thought back to the way she'd been in his arms the other night, when he'd kissed her in the elevator. She had been fire that night, not ice—but where was all that fire now?

His eyes bored into hers.

There was nothing left but embers.

From her precarious position in the Grand Canal, Jessica met Loukas's stony black gaze, which was boring into her from the side of the water. None of the crew were happy—she could tell. Not one of them, but especially not Loukas, who seemed to have been glaring at her since the shoot had got underway. The chill Venetian wind whipped around her as she tried to keep her balance, which wasn't easy when she was standing on a bobbing gondola.

She felt cold—inside and out. Around her neck hung a priceless dazzle of blue-white diamonds which shone like a beacon in the gloom of the winter day. Her newly bare neck—shorn back in London of its protective curtain of long hair—was now completely exposed to the wintry Venetian elements. Strands of the sleek new style fluttered around her chin and were starting to stick to her lip-gloss. And even though Patti the stylist stood next to her—poised with a hairbrush and a big cashmere wrap—that didn't stop Jessica from feeling ridiculously underdressed. These photos were light years away from the demure and sporty shots she usually did for the store and she felt *stupid*. No. She felt exposed.

And vulnerable.

Her eyelashes were laden down with more mascara than she'd ever worn before and consequently the smoky make-up they'd been aiming for looked as if someone had given her two black eyes. The glossy, cyclamen-pink lipstick, intended to echo the colour of the brand's iconic packaging, gave her an almost clown-like appearance. And the dress. Oh, the dress. She didn't even want to get started on the dress. It was everything she wasn't—vampy and revealing. Ebony satin fitted so closely on the bodice that she could barely breathe and cut so low that her cleavage was now an unflattering sea of goosebumps. Beneath the swish of the full skirt her knees were knocking together with a mixture of nerves and embarrassment. Because even though the city was relatively quiet in February, the odd tourist had stopped to take her photo and she hated it.

She hated trying to look *sexy and sophisticated*, which was the look the art director had told her he wanted—since she felt neither. She felt like a fraud—and wouldn't they all laugh themselves silly if they discovered that she hadn't made love to a man in eight long years?

Of course, having Loukas standing watching her wasn't helping. In fact, it was making everything a whole lot worse. Against the misty grey and white of the Venetian backdrop, the Greek stood out like a dark spectre on the bank of the canal. The light from the water caught him in its silvery gleam and the city's sense of the hidden and the deep seemed to reflect back his own unknowable personality. Two burly security guards flanked him, their eyes fixed on the fortune in gems which shimmered against her skin.

The art director looked at his watch and frowned. 'Okay, we're losing the light. Let's call it a day, shall we? Same time tomorrow, people.'

As some of the crew sprang forward to help her from the gondola, Jessica could see the art director muttering something to Loukas, who was nodding his head in thoughtful agreement. His black gaze held hers for a moment and she felt the skitter of unwanted desire whispering over her skin. Why was he even here? Why didn't he go back to London and leave her alone? Surely she might be able to come up with what they wanted if he weren't standing there, like a fire-breathing dragon, making her feel inadequate in all kinds of ways. Holding the voluminous folds of the black satin skirt of her dress, she stepped onto the bank and was handed the cashmere shawl.

'We're going to St Mark's Square for coffee, though maybe you deserve a brandy after all that,' said Patti, rubbing her hands together before putting them over her mouth and blowing on them. 'Fancy coming along once you've taken your necklace off and changed?'

'Not right now. I'm going to take Jess back to the hotel,' came a dark and silky voice from behind her.

Jessica glanced round to see Loukas walking towards her, like a character who had just stepped from an oil painting. His dark cashmere overcoat matched the dark gleam of his hair and today he seemed devoid of all colour. Today, he was all black. The hard-edged smile he glimmered at her set off faint warning bells, though she wasn't sure why.

'Because she looks frozen,' he added deliberately.

Yes, she was frozen, but, although her skin felt like ice, her blood grew heated when his fingers brushed against her neck as he unclipped the heavy diamonds and handed them over to the waiting security guard. She felt lighter once the jewels had been removed and she wrapped the shawl tightly around herself, trying to hide herself from Loukas's searching gaze. But nothing could protect her from the way he was making her feel, as self-conscious beneath that piercing stare as she had been during their journey out here.

They had taken a scheduled flight from London, which had been just about tolerable, because at least Loukas had been working while Jessica attempted to read a book. But when they had arrived and their waiting water taxi had taken them towards the city, she'd felt herself unwillingly caught up in the romance of the moment, no matter how hard she tried to fight it.

She had felt as if she were in a film as the sleek craft sped through the choppy grey waters, leaving a trail of white plume behind them, and the iconic skyline of cities, churches and domes loomed up ahead of them. She had failed to conceal her gasp of pleasure as they'd entered the Grand Canal and Loukas had turned to her and smiled. A complicit smile edged with danger and, yes, with promise.

And Jessica had shivered just as she was shivering now.

'Let's walk back to the hotel,' he said as the crew began to disperse.

Picking up the heavy skirt to prevent it from dragging on the damp bank, she looked at him. 'You really think I can walk back to the hotel wearing this?'

'You don't imagine that women in ages past had to struggle with dresses similar to that?' he mused. 'Think of the famous masked ball they hold here every February. And you'll be warmer if we walk. Come on. It isn't far.'

'Okay,' she said, and pulled the cashmere closer.

She stuck close to his side as they began to weave their way through the narrow streets, past shop windows filled with leather books and exquisite glassware and over tiny, echoing bridges. It was like being in the centre of an ancient maze and it wasn't long before Jessica had completely lost her bearings. 'You seem to know exactly where you're going,' she said.

'Unless you think I'm planning to get you lost in Venice, never to be seen again?'

She looked up at him and her heart gave a funny kind of thud. 'Are you?'

He laughed. 'Tempting, but no. Look. We're here.'

It was with something almost like disappointment that Jessica glanced up to see their hotel ahead of them, with light spilling out from the elegant porticoed entrance. Heads turned as they walked into the palm-filled foyer and she guessed that they must make a bizarre couple with her in the flowing ballgown and Loukas in his black cashmere coat. She could feel the swish of her dress brushing over the marble floor and felt her cheeks grow pink when the pianist broke into a version of 'Isn't She Lovely?' and a group of businessmen started clapping and cheering as she passed them by. She wanted to dive into the elevator but her suite was on the first floor and the sweeping staircase seemed the most sensible option for getting there. But the voluminous skirt of her dress took some manoeuvring and she was out of breath by the time she got to the top.

'Not quite as fit as you used to be?' Loukas said, his black eyes glinting.

'Obviously not, since I'm not playing competitive tennis any more, but I'm fit enough. I'm just not used to dragging this amount of material around with me.'

There was a pause as they reached her door and she fumbled with her key card to open it.

'So, are you going to have dinner with me tonight?' he asked.

She shook her head. 'Thanks for the offer, but I'm going to have a bath and try to get warm again. My hands feel like ice.' She hesitated as she looked up into his face and then swallowed. 'They didn't like what I did today, did they? I could tell.'

He shrugged. 'It was all new to you. You're used to being brisk and breezy, to wearing casual clothes and looking sporty—and suddenly you're expected to start behaving like a vamp. You're operating outside your comfort zone, Jess, but don't worry. You'll get it right tomorrow.'

'And if I don't?'

His eyes glinted again. 'We'll just have to make sure you do.' He brushed a reflective finger down over her spine. 'Have you thought how you're planning to get out of this dress? Unless you're something of a contortionist you might have something of a problem, since it has about a hundred hooks.'

Jessica was trying not to react to the brush of his finger and she cursed the restrictive fastenings intended to give her an hourglass shape. She knew what he was suggesting but the thought of him helping her undress seemed all wrong. Yet what else was she going to do? Patti and the crew were in some unknown bar in an unknown city, and, short of waiting for them to return, she certainly couldn't undo it herself.

'Would you mind?' she said casually, as if it didn't bother her one way or the other.

'No, I don't mind,' he said, just as casually, as he followed her into the suite.

It was the most beautiful place she had ever stayed in, but Jessica barely noticed the carved furniture or the beautifully restored antique piano which stood beneath a huge chandelier. Even the stunning view over the Grand Canal and the magnificent dome of the Salute church couldn't distract her from the thought that Loukas was here, in her hotel room.

'Aren't you going to turn around and look at me, Jess?' he questioned softly.

She cleared her throat, wondering if he could hear her nervousness. 'You're supposed to be undoing my dress,' she said. 'And you can't do that unless I have my back to you.'

There was a split second of a pause. She thought she heard him give a soft laugh as he unclipped the first hook, and then the second. She wanted to tell him to hurry up and yet she wanted him to take all the time in the world. She could feel the rush of air to her back as he loosened the gown and she closed her eyes as another hook was liberated. Was this how women used to feel in the days before they were free to wear short dresses and trousers, or go without a bra? A sense of being completely within a man's power as he slowly undressed her?

Her breath caught in her throat because now there was a contrast between the air which had initially cooled her skin being replaced by the unmistakable warmth of a breath. Her eyelashes fluttered. Was he... was he breathing against her bare back?

Yes, he was.

It felt like the most intimate thing imaginable. She swallowed, because now his lips were pressing against the skin and he was actually *kissing* her there.

Her eyes closed. She knew she ought to say something but every nerve in her body was telling her not to break the spell. Because this was anonymous, wasn't it? It was pleasurable and anonymous, and she didn't have to think. She didn't have to remember that this was Loukas and that there was bad history between them. She didn't have to look into those gleaming black eyes or see triumph curving his lips into a mocking smile. All she was conscious of was the feel of his lips brushing against her and the hot prickling of her breasts in response.

The dress had slid down to her hips and his hands were moving to skim their curves as if he was rediscovering them. Luxuriantly, he spread his fingers over the flesh and she thought she heard him give a sigh of pleasure. She swallowed, but still she didn't say anything, because it was easier to play dumb. To want it to continue yet not be seen to be encouraging it. Her heart began to beat even faster because now he had started brushing his fingers over her lacy thong and with that came a wave of lust so strong that it washed away the residual grains of her conscience.

'Mmm,' he said as the dress fell to the ground, pooling around her ankles and leaving her legs completely bare. He was kissing her neck and his fingers were hooking into her panties and she felt a molten rush of heat.

She knew she should stop him. But she couldn't. She just *couldn't*. It had been so long since she had done this and she was cold. So cold. And Loukas was making her feel warm. Warmer than she'd felt in a long time.

His fingers had moved from her hip and were now inside her panties, alighting on her heated flesh with a familiarity which seemed as poignant as it was exciting.

'It's been a long time,' he said almost reflectively, drifting a fingertip across the engorged bud.

Jessica's body jerked with pleasure. She wanted to say something—anything—as if to reassure herself that she was still there and that it was all real. But the words simply wouldn't come. His touch had robbed her of the power to speak. Her breath had dried in her throat and all she could think about was the hunger building up inside her and dominating her whole world. Her thighs seemed to be parting of their own accord and she felt the warmth of his breath as he smiled against her neck.

'You are very wet, *koukla mou*,' he murmured.

She swallowed as her eyes closed. 'Yes.'

'Wet for me?'

'Y-yes.'

'Have you been imagining me touching you here?'

'Yes!'

'And...*here*?'

'God, yes.' Jessica gasped, even though his words seemed to contradict his actions. Because what he was saying was provocative, but strangely cold. He was objectifying her, she realised with a brief rush of horror and she tried to pull away. To end it while she still could. But by then it was too late because she was starting to come and he was giving a low laugh of triumph as he swivelled her round to cover her mouth with his, his hand still cupping her flesh while his kiss drowned out her broken cry of surrender.

His tongue was in her mouth as she pulsated helplessly around his finger and the combination of that double invasion only increased her pleasure, until she thought she might have slid to the ground, if he hadn't been holding onto her so tightly. Time passed in a slow, throbbing haze before her eyelids fluttered open to find Loukas watching her, still with that faintly triumphant smile on his face. Slowly, he withdrew his finger and she noted that it wasn't quite steady.

'Jess,' he said and picked her up and carried her into the bedroom to lie her down on the bed.

'Loukas,' she whispered, and the tip of her tongue came out to slide over her parted lips.

Loukas felt the savage beat of his heart as he looked at her glistening mouth and his erection was so hard that it took him a moment or two before he was able to move. He wanted to tear off his clothes and just *take* her. But not yet. Not until he was in control of his feelings. Until he was certain that he was in no danger of being trapped by the powerful spell she had always been able to weave around him.

He tried to study her objectively as he shrugged off his overcoat and hung it over the back of a chair, then went back towards the bed on which she lay. Strange that she should have been so cold and uptight in front of the camera today and yet had fallen apart the moment he'd touched her. But hadn't that always been her way? He gave a bitter smile. The only time he'd ever been able to penetrate her haughty exterior—in more ways than one—was when she was naked and writhing beneath him. Because outside the bedroom, or the sitting room, or the car—or wherever else they happened to have been doing it—she had always been the very definition of cool.

But not now.

Her eyes were smoky, her face flushed with satisfaction and her thighs parted in such open invitation that he was almost tempted to bury his head between them and lick her. He thought how at home she looked, lying back against the brocade covering the ornate four-poster bed. But of course, she was. This place was classy and luxurious; it was the environment to which she was most suited. *The one in which he had never quite fitted.*

He reached out his hand and laid it over her left breast. He could feel her heart pounding beneath the lace of her provocative bra as he circled a thumb over the nipple which was peaking through the scarlet and black lace. 'You never used to wear such frivolous underwear when I was with you, *koukla mou*,' he observed silkily. 'So what happened? Did the men who followed me demand that you dress to please—or have your tastes simply changed and evolved with time?'

Jessica opened her mouth to tell him that Patti had taken her shopping after they'd been to the hairdresser, explaining that the revealing gowns wouldn't tolerate anything except the briefest of bras, and that her panties should preferably match *to get her in the mood* for the shoot. Except that it hadn't worked out that way, had it? She had stood posing like a female ice cube in the dramatic and sexy dress and had only really come to life when Loukas had touched her.

She bit her lip. And how he had touched her. She had forgotten how exquisite an orgasm could feel when it was administered by the only man she had ever really cared about. She had forgotten how weak and powerless it could make you feel. As if all your strength had been sapped. It could make you vulnerable if you weren't careful, and she needed to be careful.

She shouldn't have allowed it to happen, but now

that she had she wanted it continue. She had acted foolishly but maybe understandably—or at least, understandable to her. She was like someone who'd broken her diet by opening a packet of cookies. But why stop at one, when four would be much more satisfactory and make the sin worthwhile? She didn't want her enduring memory of sex with Loukas to be a one-sided, rather emotionless pleasuring. She wanted to make love to him properly. Hadn't she wanted that for years? She wanted to feel him inside her. Deep inside her. Filling her and heating her as nothing else could.

She reached up her hand and began to unbutton his shirt, determined to approach this as if they were equals. Because she wasn't some little virgin who'd just been seduced, and though she might lack his undoubted sexual experience, there was no reason for him to know that.

'Do you really want to talk about other men at a moment like this?' she questioned coolly, slipping free another button and rubbing her hand against his hair-roughened chest.

His mouth tightened as he leaned forward and began to tug at the belt of his trousers. 'No,' he said. 'I don't. And soon you won't be able to, because I'm going to make you forget every other man you've had sex with. You won't be able to remember a single damned thing about them, because all you'll be able to think about is *me*.'

The arrogant boast shocked her but it thrilled her, too. Nearly as much as it thrilled her to see him peel off his clothes to reveal his body in all its honed olive splendour. It was as magnificent as it had ever been but suddenly Jessica gasped because there—zigzagging over the side of his torso like a fleshy fork of lightning—was a livid scarlet scar. Her fingers flew to her lips before reaching out to touch it, as tentatively as if it might still hurt. As if it might open up and begin to bleed all over the bed.

'What happened to you?' she whispered.

'Not now, Jess,' he growled.

'But—'

'I said, not now.' His hand slid between her thighs and began to move, effectively silencing all further questioning. 'Does that kind of detail please you?' he rasped. 'Does it turn you on to think that your rough, tough bodyguard has the mark of violence on his body?'

There was something in his tone she didn't understand—some dark note which lay just beneath the mockery—and Jessica was confused. But by then he was stroking her again and his mouth was on her breast, and she was growing so hot for him that she could barely wait for him to slide on the condom and position himself over her.

She was trembling as he made that first thrust and the sensation surpassed every fantasy she'd ever had about him. But to her surprise, he was trembling, too, and for several moments his big body stayed completely still, as if he didn't trust himself to move.

She wanted to whisper things to him. Soft, stupid things. She wanted to tell him that she wished she'd married him when he'd asked her. That she'd thrown away the best chance of happiness she'd ever had. But nobody could rewrite history—and didn't they say everything happened for a reason? Even if right now it was difficult to see what that reason could possibly be.

And then all the nagging thoughts were driven from her mind because her orgasm was happening again. It built up into a crescendo and sent her into total meltdown—and the shuddered moan which echoed around the room told her that so, too, had his.

CHAPTER SEVEN

THE ROOM WAS very quiet for what seemed like a long time and, when she spoke, Jessica's words seemed to splinter the peace. She turned onto her side and stared into the face of the man beside her.

'How did you get that scar?'

Loukas stirred and stretched. Completely comfortable in his nakedness, he raised his arms and extended his powerful legs in a movement which should have distracted her, but nothing could have distracted her right then. All Jessica could see was the livid mark zigzagging over his flesh.

'How?' she whispered again, when still he didn't answer.

His face became shuttered as he drifted a fingertip over her nipple and watched it wrinkle and harden. 'As a topic for pillow talk,' he drawled, 'it's not exactly up there with telling me how much you enjoyed your orgasm.'

Jessica didn't react. He made what had happened sound so *clinical*. But maybe for him it was. Did legions of women purr the morning afterwards and tell the dark and charismatic Greek how much they had enjoyed their orgasm? She scooped back her hair and peered at him. 'Was it in Paris?' she persisted.

'Was what in Paris?' He stopped stroking.

'You told me that you were...captured there.' She hesitated. His face was still shuttered, but she persisted. 'Was it back then?'

Loukas lay back, pillowing his ruffled head on his folded arms as the chandelier glittered fractured light on their bare skin. He sensed she wouldn't give up until she had an answer and something told him he was going to find it harder to silence Jess than he would the average lover. 'No, it wasn't then,' he said dismissively.

'So...when?'

He turned his head to look at her and frowned. 'Does it matter?'

'Of course it matters.' She gave a barely perceptible sigh. 'What is it with you, Loukas? You never talk about your past, and you never did. I was with you for months and ended up knowing almost nothing about you.'

He gave the flicker of a smile. 'You knew plenty.'

'I'm not talking about the way your body works.'

He gave a short laugh. She had grown up in a land of milk and honey, in a world light years away from his. He thought about the big house with the tennis court and the bright green lawns which swept down to the sea. About privilege and belonging and all the things he'd never had. 'What difference does it make to know about my past?'

'It might make me feel as if I wasn't in bed with a stranger,' she said quietly.

It wasn't the first time the accusation had been

levelled at him, but, when Jess said it, it felt different. Come to think of it—everything about Jess felt different. 'I thought the anonymity aspect appealed to you,' he drawled. 'You certainly seemed turned on when you had your back to me earlier. For a minute I thought you might be pretending I was someone else.'

'Don't try to change the subject.'

'I'll do anything I please. Just because I've made love to you doesn't give you the right to censor my speech, or to demand answers.'

She bit her lip. 'Is it such an awful story, then?'

'Yes.' He said the word without planning and it was like an overfilled balloon being popped by the prick of a needle. Like a bruise beneath your fingernail which only a white-hot lance would relieve. 'Yes,' he repeated. 'Awful gets pretty close to it.'

'Won't you tell me?'

His instinct was to distract her—either by making love to her again, or by heading off to take a shower. Because she wanted to talk about the old Loukas, and he had spent a long time forging a new Loukas, a man as hard as the diamonds which were at the core of his fortune and a success beyond his wildest dreams.

He had uncovered secrets he would have preferred to have left alone, and had hidden them away deep inside himself. But secrets left their mark, he was discovering—a dirty mark which left a stain if you didn't expose it to the sunshine and the air. He looked into Jess's cool features, but for once her face was showing the emotions she usually kept contained. He could see the concern shadowing her eyes. He could hear an anxious softness in her voice, and something made him start talking. 'How much do you know?'

She shrugged. 'Not a lot. That you were an only child and your mother brought you up in Athens, and that you never knew who your father was.'

Loukas twisted his mouth into a grim smile. How easily a whole life could be condensed into a single sentence—black and white, without a single shade of grey in between. 'Did I tell you that we were poor?'

'Not in so many words, but I...' Her words tailed off.

'You what, Jess?' he said silkily. 'You guessed?'

She nodded.

'How?'

'It doesn't matter.'

'Oh, but it does. I'm interested.'

Reluctantly, she shrugged. 'You just always seemed so...oh, I don't know...restless, I guess. Like a shark moving through the water. Like you were always looking for something.'

It startled him how accurate her words were and Loukas nodded. Because she was right. He *had* been looking for something—he just hadn't known what it was. And then, when he'd found it...

'We were dirt poor, my mother and I,' he said, wanting to ram home the fundamental differences between them. To shock her. To convince her—and him—that all they shared was a rare electricity in between the sheets. 'Sometimes I used to hang around at the backs of restaurants to see what food they were throwing away at the end of a day's trade, and I'd take it home...' Take it home and hang around outside until his mother had finished with whoever she was currently *entertaining*. He remembered the different men who had stumbled out, some of them trying to cuff him on the mouth, while others had pressed a few coins into his hand. But Loukas had never kept those coins. He'd put them in the poor box at the nearby church… unwilling to accept money which was *tainted*, no matter how hungry he'd been. 'Although I took what jobs I could, just as soon as I was old enough—running errands, sweeping restaurants, polishing cars—anything, really.'

'And your mother?' she questioned hesitantly. 'Did she work?'

'She didn't have time to work,' he said bitterly. 'She was too busy devoting herself to whoever her current love interest was. She always had to have a man around and a child like me was only ever going to get in the way. So for the most part, I was left to my own devices.'

'Oh, Loukas,' she breathed.

'I lived from hand to mouth,' he continued grimly. 'I worked at the ferry port in Piraeus as soon as I was old enough, until I'd saved up enough money to take myself off to a new life. I didn't go back to Greece for a long, long time. I did my own tour of Europe, only it was nothing like the ones you see advertised in the glossy brochures. I lived in the shadows of Paris. I learnt to box in the Ukraine, and for a while I won amateur fights all over the continent, until Dimitri Makarov asked me to be his bodyguard.'

'And that was when you met me,' she said slowly.

Loukas nodded slowly. Yes. That was when he'd met his fairy-tale princess, with her white skin and her blue eyes and the cutest little bottom he'd ever seen. Her coolness had fascinated him; she'd been restrained and cautious—nothing like his mother or all the women he'd subsequently been intimate with. She hadn't been predatory or coquettish. In fact she'd fought against an attraction which had been almost palpable. And hadn't the fact that his princess had presented him with her virginity been like a master stroke in capturing his heart as well as his body, culminating in that proud proposal of marriage which had been thrown back in his face? He gave a bitter laugh. What a fool he had been.

'Yes,' he said, with a note of finality. 'That was when I met you.'

'And did you ever...?' She drew in a deep breath and he saw the rise of her tiny breasts. 'Did you ever see your mother again?'

Loukas flinched, because it didn't matter what hurt and what pain she had caused him—she was still his mother.

'Only once,' he said flatly. 'I'd been sending her money for years, but I couldn't face returning. And then, when she was dying I went back to find her living in a...hovel.' His voice tailed off, before taking on a bitter note. 'In thrall to her latest boyfriend—a vulture who was systematically bleeding her dry of her dignity, as well as all the money I'd sent her. I remember how weak she was when she took my hand and told me that she *loved* this particular loser. And even though she'd been a notoriously bad picker of men all her life—this one was in a class of his own. He had neglected to give her any pain relief—he'd been too busy spending her money at the casino.'

'Was that when you got the scar?' she said slowly.

Loukas nodded, realising how alien this must all sound to someone like her. *'Neh,'* he drawled, the flicker of anger not far from the surface. He remembered being young and fit and prepared to fight fairly, but his mother's lover had not. He hadn't seen the glint of steel as the knife had come flashing down out of nowhere, and at first he hadn't even registered the strange, digging sensation in his flesh, which had heralded the eruption of blood. Loukas's voice shook with rage. 'The only good thing that came out of it was that he was arrested and jailed and no longer able to steal money from my mother. But by then it was too late anyway.'

'What do you mean?' she whispered.

'She died later that week, just as I was being discharged from hospital,' he said, his face twisted with pain. 'I found all her paperwork and I understood at last why she had never wanted to talk about my father.' He met the question in her eyes. 'Like I said, she was a bad picker of men and that my father was abusive to her came as no real surprise. But the most interesting thing was that I discovered I had a twin brother.'

She tipped her head back, her eyes huge. *'A twin brother?'*

He nodded. 'Alek had been brought up by my father—a very different kind of upbringing from mine. I had him tracked down and I met him in Paris.' It had been that meeting which had made Loukas decide to lay *all* of his ghosts to rest. To make him want to move on and live his life in a different way. And hadn't Jess been the most persistent ghost of them all—the one who had hovered on the periphery of his mind like some pale and interesting beauty?

'How...' her voice trembled '...how can you possibly have discovered that you have a twin? Why didn't your mother ever tell you?'

'Because my father was powerful,' he said. 'And she was running away from him. She couldn't physically— or financially—take two tiny babies, so she chose to leave Alek.'

'How? How did she choose?'

He shook his head. 'Doesn't matter how. She knew she could never go back and so she decided to cut out that part of her life completely. To pretend it had never happened.' He gave a short laugh. 'And if I'm being objective, I think I can almost understand why. Far better to cut her losses and run, than to face up to the fact that she'd left her other son with a cruel tyrant.'

'Oh, Loukas.'

She reached her hand towards his face as if to stroke his cheek but he caught her wrist in an iron-hard grip of his own. Turning her palm upwards, he ran his tongue slowly over the salty flesh, his eyes never leaving her face.

'I don't want your pity, Jess,' he said softly. 'That's not the reason I told you.'

She trembled beneath the lick of his tongue. 'Why *did* you tell me?'

He thought about it. It was more a question of why he had kept it hidden before but now he could see that he had been ashamed. Ashamed of the circumstances which had forged him. So hungry for his cool and classy Englishwoman that he had cultured a deliberate elusiveness, so that she would accept him for his present, and not his past.

But she had not accepted him at all. He had still not

been good enough and maybe for someone like her, he never would be.

He didn't answer her question, but fixed her with a steady gaze. He remembered the way she'd breathlessly whispered that she loved him and how, for a short while, he had believed her. But words were easy, weren't they? His mother used to profess love, then leave him alone and frightened while she went out with her latest man. 'Why did you turn down my proposal?' he said suddenly.

She bit her lip and looked down at the rumpled sheets. 'Because…because I thought you were doing it to be chivalrous. To save me from my father's anger.'

'First time in my life I've ever been called chivalrous,' he said sardonically. 'But I don't think you're being entirely honest, are you, Jess? Maybe you did it to protect your fortune from a man who had nothing—who might want to marry you for all the wrong reasons?' he said, and the faint flush of colour to her cheeks told him everything he wanted to know.

'Well, there was that too,' she admitted haltingly, lifting her eyes to his as if she should be applauded for her honesty.

Loukas gave a bitter laugh. She had looked on him as someone with an eye for the main chance—able to provide her with sex, but best kept at arm's length when it came to permanency, or commitment.

And wasn't it crazy that *even now* it still hurt to realise that?

He didn't handle pain well. Physical pain was no problem, but emotional pain he found unendurable and he'd learnt that there was only one way to guarantee immunity. Don't get involved. Don't let anyone close enough to inflict it. It was a simple but effective rule as long as you stuck to it. And with Jess he'd been stupid enough to take his eye off the ball for a while.

'But you know something?' he questioned. 'You did me a kind of favour, in a way. I realised that marriage was completely wrong for someone like me.'

'Is that why you've never settled down with anyone else? Why you still live in luxury hotels, instead of having a real home?'

'Neh.' He gave a soft, cynical laugh. 'I've grown used to my life. I wouldn't have it any other way.'

'And children? What about them?'

'What about them? Why the hell would I want to bring children in the world, just to screw them up? I know what that's like and so does my twin brother.'

'Right,' she said uncertainly.

He thought he could see a flicker of darkness in her eyes—as if his words were hurting *her*. As if she wanted to reach out and stroke his pain away. And he didn't need that. He didn't need her sympathy, or understanding. He didn't want her looking at him as if he were a puzzle she could solve, because he was fine just the way he was. He didn't want her making him *feel* stuff, because life was so much easier when you didn't. There were a million things he didn't want from her and only one thing he did.

He pulled her closer, so that he could feel the warm softness of her skin. Her face was turned up to his and her lips were eagerly parted, and for a while he just teased her. He brushed his mouth over hers—back and forth—until she made a sound halfway between frustration and desire. Sliding her hand around the back of his neck, she pulled him down towards her and he felt a heady rush of sexual power as she clung to him.

This, he thought, just before he kissed her—this was all he wanted from Jessica Cartwright.

CHAPTER EIGHT

WHAT A DIFFERENCE a day could make. Or a night. A night when Loukas had seemed determined to show Jessica everything she'd been missing.

Sex.

Her throat dried.

A devastating masterclass in desire and satisfaction.

She had hardly slept a wink and by rights she should have felt terrible when she met the crew to resume shooting the following morning. But terrible was the last thing she felt. She felt *alive*. As if all her senses had suddenly exploded. The diamonds, which yesterday had hung like a millstone around her neck, today made her feel pampered and decadent as they glittered against her skin—and the close-fitting silk of her bodice no longer felt constricting. She was conscious of the way it clung to her breasts—thrusting them upwards and giving her a bit of a cleavage and reminding her of the way Loukas had licked his way over every inch of them during the sensual night they'd shared.

'Wow,' said the photographer softly as she stood in the gondola—only today she had no trouble keeping her balance, despite the rocking motion of the distinctive craft. And when she was told to pout and look

dreamy, she had no problem with that, either. In fact, it was difficult to look anything *but* dreamy when all she could think about was the man whose black eyes had grown opaque and smoky as he had lowered his head to kiss her.

But kisses could blind you to the reality and she had to keep reminding herself that it had only been about sex—*because how could it ever be anything else*? He'd made it clear that experience had hardened him. That he had changed and now there was no room in his life for marriage. She thought about the way his voice had grown cold when she'd asked about children, and—bearing in mind the things he'd told her—could she honestly blame him for not wanting any? All the things he'd told her about his childhood made her aware of just how grim his early life must have been. No wonder he'd been so reluctant to speak about it in the past. And then to discover out of the blue that he had a twin brother—a discovery like that must have rocked his world.

So she was going to have to be very mature. To accept the person he was, and if last night was the only night they would ever share, then she would accept that, too. No tears. No regrets. And definitely no recriminations. She'd had her chance a long time ago and she had blown it. She had no one to blame but herself.

This time Loukas didn't watch over the photo shoot, telling her he needed to work, before slipping away from her room in the early hours. She supposed he hadn't wanted anyone to see him leaving, knowing that it might muddy the waters if the crew discovered that the CEO was sleeping with the model.

She spent the entire day being photographed, but

that ice-cube feeling was a distant memory. The ball-gown was followed by a slinky white silk trouser suit, with nipped-in jacket and wide palazzo pants. The diamond necklace had been replaced with neat diamond studs and, with a nod to her previous career, she wore a tennis bracelet—a narrow row of diamonds, which glittered discreetly at her wrist. The last shot of the day was of Jessica wearing a monochrome mini-dress, teamed with waterproof boots as she stood in the centre of a flooded St Mark's Square, and even though her arms were covered with goosebumps she didn't feel particularly cold. Patti fed her sips of hot coffee and torn-off little pieces of croissant. Tourists gathered to watch, only today she didn't mind, and when the art director called it a day and came over to congratulate her, she experienced a feeling of real achievement. She'd done what she had set out to do. She had pulled it out of the bag and given them what they wanted. She'd shown them—and herself—that she was capable of change, and wasn't that a very empowering feeling?

They all trooped back to the hotel through the echoing streets of the darkening afternoon and Loukas was just coming down the sweeping staircase, leaving Jessica wondering whether someone had rung ahead to tell him they were on their way. Her heart pounded as she watched him move, so dark and so vital, capturing the attention of every person in the place. He walked over to talk to the art director and she tugged the cashmere wrap closer, feeling her nipples tightening beneath the soft material, afraid someone might notice and work out why. They chatted intently for a moment and then he looked round, his black gaze sweeping around until it had found her, and her heart began to race even faster as he walked across the foyer towards her.

A faint smile lifted the edges of his mouth. 'I gather you excelled yourself today,' he said.

She smiled, trying to ignore the sudden yearning deep inside her. Trying to convince herself that she only felt this way because he was a powerful, alpha male she'd spent the night with and that was how nature had conditioned her to react. 'Thanks,' she said.

'I'm tempted to ask what has changed since yesterday,' he murmured. 'But I think we both know the answer to that, wouldn't you say, *koukla mou*?'

She tilted her chin. 'Are you looking for praise?'

'Why would I need to do that when you gave me all the praise I could possibly want last night?' His lashes shuttered down to half conceal the ebony glint of his eyes. 'Would you like to repeat some of it, in case you've forgotten?'

'That won't be necessary,' she said hastily. She could see Patti and the others moving towards the elevator—presumably to pack—and her heart grew heavy as she realised that it had all come to an end. *And she didn't want it to come to an end.* 'I guess I'd better go and pack as well.'

'Well, you could. Or you and I could stay on for an extra day and give ourselves a chance to see the city properly?'

She stared at him.

His eyes glittered. 'What's the matter, Jess— doesn't the idea appeal?'

'It's not that. Surely you have...' She tried to keep

the tremor of excitement from her voice. She shrugged. 'Oh, I don't know. Work to do.'

'I'm the boss. Work can wait—while I, on the other hand…'

His words trailed off, smoky, suggestive and edged with a raw hunger which left her in no doubt what he was thinking. But it had been a long time since Jessica had engaged in sexual banter and she'd forgotten the first rule about keeping it light.

'What?' she whispered.

'I don't want to wait,' he said softly. 'And I don't intend to. I still want you. I want you so badly that I'm hard now, just standing this close to you. So hard that I want to rip those trousers from your delicious legs and put my hands where that silk has been.'

He had lowered his voice so that only she could hear, but even so Jessica found herself looking around, terrified that a passing guest would overhear, or that someone discerning would correctly interpret their body language.

'Loukas,' she said, only the word didn't come out as it was supposed to do. It came out all throatily, like a husky invitation instead of a protest.

He shook his head, as if pre-empting her objections. 'One night wasn't enough. Not nearly enough to cancel out eight long years of a slow-burning fever in my blood. A fever which has never quite gone away, no matter how many other women have graced my bed. Has it been like that for you too, Jess?' His voice dipped. 'I'm guessing so. Because you were wild for me last night. Wild,' he finished silkily.

Her instinct was to play it down. To clamp down on the feeling before it had started to grow and take hold. It was a survival mechanism which had served her well in the past. It meant she'd been able to accept a promising tennis career which had ended before it had even begun. It had enabled her to turn down his offer of marriage because she'd known that had been the right thing to do. And this time round she knew it would be best if they kept last night as a one-off. A single, amazing night they'd shared, which was never going to happen again. Because one night was easy to be objective about; any more than that and she was running straight into trouble.

She opened her mouth to say no, but something in his face was making the words die on her lips. Was it a sudden softness about the eyes which reminded her of the man he'd once been, before life had taken him and roughed him up even more?

Because something about the way he was looking at her touched a part of herself she'd thought had died a long time ago, and she was surprised he hadn't worked out for himself the reason why she'd been so *wild* for him last night. Not just because she'd been living in a sexual desert since he'd walked out of her life, but because he made her feel *stuff*. Stuff like joy and intense pleasure. Stuff like love.

She chewed on her lip. In the past she wouldn't have been able to spontaneously extend a trip abroad, because Hannah would have been at home and Jessica had always prided herself on being there for her. But Hannah was thousands of miles away and nobody else knew or cared where she was. She could think of that as isolation, or she could think of it as being free. A negative or a positive—the choice was hers.

'Okay,' she said. 'It seems a pity to come all this way and not see something of the city.'

He slanted her a conspiratorial smile. 'That's what I thought.'

Her hands were trembling as she went to her room to change into jeans, sweater and a waterproof jacket—almost glad that the day was grey and misty and she could put on normal clothes. The kind of clothes she wore at home, which made her feel more like herself and not some manufactured glamour puss.

She met Loukas back downstairs and they left the hotel, but soon after the narrow streets had begun to swallow them up, he steered her into a darkened bar.

'You need a drink,' he said firmly. 'And you missed out on lunch, didn't you?'

'It's nearly four o'clock, Loukas. We won't get lunch at this time.'

'I know that. But Venice is a city which is prepared for all eventualities.' He sat her gently down on a bar stool and nodded at the proprietor, who was polishing a glass. 'You drink a glass of local wine, which the locals call an *ombra*, and you eat some of these delicious little snacks, which are known as *cicchetti*. See? Tiny little plates of seafood, vegetables and polenta. Come on, Jess. Relax. Stop looking so uptight.' He lowered his voice. 'Pretend it's last night and I'm kissing you.'

Loukas wondered what she was thinking as she turned her remarkable eyes to his. He sensed a struggle within her, as if she was still fighting him off, and maybe it was that which drew him towards her. Was it her slight air of resistance—of *restraint*—which reinforced his growing realisation that this *thing* between them was still not settled?

Why not?

His jaw tightened. She should have been smitten with him by now—and that wasn't arrogance, it was fact. One night of sex was usually enough to guarantee adoration from whomever had shared his bed, and their history gave Jess more reason than most to have fallen under his spell. But that was the thing with her. The closer you got, the more she seemed to pull away, and all it did was to fire up his dominant hunter instincts. He sipped at his wine. Was that the reason he wanted her so much—because she kept him at arm's length unless he happened to be buried deep inside her body?

She sipped her wine, glancing round at the shadowy interior of the small bar as if soaking up the atmosphere.

'You seem to know your way around Venice pretty well,' she observed.

'I do. It was another part of my *grand tour*, even though I had nothing very much in my pockets when I first arrived.'

'So how did you survive?'

He shrugged. 'There is always work if you are prepared to do anything—and I was. I went to all the great European cities and set myself a goal. Six months in each, by which time I wanted to feel as comfortable as if I was a native of that city.'

'And was there any particular shortcut?'

'Not one that you'd probably want to hear.'

Her cheeks went pink. 'You mean—through women?'

He shrugged. 'I told you that you wouldn't like it.'

'It doesn't bother me at all.'

'Liar,' he said softly and leaned forward to brush

his lips overs hers, tasting the wine and the warmth in that brief kiss. 'Want to see some more of Venice?'

She nodded and he found himself linking her fingers through his as they started walking along the canal. Her hands were cold and despite their tennis-honed strength they felt fragile and small within his. He found himself thinking that he didn't usually do this kind of thing. He didn't wander hand in hand with a woman, pointing out the secret churches and hidden squares and feeling high with the sheer beauty of the city, almost as if he'd never really seen it before.

The afternoon became devoid of all natural light and as the streetlights began to glow, the deserted streets took on the atmospheric feel so beloved of film-makers. Loukas saw someone snap on a light in one of the great flats along the Grand Canal and a golden glow spilled down, turning Jess's hair into molten gold. They wandered off down one of the narrow streets and he was thinking about taking her to that little bar near the Rialto, when he felt her tugging at his sleeve.

'Did you hear that?' she asked.

Frowning, he shook his head.

'Listen,' she said, putting her finger over her lips.

He frowned, but all he could hear was the lap of the water and the echoing sound of music coming from a long way off. 'I don't hear anything.'

'Shh! There it is again.'

And then he heard it—would have recognised it instantly if it hadn't held such poignant memories for him. The terrified sound of a child's cry. He stiffened, every sense on full alert as he began to move purposefully in the direction of the sound. He could hear

Jess's rapid breathing beside him, just before he saw the huddled shape of a child ahead of them—a boy— his face streaked with tears, his brown eyes wide and frightened.

Jess began to run towards him, but Loukas caught her arm, speaking to her in English, in a low voice. 'Wait. Be careful,' he said.

'Be *careful*?' She turned on him. 'What are you talking about, Loukas? He's just a *child*.'

'And this could be a scam. It's a well-known method for fleecing tourists. Children used as decoys to lure unsuspecting foreigners. There are pickpockets in this city, just like everywhere else.'

Angrily, she shook his arm away. 'I don't care,' she said fiercely. 'I'm willing to take the risk of losing a few euros. I want to help him. Let me *go*!'

But he shadowed her as she ran forward and the boy turned his face upwards and choked out his frightened words.

'Aiutami,' he said. *'Aiuto.'*

Remorse flooded through Loukas as immediately he crouched and looked into the tear-filled eyes. 'I will help you,' he said gruffly, in the same language. 'Where are your parents?'

'I don't know!' cried the boy and Jess put her arms around him as if it was the easiest thing in the world, and Loukas felt his heart clench as he watched her soothing him, listening carefully to what the child said in a breathless dialect he thought might be Sicilian.

'He says he lost sight of his parents and when he heard them calling for him, he began to run,' he translated. 'Only he took the wrong turning and began to panic. He ran even faster, and that's when he realised he could no longer hear them. He couldn't hear anything. He isn't hurt, but he's frightened.'

'I'm not surprised,' she said fervently as she stroked the boy's curly hair. 'Venice is a beautiful city by day, but it must be scary if you're a child and you're lost. All that water.' She shivered. 'Tell him that we're going to help find his parents.'

Loukas nodded as he lifted the boy to his feet and began to speak in a calm, low voice before turning to her and meeting the question in her blue eyes.

'I've explained that we'll take him to the *questura*—the police,' he said. 'And that we'll probably find his parents there, waiting for him. Come on, Jess. He wants you to take his hand. Oh, and his name is Marco.'

'Marco,' she said softly as the little boy clung to her hip and wept.

CHAPTER NINE

'THAT POOR CHILD,' said Jessica as she switched on one of the lamps and the room was flooded with a soft golden light. 'He was absolutely terrified.'

'I'm not surprised,' said Loukas, shutting the door softly behind him. 'Getting lost in Venice age seven isn't something to be recommended.'

'Do you think he'll be okay?'

'He'll be fine.' He frowned. 'Are *you* okay?'

Jessica nodded, hoping her smile would convey a sense of serenity she was far from feeling. They were back in her hotel room where they'd discovered champagne sitting in an ice bucket, delivered by the grateful parents of Marco Pasolini. She and Loukas had bumped into the fraught and terrified couple outside the entrance to the police station, where they had taken the little boy, who had still been tightly holding her hand. A voluble reunion had followed, with Marco's mother alternately sobbing and scolding her young son, before scooping him into her arms and covering his face with endless kisses. His father, meanwhile—according to the translation which Loukas had provided afterwards—proceeded to offer them the use of his Sicilian villa, his ocean-going yacht or any other part of his extensive estates, any time they cared to use them.

But now that the worry and the drama had died away, Jessica was left feeling exhausted. The experience had shaken her up more than she'd realised and had only increased her growing sense of disassociation. She felt as if she shouldn't really be here, in this room, with Loukas. As if their passion of the night before had been something unplanned and probably regrettable and now, in the harsh light of day, she wasn't sure what they were supposed to do next. Would he start peeling off her clothes and expecting another acrobatic performance, like last night? She hoped not. She felt shy and inexperienced, as if she couldn't possibly live up to his expectations.

She thought about his instinctive reaction when they'd stumbled across the lost child. He had thought it was a scam.

'I'm fine,' she said, taking off her jacket and realising that her legs felt a little shaky. She sat down on a chair very suddenly and looked at him. 'Why did you jump to the conclusion that Marco was a pickpocket? That was a pretty harsh and cynical thing to do, in the circumstances.'

He gave a short and bitter laugh. 'Because I spent too many years as a bodyguard, and suspicion is something which was drummed into me. Something I learnt to live with. If you work for one of the world's wealthiest men, threats come from the most unlikely directions—something I learnt to my own cost. You learn never to trust what you see, or to believe what you hear. That nothing is ever as it seems.'

'That seems a pretty grim way to live your life.'

He raised his eyebrows. 'A cup half empty, rather than half full?'

She nodded. 'Something like that.'

'Or you could say that way you stand less chance of disappointment. If you don't have raised expectations, then they can't be smashed,' he said, his ebony gaze locking with hers. 'You were brilliant with him, by the way,' he added slowly. 'A natural.'

She heard a note of surprise in his voice, which he couldn't quite disguise. 'Something you weren't expecting?'

He shrugged. 'I never had you down as the maternal type.'

Maybe, she thought, because he must find it hard to recognise the 'maternal type', if such a thing existed. His own mother had always put the men in her life first, so could she really blame him if his perception of others was warped—if he had no real experience on which to base his judgements? Or maybe because he remembered her as single-minded and focused, letting her tennis dominate her whole life.

'I don't know if I was born that way, but it's something I learnt,' she said slowly. 'I had to. I became something of a substitute mother for my half-sister.'

'The little girl who was always hiding your hairbrush?' He frowned. 'Hannah?'

Jessica smiled. Funny he should remember that. 'That's the one. When my dad...*our* dad...and her mum were killed, I stepped in to look after her. Well, I had to really.'

'No, you didn't,' he said suddenly, another frown darkening his face. 'Presumably you had a choice and you chose to look after her. How old was she?'

'Ten.'

'And you were, what—eighteen?'

She nodded, thinking how beautiful he looked, silhouetted against the Venetian skyline. The shutters were still open and the spotlighted dome of the magnificent Salute church, which stood behind the wide band of gleaming water, could be seen in all its splendour.

'Yes,' she said. 'I was eighteen. The authorities wanted to foster her out to a proper family, but I fought very hard to keep her. I didn't...' Her words tailed off.

'Didn't what?'

She hesitated. She kept things locked inside her because that was what she'd been trained to do, just as she'd been trained to use a double-handed backhand. And when you did something for long enough it became a habit. A bit like Loukas, when he saw only danger around him. If you built a wall around your emotions you were safer—at least, that was the theory. But the rush of emotions she'd experienced today, following the incredible sex of last night, had left her feeling...

She wasn't sure. She didn't feel like Jessica Cartwright, that was for sure.

'I didn't want to let her go. Not because I loved her.' She cleared her throat. 'But probably because I didn't—at least, not at first. We'd never had an easy relationship. She was the adored child of two people who were very much in love, while I was the cuckoo in the nest—the offspring of the first marriage, a bad marriage, a marriage which should never have happened. At least, that's what I once heard my dad telling my stepmum. Hannah was always on the inside, in the warmth, while I always seemed to be out in the cold, literally, on the practice courts. And I think Hannah was a bit jealous of my tennis career. She used to hide my hairbrush, and sometimes my tennis racquet. She even threw away this stupid little mascot I carried around, until my father told me that champions didn't need mascots—they needed technique and determination.'

'So why did you fight so hard to keep her?'

'Because she was on her own and hurting,' she said simply. 'How could I not reach out to her?' But it hadn't been easy, because Jessica had been lost and hurting, too. She had missed her father. She had missed her career. And she'd missed Loukas. She'd missed him more than she could ever have imagined.

She realised she was cold. She was hugging her arms tightly around herself and wishing she hadn't taken off her jacket, especially now that Loukas's hard black gaze was sweeping over her.

'Why don't you go and take a bath?' he suggested roughly.

Awkwardly, she got to her feet. 'Good idea,' she said and went off into the bathroom, suddenly feeling self-conscious and realising that he hadn't touched her since they'd got back. Maybe he felt as cautious as she did, she thought as she upended lime and orange oil into the water and slowly lowered her aching body into the tub. Perhaps he'd realised that there was too much history for them to be able to enjoy a casual affair. Or maybe she wasn't capable of operating on that level.

Because already her feelings for him were changing. Minute by minute, she could feel it happening. She'd started to care what he thought of her. She'd started searching for emotions in his dark eyes. And it was a waste of time. He'd been completely honest about his reasons for wanting to have sex with her again—so why try to make it into something it wasn't? Embarking on a quest to make it into something it could never be was only ever going to bring her heartbreak.

She lay in the water for a long time—long enough for the skin at the ends of her fingers to become white and wrinkled. Long enough for Loukas to have grown bored with waiting, and to have made his escape, perhaps leaving behind a note scribbled on a piece of hotel notepaper. Because he certainly wasn't knocking at the bathroom door, asking her how long she was going to be.

Was he aware that a strange kind of shyness had crept over her as they'd stared at one another over the head of little Marco? That in that moment, she had glimpsed the little boy he'd once been and all the sadness he had known. She'd found herself thinking of the children she might have had with him. But Loukas doesn't want children, she reminded herself. He had been very clear about that.

Dragging a brush through her damp hair, she put on the massive bathrobe which was hanging on the back of the door and padded barefoot into her room, to find Loukas stretched out in one of the chairs, seemingly fast asleep. His eyes were closed and his face looked curiously relaxed as classical music drifted out from an unseen sound system.

She stood there, uncertain of whether or not she should wake him, when his lashes flickered apart and she was caught in the gleam of his ebony eyes.

'Hi,' he said softly. 'Good bath?'

She nodded, the lump in her throat making it impossible for her to speak because as he'd asked the innocent question it had sounded so heartbreakingly... *domestic*. It mocked her and taunted her with its implied intimacy. A real intimacy, which they'd never really shared.

There was a sudden knock on the door and she looked at him.

'Room Service,' he said, in answer to the question in her eyes

'I didn't order anything from Room Service.'

'No, but I did. Why don't you just get into bed, Jess? You look shattered. And don't look at me as if I'm the big, bad wolf, *koukla mou*.' His voice dipped. 'I am perfectly capable of being in the same room without leaping on you.'

She nodded, feeling the see-sawing of her own emotions in response to the things he was saying. She hadn't wanted sex, but suddenly she was finding that maybe she did. Only he seemed more concerned with getting his dinner!

But at least his back was turned as he answered the door, so that he wouldn't see her nakedness as she let the bathrobe slide to the floor before getting quickly into bed. It felt blissful as she sank into the mattress, the sheet cool and smooth beneath her clean skin, the duvet falling on top of her like a big, soft cloud.

She told herself she wasn't hungry but she must have been, because when he brought the food over to her—some sort of vegetable broth, followed by a toasted cheese sandwich—she began to devour it with an appetite which felt heightened. Comfort food, that was what they called food like this, and never had a description seemed more apt. After she'd finished she lay back against the feathery bank of pillows as the sound of violins filtered softly through the air.

'Better?' he questioned.

'Much.' She yawned. 'I didn't know you liked classical music.'

'Too brutish a sound for a rough, tough ex-body-guard?' His eyes glittered. 'You thought I'd be more into heavy metal?'

Too comfortable to object, Jessica smiled lazily. 'Something like that.'

'Why don't you close your eyes, Jess? Stop fighting it. You look exhausted.'

His deep accent was lulling her. It felt like velvet pressing against her skin. She wanted to ask him what he was planning, but her eyelids were heavy and she thought about his words and wondered what she was trying to fight. She drifted into a sleep which was light enough to feel the mattress dip when he got in beside her. He pulled her against him and the pleasant shock of honed muscle and warm skin told her that he, too, was naked. Did that mean he *did* want sex?

'Loukas,' she mumbled.

'Shh,' he said, his arms tightening around her waist as he pulled her even closer and the room fell into darkness as he clicked off the lamp.

She must have slept because when she drifted back into consciousness, it was to find her head pillowed comfortably against his shoulder, her lips right next to the burr of his unshaven jaw. She kissed it. She couldn't help it; her lips seemed programmed to brush over that proud curve. He mumbled something as his hand slid down to cup her bottom while the other reached behind her head and guided her lips towards his.

That first kiss was lazy. It seemed to happen in slow motion, as if they had all the time in the world. As if she'd never really kissed him properly before. And maybe she hadn't. Beneath the protective cloak of darkness it seemed that there were a million ways to explore a man's mouth, and Jessica was about to discover every one of them. She could feel him smile as, slowly, she traced the tip of her tongue over the cushioned surface. He gave a murmur of satisfaction as she pressed kiss after little kiss against him. His body felt warm and comfortable against hers and soon she began to trickle her fingertip over his chest, allowing it to continue its path inexorably downwards. But he stopped her when she reached the dark whorls of hair which lay at the base of his belly, wreathing the sudden hard jerk of his erection.

'No. Not yet,' he said urgently. 'I'm so turned on, I hardly dare risk putting on a condom.'

She swallowed, because something about his words had sent crazy thoughts splintering into her mind. 'But you will?'

'Yes, I will. Even though I long to feel myself naked inside you. My skin bare against your skin. My seed in your body.'

His words excited her, but presumably that had been his intention. They reminded her that for Loukas this was all about technique—a bit like tennis, really. It might feel deep and emotional and highly intimate, but that was her stuff. Her stupid desires. And she mustn't give into them. She mustn't.

But it was hard not to be swept away when he was kissing each of her breasts with a thoroughness which felt almost like tenderness. Or when he lifted her up effortlessly to slide her down on top of him, murmuring silky words in Greek which sounded almost *loving*. Suspecting that he would want to watch her moving up and down on him, she waited for him to reach over and put the light on—but he didn't. And the lack of a spotlight on her face meant that she could give into what she really wanted to do, and what she wanted to do more than anything was not hold back. So she tangled her fingers in this thick hair and she told him he was beautiful. And if his big body stiffened for a moment and she sensed his sudden suspicion, that was quickly forgotten when she rode him with a determination which suddenly seemed outside her own control.

'Jess,' he gasped, and she'd never heard him say her name like that before.

But then her thoughts were blotted out and her body tensed around him.

And the most stupid thing of all was that she found herself wishing that he *hadn't* worn a condom.

CHAPTER TEN

'THESE ARE AMAZING,' said Gabe Steel slowly. 'Probably the most amazing transformation I've seen all year. Cinderella doesn't come close to it.'

Loukas stared at the mocked-up advert which covered most of the advertising chief's large desk and drank in the images staring back at him. Jessica Cartwright looking like he'd never imagined she could look. Who would have thought it? He shook his head slightly. He'd stayed away on the second day of the shoot and knew the crew had been pleased with the results, but even so. Hard to believe this was the same Jess who wore classy clothes in shades of cream and taupe while her sensible ponytail bobbed behind her. The same Jess who had stood wobbling awkwardly in the gondola during the first shoot, looking like a little girl dressed up in her mother's clothes.

His throat tightened.

The black and white photos were broken only by the magenta gleam of her lips and the Lulu ribbon which lay in a gleaming swirl by her feet. Against the imposing backdrop of the iconic city, she tipped her head at an angle and looked straight into the lens. Her breasts were highlighted by the low-cut bodice, showcasing the diamonds which blazed like ice fire next to her pale skin. A gentle breeze had lifted the blonde hair so that the blunt-cut strands whipped around her chin, and her smoky eyes were emphasised by the heavy fringe.

But it was more than her beauty or the air of fragility she seemed to project, or even the way her eyes seemed full of a strange, clear light. She personified sex…that was the thing. It radiated from every pore of her body. It was there in every gesture she made. The pout of her lips was defiant and the hand slung carelessly against her jutting hip made her look like every man's fantasy come true. The teenage sweetheart was all grown up.

'What the hell happened to her?' Gabe was asking, his eyes narrowing as he looked at Loukas.

Loukas didn't answer. How could he possibly answer, when he knew it would sound like some kind of chest-thumping macho boast if he told the truth? *She looks like a woman who has just been thoroughly ravished and I should know because I was the one doing the ravishing.*

And that was another shock to the system. He hadn't expected the sex to be so good. He'd thought that once the novelty of having her in his arms again had worn off, he would realise that there were plenty of lovers more exciting than Jessica Cartwright. He'd tried to convince himself that he had built up the memory of their lovemaking in his mind to be something it wasn't. Only it hadn't turned out that way. It had been mind-blowing. Every time. He'd felt as if he were touching the stars. He'd spent his entire time in the city in a dazed and permanent state of arousal.

Was that why he had persuaded her to stay on?

Why one night had turned into two and then three? He'd intended them to fly back to England the day after they'd returned Marco to his parents, but something had stopped him and he told himself it must have been sex. But there had been something else which had made him want to prolong it, and that had been the nagging certainty that this relationship would not survive the cold light of reality. A love affair in Venice was one thing, when you could get swept away by the history and the atmosphere and the sheer beauty of the city. But life back in the UK, with their normal lives threatening to collide? No way.

He realised that Gabe was still staring at him, waiting for a reply to his question.

'I guess she grew up,' said Loukas simply.

'You know we have to capitalise on this?' said Gabe. 'Give the campaign a kick-start. Show the world that this is going to be big...'

Almost absently Loukas nodded as he studied the shot of her in the black and white dress and a pair of rubber boots, standing ankle-deep in water in a flooded St Mark's Square. They'd caught her looking up at something overhead—a bird?—and she was *giggling* and, despite being all grown up, suddenly she looked about eighteen again. Something clenched at his heart. 'How?' he questioned huskily.

'We throw a cocktail party for the press at the Granchester on Monday night, with the new look Jessica as the guest of honour.'

Loukas frowned. 'Isn't that a little short notice?'

'Not on a Monday—and not with your name attached to the invitation,' said Gabe drily. 'It's amazing the space people can find in their diaries if the person holding the party is influential enough. I'll get Patti to sort out Jessica's wardrobe and make sure she has something suitable to wear.' He frowned. 'Another dress, I think, and some of the best gems in your collection. But not diamonds this time. Let's go for something different.'

'Sapphires,' said Loukas slowly, and the thought of the darker hue contrasting with the aquamarine gleam of her eyes sent a thrill of desire skittering over his skin. 'She will wear my sapphires.'

Jessica stared at herself in the mirror. This time the dress was blue, and her jewellery gleamed as darkly as the midnight sky. She lifted her hand to her hair, watching her reflection mimicking the movement, her fingertips brushing against a small sapphire and diamond clip which glittered like starlight.

The sound of a footfall disturbed her and as she looked up to see Loukas reflected back in the glass, her heart began to pound erratically.

'You look beautiful,' he said.

She closed her eyes and shivered as he lowered his head to plant a kiss on one bare shoulder. 'Do I?'

'You know you do. You don't need me to tell you that, Jess.'

But that was where he was wrong—she *did*. She stared at his dark, bent head. She still felt like someone playing dress-up. She still felt vulnerable—especially since they'd arrived back in England and Loukas had persuaded her to stay in London. He'd told her that it was crazy not to use her luxury suite at the Vinoly Hotel, while they continued to *enjoy* one another. He had said this while trickling one finger over the swell of her naked breast and she hadn't really been in a position to say no. In fact she hadn't been in a position to do anything except make love, which was what he had been doing to her at the time.

But the reality of being in London like this didn't sit comfortably. Loukas went into the office each morning, and although she made sure that she took advantage of all that the city had to offer—including a gorgeous exhibition of Victorian embroidery—she felt like a fish out of water. As if she was waiting all the time. Waiting for him.

And Loukas seemed…well…*different*. She stifled a sigh. It wasn't something she could put her finger on. Was his lovemaking more cold-blooded than it had been in Venice, or was that just her imagination? It wasn't something she could really discuss with him without causing offence—and she didn't want to offend him. She wanted… She stared at his reflection in the mirror as he continued to kiss his way along her shoulder… She didn't know what she wanted, only that it was unlikely to involve roses and moonlight. Not from him. She sensed that for him it was already over, like when you turned an egg timer and the sand started to trickle away—the countdown had begun.

But she wasn't going to let him see her insecurities or her fears. She was going to take it all in her stride, because she was good at doing that. So as he lifted his lips from her shoulder she was able to smile so widely that she almost convinced herself she was happy. She thought about the evening ahead and sent him a slightly anxious look. 'So all I have to do tonight is chat to people and twirl around?'

'You've got it in one. Why don't you practise now?' His voice lowered. 'Twirl around. Go on.'

'Loukas.' Something in his face was turning her stomach to jelly. 'You…mustn't.'

'Mustn't what?'

Her voice sounded breathless. 'You can't kiss me now because my lipstick will—'

'Tough,' he said darkly, blotting out all her objections and kissing her so thoroughly that afterwards she had to apply the magenta-coloured gloss all over again.

But his behaviour during the short journey to the Granchester seemed to reinforce her growing insecurity. Nobody would have ever guessed they were a couple because he made no outward sign that they were anything more than working colleagues. He didn't touch her, or take her hand in his. There was no complicit smile which might indicate to the world that she was sharing his bed. Tonight she was very definitely the employee and he the boss, and she found herself thinking that their relationship had always been defined by secrecy.

A barrage of photographers was waiting outside the hotel and she kept her smile pinned to her lips as she was dazzled by the blinding wall of flash which greeted their arrival. Because she knew they weren't just here to see the jewellery. They were here to gaze in curiosity at her new, glossy image. They were hoping that she had bitten off more than she could chew, because there was nothing the press liked more than to bear witness to failure…

Inside, the Venetian photos had been blown up and mounted on the walls, so that they dominated the smaller of the Granchester's two ballrooms. Everywhere she looked she could see herself and, once Jessica had become acclimatised to the slightly surreal sensation, she found herself glancing round in disbelief. She looked so *different*. But it wasn't just the sharp new haircut or the heavier than usual make-up. It wasn't even the dress or the diamonds which made her look so unrecognisable. It was the shining look in her eyes—as if she were nursing the most beautiful secret in the world.

And Jessica realised with a jolt that she looked like a woman...if not actually *in* love, then certainly bordering on the edges of it.

But the camera lied. She knew that.

Pushing aside her confused thoughts, she tried to work the room as she knew she should. She spoke to a couple of women who worked on glossy magazines and was introduced to a man who wrote the diary section of an upmarket tabloid. But despite her outward air of confidence, she found it impossible to relax, especially as Loukas was on the other side of the room and had barely acknowledged her all evening.

She didn't dare eat anything for fear of smudging her lips and the single sip of cocktail she indulged in felt strong enough to blow her head off. This isn't my world, she thought desperately. It never really was. Everyone else seemed to know their own place in it, but not her. The smile plastered to her lips felt forced and she was terrified her conversation sounded dull to these urban high-flyers. Because they sure as hell weren't interested in talking about embroidery or growing vegetables.

It was with a feeling of relief that she saw Patti and slipped into a corner to talk to the stylist, feeling relaxed for the first time all evening, when suddenly she glanced across the room to see Loukas deep in conversation with a brunette. He'd been talking to other women, of course—she'd clocked that—but this seemed more...*intimate.*

The woman was wearing a sparkly dress so short that it made Jessica's own feel as if it had been borrowed from a museum. He was leaning his head forward to listen intently and as the woman spoke her dark hair swayed like a glossy mahogany curtain. Jessica could feel herself tensing as she saw him laugh and Patti must have noticed the direction of her glance, because she turned her head and smiled.

'Yeah. Stunning, isn't she? *And* she's French. Used to be a human rights lawyer before she started writing for one of the papers and now she's one of the best-paid feature writers in the country. Life is so unfair, isn't it?'

Don't ask it, Jessica urged herself. *Just don't ask it.*

She asked it.

'They seem to know each other very well?'

Patti smiled. 'Yeah. I think they were lovers for a while, in Paris.'

'Really?' Jessica wondered if that squeaking reply was really her voice. Was that sick pounding of her heart due to an unwanted wave of *jealousy* which she had no right to feel?

She tried not to let it spoil the rest of the evening, telling herself she wasn't even going to mention it. Even in the car on the way back to the hotel, she managed to make small talk and to look suitably pleased when Loukas told her how happy everyone was with her performance.

He brushed his hand over her waist as they stopped outside her suite and reached into her bag for her key card.

'Hey,' he said softly. 'Want to come to mine?'

'Not tonight. Would you mind?' She forced a smile. 'I'm very tired.'

'So?' He stroked a reflective fingertip over her rib-cage. 'Haven't I proved that I'm capable of letting you sleep, even if having you naked beside me drives me crazy with desire?'

'Who was that woman?'

Her blurted question seemed to come out of no-where and he raised his eyebrows. 'There were a lot of women there this evening, Jess.'

'The brunette. The one in the mini-dress.'

'Ah, yes. Maya.' He smiled. 'Her name is Maya.'

Heart pounding, she pushed open the door and walked inside and he followed her.

'Why, were you jealous?' he continued, almost conversationally.

'No.'

'Liar.' He gave a soft laugh. 'You were. You are. I can read it on your face.'

And that was Jessica's wake-up call. He wasn't *supposed* to be reading *anything* on her face, because one of her great strengths was to hide her feelings behind a cool mask. *Wasn't* it? If he'd started seeing things like jealousy in her eyes, how soon before he started seeing other things, too? Stuff she was trying to deny even to herself because she knew that it was pointless. Stuff like still caring for him when she knew there was no future in it. Stuff like falling in love with him all over again.

And then a thought occurred to her and a terrible wave of suspicion washed over her, so that she had to fight it like crazy. She knew he was ruthless. He'd told her he was ruthless. Had he...had he deliberately gone out of his way to make her fall for him, just so that he could do to her what she'd done to him all those years ago?

'Like I said, I'm very tired.'

His face darkened. 'Is Maya the reason for the icy look and frozen behaviour? Is talking to an ex-lover such a terrible thing to do when I meet her socially? What would you have me do, Jess? Tell her I'm sorry, but I happen to be sleeping with someone who wants to keep me on a leash?'

She shook her head, telling herself that she was being stupid but it didn't seem to help. *Because this was the world he operated in. A world full of sophisticated ex-lovers he bumped into at parties and then made as if it didn't matter. Because it didn't.* Not to him. A man didn't get a reputation as a playboy because he sat at home every night, nursing a cup of cocoa. Playboys had partners. Lots of them. Playboys were known mainly for the fact that they never settled down, and she needed to accept that. You didn't get a second chance in life. Not with someone like Loukas.

'Of course not,' she said. 'It was completely unreasonable and I don't know what came over me.'

He tilted her chin with his fingers so that she had nowhere to look except into the dark gleam of his eyes. 'So what shall we do to make it better?'

It wasn't easy but she gave the smile she knew was expected of her. The one with just the right amount of flirtation. One which managed to convey that she'd just had a temporary blip, but that everything was fine again.

Except that it wasn't. She felt as if she were standing on the edge of a cliff which had started to crumble and any minute now she would lose her footing and fall, if she wasn't sensible enough to take a step back.

This wasn't going anywhere. She'd known that from the beginning. So get out now, before it's too late.

Putting her arms around his neck, she drew him close and heard his soft laugh as he slid down the zip of her dress with practised fingers. She closed her eyes as his fingers found her bare skin and, automatically, she began to shiver.

Once more, she told herself.

One more night.

CHAPTER ELEVEN

SHE WAS GONE when he returned from work next evening and as Loukas looked at the single sheet of paper which was all that was left of her, he realised that it came as no great surprise. Last night in his arms, she had been mind-blowing but he'd sensed something in the way she'd kissed him before he'd left for work that morning…a certain sadness which no amount of sexual chemistry could disguise. Her lips had lingered on his in a way which had seemed wistful rather than provocative. And when he stopped to think about it, hadn't there been a little catch in her voice as she'd said goodbye?

He hadn't needed to read the few words she'd written on hotel notepaper to know that she wasn't planning on coming back.

He stared at it.

Thanks.

He frowned. For *what*, exactly? The job or the sex?

I had a fabulous time in Venice, and I'm glad that the photos were such a success, but I'm missing

Cornwall and I have a garden which is missing me.
Take good care of yourself, Loukas.
Jess.

She hadn't even put a kiss, she'd just drawn one of those stupid, smiley faces and he screwed up the sheet of paper, crushing it viciously in the palm of his hand. She'd walked out on him. She'd turned her back on him. Again. She was arrogant, she was haughty and he didn't need this.

He did not need this.

Stalking over to the drinks cabinet, he poured himself a glass of vodka and tossed it back in one deft mouthful, the way Dimitri had taught him.

Only the liquor didn't do what it was supposed to do. It didn't douse the fury which had started to flame inside him. It didn't stop him from wanting to haul her into his arms and...what?

Have sex with her?

Yes. His mouth twisted. That was what he wanted. All he wanted.

He paced around his suite, wondering why tonight it felt like a cage, despite the unparalleled luxury of the fixtures and fittings. Because he'd grown used to having her just along the corridor—was that it? And how the hell could that happen in such a short time?

Because it hadn't *been* a short time, he realised. This had been bubbling away under the surface for years.

He forced himself to concentrate on work, losing himself in the negotiations to open a branch of Lulu in Singapore's Orchard Road. And there was other good news which should have helped put Jessica Cartwright into the background of his mind. His sales team informed him excitedly that sales of precious stones in the London store alone had shot up by a staggering twenty-five per cent following the Valentine's Day advert—and they were planning to use the same advertisement on a global basis. It really *was* going to be big.

He went to the gym every night for punishing workouts, which left his body exhausted but his mind still racing. He turned down dinner invitations and threw himself into his work, which for once did not provide its all-encompassing distractions.

But life went on and the press was still going crazy. Gabe Steel phoned to say that his agency had been fielding calls from media outlets ever since Jess's piece had gone to press, since everyone was keen to discover how the sporty tennis star had transformed herself into such a vamp. Would she like to give an interview to one of the papers? Would she do a short slot on breakfast TV, or the even more popular mid-morning show? Were they planning to use her in another campaign any time soon?

'And?' bit out Loukas. 'It was supposed to be a one-off.'

'I know, but we'd be crazy not to capitalise on this,' said Gabe. 'The trouble is that nobody can get hold of her. She isn't answering her phone, or her emails. I'm thinking of sending—'

'No. Don't bother doing that. I'll go,' said Loukas, and it wasn't until he'd put the phone down that it occurred to him that Gabe hadn't questioned why the company boss should be chasing down to the other end of the country after some random model.

He set off early in the morning, just as the sun was beginning to rise and the roads were empty, save for the occasional lorry. It was a long time since he'd been to Cornwall and it brought back memories of a different life. He remembered the first time he'd seen it. His Russian boss had owned huge chunks of land there, as well as mooring one of his boats in Padstow—and the summer he'd spent there had been the most glorious of his life. For a boy brought up in the crowded backstreets of Athens, it had felt like a different world to Loukas. The wildness and the beauty. The sense of being remote. The salty air and the crash of the ocean. As the roads began to narrow into lanes and he passed through picture-perfect little villages, he thought how little had really changed.

And wasn't it funny how your feet automatically guided you to a place you hadn't seen in eight long years? The Cartwright mansion could still be seen from a distance, like some shining citadel outlined against the crisp blue of the winter sky, with its mullioned windows and its soaring roofs, and the lavender-edged gardens which swept right down to the cliffs. Across to one side, where the land was flatter, was the footpath which passed the tennis court where once he had watched Jess practise.

But when he rang the doorbell, a woman in her thirties appeared—a small child hiding behind her legs. The woman smiled at him and automatically touched her hair.

'Can I help you?'

He frowned, trying to work out who she could possibly be. 'I'm looking for Jess. Jessica.'

'Cartwright?'

'That's right.'

'She doesn't live here any more. We bought it from the people she sold it to. She's up on Atlantic Terrace now—near the cliff path. The little house right on the end, the one with the crooked chimney—do you know it?'

He didn't know it but he nodded, his mind working overtime as he thanked the woman and parked his car in the village, telling himself it was because he needed the exercise and not because he didn't want to be seen by Jess as he approached.

But that wasn't strictly true. His thoughts were reeling and he was trying to make some sense of them. Had she sold up to simplify her life, or because it was too big for her and her half-sister?

He found what was in fact a cottage and it was small. Very small. He rapped loudly on the door, but there was no reply and suddenly he wondered what he was going to do if she'd gone away. She could be anywhere. He didn't know a single thing about her daily life, he realised. He'd imagined her life staying exactly the same, while his own had moved on. It had been part of his fixed image of Jess—the upper-class blonde in her country mansion. Because wasn't it easier to be angry with a stereotype than with a real person?

He walked to the back of the property and that was where he found her, attacking the bare earth furiously with a spade. She didn't hear him at first and as he found himself looking at the denim tightening over her buttocks, it was difficult not to appreciate the sheer grace of her movements.

She must have heard him, or sensed him, because suddenly she whirled round—her face growing through a whole series of emotions but so rapidly that he couldn't make out a single one except for the one which settled there, and it was one which was distinctly unwelcoming.

She leant heavily on the spade as if she needed it for support. 'What are you doing here, Loukas?'

'Parakalo,' he said sardonically. 'Nice to see you, too.'

She seemed to remember herself and forced a cool smile.

'Sorry. It just came as a bit of a shock, you creeping up on me like that.'

'Creeping?' he echoed.

'You know what I mean.' She shrugged, but the movement seemed to take a lot of effort. 'I mean, obviously, you're not just passing.'

'Obviously.'

She looked at him with her eyebrows raised as if she wanted him to help her out, but something stubborn had taken residence inside him and he didn't feel like helping her out.

'So why are you here?'

It was a question he'd been asking himself during the four-and-a-half-hour drive but had given up on it because he couldn't seem to find a satisfactory answer. 'You haven't been answering your phone. Or your emails.'

She held her finger to her lips and began to tap them, as if considering his accusation. 'I don't think that's written into my contract.'

'Maybe it isn't,' he said, feeling a nerve beginning to flicker at his temple. 'But I don't think it's unreasonable of us to want to get hold of you, is it?'

'*Us?*'

'Zeitgeist,' he bit out, wondering what the hell was the matter with her. Why she was being so damned stubborn. And so remote. Hadn't they just spent the best part of a week being about as intimate as a man and woman could be? 'And Lulu,' he added. 'You know. The people who provided you with work.'

'I was told it was a one-off.' She gripped the handle of the spade. 'And you were the one who told me that.'

'With hindsight, I might have spoken a little hastily.'

Her gaze was steady. 'If only we all had the benefit of hindsight, Loukas.'

He frowned. He didn't want this impenetrable *wall* between them. He wanted her onside. 'The campaign has been a huge success.'

'Ah.' She smiled. 'The campaign.'

'We've been inundated with requests for interviews, TV—'

'So have I,' she said sharply. 'My answer machine keeps getting filled up with messages, even though I clear it at the end of every day.'

'But you didn't think to answer them?'

'Actually, I did. And then decided not to.' She wrapped her jacket more tightly around herself and gave an exaggerated shiver. 'I'm getting cold just standing here.'

'Then why don't you take me inside and offer me some of your legendary English hospitality?'

Jessica hesitated when she heard the sarcasm in his voice, but she could hardly say no. And the trouble was that she didn't want to say no. She wanted to know what had brought him here—appearing on her horizon like some dark avenging angel. Most of all she wanted him to kiss her, and that was where the danger lay. She had missed him so much that it had hurt and yet now that she had seen him again her heart had started aching even more. This was a lose-lose situation and his presence here wasn't going to help her in the long term. But you couldn't really turn a man away when he'd driven all this way to see you, could you?

'You'd better come in,' she said.

He followed her into the kitchen and she could sense him looking around as she put the kettle on. What did he think of her dresser, with the eclectic collection of jugs, or the cork board studded with all the postcards which Hannah had sent from her travels? Was he comparing it to his huge but cold suite at the Vinoly and did it all look terribly *parochial* to his sophisticated eye?

The wind had ruffled his black hair and he was dressed in jeans more faded than hers, along with a battered brown leather jacket. His casual clothes started playing tricks with her memory. Like a flashback, they gave her a glimpse of the man he had once been. The big bear of a bodyguard who used to watch her from the side of a tennis court. But flashbacks were notoriously unreliable—they always painted the past in such flattering shades that you wanted to be back there. And that was impossible. The past was the refuge for losers who couldn't cope with the present, and she wasn't going to be one of those losers.

She made tea and took the tray into the small sitting room which overlooked the Atlantic. She thought about lighting a fire but then decided against it, because he wasn't staying long. He definitely wasn't staying long.

'So…' She put a steaming star-decorated mug on a small table beside one of the chairs, but he didn't take the hint to sit down—he just strode over to the window and stood there, staring out at the crashing ocean, his silhouetted body dark and powerful and more than a little intimidating.

He turned back, eyes narrowed. 'Did you move because the house was too big?'

She thought about saying yes. It would be understandable, after all—especially now that it was just her. But Jessica knew that she couldn't keep hiding behind her cool mask, thinking that to do so would offer her some kind of protection. Because she'd realised that it didn't. Masks didn't stop you wishing for things which were never going to come true. And they didn't stop your heart from hurting when you fell for men who were wrong for you.

'No,' she said. 'I moved because I had to. Because my father had built up massive debts which were only revealed after he was killed in the avalanche.'

His eyes narrowed, but there wasn't a flicker of emotion on his own face. And suddenly she was glad that he hadn't come out with the usual platitudes which people always trotted out, platitudes which meant zero and somehow ended up making you feel even worse. Maybe they were more alike than she'd thought. Or maybe now that they had entered the dark worlds of death and debts, he suddenly felt on familiar ground.

He sat down then, lowering his mighty frame into a chair which up until that moment had always looked substantial.

'What happened?'

She watched as he picked up his tea and sipped it. 'Like everyone else, he was banking on me winning a Grand Slam, or three. He was very ambitious.' She shrugged. 'They say that fathers make the best and the worst coaches.'

'You didn't like him very much,' he said slowly.

His words came out of the blue. Few people would have thought it and even fewer would have dared say it. It would be easier to deny it but her chin stayed high and defiant as she met his eyes with a challenge. 'Does that shock you?'

He gave a hard smile in response. 'Very little in life shocks me, *koukla mou*.'

The soft Greek words slid over her skin, touching her at a time when she was feeling vulnerable, but she tried not to be swayed by them. She cleared her throat. 'He did his best. He did what he thought was right. It's just that he never really allowed me to have a normal life.'

'So why didn't you stand up to him?'

Recognising that his question was about more than the unbending routine of her tennis years, Jessica picked up a match and struck it to the crumpled-up paper in the grate, seeing the heated flare as it caught the logs and hoping it would warm the sudden chill of her skin. Because sometimes it was easier to be told what to do than to think for yourself. It meant you could blame someone else if it all went wrong. And it was hard to admit that, even to herself.

'There were lots of reasons why I didn't stand up to him, but I suppose what you really want to know is why I wasn't stronger when it came to you. Why I let him drive a wedge between us.' She sensed that he was holding his breath but she couldn't look at him. She didn't dare. Because if she removed her mask completely—mightn't he be repulsed by the face he saw beneath?

She threw an unnecessary log onto the fire. 'I thought we were too young to settle down and my career was very important to me.'

'But that's not the only reason, is it, Jess?'

There was a pause. 'No.' Her voice sounded quiet against the crackle of the fire. She stared into the forest of flames, losing herself in that flickering orange kingdom. 'I was an unsettled child. My parents split up when I was very young. My dad left my mum for a younger woman who was already pregnant with his child—Hannah—and my mum never really got over that. I lived with her shame and her bitterness, which didn't leave much room for anything else.'

She picked up her tea and cupped her hands around it. 'When she died I went to live with my father and that's when the tennis really kicked off. At last I had something to believe in. Something I could lose myself in. But my stepmother resented the amount of time it took him away from her and I think Hannah was a bit jealous of all the attention I got.' She gave a slightly nervous laugh. 'I mean, I'm probably making it sound worse than it was, but it was—'

'It sounds awful,' he interjected and she found herself having to blink back the sudden threat of tears, because his sympathy was unexpectedly potent.

'I'd already learnt not to show my feelings,' she said. 'And that became a useful tactic on the tennis court. Soon I didn't know how to be any other way. I learnt to block my emotions. Not to let anything or anyone in. Now do you understand?'

He nodded. 'I think so.'

'I didn't want to make you any promises I couldn't keep,' she rushed on. 'And marriage was an institution I didn't trust.'

But it had been more than that. On an instinctive level she had recognised that Loukas was a man who had been in short supply of love, who needed to be loved properly. And hadn't she thought herself incapable of that?

'There's something else,' he said. 'Something you're not telling me.'

It hurt that he could be so perceptive. She didn't want him to be perceptive—she wanted him to be brash and uncaring. She wanted him to reinforce that she'd done the right thing, not leave her wondering how she could have been so stupid.

'Jess?' he prompted.

'I thought you would leave me,' she said slowly.

'Like your father left your mother?'

'I was so young,' she whispered. 'You know I was.'

He looked at her and started speaking slowly, as if he was voicing his thoughts out loud. 'I'd like to tell you that my feelings haven't changed, but that would be strange, as well as a fabrication—because of course I feel differently eight years down the line.'

Her lips had started trembling and no amount of biting would seem to stop them. 'You do?'

He nodded. 'I still care about you, *koukla mou*. You're still the one woman who makes my heart beat faster than anyone else. Still the one who can tie me up in knots so tight I can't escape, and I don't think you even realise you're doing it.'

'So what are you saying?' she whispered.

Loukas opened his lips to speak, but an inbuilt

self-protection forced him to temper his words with caution. Just like when you were negotiating a big takeover—you didn't lay all your cards on the table at once, did you? You always kept something back.

'I'm saying that it still feels...*unfinished.* That maybe we should give it another go. What's stopping us?'

She put her mug down and pulled the scrunchy from her hair, shaking her head so that a tumble of hair fell loosely around her cheeks.

'Loads of things. We live in different worlds, for a start,' she said. 'We always did, but it's even more defined now. I'm a country girl with a simple life. The annual photo shoot in London was just something I did to finance this life. The rest of the time, I forget all about it.'

'I'm not forcing you to become the global face of Lulu if you don't want to be,' he said impatiently. 'That's not what this is all about.'

'You're missing my point, Loukas,' she said, and now she was gesturing to something he hadn't noticed before, which lay on a small table in the corner of the room. A piece of cloth covered with exquisite sewing. He narrowed his eyes. It looked like a cosmic sky, with bright planets and stars sparking across an indigo background.

'Yours?' he questioned.

She nodded. 'Mine.'

'It's beautiful,' he said automatically.

'Thank you. It's something that's become more than a hobby and I've sold several pieces through a shop in Padstow. I'm into embroidery and gardening and now that Hannah's gone away, I was even thinking of getting a cat—that's how sad I am. You, on the other hand, live permanently in a hotel and drive around in a chauffeur-driven car. You occupy a luxury suite in the centre of London and you get other people to run your life for you. We're polar opposites, Loukas. You don't have a real home. You don't seem to want one and I do. That's what I want more than anything.' Her voice trembled, as if it hurt her to say the words. 'A real home.'

CHAPTER TWELVE

LOUKAS DIDN'T ANSWER straight away. It was easier to watch the Atlantic crashing on the rocks in the distance and to listen to the crackle of the fire, rather than having to face up to what Jess had just told him. He'd never heard her be so frank and realised it must have taken a lot for her to put her feelings on the line like that. And even though he was determined to hold something back, that didn't mean he couldn't proceed with caution, did it?

'What if I told you that the reason I don't have a home is because I don't know how it works?' he said. 'And that I've never been sufficiently interested in the concept to find out?'

'Well, there you go. You've answered your own question.'

'But you could show me,' he continued, as if she hadn't interrupted.

She stared at him and there was a mutinous look in her eyes as if she didn't believe him. As if she was waiting for him to pull out the punchline and start laughing. But he wasn't laughing, he was deadly serious and maybe she picked up on that. 'Because I don't feel this thing we have between us has run its course,' he said.

'This *thing*?'

'Don't get hung up on words, Jess.' His voice deepened. 'I'm Greek, remember?'

'As if I'm likely to forget.' She tucked a strand of hair behind her ear. 'And I don't really understand what you're suggesting.'

He shrugged. 'That I move in here with you and see whether I'm compatible with home life.'

She laughed. 'But you're an international playboy.'

He gave her a slow smile. 'That could be negotiable.'

'And you have a job.'

'I also have a computer and a phone—and the ability to pull back and delegate.' He looked at her steadily. 'And it's been a very long time since I had a vacation.'

Jessica stared down at her fingernails, her initial disbelief at his suggestion morphing into a feeling of confusion. She suspected he was motivated more by ambition than any real emotion. He'd said himself this *thing* felt *unfinished* and maybe that was bugging him—because he was the kind of man who didn't like to leave things unfinished. Maybe this was all about great sex and the fact that they were still so attracted to one another. Was he banking on that attraction burning itself out, so that he could walk away? Just using the lure of *home* as a legitimate way to get his foot in the door?

Yet if he left now, what then? Would she spend the rest of her life regretting it and wondering *what if*? Too scared to face up to something which had lain beneath the surface of her life for so long, something which subconsciously might have been holding her back. There had been many times she'd wished she had the chance to do it all over again and now the opportunity was presenting itself. By allowing him access to her life, mightn't the pedestal she'd placed him on begin to crumble, freeing her from his power over her?

'If I said yes,' she said slowly, 'it could end at any time.'

'I can't guarantee—'

'No, Loukas.' She cut him off with a shake of her head, embarrassed that he thought she was trying to back him into a corner. 'I'm not asking you to pledge anything or promise anything. I'm trying to be practical because I'm a practical person.' She drew in a deep breath. 'If either of us wants out, at any time—any time at all—then we have to be able to say so. No questions. No post-mortems. Just a shrug and a smile, and a simple goodbye.'

His dark eyes gleamed. 'This is beginning to sound like my dream scenario.'

'I aim to please,' she said lightly.

He stood up and walked across the room and Jessica could almost *feel* the testosterone radiating from his powerful body.

'You certainly do. You please me very much.' His voice dipped. 'But if this is such an equal and such a *practical* arrangement, then surely I get to make a few requests myself, *koukla mou*.'

Something in the darkness of his face made her throat turn to parchment. 'Like what?' she questioned breathlessly.

'We may be playing house, but we aren't going to be constrained by house rules. We don't clock in and clock out. You won't start slamming cupboards if I'm late for dinner.'

'But you might be the one cooking dinner, and I might be the one who's late.'

'I might.' His eyes glittered. 'Just so long as you don't try to change me,' he said as his gaze travelled slowly over her body and seemed to linger there. 'And no rules about sex, either. We don't use it as a weapon or as a negotiating tool.'

'Gosh. You sound as if you've had some pretty bad experiences with women.'

'You think so?' He gave a cynical smile. 'I'd say it was the normal experience of a wealthy and attractive man who happens to be good in bed. And before you start pulling faces like that—I'm trying to be honest.' He paused. 'But again, in the pursuit of fairness—perhaps I should ask you the same thing. Have you had bad experiences with men?'

She hadn't been expecting the question and therefore hadn't prepared an answer, but now was not the time to make the announcement that there hadn't *been* anyone except for him. Apart from making her look hopelessly out of touch, mightn't it also make him wary? He might realise that nobody else had come close to making her feel the way he had done. That she had fallen for him big time. That she was expecting a whole lot more than he could ever give.

So she smiled. 'I thought we were going to have fun,' she said. 'Not rake up stuff about the past. The past has gone, Loukas, and this is what we're left with.'

'So it is.' He pulled her to her feet, tipping her chin upwards so that there was nowhere to look except at him, and when he spoke again his voice had deepened and suddenly it no longer sounded steady. 'I want you, Jess.'

'Let's go upstairs to bed,' she whispered.

He shook his head. 'I don't want to go anywhere. Draw the curtains.'

Her hands were trembling as she did as he asked, turning back to see his face looking shadowed in the suddenly subdued lighting broken only by the dancing flicker of the fire.

'Loukas,' she said uncertainly, and suddenly he was all over her. His hands were fumbling with the zip of her jeans, yanking them down to her ankles before impatiently tugging them off and hurling them to one side. He was peeling her sweater over her head and she was urging him on—silently positioning her body to make access easier. She shrugged the leather jacket from his broad shoulders and heard it slide to the floor. She eased the zip of his jeans down, but he was so aroused—the hard ridge of him so *big* beneath her still-trembling fingers—that he pushed her hand away.

'No. Let me,' he said succinctly, before freeing himself.

She gasped as he did so and it felt so deliciously decadent to be stripping off in the shadowy firelight that she reached down to cradle him in her hands but, again, he pushed her away—rapidly disposing of his own remaining clothes until they were both naked before the golden flicker of the flames.

'Now,' he said, but his voice sounded so tight and urgent that it was almost as if she had never heard him speak before. She was breathless and wet as he eased the condom on himself with an exaggerated amount of care, as if only by doing that could he hang onto a self-control which seemed perilously close to deserting him. And then he positioned himself over her, that first deep thrust making her moan and his subsequent rhythm making her moan ever more. Until he stopped and a mumbled protest fell from her lips.

'L-Loukas—'

'Open your eyes,' he ordered. 'Open your eyes and look at me.'

Reluctantly she let her lashes flutter apart to meet his smoky black gaze, afraid of what he might be able to read when all her defences were down. She tried to tell herself that this was what every woman felt when she was having sex with a man, but on some fundamental level she knew that wasn't true. Because surely it wasn't normal to feel as if your heart were on fire. As if you wanted to burst with joy. Those were the feelings you associated with love.

But Loukas wasn't looking for love. The reason he wanted her to open her eyes was to gauge her level of satisfaction, and there was no hiding *that*.

Her lashes flickered open completely, and he smiled.

'That's better,' he said. 'Tell me what you like, Jess. Tell me what you want me to do to you.'

She wondered what he expected—a verbal map to indicate just which zones she found most erogenous, or an expressed preference for a different position? But in reality, there was only one thing Jessica wanted Loukas to do to her.

'Just kiss me,' she said, because that was the closest she could get to asking him to love her.

CHAPTER THIRTEEN

BE CAREFUL WHAT you wish for.

Jessica stood at her bedroom window, watching Loukas in the garden below as he chopped logs and added them to the growing pile. It made for a compelling image. His strong arms swung in an arc as the blade splintered into the wood—drawing attention to the honed definition of muscles rippling across his shoulders and his broad back.

Her throat dried. How many times had she longed for a scenario like this, in those lonely moments when her fantasies about him wouldn't respond to censorship, no matter how hard she'd tried? She'd dreamed of Loukas being back in her life and in her bed—with the freedom to conduct their relationship openly in a way which had never been possible before. And now she had it. No more moments of passion sandwiched in between the strictures of her career and the demands of his billionaire boss. Now *he* was the billionaire—although she no longer had a career, she thought wryly. Still. It should have been great. It should have been almost perfect.

So why the questions which still whirled around in her mind, which felt as if they had no real answers?

Ever since he'd moved into her Cornish cottage, they'd behaved like a couple. They'd done stuff. The normal stuff which other people did. They'd cooked dinner and shopped for food, and at first it had been disorientating to see Loukas in the local store, standing among all the villagers and the occasional tourist. People stopped what they were doing and turned to look at him and it was easy to see why. With his leather jacket and faded jeans, he looked larger than life—tall and indomitable. A dark, head-turning presence who seemed to come from a very different world.

Because he had. That was exactly what he had done. He'd known violence, rejection, pain and despair and those things had given him an edge which marked him out from other men. No wonder everyone else had always seemed so pale and so tame in comparison. No wonder no other man had ever been able to coax her into his bed.

Very quickly Jessica discovered that she liked having him around. She liked being part of a couple and doing coupley things. It made life more interesting to have a man to watch a scary film with, and play the old-fashioned board games which she taught him and which he was soon winning. She liked the feel of his warm, naked body when she got into bed at night and his arms wrapped around her waist when she woke up in the morning. She liked knowing they could make love whenever and wherever they liked.

But she was also aware of the subtle boundaries which surrounded them. The unspoken, instinctive restrictions. They never talked about the future and they never used the word love. He might have seamlessly slotted into having a home, but it still felt like *her* home, not his. As if he had invested nothing in it, nor was he planning to. Of course he hadn't. Because, when she stopped to think about it for long enough, could she really imagine Loukas Sarantos living the rest of his life in some rural Cornish outlet?

And despite his intention to delegate, his other life soon began to snap around at his heels, like a puppy demanding to be played with. It started with the odd phone call here and there and the beginning of a mounting pile of emails which needed to be dealt with. Soon there were conference calls, which he told her he had to take.

Jessica usually absented herself for those. She would go out into the garden, hearing his deep voice drifting through the open window—often speaking Greek—while she stared down at the bare soil and wondered when the first daffodils would push through and show that spring was nearly here.

She had just straightened up from plucking a weed from the ground after one such call, when she felt the warm caress of Loukas's hand splaying over her denim-covered buttock and she gave a little shiver of pleasure.

She threw the weed onto the compost heap. 'Everything okay?'

'The conference call was fine. And then my brother rang.' There was a pause. 'My twin.'

Jessica turned around, hearing his deliberate emphasis of the word and knowing just why he did that. She guessed it was still weird for him to acknowledge that he actually *had* a twin—the amazingly successful Alek Sarantos. She knew that contact between the two men had been minimal, but maybe that wasn't so surprising, since neither had known about the other's existence until they were grown men.

'How is he?'

He shrugged. 'He's okay. Actually, he's in London.'

'Oh.' Wasn't it stupid that just the mention of the city sounded vaguely *ominous*, as if it posed some kind of threat? She felt as if his other world—the one she wasn't part of—was beginning to inch towards them. Her smile didn't slip. 'That's nice.'

'Mmm. He wants me to have dinner with him. I thought I'd stay up for a few days. Do a little work while I'm there.' He narrowed his black eyes. 'You could always come with me.'

She lifted her hand to his face, her fingertips drifting over the sculptured outline of his unshaven jaw and feeling its rough rasp. Yes, she could. She could accompany him to London, a trip which would require a frantic mental inventory about what to wear. She could gatecrash his meeting with his newfound brother and inhibit their burgeoning relationship. She could hang around the Vinoly while he went into the office, or dutifully kill hours doing cultural things with which to impress him when he got home.

She got a sudden scary glimpse of how the future might look, once the initial wild sexual excitement had started to fade. He would probably start making more trips to London and each time he came back, it would be a little harder for them to reconnect. That was how these things worked, wasn't it? How long before he told her he was moving back permanently to the city, to the rented hotel suite he called home? Deep-down she knew she didn't fit into his life in London and that was his base.

So shouldn't she start getting used to that—with pride and with dignity?

'You need some time on your own with Alek,' she said. 'I'll stay here.'

His mouth tightened. 'Right.'

She saw the sudden flinty look in his eyes. Did it matter to him if she accompanied him or not?

So ask him. Just go right ahead and ask him.

But the different ways of phrasing such a question were really only a disguise for the one which could never be asked.

How do you feel about me, Loukas?

A more confident woman might have come right out and said it. A more sexually experienced one almost certainly would have done. But Jessica had been protecting herself from pain for so long that she would sooner have walked barefoot across the rough cliff path than risk getting hurt again.

'When will you leave?' she said as they began to walk back towards the house.

'I'll leave immediately. Why hang around? There's just one thing I need to do first.'

She turned her face up to look at him. 'What's that?'

'I'll show you.'

He linked his fingers with hers and led her inside, taking her straight upstairs and stripping off her clothes with speed rather than finesse. His eyes were still flinty and his mouth hardened into an odd kind of smile just before he drove it down on hers in a punishing kind of kiss.

He entered her urgently and as Jessica clung to his thrusting body she was filled with a terrible sense of *sadness*—as if she'd just failed a test she hadn't even known she was taking.

The house was quiet after he'd left. It was the first time she'd been without him for weeks. Long, lazy weeks which now seemed to have passed in a flash. She kept looking up, expecting to see him, telling herself it was crazy how quickly she had become used to having him around.

She kept busy, working hard on her embroidery and selling a small piece privately, before hearing about the possibility of a commission for a much larger piece. She gardened and made bread and went for long clifftop walks. Then she took a call from an excited Hannah, who told her that she'd met a young Australian vet in Bali.

'Oh, Jess,' she sighed. 'He's gorgeous. You'd really like him. He wants me to go to Perth next. That's where his folks live.'

'That sounds lovely,' said Jessica, even though inside she wanted to scream, *Please don't fall in love with a man from the other side of the world, so that I probably won't see you very much.*

Because you shouldn't use your own selfish needs to try to change someone else's behaviour, should you? Wasn't that one of the reasons why she never dared bring up the subject of the future with Loukas—because she sensed there could never be any compromise about their different lifestyles? Or because she wasn't sure if his feelings for her went any deeper than a powerful sexual attraction? She thought about him, miles away in London, and her heart clenched. Did he miss her, she wondered, and did he have any idea how much she missed him?

She spoke to him that evening and the sound of laughter and glasses clinking in the background made her feel very alone. And it was her own stupid fault. She thought that if he'd suggested her joining him, she would have been booking her ticket from Bodmin station quicker than a flash. But he didn't. Just as he didn't know *exactly* when he would be back.

'Soon,' he said.

But *soon* was inconclusive. *Soon* gave her the chance to dwell on all the things which were nagging away inside her. Maybe his brother was lining him up with a nice Greek girl. Maybe the lure of London had enticed him back and the thought of returning to this quiet little hamlet had filled him with horror.

Or just maybe he was missing her as much as she was missing him. What if that was a possibility? And once she allowed herself to consider *that* possibility, it altered everything. It scared her. It excited her. It made her feel as if she were floating three inches about the ground. She thought about some of the things he'd told her. About a mother who had always put other men before her son. Didn't that mean he would be reluctant to trust the love of women—or wary about putting his own feelings on the line? So wasn't it time to start grabbing at a little emotional courage—to dare show Loukas that she wanted him? To stop worrying about the fear of rejection and tell him she cared.

A text arrived from him in the early hours and she stared at it sleepily.

Back tomorrow. ☹ xxx

She woke, still with that walking-on-air feeling. She cleaned the house from top to bottom and swept the path. At the village store, she bought coffee, bread and wine—and when she got home went out into the garden, snipping off bright stems of foliage to cram into a beautiful blue and white vase. When he arrived she would tell him she'd missed him. Or ask him whether he wanted her to return to London with him. Because home was where you made it, wasn't it? She might not particularly like London, but wouldn't she rather live there with him than live in the countryside without him? Couldn't she show him that she could be adaptable?

She'd just washed the mud from her hands when the phone started ringing and eagerly she snatched it up, surprised but pleased to hear Patti, the spiky-haired stylist from Zeitgeist, on the end of the line and remembering the conversation they'd had at the launch party.

'If you're ringing about meeting for coffee, then it'll have to wait,' said Jessica. 'I'm in Cornwall.'

'Oh, okay.' There was a pause. 'Jessica…this might sound like a crazy question but I don't suppose Loukas is with you, is he?'

Afterwards, Jessica would think how strange the human brain was—that it could sift out a single word from a sentence and focus on that alone.

'Why would it be crazy?' she asked, because maybe it was time to stop pretending this wasn't happening. To start acknowledging that she and Loukas were in some sort of *relationship*.

'Oh, just that someone at Lulu said they thought you two were dating.'

'I don't know that I'd exactly describe it as dating. But, well, yes. He's been staying here.'

'So it worked,' said Patti, in a flat kind of voice.

'What worked?'

'It doesn't matter.'

'Oh, come on, Patti—you can't do that. You can't half say something and then leave me wondering the worst.'

There was a pause. 'I like you, Jessica. I like you very much.'

'And I like you, too. Mutual admiration society established. So what aren't you telling me?'

Another pause. 'Remember when the photos weren't working that first time in Venice? You know—when you were all wooden in front of the camera.'

'Yes, I remember. What about it?'

Patti's voice sounded hesitant. 'It's just that the art director said that what they really needed was for you to look like a woman who had just had sex. And the next day you did. The photos were absolute dynamite and everyone thought…'

'Everyone thought, what—that Loukas had taken the suggestion literally?'

'Something like that,' said Patti uncomfortably. 'And I wouldn't say anything, but… Well, it's just that he has such a reputation, and I'd hate to see you getting hurt. I'm sorry. Maybe I shouldn't have said anything.'

'No,' said Jessica, with soft urgency. 'You should. Don't worry about it, Patti. You did exactly the right thing. You told me something I needed to know.'

She couldn't settle to anything after that. Loukas rang to say he was on his way back and she slumped down into the chair, her embroidery untouched and nothing really registering until she saw the low flash of winter sun glinting from his windscreen.

Her heart had started pounding and her palms were

clammy. Wiping them down over her jeans, she prepared to greet him. And even while her heart was feeling the pain, she was running the whole scene like a film through her mind. This is the last time I'll see him drive up here like this, she thought. The last time he'll walk up this little path with the sun glinting off his black hair. The last, dying moments of being a couple were almost upon her and Jessica could barely summon up a smile with which to greet him.

But she didn't want this to turn into some kind of awful screaming match. She'd witnessed enough of those before her parents' divorce to put her off displays of high emotion for ever. She would be very calm and very dignified. It might even come as something of a relief to Loukas. For all she knew, he might have been trying to work out a diplomatic way of ending it himself. She wasn't going to do accusations, or regret. She would do it neatly and without a scene, just as she'd promised right at the beginning.

His sleek car came to a halt and he got out. She saw those impossibly long legs unfolding themselves and the expression on that dark and rugged face making her feel...

She gave herself a mental shake. She wasn't going to *feel* anything. It was safer that way.

The crunch of the gravel was replaced by the sound of a door being opened and closed and then suddenly he was standing in front of her, framed in the doorway, like some dark and golden statue come to life.

'Hello, Loukas,' she said.

'Hello, Jess.'

Loukas waited for her to jump out of the chair and fling her arms around him. But she didn't. She just sat there in her jeans and sweater staring up at him, with those extraordinary aquamarine eyes narrowed and giving nothing away.

She never gave anything away, did she?

'Did you have a good trip?'

'Good in parts,' he said, just about to tell her that he'd missed her when something stopped him, only he wasn't sure what. He stared into her tense face. Perhaps he was starting to get a good idea.

He looked around the room, noticing the spray of berried branches in a blue and white vase and he narrowed his eyes in surprise, because that wasn't usually the kind of detail he noticed.

'So how was your brother?'

'Is my brother the reason you're sitting there looking so uptight?' he questioned. 'Is my brother the reason you haven't kissed me, or looked as if you're pleased to see me?'

'I'm very pleased to see you.'

'Liar,' he said softly. 'Or maybe you're just not as good at hiding your feelings as you used to be. Are you going to tell me what's bugging you, Jess—or are we going to play a game of elimination?'

She shook her head as if she was having some kind of silent tussle with herself and when she spoke, it was as if she was picking her words with care.

'Let me ask *you* a question, Loukas. How important was it to turn the company around, when you bought Lulu?'

He shrugged. 'Very important—naturally. I'm a businessman and success is part of the deal—the biggest and most measurable part there is.'

She nodded as if his answer had just reinforced

something she already knew, and suddenly her hands were clenching into fists so tight he could see the whitening of her knuckles.

'Did you have sex with me just to get me to relax for the photo shoot?' she hissed.

'What?'

'You heard me perfectly well. Don't try to think up a clever answer—just tell me the truth.'

'You seem to have already decided for yourself what the truth is, without bothering to reference me first,' he snapped. 'Where the hell has all this come from?'

'It doesn't matter where it came from. Just that I heard that after the first disastrous shoot in Venice, the art director said I needed to look as if I'd just had sex.' Her cheeks were flushed and her eyes defiant as she stared him full in the face. 'And so…'

Her words tailed off and he felt his heart clench with anger. 'And so you thought that I would make the ultimate sacrifice for the sake of the company? That I'd take you to bed and loosen you up, thus ensuring that we had the requisite sultry photos to headline the new campaign. Is that what you thought, Jess?'

She opened her mouth and then closed it again, before nodding her head so vigorously that her blonde hair shimmered up and down.

'Yes,' she said fervently. 'That's exactly what I thought because it's the truth, isn't it, Loukas?'

He stared at her for a long moment and then he began to laugh.

CHAPTER FOURTEEN

FEELING WRONG-FOOTED, Jessica stared into Loukas's face—wondering how he had the *nerve* to laugh at a moment like this.

'What's so funny?' she demanded.

Only now the smile had gone. It had died on his lips, leaving nothing in its place but a look of withering contempt.

'You are,' he said. 'You're priceless. Do you really think that I would have cold-bloodedly had sex with you, just to make a better photo? I've heard of naked ambition, but really! Just how far do you think my dedication to the company goes, Jess? Do you think I would have done the same if I'd only just met the model, or found her physically repulsive? That I'd be acting like some kind of male whore?'

She glared at him. How dared he try to turn this round? 'You were talking to loads of different women at the party!' she accused. 'You know you were. Just not to me. But then, you've been hiding me away like a dirty secret, haven't you? You acted like you barely knew me at the party. Like we were strangers!'

He frowned. 'Because I didn't think either of us were ready to go public right then. And yes, I was talking to other women there—but it doesn't automatically follow that I was planning on having sex with them.'

Her eyes bored into his. 'Not even Maya?' she accused.

'Maya?' he echoed blankly, until his face cleared. 'Oh, Maya. You mean my ex-lover? Why, would you have had me blank her and be rude to her by ignoring her? That isn't the kind of behaviour I'd expect from a classy lady like you, Jess.'

His sarcasm washed over her and she glared at him. 'You hired me for all kinds of reasons,' she bit out. 'But I got the distinct impression that the main one was because you wanted to get even with me. That you'd never quite forgiven me for everything that happened before. And please don't try and make out I'm a fool, Loukas—or that I imagined it. You did. You know you did.'

There was a pause before he answered and then he sucked in a breath and nodded his head slowly. 'At the beginning, maybe I did,' he said. 'But things change, Jess—only you seem to be blind to them. You only ever see the shallow stuff—you never dare scratch beneath the surface, do you? When we reconnected again after all those years I agree that initially I felt a mixture of anger and lust. And if you really want the truth, I thought that getting you out of my system was going to be simple.'

'By sleeping with me?' she demanded.

'*Neh.* By sleeping with you.' He gave a cynical laugh. 'Actually, sleeping had nothing to do with it. I wanted you wide awake and very present. I wanted to do something that I'd been unable to forget and that was to have sex with you again. But you fought me all the way. You didn't just fall into my arms, even though I knew you wanted to. You forced me to get to know you again and to realise—'

'Realise what?'

'It doesn't matter.' He shook his head and his voice had grown cold now—as cold as the icy glint from his eyes. 'None of it does. Doesn't matter that I indulged you—'

'Indulged me?'

'Neh. I treated you with kid gloves,' he gritted out. 'I was cautious and careful. I put my business on hold and came to live with you here because I know you don't like London, but it still wasn't enough, was it? Because nothing is ever enough for you, Jess. You couldn't wait to think the worst of me—to give you a reason not to trust me. A reason to send me away and lock yourself away again—with all your beauty and your warmth hidden behind the frozen front you present to the world.'

'Loukas—'

'No!' he flared impatiently. 'I don't intend to spend my life tiptoeing around you, while you imagine the worst. Believe what you want to believe, because I'm done with this. And I'm done with you.'

His tone was harsh and Jessica stared at him, wondering what he was doing, then realised he was tugging his car keys from the pocket of his jacket and preparing to leave.

He was preparing to leave, only this time the look on his face told her he would never come back.

'Loukas,' she said again, fingertips flying to her mouth in horror. But her gasped word didn't stop him or make his stony face relax. He was opening the front door and the chill March wind was whistling through the door as he walked out, sending the temperature plummeting.

Frozen, he'd called her, and she *felt* frozen. Frozen enough to feel as if she were encased in ice when she heard a door slam and the sound of an engine firing into life. She turned her head to see the car bumping over the grass onto the unmade road, with Loukas's stony profile staring straight ahead.

He was going.

He was going.

'Loukas!' She ran outside and the cry was torn from her throat as she screamed it into the wind, but if he heard her, he didn't stop. And if he saw her that made no difference either, because the car continued to move forward. Waving her arms in the air, she started to run after it. To run as she hadn't run in years. It was like running across the court for a ball she knew she would never reach, only...

The last time that had happened she had ruptured her cruciate ligament and ended her career with a sickening snap, but this time she couldn't move as fast as her teenage self and her footsteps slowed to a stumbled halt. This time all that she had ruptured was her heart, yet somehow the pain seemed just as intense.

Sinking to her knees on the damp ground, she buried her face in her hands and began to cry, great sobs welling up from somewhere deep inside her chest until they erupted into a raw howl of pain. She wept at her own stupidity and timidity—at her lack of courage at going after something she realised now was irreplaceable. She could have had him—the only man she had ever cared about—but she'd been too proud and too stupid and too scared to give it a go. Too afraid of being hurt to take a risk, when everyone knew that love never came without some element of risk.

Hot tears dripped through her frozen fingers, drying instantly in the chill wind, and as she began to shiver she knew she couldn't stay there for ever. Her teeth chattering, she rose slowly to her feet, blinking away tears as she stared into the distance and saw the dark shape of a distinctive car parked on the clifftop and her heart missed a beat.

Loukas's car.

She blinked again as she realised that her eyes weren't playing tricks on her, but that it was definitely *his* car and he hadn't gone.

He hadn't gone.

With stumbling steps she began to run—expecting at any moment to see it disappear into the distance in a swift acceleration of power. But it didn't and her stride became longer—her panting breath making clouds of vapour in the chill air as she began to make silent pleas in her head. *Please don't go. Please just give me one more chance and I'll never let you down again.*

Out of breath, she reached the car at last. He was sitting perfectly still, staring straight ahead until she began to rap on the window and then he turned his head to look at her. His black eyes were flinty and his dark features were unreadable, but these days such a look was rare. She remembered the night when she'd been exhausted and wrung out in Venice. When he'd put her to bed and fed her melted cheese. When he'd made her feel safe and cherished as well as desired, and her heart swelled with an immense feeling of love and longing.

'Don't go,' she mouthed, through the glass. 'Please.'

He didn't say a word as he took the key from the ignition and climbed out of the car. He stared down at her for a long moment and then the flicker of a smile appeared on his lips.

'I wasn't,' he said, 'planning on going anywhere. I just needed time to cool down, before I said something I might afterwards regret.'

'Oh, Loukas,' she said, her words still muffled from all the crying she'd done.

But as Loukas looked at her he knew it had been more than that. He'd wanted to see if she would come after him, and she had. He'd wanted to show her that he had staying power. He needed her to know that she could trust him, because without that there could be no real love. And he knew he really couldn't hold back any longer.

'Because what I really want to say is that I love you, Jess,' he said simply. 'I love you. Completely, absolutely and enduringly.'

'Oh, Loukas,' she said as she flung her arms around his neck and pressed her cold face to his. 'I feel exactly the same about you. I love you so much, and I've made such a mess of showing you.'

'Then show me,' he said fiercely. 'Show me now.' And when she lifted her face to his, her eyes were very bright as he brushed his lips over hers.

The kiss deepened. He kissed her until they were both breathless and when he pulled away they were smiling—as if they'd just allowed themselves to see something which had been there all the time. He put her into the car and snapped her seat belt closed and when he'd parked outside her cottage, he took her hand

and led her inside. He made coffee and smoothed the hair from her eyes and it was only when she was sitting snuggled up against him on the sofa that he looked down at her gravely.

'But there are a few things we need to get cleared up before we go any further.'

'Mmm?' she said dreamily, her head resting against his shoulder.

'Just for the record—I know you aren't a city girl,' he said. 'And you don't have to be, because all I want to do is to marry you and make a home with you. Where that home will be is entirely up to you.'

'Loukas—'

'No, Jess,' he said. 'Hear me out. I need you to know that I'm not saying any of this in reaction to what has just happened. I need you to know that I've been thinking about this and have wanted it for a long while.'

She opened her eyes wide. 'You have?'

'I have. When I was in London I talked to my brother about it, in a way I've never talked to anyone.' He smiled. 'Except maybe you. I told him that I was in love with you but that I thought you were scared because you kept pushing me away every time I tried to get closer.'

She sniffed again. 'And what did he say?'

'He said that deep down most people are scared of love, because they recognise it has the power to hurt them like nothing else can. And that there are no guarantees in life.'

'You mean that nothing is certain?'

'Absolutely nothing,' he agreed, and now she could see the pain in his own eyes. 'But we both know how important it is to succeed at this. We've both had things happen which make it hard for us to believe it ever can, but I know it can. I think we both want this relationship to work more than we've ever wanted trophies, or money in the bank, or houses and cars.' His voice deepened. 'I know I do.'

'So do I,' she said in a squeaky voice which sounded perilously close to more tears.

'Because at the end of the day, love is the only thing which matters, and it is important that we mark that love.' He reached into his pocket and pulled out a familiarly coloured magenta box, tied with the distinctive Lulu ribbon. 'Which is why I want to ask you to be my wife.'

She swallowed. 'You've already bought me a ring?'

His face was grave. 'Well, I had the choice of some of the world's finest jewels.'

He flipped open the box and Jessica blinked. She had been expecting to be dazzled by diamonds, but all that lay on the indigo velvet was a small, metal ring-pull—the type you found on a can of cola.

She looked at him in surprise, with the first flicker of amusement tugging at her lips. 'And this is my engagement ring?'

He shrugged. 'Everything seemed such a cliché. Aquamarine to match your eyes, or diamonds for their cold and glittering beauty? With a whole empire at my disposal I was spoilt for choice—and I gather that, these days, the trend is to let women choose what they really, really want.'

'Put it on,' she said fiercely, and as he slid the worthless piece of metal onto her finger she saw that it was trembling. And she thought that being with Loukas Sarantos made a mockery of the steady hands which had once been her trademark. But she was smiling as she cupped his face in her hands and pressed her own very close.

'I don't want your diamonds,' she whispered. 'You're the only thing I really, really want. Your love and your commitment. They are more precious to me than all the jewels in the world, and I will treasure them and keep them close to my heart. Because I want you to know that I love you, Loukas Sarantos. I always have and I always will. A diamond isn't for ever. Love is.'

EPILOGUE

'Happy?' Loukas nuzzled his mouth over Jess's bare shoulder and felt her wriggle luxuriously.

Turning her head towards his, she smiled.

'Totally,' she sighed.

'Sure?'

'How could I not be?' She traced his mouth with a tender finger. 'You're my husband and I'm your wife. Your pregnant wife.'

He saw the way that her eyes flashed with joy and that pleased him. It pleased him that he could read her so well—and that these days she was happy to let him. And he recognised you couldn't change the past overnight. You had to work at things. No pain—no gain.

And yet the gain.

Ah, the gain.

He sighed with contentment as he stared out of the window, where the massive Greek sun was beginning its scarlet and vibrant ascendancy. The most dazzling sunrises he'd ever seen had been here, on the island where he'd been born and then taken away from as a wriggling baby, too young to remember its powdery white sands or the crystal seas after which it had been named.

Until now.

Kristalothos was one of the most beautiful places he'd ever seen, although he'd been reluctant to return at first, because it symbolised a dark time of his life. But Jess had gently persuaded him that it would be healthy to lay this particular ghost to rest.

His first trip back had been with his twin, Alek— just the two of them, when they'd stood and stared at the luxury hotel which had replaced the fortress in which Alek had grown up. It had been razed to the ground and now, as a luxury hotel, it was a place of light, not shade. And the two brothers had swum and fished, and listened to the night herons as they'd gathered around the lapping bay. And they'd talked. They'd talked long into the night, having conversations which had been over thirty years in the making.

Loukas had gone home to Jess and told her that the island was a paradise and when she'd suggested spending part of their honeymoon there during their tour of the Greek islands, he had readily agreed. He wanted to show her the place of his birth and to share it with her. He wanted to share pretty much everything with her.

He looked at the platinum and diamond wedding band which gleamed on her finger. It had been the most amazing wedding—especially for a man who didn't like weddings. But he had liked his own. He had liked making those solemn vows and declaring to the world that Jessica Cartwright was his. She had always been his, and she would remain so for as long as he drew breath.

Hannah had been their bridesmaid—resplendent in

a blue silk dress which had contrasted with her gap year tan—overjoyed to have the big brother she'd always longed for.

Alek had been his best man and his wife, Ellie, Jess's matron of honour. And their young son, named Loukas after his uncle, had been the cute hit of the day as he had toddled down the aisle as pageboy behind the bride.

One of the first things Loukas had done was to terminate the contract on his suite at the Vinoly. He had told Jess he was prepared to work as much as possible from the west of the country, if she really wanted to stay there. But Jess had changed, just as much as he had. She hadn't wanted to be apart from him for a second longer than she needed to be, and she'd agreed to live in London, just so long as they had a garden.

So now they were in Hampstead, with not only their own garden, but a huge heath nearby, on which they would soon be able to take their son or daughter in a big, old-fashioned pram.

'Are you?'

Her soft voice broke into his thoughts and he stirred lazily as he met her questioning look. 'Am I what?'

'Happy.'

He smiled as he placed a hand over her still-flat belly and looked up into her shining eyes. 'I love you, Jess Sarantos,' he said. 'I love you more than I ever thought I could love anyone and you're now my wife. Does that answer your question?'

'It does,' she murmured and gave a contented little wriggle as he continued to stroke her belly with that same seductive, circular movement. She closed her eyes. 'Mmm. That's nice. Any ideas about what you'd like to do today?'

'More of the same,' he said, his husky words made indistinct by the lazy pressure of his kiss. 'Just more of the same.'

* * * * *

MILLS & BOON®
Hardback – July 2015

ROMANCE

The Ruthless Greek's Return	Sharon Kendrick
Bound by the Billionaire's Baby	Cathy Williams
Married for Amari's Heir	Maisey Yates
A Taste of Sin	Maggie Cox
Sicilian's Shock Proposal	Carol Marinelli
Vows Made in Secret	Louise Fuller
The Sheikh's Wedding Contract	Andie Brock
Tycoon's Delicious Debt	Susanna Carr
A Bride for the Italian Boss	Susan Meier
The Millionaire's True Worth	Rebecca Winters
The Earl's Convenient Wife	Marion Lennox
Vettori's Damsel in Distress	Liz Fielding
Unlocking Her Surgeon's Heart	Fiona Lowe
Her Playboy's Secret	Tina Beckett
The Doctor She Left Behind	Scarlet Wilson
Taming Her Navy Doc	Amy Ruttan
A Promise...to a Proposal?	Kate Hardy
Her Family for Keeps	Molly Evans
Seduced by the Spare Heir	Andrea Laurence
A Royal Amnesia Scandal	Jules Bennett

MILLS & BOON®
Large Print – July 2015

ROMANCE

The Taming of Xander Sterne	Carole Mortimer
In the Brazilian's Debt	Susan Stephens
At the Count's Bidding	Caitlin Crews
The Sheikh's Sinful Seduction	Dani Collins
The Real Romero	Cathy Williams
His Defiant Desert Queen	Jane Porter
Prince Nadir's Secret Heir	Michelle Conder
The Renegade Billionaire	Rebecca Winters
The Playboy of Rome	Jennifer Faye
Reunited with Her Italian Ex	Lucy Gordon
Her Knight in the Outback	Nikki Logan

HISTORICAL

The Soldier's Dark Secret	Marguerite Kaye
Reunited with the Major	Anne Herries
The Rake to Rescue Her	Julia Justiss
Lord Gawain's Forbidden Mistress	Carol Townend
A Debt Paid in Marriage	Georgie Lee

MEDICAL

How to Find a Man in Five Dates	Tina Beckett
Breaking Her No-Dating Rule	Amalie Berlin
It Happened One Night Shift	Amy Andrews
Tamed by Her Army Doc's Touch	Lucy Ryder
A Child to Bind Them	Lucy Clark
The Baby That Changed Her Life	Louisa Heaton

MILLS & BOON®
Hardback – August 2015

ROMANCE

The Greek Demands His Heir	Lynne Graham
The Sinner's Marriage Redemption	Annie West
His Sicilian Cinderella	Carol Marinelli
Captivated by the Greek	Julia James
The Perfect Cazorla Wife	Michelle Smart
Claimed for His Duty	Tara Pammi
The Marakaios Baby	Kate Hewitt
Billionaire's Ultimate Acquisition	Melanie Milburne
Return of the Italian Tycoon	Jennifer Faye
His Unforgettable Fiancée	Teresa Carpenter
Hired by the Brooding Billionaire	Kandy Shepherd
A Will, a Wish...a Proposal	Jessica Gilmore
Hot Doc from Her Past	Tina Beckett
Surgeons, Rivals...Lovers	Amalie Berlin
Best Friend to Perfect Bride	Jennifer Taylor
Resisting Her Rebel Doc	Joanna Neil
A Baby to Bind Them	Susanne Hampton
Doctor...to Duchess?	Annie O'Neil
Second Chance with the Billionaire	Janice Maynard
Having Her Boss's Baby	Maureen Child

MILLS & BOON®
Large Print – August 2015

ROMANCE

The Billionaire's Bridal Bargain	Lynne Graham
At the Brazilian's Command	Susan Stephens
Carrying the Greek's Heir	Sharon Kendrick
The Sheikh's Princess Bride	Annie West
His Diamond of Convenience	Maisey Yates
Olivero's Outrageous Proposal	Kate Walker
The Italian's Deal for I Do	Jennifer Hayward
The Millionaire and the Maid	Michelle Douglas
Expecting the Earl's Baby	Jessica Gilmore
Best Man for the Bridesmaid	Jennifer Faye
It Started at a Wedding...	Kate Hardy

HISTORICAL

A Ring from a Marquess	Christine Merrill
Bound by Duty	Diane Gaston
From Wallflower to Countess	Janice Preston
Stolen by the Highlander	Terri Brisbin
Enslaved by the Viking	Harper St. George

MEDICAL

A Date with Her Valentine Doc	Melanie Milburne
It Happened in Paris...	Robin Gianna
The Sheikh Doctor's Bride	Meredith Webber
Temptation in Paradise	Joanna Neil
A Baby to Heal Their Hearts	Kate Hardy
The Surgeon's Baby Secret	Amber McKenzie

MILLS & BOON®

Why shop at millsandboon.co.uk?

Each year, thousands of romance readers find their perfect read at millsandboon.co.uk. That's because we're passionate about bringing you the very best romantic fiction. Here are some of the advantages of shopping at www.millsandboon.co.uk:

* **Get new books first**—you'll be able to buy your favourite books one month before they hit the shops

* **Get exclusive discounts**—you'll also be able to buy our specially created monthly collections, with up to 50% off the RRP

* **Find your favourite authors**—latest news, interviews and new releases for all your favourite authors and series on our website, plus ideas for what to try next

* **Join in**—once you've bought your favourite books, don't forget to register with us to rate, review and join in the discussions

Visit **www.millsandboon.co.uk**
for all this and more today!

THE BRITISH MUSEUM
ELEPHANTS

Toomai of the Elephants · p 217

David Gentleman

THE BRITISH MUSEUM
ELEPHANTS

EDITED BY

Sarah Longair

THE BRITISH MUSEUM PRESS

For Malcolm, Deborah and Mark

First published in 2008 by The British Museum Press
A division of The British Museum Company Ltd
38 Russell Square, London WC1B 3QQ

www.britishmuseum.org

A catalogue record for this book is available from the British Library

ISBN 978-0-7141-5075-8

Text is reprinted by kind permission of the copyright holders (see pages 94–5)

Frontispiece: David Gentleman, 'Toomai of the Elephants'.
Pen, ink and watercolour, study for an illustration to an edition of Rudyard Kipling's
Jungle Book published by Limited Editions, New York, in 1968

Photography by the British Museum Department of Photography and Imaging
Designed and typeset in Centaur by Peter Ward
Printed in China by C&C Offset Printing Co., Ltd

INTRODUCTION

ELEPHANTS have captivated, astonished, intrigued and terrified humans in equal measure since the earliest encounters between them. Their enormous size and striking physical features of tusks, trunk and large, flapping ears make them unique in the animal kingdom. The power that they are able to wield commands respect, as alluded to in the greeting of a Yoruba hunter: 'one-armed spirit, spirit that shatters the forest, render of trees, child of the forest destroyer, offspring of the coconut-breaker, elephant who kneels in a huge mass, you with indestructible tusks, you whose mouth utters a laugh that enjoins respect.' Other characteristics that have fascinated humans include their remarkable intelligence and discernible emotions. Despite their significant physical differences, humans feel an affinity with elephants, revering and loving the giant mammals for their loyalty and displays of familial affection. When the Roman general Pompey designed games to amuse the crowd by pitting elephant against elephant in a fight, Cicero noted that many of the spectators were dismayed and felt 'an impulse of compassion' for the animals as there was 'something human about them'.

The first members of the Elephantidae family, the ancestors of those we know today, roamed the earth around 5 million years ago, although proboscideans had existed for over 50 million years. About 5,000 years ago, after the mammoths died out, only the Asian and African elephants remained. The Asian elephant has been tamed by man for over two thousand years, whereas in Africa this has been far less common. In Asia mahouts have for centuries trained elephants from a young age to work on the land, for example dextrously clearing trees with their trunks. Their role in ceremonial display has been recorded in miniature paintings from across Asia, showing ornately decorated creatures surmounted by magnificent howdahs carrying rulers and dignitaries. Another crucial example of their use by humans has been in war. The Greeks encountered them on the battlefield and numerous writers described their formidable presence. Two particular moments from Antiquity entered Western legend: Alexander's defeat of the Indian king Porus, and his subsequent adoption of elephants as an emblem and in battle, and Hannibal's crossing of the Alps accompanied by thirty-seven elephants. The elephants brought to Europe during this period were the first proboscideans on that continent since the extinction of the mammoth.

Symbolically, the elephant has various meanings across different cultures. Their sheer size has long led them to be associated with power and royalty in several African and Asian societies. The gentle nature of so large an animal, and the discerning use of its power, provides an example of leadership alluded to in many West African proverbs. Elephants play an important part in the spiritual beliefs of many African societies, and thus are symbolically depicted on objects or invoked through masking traditions, such as those of the Bamileke of the Cameroon grasslands. The white elephant, a rare genetic variety, features widely in the mythology of several cultures; for example, Buddha's conception took place when his mother, Maya, dreamed that a white elephant entered her side. In Thailand and Burma, ownership of a white elephant by the ruler means he will rule with justice and enjoy peace and prosperity. The elephant-headed Hindu god, Ganesha, is one of the most popular deities, depicted widely in material culture, both historic and contemporary. In Christian Europe, the loyalty of the elephant to its partner, as described by St Francis de Sales, the French Renaissance churchman, led to it becoming a symbol of chastity.

Elephants appeared sporadically in Europe during the medieval period: the thirteenth-century chronicler Matthew Paris noted the arrival in London of an elephant – a gift from Louis IX of

Elephant masks from the Bamileke people in the Grasslands of Cameroon, used by the elephant secret society and in dances and ritual performances. Early 20th century

France to Henry II — which was kept in the Tower and reputedly died from drinking too much wine. The animals were also brought back from travels as curiosities. Throughout the fifteenth century, a period of greater interaction with the world beyond Europe, elephants became synonymous with the exotic and the unknown. As Jonathan Swift observed, cartographers making 'Afric maps' would place elephants 'for want of towns'. The elephant came to represent 'to the Orient', depicted by European artists with varying degrees of accuracy. During the nineteenth and twentieth centuries elephants became increasingly familiar in Europe as they were installed in zoos and circuses, striking awe in spectators and featuring in many novels and stories of the period.

In Africa and Asia elephants have always been hunted for their meat and, more significantly, for their most precious commodity to man: the ivory of their tusks. Prized objects have been created from ivory all over the world and the expansion of the lucrative trade in the commodity was a driving force in increasing contact with many parts of Africa. The pureness of its colour and its suitability for detailed carving made it a valuable and much admired material. On both the West and East African coasts, elephants were slaughtered in ever greater numbers to serve the seemingly insatiable Western desire for ivory. In the twentieth century, awareness of animal conservation has developed. After early decimation through hunting, the elephant population has stabilized with strict international law against the ivory trade and their homelands are now protected.

The combination of the elephant's wisdom, power and loyalty makes it the most beguiling and admirable of creatures, which continues to fascinate us. Encounters with elephants evoke wonder among visitors to safari parks, which now protect them from poachers and hunters. These same characteristics have been described for centuries by writers, travellers, storytellers, craftsmen and artists, a selection of which have been collected together in this book. All but one of the objects illustrated are drawn from the collections of the British Museum, which span many cultures and periods in history. Here we can see how humans across the world have for centuries attempted to understand and pay homage to this unique and most beloved member of the animal kingdom.

Nature's great masterpiece,
    an Elephant.
The only harmless great thing;
    the giant of beasts.

JOHN DONNE (1572–1631)
From *The Progress of the Soul*, 1601

Rembrandt van Rijn, *An elephant*.
Black chalk and charcoal,
The Netherlands, *c.* 1637

9

I have a memory like an elephant.
In fact, elephants often consult me.

NOEL COWARD (1899–1973)

Detail of a beadwork wall-hanging.
Gujarat, India, *c.* 1920

Detail of an engraved two-sided copper plate
showing board games in use at the Mysore
court, 19th century

One of the first things an infant elephant has to discover is how to use its trunk. When it is only a month or two old, the long dangling object in front of its face is obviously a puzzle to it. It will shake its head and observe how this curious appendage flops about. Sometimes it trips up over it. And when it goes down to a water hole to drink it crouches down and awkwardly sips with its mouth. Not until it is four or five months old does it discover the remarkable fact that water can be sniffed up into a trunk and that, if you blow out, you can hose it into your mouth. And that discovery, of course, leads to a whole new set of possibilities for games.

DAVID ATTENBOROUGH (b. 1926)
From *The Trials of Life*, 1990

When the king heard these words, he commanded the brahmans to be sent for, learned in the vedas and skilled in the interpretation of çāstras. And Māyā, standing before them, spoke to the brahmans and said: 'I have seen a dream, expound the meaning thereof unto me.' And the brahmans spoke: 'Relate, o queen, what dream thou hast seen; after hearing it we may understand it.' Then the queen answered: 'Like unto snow and silver, exceeding the glory of sun and moon, with stately pace and well-built, with six tusks and noble, his limbs as firm as diamond and full of beauty, a splendid elephant has entered my womb. Reveal to me the meaning of this.'

On hearing these words, the brahmans spake as follows: 'Behold a great joy shall befall thee, it brings no misfortune to your race. A son shall be born unto thee, his body adorned with tokens, worthy descendant of the royal race, a noble ruler of the world. When he forsakes love, royal power and palace and without giving any more thought to whom wanders forth in pity for the whole world, he will become a Buddha to be honoured by the three worlds and he will make glad the universe with the marvellous nectar of immortality.'

From the *Lalitavistara Sutra* (Life of the Buddha), transl. N.J. Krom

The Dream of Maya. Detail of a silk painting showing scenes from the life of the Buddha. From Cave 17, Dunhuang, China, Tang dynasty, 9th century AD

After Parvati created her son Ganesha, the young boy prohibited anyone from seeing his mother, even her husband, Shiva. He fought Vishnu and Shiva's attendants, the Ganas, and finally encountered Shiva himself, whose trident Ganesha broke . . . At last Shiva struck off Ganesha's head while he was engaged with Vishnu.

While the Ganas rejoiced at Ganesha's death, Parvati was inconsolable, and proceeded to create other beings for the express purpose of counteracting the settled destiny of the world and anticipating its destruction. Narada and the Ganas interfered and prevailed on Parvati to desist, to which she assented only on the condition that Ganesha was revived. But, his head being lost, they were obliged to cut off that of the first animal coming to them the next morning from the north, by Shiva's advice. It proved to be an elephant with one tooth. His head was accordingly fixed on Ganesha's shoulders. Shiva revived him by certain mantras of the Vedas. Shiva then adopted Ganesha, and all the Ganas agreed that he should be worshipped the first of all of them.

The Story of Ganesha, from the *Siva-Purana*,
adapted from a translation by J. Hindley

Stone sculpture of Shakti-Ganesha,
elephant-headed god from a temple of the sun.
Orissa, India, 13th century

About them frisking playd
All Beasts of th' Earth, since wilde, and of all chase
In Wood or Wilderness, Forrest or Den;
Sporting the Lion rampd, and in his paw
Dandl'd the Kid; Bears, Tygers, Ounces, Pards
Gambold before them, th' unwieldy Elephant
To make them mirth us'd all his might, and wreathd
His Lithe Proboscis;

JOHN MILTON (1608–74)
From *Paradise Lost*, 1667

Earthenware painted dish showing Adam and Eve in the Garden of Eden.
Probably made in the Netherlands, 17th century

Love will draw an elephant through a key-hole.

Samuel Richardson (1689–1761)
Lovelace, in *Clarissa*, 1748

Lakshmi, Hindu goddess of love, wealth, fortune and beauty, with elephants. Painting on paper, Bundi, Rajasthan, India, *c.* 1780

The Indian elephant is known sometimes to weep.

CHARLES DARWIN (1809–82)
From *The Expression of the Emotions in Man and Animals*, 1872

Rectangular limestone block carved on one long
face with a pair of elephants carrying garlands in
honour of a stupa. From the Buddhist temple at
Amaravati, India, late 2nd–early 3rd century AD

From *The Stolen White Elephant*, 1882

The narrator goes to Inspector Blunt in New York when the white elephant, a gift from the King of Siam that he was conveying to Her Majesty, was stolen.

He took a pen and some paper. 'Now – name of the elephant?'

'Hassan Ben Ali Ben Selim Abdallah Mohammed Moisé Alhammal Jamsetjejeebhoy Dhuleep Sultan Ebu Bhudpoor.'

'Very well. Given name?'

'Jumbo.'

'Very well. Place of birth?'

'The capital city of Siam.'

'Parents living?'

'No – dead.'

'Had they any other issue besides this one?'

'None. He was an only child.'

'Very well. These matters are sufficient under that head. Now please describe the elephant, and leave out no particular, however insignificant – that is, insignificant from *your* point of view. To men in my profession there *are* no insignificant particulars; they do not exist.'

I described; he wrote. When I was done, he said:

'Now listen. If I have made any mistakes, correct me.'

He read as follows:

'Height, 19 feet; length, from apex of forehead to insertion of tail, 26 feet; length of trunk, 16 feet; length of tail, 6 feet; total length, including trunk and tail, 48 feet; length of tusks, 9½ feet; ears in keeping with these dimensions; footprint resembles the mark left when one up-ends a barrel in the snow; the color of the elephant, a dull white; has a hole the size of a plate in each ear for the insertion of jewelry and possesses the habit in a remarkable degree of squirting water upon spectators and of maltreating with his trunk not only such persons as he is acquainted with, but even entire strangers; limps slightly with his right hind leg, and has a small scar in his left armpit caused by a former boil; had on, when stolen, a castle containing seats for fifteen persons, and a gold-cloth saddle-blanket the size of an ordinary carpet.'

There were no mistakes. The inspector touched the bell, handed the description to Alaric, and said:

'Have fifty thousand copies of this printed at once and mailed to every detective office and pawnbroker's shop on the continent.'

MARK TWAIN (1835–1910)

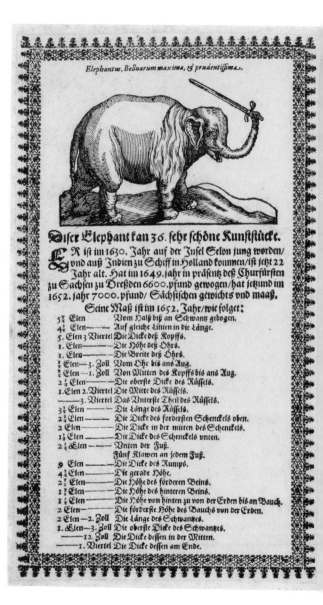

Elephantus, Belluarum maxima, & prudentissima. Woodcut depicting an elephant holding a sword with its trunk, with a list of the elephant's measurements. German, 1652

From *Hyde Park at Night, Before the War*, 1916

Not too near and not too far
Out of the stress of the crowd
Music screams as elephants scream
When they lift their trunks and scream aloud
For joy of the night when masters are
Asleep and adream.

D.H. LAWRENCE (1885–1930)

SUMMER FASHIONS for

View in the Zoological Gardens, Regent's Park, London.
Colour aquatint and etching, published
by Benjamin Read, London, 1837

VIEW IN THE ZOOLOGICAL GARDENS REGENTS PARK LONDON.

READ & H. BODMAN, 12, Hart St. Bloomsbury Sq.e & 95, Strand LONDON also Broad Way New York AMERICA.

We use the word 'monument', although in fact it was no more than a preliminary sketch; but a sketch on the grand scale, the prodigious corpse of a Napoleonic aspiration which successive adverse winds have borne further and further away from us until it has lapsed into history; but the sketch had a look of permanence which was in sharp contrast to its provisional nature. It was an elephant some forty feet high, constructed of wood and plaster, with a tower the size of a house on its back, that once had been roughly painted green but was now blackened by wind and weather. Outlined against the stars at night, in that open space, with its huge body and trunk, its crenellated tower, its four legs like temple columns, it was an astonishing and impressive spectacle. No one knew precisely what it meant. It was in some sort a symbol of the popular will, sombre, enigmatic, and immense; a sort of powerful and visible ghost confronting the invisible spectre of the Bastille.

VICTOR HUGO (1802–85)
From *Les Misérables*, 1862, transl. Norman Denny

Chess piece with a king mounted in a
howdah on an elephant. Painted and gilded ivory,
late Mughal dynasty, 19th century

Elephants wander in the midst of the charming groves,
that are filled with the cries of intoxicated peacocks in
the grass, sprinkled with ladybirds and planted with
Nipa and Arjuna trees.

From *The Ramayana of Valmiki*, transl. Hari Prasad Shastri

The month of Bhadon (August–September), from a *baramasa* series.
Krishna and Radha are depicted with two standing girls,
three elephants in a pool and peacocks. Painting on paper,
Jaipur, Rajasthan, India, *c.* 1800

The ears of a chief are as big as those of an elephant.

Proverb of the Akan people of West Africa, describing how a
chief is a good listener and hears the voices of his subjects

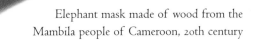

Elephant mask made of wood from the
Mambila people of Cameroon, 20th century

Aut Viam Inveniam Aut Faciam.
(I will either find a way, or make one.)

HANNIBAL (247–183 BC), attrib., in response
to the claimed impossibility of crossing the Alps
with elephants

William Clarkson Stanfield, *A difficult passage:
Hannibal crossing the Alps*. Brown and grey wash
over graphite, England, 19th century

From *The Elephant's Child*

In the High and Far-Off Times the Elephant, O Best Beloved, had no trunk. He had only a blackish, bulgy nose, as big as a boot, that he could wriggle about from side to side; but he couldn't pick up things with it. But there was one Elephant – a new Elephant – an Elephant's Child – who was full of 'satiable curtiosity, and that means he asked ever so many questions. And he lived in Africa, and he filled all Africa with his 'satiable curtiosities.

RUDYARD KIPLING (1865–1936)
From *Just So Stories*, 1902

White marble sculpture of a crouching elephant.
Jaipur, Rajasthan, India, late 18th century

From *On Poetry: a Rhapsody*, 1733

So geographers in Afric-maps
With savage pictures fill their gaps
And o'er unhabitable downs
Place elephants for want of towns.

JONATHAN SWIFT (1667–1745)

Map of Africa, from *Le Grand Atlas,
ou Cosmographie Blaviane, en la quelle est
exactement descritte la Terre, la Mer, et le
Ciel*, X, Amsterdam, 1663

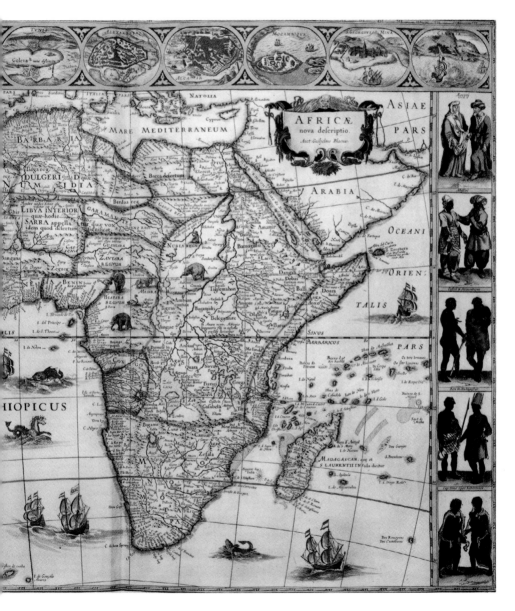

39

HECTOR TROIANVS· ALEXANDER MACEDO· IVLIVS CAESAR·

Inter ethnicos hi tres nobilitatis palmam ferunt·

Harmen Jansz. Muller, after Maarten van Heemskerck, *Alexander of Macedonia sitting on an elephant, flanked by Hector of Troy and Julius Caesar.* Engraving from the series 'The Nine Worthies', published by Hieronymus Cock, The Netherlands, *c.* 1567

From *The Prophecy of Capys*

The Greek shall come against thee,
        The conqueror of the East.
Beside him stalks to battle
        The huge earth-shaking beast,
The beast on whom the castle
        With all its guards doth stand,
The beast who hath between his eyes
        The serpent for a hand.

Thomas Babington Macaulay (1800–59)
From *Lays of Ancient Rome*, 1842

42

Be humble as the blade of grass that is being trodden underneath
the feet. The little ant tastes joyously the sweetness of honey and sugar.
The mighty elephant trembles in pain under the agony of sharp goad.

JOHN RUSKIN (1819–1900)

Embossed silver roundel of three figures riding
on an elephant, dating from *c.* 2nd century AD,
found in Rawalpindi, Pakistan

When elephants fight, it is the grass that suffers.

Proverb of the Swahili people of East Africa

An elephant killing another after an engagement
in which he has oversett his antagonist.
Album leaf, Mughal style, 18th century

When the washing is finished, he slings his nurses up to his neck with his trunk, or gives them a 'leg-up' behind in the friendly fashion peculiar to him, and shuffles back to the serai or yard to be dressed. If the occasion be a very grand one, a day or two will be consumed in preparations. First the forehead, trunk, and ears are painted in bold patterns in colour. This is a work of art, for the designs are often good, and the whole serai, excepting always the elephant itself, is deeply interested. His mind and trunk wander; he trifles with the colour pots; so with each stroke comes an order to stand still. Some mahouts are quite skilful in this pattern work. Then the howdah pad is girthed on with cotton ropes riding over flaps of leather to prevent the chafing to which the sensitive skin is liable. The howdah itself, a cumbrous frame of wood covered with beaten silver plates, is slung and tied with a purchase on the tail-root, and heavy cloths broidered in raised work of gold and silver thread are attached, hanging like altar cloths down the sides . . . At last, my lord the elephant is ready.

JOHN LOCKWOOD KIPLING (1837–1911)
From *Beast and Man in India*, 1904

Gazi Pir riding an elephant. Register from the Gazi scroll, Bengal, India, *c.* 1800. Such scrolls were used by itinerant storytellers to illustrate spoken or sung narration of myths.

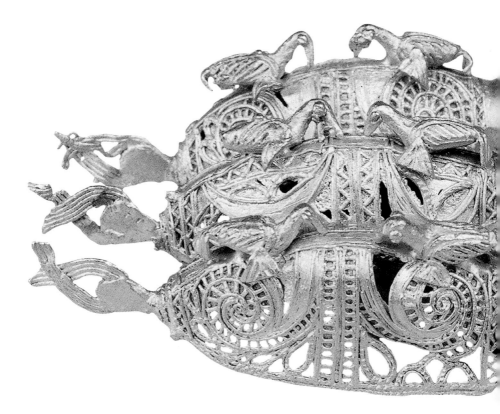

Though an elephant's tail is short,
it can nevertheless keep flies off the elephant.

Proverb of the Akan people of West Africa. This proverb
suggests that despite any apparent shortcomings,
the chief is prepared to solve all problems.

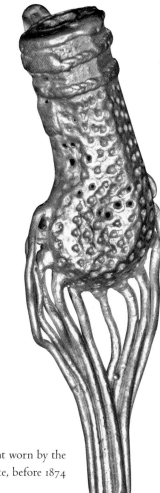

(*left*) Gold ornament of three elephants for an Asante chief, before 1874

(*right*) Gold elephant's tail pendant worn by the Asantehene, king of the Asante, before 1874

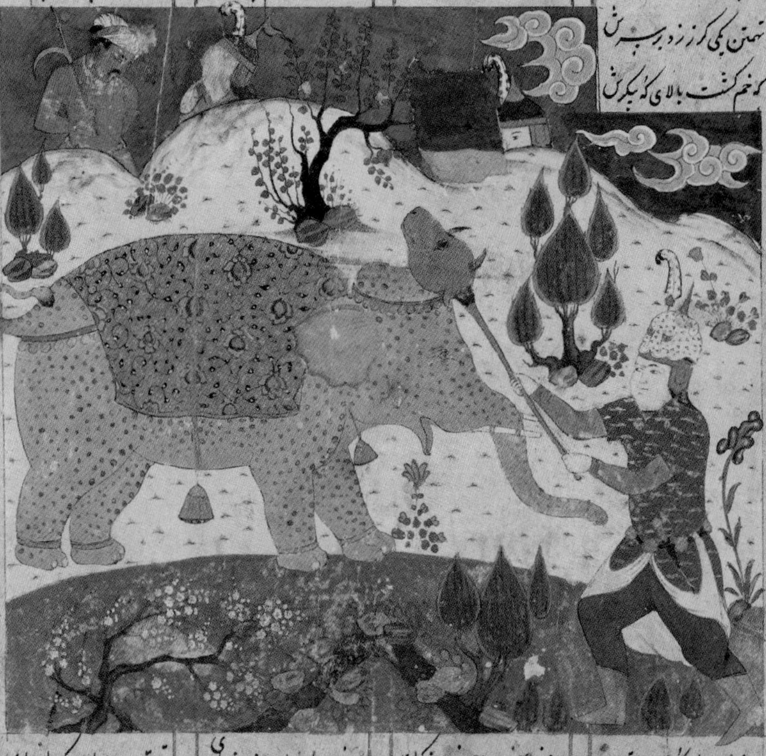

One night Rustem was awakened out of his sleep by a great noise, and cries of distress, when starting up and inquiring the cause, he was told that the white elephant had got loose, and was trampling and crushing the people to death. In a moment he issued from his apartment, brandishing his mace; but was soon stopped by the servants who were anxious to expostulate with him against venturing out in the darkness to encounter a ferocious elephant.

Impatient at being thus interrupted he knocked down one of the watchmen, who fell dead at his feet, and the others running away, he broke the lock of the gate, and escaped. He immediately opposed himself to the enormous animal, which looked like a mountain, and kept roaring like the river Níl. Regarding him with a cautious and steady eye, he gave a loud shout, and fearlessly struck him a blow, with such strength and vigour, that the iron mace was almost bent double. The elephant trembled, and soon fell exhausted and lifeless in the dust. When it was communicated to Zál that Rustem had killed the animal with one blow, he was amazed, and fervently returned thanks to heaven. He called him to him, and kissed him, and said: 'My darling boy, thou art indeed unequalled in valour and magnanimity.'

FIRDAUSI (AD 935–1020)
From the *Shahnameh* (Book of Kings), transl. James Atkinson

The boy Rustam slays a white elephant. Manuscript painting from the *Shahnameh* of Firdausi, Persian, *c.* 1560

And other authorities have dwelt on the age of the animals and say that they are very long-lived; but our party too say that they came on an elephant near Taxila, the greatest city in India, who was anointed with myrrh by the natives and adorned with fillets. For, they said, this was one of those who fought on the side of Porus against Alexander; and, as it had made a great fight, Alexander dedicated it to the Sun. And it had, they say, gold rings around its tusks or horns, whichever you call them, and an inscription was written on them in Greek, as follows: 'Alexander the son of Zeus dedicates Ajax to the Sun.' For he had given this name to the elephant, thinking so great an animal deserved a great name. And the natives reckoned that 350 years had elapsed since the battle, without taking into account how old the elephant was when he went into battle.

PHILOSTRATUS (AD *c.* 172–*c.* 250)
From *The Life of Apollonius of Tyana*, transl. F.C. Conybeare

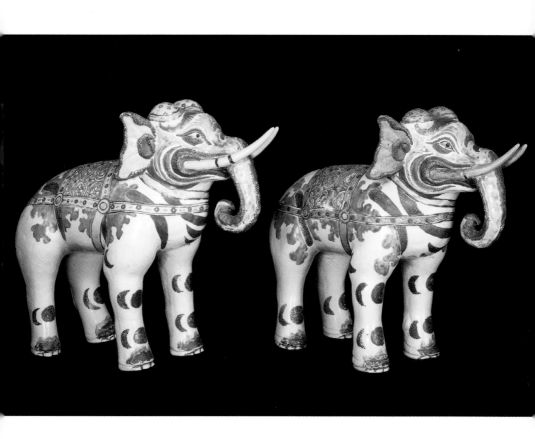

Pair of porcelain model elephants.
Japan, Edo period, late 17th century

A true philosopher is like an elephant; he never puts the second foot down until the first one is solidly in place.

BERNARD LE BOVIER DE FONTENELLE (1657–1757)
From *Entretiens sur la pluralité des mondes*, 1686

Marius Bauer, *Elephants in Hyderabad*.
Drypoint, Dutch school, *c.* 1882–1924

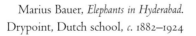

The Elephant is Slow to Mate

The elephant, the huge old beast,
    is slow to mate;
he finds a female, they show no haste
    they wait
for the sympathy in their vast shy hearts
    slowly, slowly to rouse
as they loiter along the river-beds
    and drink and browse

and dash in panic through the brake
    of forest with the herd,
and sleep in massive silence, and wake
    together, without a word.
So slowly the great hot elephant hearts
    grow full of desire,
and the great beasts mate in secret at last,
    hiding their fire.

Oldest they are and the wisest of beasts
    so they know at last
how to wait for the loneliest of feasts
    for the full repast.
They do not snatch, they do not tear;
    their massive blood
moves as the moon-tides, near, more near
    till they touch in flood.

D.H. LAWRENCE (1885–1930)

Mahouts rounding up elephants. Album leaf,
Mughal style, 18th century

An elephant has fallen out of society.

Saying of the Bini people of West Africa, used when an
important man dies, as the elephant is considered the lord
(*ogie*) among animals

Bronze lid of a bowl, with four elephant heads ending
in human hands. Benin, Nigeria, 16th century

59

The elephant's a gentleman.

RUDYARD KIPLING (1865–1936)
From the poem *Oonts*, 1890

John Doyle, *A lesson in elephant riding*. Pen, brown ink
and graphite on paper, 1844. A study for a satirical
print in the series 'Political Sketches', published by
Thomas McLean, 1821–51

62

In no animal is this part so peculiar as in the elephant, where it attains an extraordinary size and strength. For the elephant uses its nostril as a hand; this being the instrument with which it conveys food, fluid and solid alike, to its mouth. With it too it tears up trees, coiling it round their stems. In fact it applies it generally to the purposes of a hand.

ARISTOTLE (384–322 BC)
From *De Partibus Animalium*, transl. William Ogle

Bronze incense burner in the shape of an elephant.
Mughal dynasty, *c.* 17th century

From *Mulliner's Buck-U-Uppo*

My dear Augustine

I am writing in some haste to tell you that the impulsiveness of your aunt has led to a rather serious mistake. She tells me that she dispatched to you yesterday by parcels post a sample bottle of my new Buck-U-Uppo, which she obtained without my knowledge from my laboratory. Had she mentioned what she was intending to do, I could have prevented a very unfortunate occurrence.

Mulliner's Buck-U-Uppo is of two grades or qualities – the A and the B. The A is a mild, but strengthening, tonic designed for human invalids. The B, on the other hand, is purely for circulation in the animal kingdom, and was invented to fill a long-felt want throughout our Indian possessions.

As you are doubtless aware, the favourite pastime of the Indian Maharajahs is the hunting of the tiger of the jungle from the backs of elephants; and it has happened frequently in the past that hunts have been spoiled by the failure of the elephant to see eye to eye with its owner in the matter of what constitutes sport.

Too often elephants, on sighting the tiger, have turned and galloped home: and it was to correct this tendency on their part that I invented Mulliner's Buck-U-Uppo 'B'. One teaspoonful of Buck-U-Uppo 'B' administered in its morning bran-mash will cause the most timid elephant to trumpet loudly and charge the fiercest tiger without a qualm.

Abstain, therefore, from taking any contents of the bottle you now possess.

P.G. WODEHOUSE (1881–1975)
From *Meet Mr Mulliner*, 1927

A nobleman and attendants mounted on an elephant attacked by a tiger.
Gouache on paper, Rajasthan style, India, *c.* 1790–1810

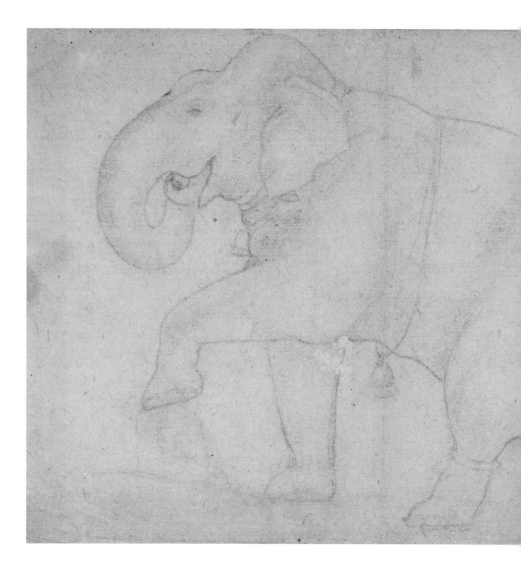

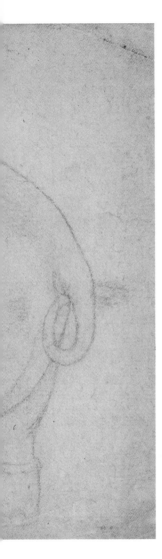

The largest land animal is the elephant, and it is the nearest to man in intelligence: it understands the language of its country and obeys orders, remembers duties that it has been taught, is pleased by affection and by marks of honour, nay more it possesses virtues rare even in man, honesty, wisdom, justice, also respect for the stars and reverence for the sun and moon. Authorities state that in the forests of Mauretania, when the new moon is shining, herds of elephants go down to a river named Amilo, and there perform a ritual of purification, sprinkling themselves with water, and after thus paying their respects to the moon return to the woods carrying before them those of their calves that are tired.

PLINY THE ELDER (AD 23–79)
From *Natural History*, transl. H. Rackham

An elephant. Pencil on paper, Rajput style, India, 18th century

From *The Sphinx*, 1841

Erect as a sunbeam,
Upspringeth the palm;
The elephant browses,
Undaunted and calm;

RALPH WALDO EMERSON (1803–82)

Seal and inscription dating from 2600–1900 BC,
found in Pakistan. Similar seals have been found
that show early evidence of elephants being used
as domesticated animals.

Sakao Moriyasu, detail of a *makimono* or handscroll with scenes
of an elephant playing with children, being ridden, eating,
fording a river, ascending a mountain path, and drinking.
Ink on paper, Japan, mid-19th century

From *Endymion*, 1818

He cannot see the heavens, nor the flow
Of rivers, nor hill-flowers running wild
In pink and purple chequer, nor, up-pil'd,
The cloudy rack slow journeying in the west,
Like herded elephants; . . .

JOHN KEATS (1795–1821)

In these circumstances the elephants were of the greatest service to him; the enemy never dared to approach that part of the column where they were placed, being terrified of the strangeness of their appearance.

POLYBIUS (*c.* 203–210 BC), describing the impact of elephants in Hannibal's army. From the *Histories*, transl. W.R. Paton

Black-glazed pottery pourer (*askos*) in the form of an elephant, probably inspired by the elephants brought to Rome by Hannibal. Roman, from Vulci (now in Lazio, Italy), 4th–3rd century BC

The Borradaile oliphant, a sounding horn carved from an
elephant tusk. Byzantine, 11th century. The term 'oliphant',
the old French word for elephant, derives from *The Song of Roland*.

'Sound Olifant, Roland my comrade, and straightway shall Charlemagne hear:
He is threading the mountain-gorges still – O yet is he near.
Full soon, mine honour I pledge thee, will the banners of France appear.'
'Now God forbid,' cried Roland, 'that for any heathen born
It shall ever be said that Roland hath stooped to sound his horn!
Shall I be on the lips of my kinsmen a byword, a shame, and a scorn?
No! in the mighty battle, in the heart of its tempest-roar,
Sword-strokes will I smite a thousand – ay, and seven hundred more!
Ye shall see Sword Durendal streaming and steaming with paynim gore.
The Franks, please God, like vassals shall battle, like knights without stain;
But none shall redeem from destruction the caitiff hordes of Spain.'

From *The Song of Roland*, mid-12th century, transl. Arthur S. Way

76

The elephant, not only the largest but the most intelligent of animals, provides us with an excellent example. It is faithful and tenderly loving to the female of its choice, mating only every third year and then for no more than five days, and so secretly as never to be seen, until, on the sixth day, it appears and goes at once to wash its whole body in the river, unwilling to return to the herd until thus purified. Such good and modest habits are an example to husband and wife.

St Francis de Sales (1567–1622)
From *Introduction to the Devout Life*, 1609, transl. Michael Day

Matteo de' Pasti, Cast bronze medal of Isotta degli Atti, faithful mistress of the Lord of Rimini, with an elephant – a symbol of fortitude and chastity – on the reverse. Rimini, 1446

Proboscis, *n.* The rudimentary organ of an elephant which serves him in place of the knife-and-fork that Evolution has as yet denied him. For purposes of humor it is popularly called a trunk.

AMBROSE BIERCE (1842–1914)
From *The Devil's Dictionary*, 1911

William Vaughan, detail of plate 6 of *A Booke Containing such Beasts as are most Usefull for such as practice Drawing, Graveing, Armes Painting, Chaseing, and for severall other occasions.* Engraving, published in London, 1664

R.H 74

From *Young Night-Thought*

So fine a show was never seen,
At the great circus on the green;
For every kind of beast and man
Was marching in that caravan.

Robert Louis Stevenson (1850–94)
From *A Child's Garden of Verses*, 1913

Roger Hilton, *Grey elephant decorated
with stripes and spots*. Gouache on paper,
inspired by the circus at Antibes, 1974

The elephant hath joints, but none for courtesy;
his legs are legs for necessity, not for flexure.

WILLIAM SHAKESPEARE (1564–1616)
Ulysses, in *Troilus and Cressida*, act 2, scene 2

Henri de Toulouse-Lautrec, print for the cover of
L'Estampe originale, showing a stage with curtain
down and a decorative elephant on a plinth.
Lithograph on paper, published in Paris, March 1895

Mars 1895
"L'Estampe originale"
Album de clôture

Albert Besnard
Eugène Carrière
Alexandre Charpentier
Walter Crane
Gandara
Constantin Meunier
Camille Pissarro
Puvis de Chavannes
H. de Toulouse-Lautrec
Odilon Redon
Renoir
Pierre Roche
Félicien Rops
Willette

André Marty, éditeur
imp. Edw. Ancourt, 83, R. à Paris

The Blind Men and the Elephant

It was six men of Indostan
To learning much inclined,
Who went to see the Elephant
(Though all of them were blind),
That each by observation
Might satisfy his mind.

The First approached the Elephant,
And happening to fall
Against his broad and sturdy side,
At once began to bawl:
'God bless me! but the Elephant
Is very like a wall!'

The Second, feeling of the tusk
Cried, 'Ho! what have we here,
So very round and smooth and
      sharp?
To me 'tis mighty clear
This wonder of an Elephant
Is very like a spear!'

The Third approached the animal,
And happening to take
The squirming trunk within his
      hands,
Thus boldly up he spake:
'I see,' quoth he, 'the Elephant
Is very like a snake!'

The Fourth reached out an eager
      hand,
And felt about the knee:
'What most this wondrous beast is
      like
Is mighty plain,' quoth he;
''Tis clear enough the Elephant
Is very like a tree!'

The Fifth, who chanced to touch
      the ear,
Said: 'E'en the blindest man
Can tell what this resembles most;
Deny the fact who can,
This marvel of an Elephant
Is very like a fan!'

The Sixth no sooner had begun
About the beast to grope,
Than, seizing on the swinging tail
That fell within his scope.
'I see,' quoth he, 'the Elephant
Is very like a rope!'

And so these men of Indostan
Disputed loud and long,
Each in his own opinion
Exceeding stiff and strong,
Though each was partly in the right,
And all were in the wrong!

Moral:
So oft in theologic wars,
The disputants, I ween,
Rail on in utter ignorance
Of what each other mean,
And prate about an Elephant
Not one of them has seen.

JOHN GODFREY SAXE (1816–87)
The poem echoes an Indian parable
often recounted by Mahatma Gandhi

Glazed porcelain figure of
a standing elephant. China,
Qing dynasty, 1800–78

I shall endure hard words even as the elephant in battle endures the arrow shot from the bow; the majority of people are, indeed, ill natured. They lead a tamed elephant into battle; the king mounts a tamed elephant. The tamed is the best among men, he who endures patiently hard words.

The Dhammapada (Sayings of the Buddha), transl. S. Radhakrishnan

An elephant and his mahout being attacked by a
spearman on a horse. Watercolour on paper,
Mughal dynasty, late 16th century

From *The Elephant*

Here comes the elephant
Swaying along
With his cargo of children
All singing a song:
To the tinkle of laughter
He goes on his way,
And his cargo of children
Have crowned him with may
His legs are in leather
And padded his toes;
He can root up an oak
With a wisk of his nose;
With a wave of his trunk
And a turn of his chin
He can pull down a house,
Or pick up a pin.
Beneath his gray forehead
A little eye peers;
Of what is he thinking
Between those wide ears?
What does he feel?

HERBERT ASQUITH (1881–1947)

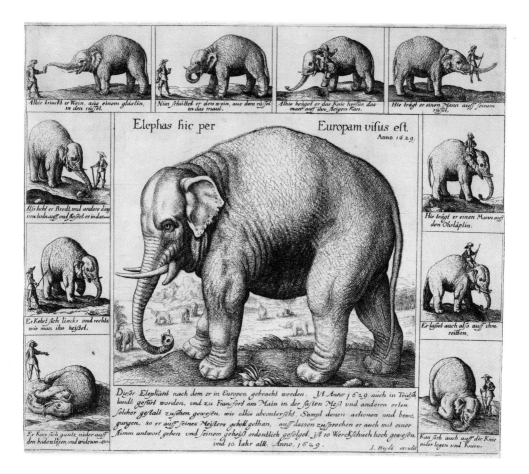

Wenceslaus Hollar, print for the exhibition of an elephant in
Frankfurt am Main, showing the animal performing
various tricks and being ridden. Etching, Strasbourg, 1629

There is an old African legend about the majestic bull elephant.
When he realizes that death is near, he returns deep into the darkest forest.
There he dies hidden from the world.

<small>Robert Baden-Powell (1857–1941) upon his
retirement to Nyeri, Kenya, in 1938</small>

Wooden coffin in the form of an elephant.
Made in the workshop of Paa Joe in Accra,
Ghana, 2000

The elephant is a friend to man
More than the dog, it's constant.
And now indeed our turn has come
    to be the Friend of the Elephant.

From the song *Friends of the Elephant*,
composed by Paul Hippeau for the 1906
banquet of the Society of the Friends of
the Elephant. The society was founded
in Paris in 1905 to champion the rights of
the elephant against slaughter.

A man feeding an elephant. Painting on
paper, Mughal style, *c.* 1620

FURTHER READING AND SOURCES

Text reprinted by permission of the copyright holders (original page numbers in italic)

ARISTOTLE, *De Partibus Animalium*, transl. William Ogle, Clarendon Press, Oxford, 1912
  (*p. 658*)

ASQUITH, Herbert, *Poems 1912–1933*, Sidgwick & Jackson, London, 1934 (*pp. 51–2*):
  © Herbert Asquith 1934, by permission of Pan Macmillan, London

ATTENBOROUGH, David, *The Trials of Life*, Collins, London, 1990 (*p. 50*): by permission of
  the author

BEN-AMOS, Paula, 'Men and Animals in Benin Art', *Man* (vol. XI, no. 2, June 1976, *p. 247*)

BIERCE, Ambrose, *The Enlarged Devil's Dictionary*, ed. Ernest Jerome Hopkins and with preface
  by John Miles, Penguin Modern Classics, London, 2001 (*p. 255*)

DARWIN, Charles, *The Expression of the Emotions in Man and Animals*, John Murray, London,
  1872 (*p. 176*)

DONNE, John, *The Complete English Poems*, ed. A.J. Smith, Penguin, London, 1973 (*p. 189*)

EMERSON, Ralph Waldo, *Poems*, Houghton Mifflin, Boston, 1904 (*p. 20*)

FIRDAUSI, Abu al-Qasim Hasan, *The Shahnameh of the Persian poet Firdausi*, transl. and ed. James
  Atkinson, John Murray, London, 1832 (*pp. 97–8*)

FONTENELLE, Bernard le Bovier de, *Entretiens sur la pluralité des mondes*, with introduction by
  François Bott, Editions de l'Aube, La Tour d'Aigues, 1994 (*p. 133*)

HINDLEY, J. (ed.), *Extracts, Epitomes and Translations from Asiatick Authors*, vol. 1, Black, Parry and
  Kingsbury, London, 1807

HUGO, Victor, *Les Misérables*, transl. Norman Denny, Penguin Classics, London, 1976
  (*pp. 256–7*): © The Folio Society 1976, by kind permission of The Folio Society

KEATS, John, *The Complete Poems*, ed. John Barnard, Penguin, London, 1973 (*p. 141*)

KIPLING, John Lockwood, *Beast and Man in India: a popular sketch of Indian animals in their relations
  with the people*, Macmillan, London, 1904 (*pp. 256–7*)

KIPLING, Rudyard, *The Complete Barrack Room Ballads of Rudyard Kipling*, ed. John Whitehead,
  Hearthstone Publications, Munslow, 1995 (*pp. 46–7*)

KIPLING, Rudyard, *Just So Stories*, with introduction by Jonathan Stroud, Puffin Classics,
  London, 2008 (*p. 53*)

KROM, N.J. (transl. and ed.), *The Life of Buddha on the stupa of Barabudur according to the Lalitavistara
  text*, Martinus Nijhoff, The Hague, 1926 (*p. 21*)

LAWRENCE, D.H., *The Complete Poems of D.H. Lawrence*, ed. Vivian de Sola Pinto and Warren
  Roberts, Penguin, Harmondsworth, 1977 (*pp. 70, 465*)

MACAULAY, Thomas Babington, *Lays of Ancient Rome and other Historical Poems*, with introduction by G.M. Trevelyan, Longman, London, 1928 (*pp. 146–7*)

MILTON, John, *The Complete Poems*, ed. John Leonard, Penguin, London, 1998 (*p. 200*)

PHILOSTRATUS, *The Life of Apollonius of Tyana*, transl. F.C. Conybeare, Harvard University Press, Cambridge, MA, 1960 (*p. 147*)

PLINY, *Natural History*, transl. H. Rackham, book VIII, vol. 3, Heinemann, Cambridge, MA, 1967 (*p. 3*)

POLYBIUS, *The Histories*, transl. W.R. Paton, book III, vol. 1, Harvard University Press, Cambridge, MA, 1967 (*p. 129*)

RADHAKRISHNAN, S. (transl. and ed.), *The Dhammapada*, Oxford University Press, New Delhi, 1950 (*p. 160*): by permission of Oxford University Press India, New Delhi

RICHARDSON, Samuel, *Clarissa, or, The history of a young lady comprehending the most important concerns of private life*, with introduction by Florian Stuber, vol. 8, AMS Press, New York, 1990 (*p. 149*)

ROSS, Doran H., *Elephant: the Animal and its Ivory in African Culture*, Fowler Museum of Cultural History, UCLA, Los Angeles, 1992 (*pp. 86, 141, 162–4*)

ST FRANCIS DE SALES, *Introduction to the Devout Life*, transl. Michael Day, Burns & Oates, London, 1956 (*pp. 193*): by kind permission of Continuum International Publishing Group

SAXE, John Godfrey, *The Poems of John Godfrey Saxe*, James R. Osgood & Company, Boston, 1873 (*pp. 135–6*)

SHAKESPEARE, William, *The Riverside Shakespeare*, ed. G. Blakemore Evans and J.J.M. Tobin, Houghton Mifflin, Boston, 1997 (*p. 499*)

SHASTRI, Hari Prasad (transl. and ed.), *The Ramayana of Valmiki*, Shanti Sadan, London, 1957 (*p. 240*): by permission of Shanti Sadan (*www.shantisadan.org*)

STEVENSON, Robert Louis, *Selected Poems*, ed. Angus Calder, Penguin Classics, London, 1998 (*p. 65*)

SWIFT, Jonathan, *The Complete Poems*, ed. Pat Rogers, Penguin, Harmondsworth, 1983 (*p. 526*)

TOPSELL, Edward, *The Historie of Foure-Footed Beastes, Describing the True and Lively Figure of Every Beast*, fascimile, Theatrum Orbis Terrarum, Amsterdam, 1973 (*p. 190*)

TWAIN, Mark, *The Stolen White Elephant Etc.*, Chatto & Windus, London, 1882 (*pp. 3–5*)

WAY, Arthur S. (transl.), *The Song of Roland*, Cambridge University Press, Cambridge, 1913 (*pp. 41–2*)

WODEHOUSE, P.G., *Meet Mr Mulliner*, Hutchinson, London, 1987 (*p. 57*): by permission of the Random House Group Ltd

play forever on video and

Disney
DVD

Published by Ladybird Books Ltd.
A Penguin Company
Penguin Books Ltd., 80 Strand, London WC2R 0RL
Penguin Books Australia Ltd., Camberwell, Victoria, Australia
Penguin Books (NZ) Ltd., Private Bag 102902, NSMC, Auckland,
New Zealand
LADYBIRD and the device of a ladybird
are trademarks of Ladybird Books, Ltd.
4 6 8 10 9 7 5
Printed in Italy

CLASSIC

LADY AND THE TRAMP

Ladybird

One Christmas morning, Jim Dear gave his wife, Darling, a very special present. It was wrapped in a box and tied with a pink ribbon.

When Darling opened it, a tiny cocker spaniel puppy peeped out at her.

"How sweet!" cried Darling. "What a perfectly beautiful little lady." And that was how Lady got her name.

Lady loved her new home. She had a big garden to play in and bones to bury. Her best friends, Jock and Trusty, lived nearby. Jock was a small, black Scottish terrier. Trusty was a big, brown bloodhound.

When Lady was six months old,
Darling gave her a smart, blue collar.
The little spaniel rushed off to show
Jock and Trusty.

"My, you're a full grown lady now!"
said Jock.

Lady felt that she was the luckiest,
happiest dog in the whole world.

9

A few weeks later, Jock and Trusty
found Lady lying by her water bowl.
She looked *very* sad.

"What's wrong, lassie?" asked Jock.

Lady explained that Jim Dear and
Darling seemed cross with her – but
she didn't know why.

"I wouldn'a worry," Jock said.
"Darling is expecting a wee bairn."
Lady looked puzzled.

"He means a baby," explained
Trusty.

"Oh!" said Lady, still puzzled.
"What's a baby?"

"A baby," Jock began, "is a cute little bundle of…" But before he could finish, a voice behind him said, "…trouble."

12

Lady turned round to see who had
spoken. Walking towards her was
a scruffy but handsome mongrel
called Tramp. "Remember, when a
baby moves in, the dog moves out!"
he warned.

The baby was born that spring. Jim Dear and Darling were overjoyed. And so was Lady.

Sometime later, Jim Dear and Darling went away to visit friends. Aunt Sarah came to look after the baby. She brought her two Siamese cats with her.

The cats were sly and mischievous. They raced through the house frightening the canary, ripping the curtains and upsetting the goldfish bowl!

When Aunt Sarah saw the mess, the cats made it look as though it was all Lady's fault.

Aunt Sarah was very angry. In fact,
she decided to buy a muzzle to
restrain the little dog. So she took
Lady to a pet shop that very day.

As an assistant placed a muzzle over
Lady's head, Lady panicked. She
managed to wriggle free and leapt off
the shop's counter. She ran out of the
door into the busy road. Cars and
lorries whizzed by.

As she dashed across the road, Lady was nearly knocked down by a car. Terrified, she ran into a side street.

Suddenly, a pack of stray dogs jumped out and began chasing her. Lady fled down an alley to try and escape but a huge fence blocked her way – she was trapped!

Just as the dogs were about to attack
her, Tramp jumped over the fence.
He was a very fierce fighter and
quickly forced the other dogs back
the way they had come. Lady had
been saved!

Tramp walked back to Lady, who was shaking with fear. "Oh! You poor kid," he said, looking at her muzzle. "Come on. We've got to get that thing off."

Tramp led Lady to a nearby zoo where they soon spotted a beaver. He was gnawing through some logs to build a dam.

Tramp persuaded the beaver to use his strong, sharp teeth to bite through Lady's muzzle. In a second, the muzzle dropped off and Lady was free again!

As the stars began to twinkle in the sky, Tramp said, "Come on, it's supper time." He led Lady to the back door of Tony's Italian restaurant.

"Hey, Joe! Look'a who's here!" called Tony to his chef. "Bring them the best'a spaghetti in'a town!"

While Tony and Joe played soft romantic music, Lady and Tramp shared a delicious meal.

What a wonderful night, thought Lady, beginning to chew a strand of spaghetti. Suddenly, her lips met Tramp's – they were both eating the same strand! Lady blushed and the two dogs gazed dreamily at each other. They were falling in love.

After supper, Tramp took Lady for a
stroll in a park. As a reminder of the
evening, the two dogs put their paw
prints side by side in some wet
cement. Later that night, they fell
asleep together under the stars.

The next morning, Lady woke with a start. "Oh, dear!" she said, as she suddenly remembered, "I must go home to look after the baby."

Tramp tried to persuade Lady to stay with him but she was determined to go home. Finally, Tramp agreed to show Lady the way back.

As they approached Lady's home, Tramp spotted a hen house. "Ever chased chickens?" he asked Lady.

"Certainly not!" Lady replied.

"Then you've never lived!" cried Tramp. "Follow me!"

Tramp began chasing the chickens around the farmyard. Feathers flew everywhere! Lady was horrified.

Suddenly, there was a gunshot. "Come on!" shouted Tramp as he squeezed under a fence. "That's the signal to get going!"

Tramp and Lady dashed round the corner. They splashed through a stream and jumped over ditches. Tramp was racing ahead. When he turned round, Lady was nowhere to be seen – she had been caught by a dog catcher!

Poor Lady was taken off to the dog
pound – a dark, terrible place where
all the unwanted dogs were locked
up. Lady's eyes filled with tears as
the door of her cell clanged shut
behind her.

Later that day, Lady was surprised to
find out that all the other dogs knew
about Tramp. It seemed he had lots
of other girlfriends. Lady felt sad and
disappointed. She had thought she
and Tramp had a special friendship.
She decided to try to forget him.

Before long, Aunt Sarah came to collect Lady from the dog pound. She was very cross with Lady for running away. When they got home, she chained Lady to a kennel in the garden.

That evening, when Tramp came to visit, Lady refused to speak to him. As Tramp left, Lady felt so unhappy that she lay down in the kennel and cried.

Suddenly, she noticed two eyes glinting in the shadows. A huge rat was scurrying towards the house! Lady barked and tried to chase it away – but her chain held her back.

Luckily, Tramp heard Lady barking. He ran back to see what was wrong.

33

"It's a rat!" cried Lady. "It ran up the side of the house and into the baby's room." In a flash, Tramp was inside the house, running up the stairs and through the nursery door.

The rat was about to jump into the baby's cot when Tramp leapt at it. The cot toppled over and the baby began to cry. Tramp chased the rat around the room.

There was a terrible fight. Finally,
Tramp trapped the rat and killed it.

Outside, Lady managed to pull free
from her chain. She raced inside the
house and upstairs to the nursery.

But Aunt Sarah had heard the commotion and had come rushing into the nursery. "Merciful heavens!" she cried, staring at the mess.

The dead rat was hidden behind the curtains. Aunt Sarah only saw Lady and Tramp and immediately blamed them.

"You vicious brutes!" she shouted, pushing Tramp into a cupboard with her broom. Then she dragged Lady downstairs and locked her in a dark, damp cellar.

Aunt Sarah telephoned the dog pound and ordered them to come and take Tramp away.

As Tramp was being led to the
pound wagon, Jim Dear and Darling
arrived back home. They rushed
inside the house and were met by
Lady, who had managed to escape
from the cellar.

Lady began barking wildly and led Jim Dear up to the nursery.

She showed him the dead rat behind the curtains. Lady knew in her heart that Jim Dear would understand that Tramp had killed the rat and saved the baby.

Meanwhile, Jock and Trusty were following the scent of the pound wagon. They were determined to try and free Tramp.

When they finally caught up with the wagon, Trusty barked at the horses. The horses reared up and the wagon overturned. It crashed to the floor, trapping Trusty's leg beneath. Then the wagon door sprung open and Tramp leapt free.

Suddenly, a taxi drove up with Lady and Jim Dear in it.

Luckily, Jim Dear had realised that
Tramp had rescued the baby. From
that day, Tramp was welcomed into
Jim Dear and Darling's home forever.

*   *   *

A few months later, at Christmas,
Jock and Trusty, whose broken leg
was mending well, came to visit
Lady and Tramp. As they arrived,
four little puppies ran to greet them.

"They've got their mother's eyes,"
said Trusty. He looked fondly at
three of the tiny puppies.

"Aye, but there's a bit of their father in them too," said Jock, trying to stop the fourth puppy chewing his coat!

Behind the puppies sat Lady and Tramp. Tramp looked over at his family and smiled. He knew they would all live happily ever after.

Yours
to own
on Disney
DVD
Walt Disney
CLASSICS
Magical stories to

DERTIG GRADEN IN DE SCHADUW

Martin Bril

Dertig graden in de schaduw

Zomerverhalen

2009 Prometheus Amsterdam

'Monica's blues' en 'Blauwe schoenen' verschenen eerder in *De heetste dag van het jaar*, een gelimiteerde uitgave van Magazijn de Bijenkorf BV uit 2006, en werden voor deze uitgave door de auteur geredigeerd. 'Wachten op onweer' en 'Twee dagen voor kerst' verschijnen voor het eerst in boekvorm.

Eerste druk juli 2009
Tweede druk juli 2009
Derde druk augustus 2009

Omslagontwerp Hugo Zwolsman
Foto omslag Henryk T. Kaiser/Rex Features Ltd.
Foto auteur Anneke Stehouwer
www.uitgeverijprometheus.nl
ISBN 978 90 446 1464 0

Monica's blues

Monica dobberde. Ze wist dat ze in bed lag, en dat ze sliep, maar toch dreef ze ook in het water – de zee, een lauwe, kalme zee. Ze hoorde haar moeder zingen. *Aus der Tiefen rufe ich, Herr, zu dir.*

Een zuivere sopraan.

Bach was haar moeders lieveling. Maar ze was opgehouden met zingen toen Robert verongelukte, drie jaar geleden. Het volgende moment wist Monica weer zeker dat ze sliep, en dat het maar een droom was: Robert die bij een open raam piano-speelde, zijn haar in de war, alsof hij net uit bed kwam.

Halfslaap.

Af en toe was ze ver weg, maar soms zat ze even rechtop in bed naar de wekker te kijken. Het ene moment was het 3.41 uur, daarna 4.12 uur. De tijd nam een loopje met haar, of de slaap speelde met de tijd – slapende minuten in een stro-perige nacht. *Gottes Zeit ist die allerbeste Zeit.* Daar had je mama weer, en Robert aan de piano. Ze draaide zich maar weer om.

Linkerzij, rechterzij.

Linkerzij, rechterzij.

Eigenlijk droomde ze nooit, of nou ja: ze droomde natuurlijk wel, maar zodra ze wakker was, wist ze niet meer wat er was gebeurd. Slaap was een toestand van genade. Daarom was ze zich nu zo bewust van de beelden die passeerden, de korte flitsen als ze wakker was, de diepte waar ze in viel als ze zich had omgedraaid. Haar vader kwam voorbij. Hij droeg een korte broek en trok een oude bolderkar vol kinderen. Ze zag zichzelf tussen twee blonde jongens zitten, haar broers.

Jacques verscheen, haar baas. Ze was verliefd op hem, dronken van verliefdheid, maar hij was homo. Ze glimlachte (in haar droom of in het echt?); ze was helemaal niet verliefd op Jacques, nooit geweest ook. Ze moest er niet aan denken. Een seconde later fietste ze over de dijk, richting de IJsselbrug. Naar school ging ze, en daar wachtte Leonard. Hij had lang haar en schreef gedichten voor haar.

Moontje, Monicabella.

Ze moest plassen en ze had dorst, maar ze bleef liggen. Ze herinnerde zich de wekker van haar jeugd – een grote oranje van de HEMA. Met twee grote bellen bovenop en een zilveren hamertje dat als een bezetene heen en weer ratelde als hij afging. Soms kon ze 's avonds niet in slaap komen, zo hard tikte dat ding. Maar als je geconcentreerd naar de tijd luisterde, kwam de slaap vanzelf.

Ze sloeg het klamme laken van zich af, en omhelsde het kussen dat naast haar lag, een vers, zacht kussen. Een van de voordelen van het alleen-zijn: plenty kussens in bed. Ze sloeg het laken weer over zich heen en dobberde weg.

5.11 uur, weer wakker.

Kennelijk kwam ze uit een diepe, droomloze episode nu, want volkomen gedesoriënteerd wist ze ineens zeker dat ze niet thuis, maar in een hotelkamer lag, ergens in een ver, goedkoop buitenland, Spanje, Portugal, Griekenland. Zo warm en klam was het, en zo brutaal waren de geluiden. Het kreunen, het piepen van een bed, de onderdrukte kreten, het natte slaan van naakt vlees tegen naakt vlees, een hoofdsteun die tegen de muur bonkte. Alleen in goedkope hotels kon je zo meegenieten. Ze herinnerde zich de eerste keer dat ze het had gehoord, in een hotelletje in Perpignan. Nienke was ook wakker geworden. Giechelend hadden ze in het donker liggen luisteren. Achttien waren ze, voor het eerst alleen op vakantie, allebei nog maagd, een en al hunkering. 'Girls Just Want to Have Fun' zongen ze die zomer. Ze zagen eruit als Cyndi Lauper.

Inmiddels kon ze de geluiden thuisbrengen: ze kwamen van beneden, bij Laura vandaan. Ze dacht: het moet niet gekker worden. Ze stond op om de balkondeuren dicht te doen. Ze deed dat niet zachtjes, zoals ze het normaal zou doen, maar met een fikse bons, in de hoop dat ze zich beneden zouden realiseren dat boven de buurvrouw wakker was en luisterde, maar de seks ging natuurlijk door, minder goed hoorbaar, dat wel.

Ze probeerde weer in slaap te komen, maar nu werd ze gehinderd door een rondzoemende mug. Het was 5.24 uur. Ze dacht opnieuw aan Nienke, die ze al zeker tien jaar niet gezien had. Na die zomer in Spanje, en al die leuke Spaanse jongens op wie ze verliefd waren geweest, was Nienke in Nijmegen en Monica in Amsterdam gaan studeren.

Ze hadden nog een tijd contact gehad, maar het was verwaterd, zoals dat ging. Waarschijnlijk was ze goed getrouwd en reed ze in een terreinwagen. Op de begrafenis van Robert was ze niet gekomen. Misschien moest ze het eens op Schoolbank.nl proberen – wie weet zocht Nienke háár wel. Ze waren toch echt erg close geweest. Gek dat zoiets over kon gaan, eigenlijk.

Monica legde een *Marie Claire* over de grote, rode cijfers van de wekkerradio. Het laken plakte aan haar lichaam, haar nek was nat van het zweet. Ze hoorde in de verte een man, zwaar en ritmisch. Het ging niet lang meer duren. Ze zwaaide haar benen uit bed en stommelde naar de badkamer.

Terwijl ze plaste, kwamen ze beneden met veel kabaal klaar. Monica trok snel door. Ondanks haar ergernis en gêne voelde ze ook een kleine steek van jaloezie. Het was al een tijd geleden dat ze een man in haar bed had gehad. En ineens had ze er zin in.

Ook dat nog.

Ze was negenendertig. Volgend jaar veertig, een mijlpaal. Ze was drie jaar geleden van Ben gescheiden, na een huwelijk van zeven jaar, en had sindsdien een serie vriendjes gehad, zoals ze ze gemakshalve maar noemde, lekker vrijblijvend, sommigen voor één nacht, anderen voor langere tijd.

Ze had niet de behoefte zich opnieuw te binden, het woord alleen al – ze werd er misselijk van. In tegenstelling tot andere singles van haar leeftijd was ze niet actief met daten, of op internet. Ze moest er niet aan denken. Ze kende mannen genoeg. Ze dacht zelden aan kinderen, en als ze er al aan dacht, had ze het gevoel dat ze ze niet wilde. Er waren al zo veel kinderen, en ze had er het geduld niet voor.

Haar huwelijk met Ben was erop stukgelopen; hij wilde per se wél kinderen, en hij vond dat zij dan moest stoppen met werken, al zei hij dat maar zelden hardop, want dat durfde hij niet. Monica's werk bracht bovendien meer geld in het laatje dan het zijne. Toen bleek dat hij haar vriendin Belinda zwanger had gemaakt, had ze hem het huis uit gezet. Dat was nog vrij makkelijk gegaan ook, en met terugwerkende kracht was ze Ben een karakterloze slappeling gaan vinden. Hoewel hij een goeie minnaar was geweest – vooral als hij een blowtje had gerookt. Met Belinda was ze goede vriendinnen gebleven.

Ze was één keer zwanger geweest, aan het begin van hun

huwelijk. Ze had het Ben niet verteld en het weg laten halen. Robert had haar vergezeld naar een kliniek aan de rand van het Oosterpark waar ze een lange ochtend hadden zitten wachten in een kamer vol timide meisjes in trainingspak, in gezelschap van stuurs kijkende moeders. Al wachtend had ze ruimschoots de tijd over haar beslissing na te denken, en één of twee keer was ze bijna opgestaan om weg te lopen, maar uiteindelijk was ze toch de behandelkamer in gegaan. Robert had al die tijd haar hand vastgehouden. 'Ik ben hier al twee keer eerder geweest,' had hij haar op een gegeven moment toegefluisterd, 'en het is een eitje, zus, echt.' Dat was het ook, al was het ook beschamend om wijdbeens in zo'n absurde stoel te liggen, een dokter en een assistente met een zoemend apparaat over je kut gebogen. Later had Robert haar nog wel eens gevraagd waarom Ben er niets van mocht weten, maar een goed antwoord had ze daar nooit op gehad.

Ze stond op van de wc.

De bril plakte aan haar billen, die de laatste tijd wat slap begonnen te worden. Beneden was het stil. Ze zette de douche aan. Soms masturbeerde ze onder de douche, maar nu had ze er geen zin in. Ze liet het water langs haar lichaam stromen, zeepte haar borsten in met een Sisley-douchegel die naar tuinkruiden rook, vooral naar dille. Ze speelde een beetje met haar tepels, die extra gevoelig waren omdat ze ongesteld moest worden. Haar borsten waren best in orde. Een volle B, een perfect decolleté, als ze de juiste bh droeg. Een beetje hangend waren ze inmiddels, maar ze was niet van plan er iets aan te doen. Willem was gek op haar borsten geweest – 'de jongens', noemde hij ze.

Ach ja: Willem, getrouwd, drie kinderen, een grote speler in de telecom. Twee maanden geleden had hij een punt achter hun relatie gezet. Hij was groot en lelijk, en al tegen de zestig, maar ze had erg met hem gelachen – een rare, hoge, hinnikende lach had hij. Ze geloofde nog steeds niet dat hij de waarheid had gezegd toen hij ermee ophield, want hij was geen man die zich door zijn geweten dwars liet zitten, zoals hij beweerde. Waarschijnlijk was hij gewoon op haar uitgekeken, of had zijn vrouw geen zin meer het door de vingers te zien.

Een beetje pijn deed het wel. Ze miste vooral de seks – altijd in hotelkamers, altijd overdag, van twaalf tot twee, van vijf tot zeven, dat soort uren. Tot het einde toe hadden die korte uren altijd heel lang geleken, diep en innig. Ze neukten, ze aten sushi die zij had meegebracht, ze keken televisie, ze namen hun werk door, ze neukten, ze douchten, ze dronken en lachten – als je je volledig op elkaar concentreerde, had je aan een paar uur genoeg. Op z'n minst was dat een mooie illusie. Maar uiteindelijk had het dus niet gewerkt, hoewel ze nog wel contact met elkaar hadden – telefonisch, hij vanuit de auto, zij vanuit de auto.

Ze deed de douche uit en droogde zich af met een verse, stugge handdoek. Als ze nou verstandig was, legde ze even een schoon laken over het bed, dan kon ze vast nog een paar uur lekker slapen, het was tenslotte zondagochtend, Bens favoriete moment, trouwens; zeker in het begin van hun huwelijk had hij de gewoonte op zondagochtend zachtjes bij haar binnen te schuiven, een ideale manier van wakker worden.

De laatste jaren sliepen ze met de ruggen naar elkaar toe, hij op zijn linkerzij, zij op haar rechterzij, en gebeurde het nog maar zelden dat ze wakker werd met haar billen in zijn schoot. Seks was een gek ding – af en toe herinnerde je je er een flard van, maar groots, meeslepend en onvergetelijk was het zelden. Wel erg lekker, daar niet van, maar dat was dineren bij Parkheuvel of Kaatje bij de Sluis ook.

Ze ging weer liggen. Buiten kwetterden de vogels. Een streep zonlicht viel de slaapkamer binnen. Om tien uur had ze afgesproken met haar vriendinnen, op het strand van Bloemendaal, bij Parnassia, lekker voor de drukte uit. Donna moest uit Den Haag komen, Julia uit Oegstgeest. Ze had ze al weken niet gezien, en had er zin in, kletsen en geiten met de meiden, roseetje erbij, lachen om al die domme gezinnen om hen heen. Maar nu eerst nog wat slapen. Of zou ze opstaan en er over een uurtje al heen gaan? Ze kon daar ook slapen.

Ze liet even twee vingers over haar clitoris gaan, maar ging er niet mee door, omdat ze koel wilde blijven. Dat was moeilijk genoeg. Het was al een paar dagen dertig graden, en vandaag beloofde het nog warmer te worden. De hitte was nauwelijks meer het huis uit te krijgen. Net toen ze wegdommelde, wegzakte in onverwachte tevredenheid, ging beneden Laura's baby huilen.

Shit.

Laura was vijfentwintig. Via een uitzendbureau was ze twee jaar geleden bij de zaak binnengekomen. Monica had haar meteen leuk gevonden: een spontane, snelle, grappige meid, en een goeie receptioniste. Een tijdje later bleken ze te sporten bij dezelfde sportschool, en van het een kwam het ander: af en toe gingen ze na afloop samen wat eten, twee vrouwen, allebei alleen. Al snel bleek dat ze geweldig met elkaar konden lachen. En Laura had bovendien een scherpe, genadeloze kijk op de mensen in het bedrijf; ze zag dingen die Monica niet zag, en durfde alles te zeggen. Monica moedigde haar niet echt aan, maar remde haar ook niet af. Ze vond het fascinerend om te zien hoe Laura de grenzen opzocht.

En toen was Laura zwanger; ze vertelde het op een avond aan de bar in de sportschool. Ze hadden allebei een glas wortelsap voor zich. 'Van wie?' vroeg Monica meteen.

'Ooh, een Italiaan,' zei Laura, alsof het logisch was om van een Italiaan zwanger te raken – waar anders van? 'Hij heeft een restaurant. We hebben er wel eens gegeten, weet je niet meer? Die pasta die niet gaar was? Hij is lief.'

Monica was verbaasd. Ze wist wel een beetje van Laura's privéleven, maar niets van de Italiaan, en ook niet van een kinderwens. De ongare pasta kon ze zich herinneren, een hele discussie over wat nou *al dente* was, best vermakelijk eigenlijk, en de ober had hen uitgebreid op grappa getrakteerd.

Regelmatig had Laura haar verteld over haar avonturen in de liefde. Nu eens een deejay, dan weer een jongen van de Filmacademie, maar nooit was ze tot over haar oren verliefd, laat staan dat ze echt een relatie wilde. Mannen waren leuke verhalen waar je in plonsde, en dan weer uit stapte, zo zag Laura het – in afwachting van de grote liefde die ongetwijfeld langs zou komen, dat kon niet anders, want een schoonheid was ze, met lange, blonde krullen, een prachtig lijf en ogen waar zelfs Monica niet al te lang in moest kijken. 'Ooh, ooh, een Italiaan,' had ze gezegd.

'Ja, dom, hè? Maar je moet het een keer hebben meegemaakt, vind je niet? Heb jij nooit een Italiaan gehad?'

'Jawel, maar ik werd er niet zwanger van. En nu?'

'We willen het houden,' zei Laura, 'en we gaan samenwonen. Zijn moeder is helemaal door het dolle heen – die zit al sokjes te breien.' Een paar weken later nam Laura een paar dagen vrij om die sokjesbreiende moeder te ontmoeten; ze vloog met haar vrijer naar Rome, en kwam nog enthousiaster terug. 'Zulke lieve mensen, je gelooft het gewoon niet!'

Monica geloofde het meteen.

Ze wist ook hoe het verder zou gaan, en zo ging het ook verder. Laura trok bij haar Luigi in, zei haar baan op en werkte tot de dag van de bevalling in de bediening van Luigi's restaurant. Twee maanden nadat de baby was geboren, wilde ze bij hem weg – hij had toch meer belangstelling voor zijn vrienden en zijn scooter dan voor haar. De baby, een meisje dat Orvieta was genoemd, deed hem niets. Zonder erover na te denken, had Monica Laura toen de leegstaande verdieping in haar huis aangeboden, op voorwaarde dat Roberts vleugel bleef staan. Na zijn dood had ze die hierheen verhuisd, vaag van plan zelf piano te leren spelen, maar daar was het nooit van gekomen. Laura had geaarzeld – ze was niet het type om liefdadigheid te accepteren –, maar was er uiteindelijk ingetrokken, 'tot ik zelf iets heb'. Dat was inmiddels een jaar geleden en het leek er niet op dat Laura en Orvieta op korte termijn zouden vertrekken – het was veel te gezellig.

Aanvankelijk was het de bedoeling geweest dat Laura ook terug zou komen bij de zaak, maar daar zag ze van af, omdat het toch leuker was voor de kleine te zorgen. De tijd die ze over had besteedde ze aan het schrijven van korte verhalen die ze af en toe aan Monica voor kwam lezen. Dan zat ze op het aanrecht terwijl Monica kookte, of op de wc in de badkamer, terwijl Monica in bad lag.

Bizarre verhalen trouwens, over Laura's jeugd op de Veluwe, haar heerszuchtige vader die beroepsmilitair was en te veel dronk, haar moeder die het grootste deel van de dag in bed lag met hoofdpijn en 's nachts in haar duster door het dorp zwierf, haar twee broers die helemaal in de EO waren, haar schooltijd die verpest was door een leraar Duits die zijn handen niet thuis kon houden, haar eerste vriendje, een Turkse jongen uit Amersfoort, die een snackbar overviel om een knots van een ring voor haar te kunnen kopen, haar hartsvriendin, Alma, die zichzelf verhing in de slaapkamer van haar ouders – 'de enige kamer in huis met balken' –, haar vlucht naar Utrecht, en later naar Amsterdam waar ze terechtkwam in de housescene en een tijdje optrok met de jongens die al die grote feesten organiseerden, een van hen reed zich later in een Porsche dood bij de RAI, tegenover het No-votel waar Monica wel eens afsprak met Willem. Voor iemand die nog maar vijfentwintig was, had Laura een hoop meegemaakt – of ze had een heel levendige fantasie. Het maakte Monica niet echt uit, ze was gek op Laura.

De baby was oké.

Monica had er nauwelijks last van. Ze vond het wel grappig om te zien hoe Laura ermee omging, maar het deed haar weinig. Ze voelde in ieder geval niet de neiging zich als een soort peettante op te stellen, waar ze wel even bang voor was geweest. Laura was ook slim genoeg om haar erbuiten te laten; ze vroeg Monica niet om op te passen, bijvoorbeeld, en ook als gespreksonderwerp hield ze Orvieta een beetje buiten beeld – niet alleen om te voorkomen dat ze zo'n jonge moeder werd die alleen maar over luieruitslag en toeschietende melk kon praten, maar ook om Monica te sparen, wat weer niet hoefde, maar wat wel subtiel en attent was.

Soms gingen ze er toch met z'n drietjes op uit, naar de markt, of een hapje eten, de baby bij Laura in een zakje op de buik, of in de wandelwagen. Het maakte bij Monica een vage melancholie los, en daar werd ze onrustig en geïrriteerd van. Alsof zij óók een kind zou moeten willen – het was net alsof de wereld een beetje verwijtend naar haar keek als ze met Laura en de baby op stap was, nee, niet verwijtend, maar met een soort medelijden; alsof Laura het kind had dat Monica had moeten hebben. Bullshit natuurlijk, maar toch, er zat iets niet helemaal lekker.

Orvieta was normaal gesproken een stille, rustige baby, maar nu huilde ze met lange, felle uithalen. Het was eigenlijk voor het eerst dat Monica haar zo hard hoorde huilen. Als het kind vanaf het begin zo veel herrie had gemaakt, had ze Laura er meteen uit gezet, bedacht ze grimmig. Ze hoorde gestommel, en even later was het huilen voorbij – Laura had de kleine uit haar bedje gevist en aan de borst gelegd, of een schone luier gegeven, zoiets.

Monica probeerde zich een voorstelling van de man te maken die haar gezelschap hield – of zou hij al vertrokken zijn? Of was het Orvieta's vader? Dat laatste kon ze zich niet voorstellen, Luigi had nooit meer iets van zich laten horen. Lag er dan nu bij Laura een behaarde kerel in bed die slaperig toekeek hoe zijn liefje van die nacht uit de aangrenzende kamer ineens een huilende baby tevoorschijn haalde? En waarom was de man in haar verbeelding behaard? Misschien was het George Clooney wel, of Brad Pitt – maar ook die konden natuurlijk haar op hun rug en hun schouders hebben.

Ze stond op. *Ich habe genug*, dacht ze cynisch. De lievelingscantate van haar moeder, en een van Monica's eigen krakers in tijden van stress en tegenslag. 'Kom nou eens met wat anders, schat, iets in het Engels of het Frans of zo,' plaagde Jacques haar altijd. Om hém te pesten, zei-zong ze het dan nog een keer – '*Ich habe genug*', met de trillende, omhoog klimmende a die ze van haar moeder kende. God, wat had ze die manier van zingen gehaat toen ze jong was.

Het was 6.30 uur.

Nog veel te vroeg om naar het strand te gaan, maar ze had genoeg te doen. De kranten en tijdschriften lezen, wat strijken, de koelkast schoonmaken, want er had een meloen in liggen rotten, e-mails beantwoorden, haar bankafschriften van de laatste weken openen en in hun map doen, rekeningen betalen, de vensterbanken afstoffen. Ze trok een dun jurkje aan, eigenlijk een onderjurk waarin ze ook wel eens sliep, en ging aan de slag. Ze draaide intussen de laatste cd van Jack Johnson, de ultieme zomermuziek die je de laatste tijd overal

hoorde. *Where'd all the good people go? I've been changing chan-*
nels, I don't see them on the TV shows. Where'd all the good people
go? We got heaps and heaps of what we sow. Ja, waar waren de
goede mensen gebleven? Dat vroeg Monica zich ook wel eens
af, die schaarse keren dat ze tv keek – allemaal plastic, allemaal grote grijnzen. Ze zong af en toe wat met Jack mee, zo
noemde ze hem, in gedachten. Jack, hij was haar erg dierbaar.
Hij deed haar aan Robert denken.

Na een tijdje had ze er genoeg van en schakelde ze over op
de radio. Ze draaide wat aan de knoppen, tot ze ergens in 'Love
Is a Battlefield' van Pat Benatar viel – dat deed haar weer aan
die vakantie met Nienke denken. Ze draaide verder en kwam
bij een gesprek over het ringen van valken dat zich afspeelde
op een 120 meter hoge schoorsteen van een elektriciteitscen-
trale op de Maasvlakte, en daarna bij opgewonden praatjes
over een poema die al een paar dagen over de Veluwe zwierf.
Ze deed de radio uit. Op haar computer tikte ze even de naam
en achternaam van Nienke in. Nienke Buitelaar. Het leverde
een paar gekke hits op, maar niet de oude vriendin die ze
zocht, en ze schudde Nienke van zich af.

Wat moest ze aan?

Dat was een kwestie waar ze nog wel eens wat tijd aan wilde
besteden, maar de dag beloofde zo warm te worden dat er
maar weinig mogelijkheden waren. Een bikini en een dun zo-
merjurkje. Slippers, een bandana om haar haar. Daar was ze
in vijf minuten klaar mee.

Ze pakte haar tas, de nieuwe *Elle*, de *Wad*, een buitenlands
designblad (kon ze toch nog een beetje werken), *Sonny Boy* van
Annejet van der Zijl, een boek waar ze al een paar keer in was
begonnen, en waar al haar vriendinnen laaiend over waren,
een paar flessen Evian, zonnebrandcrème, lippenbalsem, tam-
pons, een handdoek, haar telefoon. In haar iPod had ze geen
zin; altijd maar muziek om je heen was niet goed voor je.

Toen ze klaar was, was het vijf voor acht. Ze zette een espresso voor zichzelf, at yoghurt met muesli en een perzik. Ze vond zichzelf ineens een beetje belachelijk. Kwart over acht, naar het strand, ze leek wel gek. Ze maakte nog een espresso, en warmde melk op – een cappuccino dan maar, op het balkon van de slaapkamer; treuzelen, haar teennagels lakken.

In de binnentuin was het nog stil. Sinds kort had ze nieuwe achterburen: een stel met twee kleine jongetjes die als ze maar even de kans kregen met plastic zwaarden en brandweerhelmpjes op hun donkere koppies over de daken van de schuren in de tuin holden. Nu was het nog te vroeg, hoewel: de keukendeur van de achterburen stond al open, en vader liep in een korte broek op en neer met een dienblad, die gingen in de tuin ontbijten. De jongetjes waren er ook, bleek even later, ze hingen in de enige boom die de buren in hun tuin hadden staan. Daar hadden ze zich verstopt, en vandaar dat ze stil waren. Maar zodra hun vader hen gespot had, begonnen ze te schreeuwen. Pap stond er hulpeloos bij, in zijn korte broek. Hij had van die witte, behaarde benen.

Monica lakte haar nagels, oranje, en probeerde zich niet te ergeren. Er was zo veel lelijkheid; als je er oog voor had, werd je er niet goed van. De kunst was, had ze van Jacques geleerd, om het van je af te laten glijden. 'Concentreer je op wat mooi is, schat,' zei hij dan, als ze weer eens stuiterend van adrenaline en ergernis het kantoor binnen kwam, 'kijk desnoods naar je eigen handen, die zijn mooi.' Ze dacht even dat ze beneden stemmen hoorde, maar verdreef het idee door snel naar binnen te gaan, maar toen ze er was, wist ze niet wat ze er moest doen. Ze plofte op de bank neer en voelde zich moe. Ze keek om zich heen. Ze had het goed voor elkaar, een leuk, gezellig huis. Maar soms, als alles aan kant was, zoals nu, vond ze dat het er kaal en een beetje zielloos uitzag.

Goed, dat was dan maar zo. Ze stond op, opende de deur en liep naar beneden.

Op de trap deed ze rustig aan, een gewoonte. Laura en de kleine sliepen meestal als ze naar haar werk ging. Maar nu hoorde ze geluiden achter de deur, een donkere mannenstem, Laura's lach. Wat de man zei, kon ze niet verstaan. Ze had ineens haast, merkte ze. Maar halverwege de laatste trap hoorde ze pianoklanken.

Shit, hij zat achter de vleugel.

Haar eerste impuls was onmiddellijk terug naar boven hollen en op de deur bonzen. Niemand mocht aan Roberts vleugel komen. Hij was niet eens gestemd, trouwens. Het eerste jaar had ze dat nog om de drie maanden laten doen. Af en toe had ze er zelf achter gezeten, in dat lege appartement, waar verder alleen een paar dozen met spullen van haar overleden broer stonden.

Een paar dagen na zijn begrafenis had ze met twee vriendinnen zijn huis in Utrecht leeggeruimd. Behalve muziekinstrumenten, versterkers, keyboards en computers, had hij eigenlijk alleen boeken, platen en cd's gehad. Monica had er een dag in gegrasduind, bijna alle boeken door haar handen laten gaan – boeken die gesigneerd waren, waar opdrachten in stonden, of aantekeningen van haar broer, en boeken waarvan ze wist dat ze veel voor hem betekenden en die ze zelf ook wel eens zou willen lezen, had ze apart gelegd. Hetzelfde had ze met de muziek gedaan. Een paar van Roberts lievelingsplaten, voor zover ze dat wist, had ze in laten lijsten, de hoezen, met plaat en al – die hingen in haar werkkamer. *Waltz for Debby* van Bill Evans, *A Love Supreme* van John Coltrane, *Closer* van Joy Division.

Ze aarzelde.

De man die op de vleugel speelde, kon het nog ook, dat was

het ergste. Hij speelde een romantisch, jazzy riedeltje, niets bijzonders. Robert zou er zijn hand niet voor hebben omgedraaid. Monica holde de trap af, opende de voordeur en sloeg hem hard achter zich dicht. Het was stil op straat, doodstil, en al erg warm. Vaag hoorde ze nog steeds de pianomuziek. Moest ze teruggaan, en Laura vragen haar lover niet op de vleugel te laten spelen? Waarom deed ze zo kinderachtig? Er gingen weken voorbij zonder dat ze ook maar een minuut aan Robert dacht, en vandaag hield het maar niet op. Misschien kwam het omdat ze ongesteld moest worden. Dan was ze snel sentimenteel.

Ze haalde diep adem en liep naar haar auto – Jacques' cadeautje toen ze vorig jaar tien jaar bij de zaak zat, een BMW-Z3, zwart als de nacht, en zwart als haar haar, als ze de grijze haren er tenminste uittrok, wat ze toch minstens een keer per week deed. Ze was gek op het autootje – altijd gek op auto's geweest, net als Robert, die een zwak voor oude Mercedessen had, zigeunerwagens. In zo'n auto was hij ook verongelukt, in de buurt van Apeldoorn, bij Brummen, het kanaal in gereden, na een of ander dom optreden op een feest. Of hij had gedronken kon de politie niet zeggen, ze hadden geen bloedonderzoek gedaan. Er waren verder geen slachtoffers, behalve een boom langs het kanaal – daar had de Mercedes een stuk schors afgeschaafd voor hij in het water terecht was gekomen. Monica was er op een zwak moment eens naartoe gereden. Lekker huilen op een zondagmiddag. Het had niet geholpen. Maar hulp was ook iets waar ze niet in geloofde. Had ze helemaal niet nodig.

*

Ze reed de bekende weg. Langs Geuzenveld en de vaart naar Halfweg. Uitbundig glinsterende vliegtuigen in de blauwe lucht vlogen aan op Schiphol. Ze had bijna zin om erheen te rijden en de eerste de beste vlucht naar Verweggistan te nemen. Door de kronkelende bocht bij de suikerfabrieken, recht op het Rottepolderplein af, Haarlem in de verte, bijna geen verkeer op de weg. De radio keihard aan. 'Watskeburt'. Eminem. 'Let's Get Down to Business'. De stoplichten in Haarlem, de Amsterdamse Poort links, rechtsaf onder het spoorviaduct door, de gevangenis, onder het spoor door de brug over het Spaarne, achter het station langs, de Julianalaan, de watertoren – hoe vaak had ze deze route al niet gereden?

De Zeeweg.

Met z'n heerlijke bochten. Alleen daarom al moest je vroeg naar het strand gaan; met het dak open over de Zeeweg, de zoute wind in de haren, luidkeels zingen. *Hé, kleine meid op je kinderfiets, de zon draait steeds met je mee.* Herman van Veen. Wat een leven, waarom had ze eigenlijk geen leuke man? *What went wrong?* Niets. Zelfs de leukste man liet scheten, smakte bij het eten en kwam te snel klaar. *Fuck them all.*

Bloemendaal.

Vlaggen, wind.

Zon in de rug.

Wandelaars, honden.

Maar om halfelf was het druk op het strand en was het eigenlijk al te heet. Het eerste uur had ze nog rustig kunnen liggen, beetje lezen, beetje doezelen, beetje kijken, maar inmiddels waren er steeds meer mensen in de buurt komen liggen. De dichtstbijzijnde buren waren een vader en zijn kleine zoontje; ze hadden voortdurend ruzie. De vader wilde op een gegeven moment voetballen, maar na twee keer de bal over en weer te hebben geschopt, liet het jongetje zich weer op de handdoeken vallen. 'Met Ruud gaat het veel beter,' zei hij verbeten.

De vader, een lange, bleke man met een ouderwets lubberende zwembroek, ging naast hem zitten. 'Ik ben Ruud niet,' zei hij.

'Nee, jij bent Ruud niet,' zei het jongetje, een wreed kereltje met rood haar.

'Ik ben je vader. Zullen we een ijsje gaan halen?' stelde de man voor. Zweet glinsterde op zijn voorhoofd.

'Ik heb geen zin in een ijsje. Ik wil vliegeren.'

'Er staat geen wind,' kreunde zijn vader.

'Ruud zei dat het hartstikke goed weer was om te vliege-ren.'

Monica schoot in de lach.

De man keek haar kwaad, en toen vertwijfeld aan. 'Het valt niet mee om géén Ruud te zijn,' zei hij met een glimlach.

'Ach,' zei Monica, 'als iedereen een Ruud was, was er geen reet aan.'

De man lachte.

Het jongetje vloekte en rommelde in zijn tas. Er kwam een telefoon tevoorschijn.

'Wat ga je doen?' vroeg zijn vader.

'Mama bellen. Misschien kan Ruud me komen halen,' zei het jongetje.

Monica kon het niet langer aanzien en stond op. Op dat moment ging haar eigen telefoon. Ze bukte om hem te pak-ken, en zag nog net hoe in de ogen van de buurman vage hoop omsloeg in berusting. Ach god, dacht ze, terwijl ze op haar display zag dat het Donna was. Ze liep richting water-kant.

De dames gingen het niet redden.

Donna had Julia opgepikt, maar onderweg hadden ze een klapband gekregen. Nu stonden ze langs de A4 te wachten op de wegenwacht, want ze hadden geen krik bij zich.

'Hè, jammer,' zei Monica, maar ze vond het niet zo heel erg, want het begon toch al veel te druk te worden. Ze ging liever vroeg naar huis. Daar was het koel. Donna ratelde gezellig door: hoe eng het was, zo'n klapband, hoe heet het was, langs de weg, en hoe druk, en dat ze het niet vertrouwden om helemaal naar Bloemendaal te rijden op zo'n dom thuiskomertje, en dan ook nog terug, en dat Julia natuurlijk meteen hysterisch was gaan huilen en dat het voorlopig nog wel mooi weer bleef, dus dat ze maar snel een nieuwe afspraak moesten maken, jammer jammer, ze hadden zich er zo op verheugd. Monica wilde nog voorstellen die avond dan maar af te spreken, in Leiden, maar ze hield het voor zich. Ze had een vreemd verlangen naar eenzaamheid.

'Juul wil je spreken,' zei Donna.

'Wat een zeperd, hè,' riep Julia, die een merkwaardige, hoge stem had waar Monica altijd even aan moest wennen. 'We zitten lekker te kletsen, ik steek net een sigaretje op, horen we een knal, nou ja, die sigaret valt in m'n kruis natuurlijk, zo'n gat in m'n nieuwe jurkje, zo'n Donna Karan-dingetje. Nou ja, we leven nog. Hoe is het met jou?'

'Goed, schat,' zei Monica.

'Moet je horen, ik bel er later nog wel even over, maar ik heb toch zoiets geks met Marc meegemaakt, dat moet je horen.' Typisch Julia: zeggen dat ze iets ging zeggen en het dan níet zeggen, want ze ging het *later* zeggen.

'Vertel op,' drong Monica aan.

Voor haar in de rimpelloze zee stonden twee vrouwen aan de achterkant van hun bikinibroekjes te frunniken – vingers tussen het elastiek die de dunne stof uit de bilspleet plukten om die over de billen te vlijen, de een droeg een topje, de ander niet. Ze waren in druk gesprek verwikkeld. Aan de billen te zien waren het zussen. Er kwam een man bij staan met een strak, fluorescerend blauw zwembroekje en een enorme tatoeage op zijn rode rug. Hij kneep zonder pardon in de dichtstbijzijnde kont.

Julia vertelde intussen over Marc, een fysiotherapeut die Monica een keer ontmoet had en die ze niet aardig had gevonden – het was op een feestje en Marc was er met Julia, maar flirtte nogal nadrukkelijk met andere vrouwen, onder wie Monica. Hij had bovendien ontzettend uit zijn mond geroken. Toch had Juul het een tijdje met hem uitgehouden, maar nu was hij dus te ver gegaan, vertelde ze, want ze had hem in zijn eigen praktijk betrapt met een ander. 'Je gelooft je ogen niet, joh, het was net een pornofilm,' kirde Juul. 'Hé, daar is de wegenwacht, ik hang op, lieverd. Bel je later!'

Monica liep een stukje de zee in. Het water was lauw. Ze draaide zich naar de dames naast haar. De toploze stond het dichtstbij – ze had grote borsten, bollen vol siliconen en piercings in haar tepels, kleine boutjes die schitterden van de zonnebrandolie. 'Wil je even mijn telefoon vasthouden?' vroeg Monica. *Ich habe genug*, flitste het door haar heen, en ze moest oppassen dat ze niet naar de tepels ging staren.

'Tuurlijk, mop, ga je zwemmen?'

Monica knikte en gaf haar telefoon af.

Ze liep met stevige passen de zee in. Een vliegtuigje met Bacardi-reclame knetterde laag over. Ze liep door tot het té diep was om verder te lopen, en zwom toen net zo lang tot ze niemand meer zag en rustig op haar rug kon dobberen; het bomvolle strand in de verte, alleen.

Toen ze terugkwam op het strand, stond de vrouw met de piercings ongeduldig op haar te wachten. 'Het had niet veel langer moeten duren,' beet ze Monica toe, terwijl ze de telefoon teruggaf.

'Sorry, bedankt,' mompelde Monica.

'Is goed,' zei de vrouw, en ze liep weg.

Monica ging op zoek naar haar plekje. Het leek wel alsof het twee keer zo druk was geworden. Wat een gekkenhuis. Uiteindelijk vond ze haar handdoek. Ze strekte zich uit.

Opdrogen, ontspannen, relax. *Don't do it*, zong Frankie Goes to Hollywood er in haar hoofd achteraan. Toch was het de gesel van de moderne tijd, volgens Willem, relaxen – iedereen wilde maar niks doen. Ze glimlachte bij de herinnering. Ze hoorde het hem zeggen.

Misschien moest ze naar het naaktstrand, verderop – daar was het beslist een stuk rustiger. Aan de andere kant: naakte lichamen waren nog erger dan miniem bedekte lichamen. De laatste keer dat ze er had gelegen, een jaar geleden of zo, met Julia, hadden ze uitzicht gehad op een dikke vrouw die met provocerende wellust voortdurend haar grote, hangende borsten insmeerde met Nivea, en toen ze verhuisden, kwamen er twee nichten bij hen in de buurt liggen, eentje met een erectie. Ja, lachen was het, het naaktstrand, maar als je er alleen ging liggen, had je binnen een mum van tijd aanspraak van een of andere halvegare die in de duinen een vluggertje wilde maken.

In haar tas hoorde ze haar telefoon pingelen: er kwam een sms'je binnen. Het ging niet lang meer duren of ze had een leesbril nodig voor die kleine lettertjes op het schermpje van haar Motorola. Toen het fenomeen net bestond, kon ze er geen genoeg van krijgen, maar de laatste tijd belde ze liever gewoon – al dat geklungel met die kleine knopjes, haar nagels waren er ook te lang voor: zette ze haar vingertop op een toets, prikte haar nagel in de toets erboven. Ja, van die dingen. Ze viste haar telefoon uit haar tas.

Laura natuurlijk.

'Ben je thuis?'

'Nee,' sms'te ze terug – geen zin in geintjes.

'Waar dan?'

'Strand.'

'Gaat het goed met je?'

'Tuurlijk.'

'Jammer.' Dat was nou echt Laura, en Monica glimlachte.

'Jij? Lekker geneukt?'

'Ja, jij niet, of wel?'

'Nee. Geen oog dichtgedaan.'

'Echt niet?'

Ineens had ze er geen zin meer in, en ze belde Laura. 'Schat, wat een herrie was dat vannacht. Is-ie leuk?'

'Hij is zo dom, ongelooflijk,' kirde Laura. 'Sorry, hoor. Had je er echt last van? Orvieta sliep er dwars doorheen. Hè, kut. Wat gênant.'

'Geeft niet. Wat is het voor man?'

'Hij speelt bongo en hij heet Xavier. Hij komt uit Zuid-Amerika. Ik versta geen woord van wat-ie zegt. Maar jezus, Moon, ik wist niet dat het zo lekker kon zijn. Heb jij wel eens een bongospeler gehad?'

'Ik haat bongo's,' zei Monica – die ineens voorzag dat Xavier, de naam alleen al, bij Laura in zou trekken –, hoe kreeg ze in godsnaam die meid haar huis uit? 'En ik vind het helemaal vervelend als-ie pianospeelt.'

Het werd stil op de lijn.

'Sorry,' zei Laura uiteindelijk, met een klein stemmetje. 'Dat was dom, ja, maar hij zat erachter voor ik het in de gaten had.'

'Ik heb slechte herinneringen aan piano's,' ging Monica verder. Waar had ze het over? Had ze het te heet of zo? Ze nam een slok water.

'Verkoop hem dan, hij staat mij ook alleen maar in de weg,' flapte Laura eruit.

'Hij is van mijn broer geweest.'

'Dat weet ik, lieverd, daarom moet je hem ook wegdoen. Je broer is dood, die kan er niet meer op spelen, en als anderen erop spelen, moet je aan je broer denken. Weg ermee, zou ik zeggen.'

'Dank je.'

'*You're welcome,*' lachte Laura, en Monica hoorde hoe in Amsterdam de hand even over de microfoon ging om iets de huiskamer in te roepen. Verbeeldde ze het zich, of hoorde ze even een flard pianomuziek?

'Hij zit erachter, hè?'

'In z'n blote reet, ja, schandelijk,' reageerde Laura luchtig, 'maar ik heb hem verboden te spelen.'

'Goed.'

'Ik hoor je denken dat je straks een pianist in huis hebt,' vervolgde Laura, 'maar maak je geen zorgen, hoor, hij is zo weer weg. Orvieta vindt hem eng.' Laura lachte schaterend. 'Waar ben je, Zandvoort?'

'Parnassia,' zei Monica, 'maar niet lang meer, want het is hier verschrikkelijk en de meiden komen niet.' Ze keek om zich heen. Een deinende massa vlees, tentjes, windschermen, koelboxen, roodverbrande blote kinderen, kratten bier, strandballen, vliegers, gettoblasters, haringkarren, terreinwagens, vrijende stelletjes, parasols, nijvere vaders die diepe kuilen groeven met hun zoontjes die al snel iets anders aan het hoofd hadden, maar de vaders groeven door, Hollandse vrouwen met putten in hun dijen en praktisch haar – altijd blond. Ze was blij dat ze anders was. 'Heet-ie echt Xavier? Is het een neger?' vroeg ze.

'Ja. Goed, hè? Xavier. Een perfecte naam. Als ik een jongetje had, zou ik hem ook Xavier noemen. Nee, het is geen neger, ik val niet op negers, dat weet je toch?' Laura giechelde – en op de achtergrond hoorde Monica Orvieta, of was het Xavier die iets in Laura's oor fluisterde?

'Zie je later, *take care,*' zei Monica, en ze hing op. Ze bleef nog een uurtje liggen, maar toen pakte ze haar spullen in en sjouwde ze door het hete zand naar het duinpad. In de koelte van het strandpaviljoen dronk ze een glaasje rosé en daarna ging ze op zoek naar haar auto op het parkeerterrein. Toen ze hem gevonden had, trok ze haar bikini uit en schoot ze haar jurkje aan. Ondergoed was ze vergeten.

Ach wat, dacht ze toen ze wegreed, ik ga even bij ze langs. Haar ouders woonden in Heemstede, vlakbij. De Zeeweg stond volkomen vast, maar aan haar kant van de weg was het rustig.

Aan het einde, vlak voor Haarlem, bij de watertoren, sloeg ze rechts af, richting Kraantje Lek en Aerdenhout. Dit was niet het terrein van haar jeugd, maar zo voelde het wel. Haar ouders woonden al twintig jaar in Heemstede, en Monica zelf al twintig jaar in Amsterdam. Door de jaren heen was ze hier veel geweest. Wandelen in de herfst, pannenkoeken en donker bier bij Kraantje, 's zomers picknicken in Elswout, luieren onder de bomen. De wind speelde door haar haar, Jack Johnson zong over de goede mensen die er niet meer waren, en ze zong met hem mee. Het leven was best in orde, tot op zekere hoogte. Moest ze niet even bellen dat ze eraan kwam?

Natuurlijk niet.

Haar ouders waren er altijd, daar waren het ouders voor. Ze zag er ineens een beetje tegen op. Hoe ouder ze werden, haar vader en moeder, hoe vreemder ze zich gedroegen. Vroeger was het een innig echtpaar geweest, van die mensen die alles samen deden, maar de laatste jaren waren ze uit elkaar gegroeid – haar moeder bewoonde een deel van het huis, haar vader een ander deel. Ze gingen nauwelijks meer met elkaar om.

Haar vader, dik in de zeventig, bleef geloven in de toekomst en de vooruitgang. Nieuwe keukens, nieuwe televisies, nieuwe auto's, nieuwe meubels – hoe nieuwer alles was, hoe beter, en des te verder weg het verleden. Haar moeder daarentegen hechtte steeds meer aan haar oude spulletjes:

de piano, haar boeken, het radiomeubel dat ze op hun koperen bruiloft hadden gekregen, zelfs oude kleren. De dood van Robert had alles nog eens verhevigd, en de kleinkinderen, de kinderen van Nico en Joke, zagen ze maar een paar keer per jaar, misschien was dat nog wel het grootste verdriet. Oude mensen en kleine kinderen, er was geen peil op te trekken.

Ze deed het rustig aan. Ze had geen haast. Stiekem hoopte ze dat ze nog van gedachten zou veranderen. Ze hoefde helemaal niet bij haar ouders langs. Ze werd niet verwacht, tenslotte. Maar ze reed er toch recht op af, ondertussen naar de radio luisterend: een gesprek over een ontsnapte tbs'er die een oude zonderling uit de Jordaan had vermoord. Daarna werd er een liedje gedraaid van een Belgische zangeres die ze niet kende, maar die haar zomaar vreselijk ontroerde, terwijl ze daar zo onder het bladerdek van oude bomen reed: *Dans me naar de toekomst in een roes van rode wijn.*

Wat een zangeres.

Ze hield het stuur vast tussen haar knieën en krabbelde de naam op een papiertje: Yasmien, Yasmine. *Dans me naar de toekomst in een roes van rode wijn.* Had ze zelf een toekomst? Natuurlijk had ze een toekomst. Maar alleen.

Was ze daar blij mee?

Natuurlijk was ze daar blij mee – het had geen zin er ongelukkig mee te zijn. Doorbijten, plezier maken. En gas gaf ze, om over die mooie, lange, statige lanen te blazen. Dak open, kop in de wind.

De oprit was leeg, daar schrok ze van. Ze had op z'n minst haar vaders Mercedes verwacht. Langzaam draaide ze het grind op. Of zou ze snel achteruitrijden en ervandoor gaan? Het kon nog. Ze stopte en stapte uit. Ergens vlakbij hoorde ze de geluiden van een zwembad, gejoel, geplons – ooh ja, daar had ze papa wel eens over gehoord; de nieuwe buren hadden een enorm zwembad in de tuin aangelegd, en ze waren ook nog van evangelischen huize, kinderen genoeg.

De keukendeur was open. Goeie ouwe gewoonte. 'Mam!' riep ze. Ze voelde zich een beetje belachelijk. Maar unheimisch was het ook – de stilte in het huis. 'Pap!' riep ze vervolgens, maar ook daar reageerde niemand op. Waar waren ze?

Op het aanrecht stonden twee espressoapparaten en een Senseo-machine. Monica glimlachte. Ze kon zich de situatie voorstellen. Haar vader was afgeknapt op het Senseo-apparaat, en had een espressomachine gekocht. Van de weeromstuit had haar moeder het Senseo-apparaat natuurlijk hemelhoog geprezen: als papa die koffie niet te drinken vond, vond zij hem juist heerlijk. Helaas was de espressomachine die hij vervolgens kocht een teleurstelling, maar om dan maar weer terug te vallen op de Senseo, of erger nog, op het ouderwetse koffiezetapparaat, met zakjes (Monica zag het staan, in een hoek achter de fruitmand), dat zou een nederlaag betekenen, en dus had haar vader een nog beter en duurder espressoapparaat gekocht. Intussen was het goed mogelijk dat hij stiekem weer Senseo-koffie dronk, of zich in alweer een nieuw systeem aan het verdiepen was.

Tsja, oude mensen.

Ze dwaalde door het stille huis. Ze voelde zich een indringer. Dit was niet het huis waar ze was opgegroeid, al kwam ze zichzelf wel een paar keer tegen: op de mantel van de haard, samen met Nico, vrij recente foto's, naast een rijtje van de kinderen van Nico en Joke, en in de gang, waar een hele wand vol kinderfoto's was. Verder herkende ze niets, behalve de stoel van haar vader, een Eames-loungechair met ottoman die hij zichzelf op zijn vijftigste verjaardag cadeau had gedaan, omdat het, zoals hij het zelf uitdrukte, 'tijd was om te zitten', en de breimand van haar moeder, een grote, rieten mand met een leren deksel waar ze ooit haar bollen en pennen in bewaarde, en nu tijdschriften, zag Monica – ze kon het even niet laten om te checken of haar moeder nog breide.

Ze ging in haar vaders stoel zitten.

Vroeger streng verboden: papa's stoel. Het was toen een heel andere geweest, een groot, donkerbruin, leren geval, en hij had in een ander huis gestaan, maar de kinderen mochten er niet in zitten, zeker niet als hij zelf thuis was, en als ze het wel deden, als hij er niet was, vaak, joeg hun moeder hen eruit. 'Niet in papa's stoel zitten,' riep ze dan, waarschijnlijk eerder uit gewoonte dan dat ze er werkelijk bezwaren tegen had, want als Robert gewoon bleef zitten, gebeurde er niets, behalve als hij zijn voeten op de salontafel had liggen – dat mocht écht alleen papa. En iedere avond na het eten gebeurde dat ook: hij ging met de krant in zijn stoel zitten, legde zijn lange benen op tafel, sloeg de krant open en viel in slaap, tot het tijd was voor het *Journaal*.

Ze stond op.

'Oké,' zei ze tegen zichzelf.

Ze was moe.

Haar jurk plakte aan haar lichaam.

Ze liep de trap op naar de kamer van haar moeder. Ze stelde zich voor dat haar ouders boven dood in bed lagen, een leven lang samen, dan ook in de dood. Maar in de slaapkamer stond alleen het grote bed, keurig opgemaakt. Zo mooi als haar moeder had Monica nooit een bed kunnen opmaken. Ze sloot de deur snel, en gleed haar moeders kamer binnen, de piano-kamer, want daar gaf mama haar lessen: pianoles. Ook in het huis waar Monica was opgegroeid had mama lesgegeven, om gek van te worden. Op woensdagmiddag een stroom kinderen die allemaal een halfuur bleven en allemaal dezelfde deuntjes uit *Folk Dean* speelden. De meesten haakten al snel af, en jaar in jaar uit klonk dus dezelfde muziek in het huis, haperend, onzeker, aarzelend. Af en toe zat er een kind tussen dat langer doorging, en beter leerde spelen. Dan klonken Chopin en Mozart.

De beste leerling die haar moeder ooit had gehad, was Robert, haar jongste zoon: die speelde zo goed, en zo bezeten, dat hij naar het conservatorium kon. Maar daar keerde hij zich van de klassieke muziek af, en dook hij de jazz in, tot mama's verdriet natuurlijk, al bleef hij als hij thuiskwam nog altijd Bach spelen, zijn favoriet – *Das wohltemperierte Klavier*, 'de goedgemutste piano', zoals hij het gekscherend noemde, en cantates voor mama, die zo graag zong.

Was Gott tut, das ist wohlgetan, soms floepten de titels moeiteloos Monica's hoofd binnen, en ze moest er altijd een beetje om lachen. Naast jazz begon Robert in de popmuziek; hij speelde in diverse bandjes, nooit met veel succes, want hij was een einzelgänger pur sang, en iemand met een hang naar verslavingen: hij dronk, hij snoof speed en cocaïne. Hoe vaak hij niet bij Monica langs was gekomen om geld te lenen, ontelbaar. Een vrouwenman ook, altijd gelazer met wijven.

Ach, Robert, broertje.

Het was donker in de kamer. De gordijnen waren dicht. Het rook er muf. Over de piano, een kleine vleugel, lag een grote, witte doek. Erbovenop: stapels boeken, tijdschriften, een bos oude rozen. Monica ging op de kruk zitten en opende langzaam de klep. Zij en Nico hadden zich altijd tegen pianospelen verzet. Nico had nog een blauwe maandag gitaar gespeeld, maar hij was niet muzikaal, en vooral ongeduldig. Monica was wel muzikaal, maar ze wilde niet. In haar studententijd had ze een tijdje in een koor gezongen, zingen vond ze leuk – net als zwemmen, of hardlopen – je kon jezelf erin verliezen.

'Ik besta alleen als ik speel,' had Robert wel eens tegen haar gezegd, 'dan voel ik mezelf gewoon verdwijnen.' Ze liet haar vingers over de toetsen gaan, maar drukte ze niet in. Het ivoor voelde koud. Sommige toetsen droegen de sporen van jarenlang gebruik; haar moeders vingertoppen hadden er gladde, minuscule welvingen in achtergelaten.

'Oké,' zei ze opnieuw, hard. 'Oké, Robert, je bent dood.'

Verdwenen, dacht ze erachteraan.

Ze stond op. Ze had dorst. En ze moest plassen, ineens. Hoe kon het toch dat ze altijd moest plassen als ze dorst had? Kreeg ze dorst omdat ze moest plassen, of moest ze plassen omdat ze dorst had? En was piesen niet eigenlijk een veel vrouwelijker woord – dat klonk zoals het was, piesen. Nee, sassen, dat was het woord, zó klonk het. Ze zou het Laura eens vragen – die had uitgesproken ideeën over dat soort dingen.

Ze had geen zin in haar ouders' badkamer, en haastte zich de trap af, naar het toilet in de hal. Het was daar koud, bijna ijzig. Aan de muur een kalender. Niemand jarig deze maand. Ze liet haar water lopen. Heerlijk had Willem het gevonden als ze in een hotelkamer naar de wc ging en de deur open liet staan. 'Harder,' riep hij dan vanaf het hotelbed, lui op zijn rug, de dikke buik deinend, een sigaret in zijn hand, 'klateren, schat!' Goed, ze klaterde – voor hem, ach wat, voor iedereen. Mannen, kinderen waren het.

Even later stond ze ernaar te kijken, de kinderen die ze zelf waren geweest: Nico de oudste, zij de middelste, Robert de jongste. Een hele wand had haar moeder ingericht.

Babyfoto's.

Vakantiefoto's.

Schoolfoto's.

Kiekjes, portretten.

Nico trots bij het Volkswagenbusje vol spullen toen hij

het huis uit ging om te studeren, Robert op het podium van zijn school, achter de piano natuurlijk, Monica met vlechten, Monica met strikjes in het haar, Monica op haar eerste brommer, een Puch Maxi, Robert in een korte broek, een jaar of twaalf, in de sneeuw op de Brennerpas, Nico met een vis in zijn armen, ergens in Italië, het hele gezin op het San Marcoplein in Venetië – een vlucht duiven op de achtergrond, de jongens in broeken met wijde pijpen, Monica in een lange hippiejurk, pa en ma trots in het midden, vader met zo'n dwaas polstasje, moeder met een Jackie Kennedy-zonnebril op haar neus.

Een groot zwart-witportret van Robert, een jaar of dertig, op zijn mooist: sigaret in zijn mondhoek, openstaand overhemd, krullend borsthaar, ironische oogopslag, een jongen om verliefd op te worden, een fotomodel. Een kleurenfoto van Nico en Joke op het feest van hun huwelijk: dansend, lachend, zwierend – zij met haar klassieke Hollandse blonde haar in zijn stevige Hollandse armen. Een foto van Monica op Schiphol – terugkomend van haar eerste, echte reis, naar Indonesië; jeans, paardenstaart, T-shirtje, een enorme rugzak, een grijns van oor tot oor. Op de achtergrond een rode ballon met I LOVE YOU – maar die had niets met haar te maken, toevalstreffer van papa, de fotograaf. Op mooi Ameland: twee blonde jongetjes en een meisje met vlechtjes in een bolderkar, voortgetrokken door een lachende, sterke man met zwart, golvend haar. De statige trouwfoto van Nico en Joke, op de trappen van het stadhuis van Gouda. Robert en Nico samen, allebei in smoking en vlinderstrik, geen idee bij welke gelegenheid die foto was gemaakt. Monica in haar eerste auto, een gele Ford Escort, zelf verdiend, drieëntwintig was ze, en wild.

De onbenulligheid, dacht ze, meewarig.

Levens, verhalen, kleine feiten, grote feiten.

Alles hing ervan af wie ernaar keek.

En hoe er dan werd gekeken.

Haar eigen trouwfoto, met Ben, hing er niet. De zeven jaren met Ben ontbraken sowieso – grappig. Haar moeder had Ben altijd aardig gevonden, haar vader niet. Hij had er nooit iets over gezegd, maar ze voelde het aan hem. Hij was bang dat Ben haar niet gelukkig zou maken. Nou, dat had Ben ook niet gedaan, maar óngelukkig ook niet – zeven jaar Ben, ze kon zich er nauwelijks iets van herinneren. Hoe heette die zangeres van daarnet ook alweer? *Dans me naar de toekomst.* Ze mummelde het, en besloot een briefje voor haar ouders achter te laten – wel zo aardig.

Terwijl ze het schreef, op de achterkant van een bankenveloppe, aan de keukentafel, ging de telefoon. Ze schrok enorm, maar nam niet op. Nadat hij drie keer was overgegaan, sloeg in haar moeders kamer boven het antwoordapparaat aan. Haar vader haatte die dingen, want dan moest hij terugbellen, maar haar moeder had er ooit eentje gekocht, toen ze nog lesgaf.

Vaag hoorde ze een stem iets inspreken, en even, in een flits, dacht ze dat ze de stem van Nico herkende. Ze stond op en liep het huis uit.

*

Tegen drieën was ze terug in de stad. De straat lag er stil en verlaten bij, de hele stad, stoffig en trillend. Iedereen was naar het strand. Monica parkeerde een paar plekken voor haar huis en vlak voor ze de motor uit wilde doen, zag ze haar voordeur opengaan. Een lange jongen in een korte broek stapte naar buiten, gevolgd door de grote driewieler met Orvieta en Laura in een klein, wit jurkje dat haar heupen benadrukte, 'child-bearing hips', noemde ze dat zelf, zo'n typische Laura-uitdrukking.

Ze gingen de andere kant op. De jongen had een paardenstaart, brede schouders en gespierde, bruine armen. Het was zo snel niet te zien hoe oud hij was, een jaar of dertig, achter in de twintig. Ook zijn benen waren bruin, en ondanks het feit dat Monica een hekel had aan korte broeken had hij een lekker kontje. Ze sloegen de hoek om, en weg waren ze. Ze wachtte nog even met uitstappen om naar 'Feel' van Robbie Williams te luisteren. Ze voelde zich ontzettend moe worden en overwoog of ze een uurtje zou gaan sporten. Lekker rustig zou het in de sportschool zijn.

Nee, slapen.

In huis was het warm, maar in de slaapkamer kon ze de balkondeuren openzetten. Ze nam een koude douche en een halve slaaptablet en ging liggen. Ergens buiten in de binnentuin koerde een duif, en in de verte bromde een vliegtuigje, meer zondagmiddag kon het niet zijn, of er zou een ijscoman met een ouderwetse kar en een rinkelende bel langs moeten komen. Ze dobberde weg.

Ze werd in paniek wakker, omdat ze niet wist hoe laat het was, want er lag een *Marie Claire* over de wekker heen. Ze sloeg hem aan de kant, en het bleek 19.09 uur te zijn. Ze had honger, stond op en trok haar kimono aan. Vervolgens had ze hoofdpijn en niets in de koelkast, nou ja, roomijs van Hertog, een doos aardbeien op het randje van bederf, een beker Griekse yoghurt en een pot augurken. Vanuit de binnentuin trok rook het huis binnen; achterburen die aan het barbecueën waren.

Shit, shit, shit.

Ze kon er slecht tegen als ze met zichzelf te doen kreeg. Ze had een goed leven, ze was zo vrij als ze maar wilde, ze had leuke vrienden en vriendinnen, een topbaan. Als ze alleen was, wilde ze zich niet eenzaam voelen. En ze wilde al helemaal geen onderbuurvrouw die onstuimig lag te neuken, want ook dat hoorde ze ineens weer: Laura en haar pianospelende bongospeler, die waren er ook weer. Het kon toch niet waar zijn! Maar waarom niet? Zelf had ze ook wel minnaars gehad die er geen genoeg van kregen, en waar zíj ook geen genoeg van kreeg. Wat liep ze nou te mutsen? Ze stampte door het huis, en maakte iets te eten klaar. Pasta en saus had ze altijd wel in huis, en ijs toe, een glaasje sancerre erbij, de televisie aan, de avond kwam wel om. Morgen vroeg weer op, lekker werken – een drukke dag.

Maar ze kon haar draai niet vinden – en dronk van de weeromstuit de hele fles wijn leeg. Ze belde met Heleen in Haarlem die geen tijd had om uitgebreid te kletsen omdat ze naar een feestje moest en zich aan het verkleden was. Ze stuurde Laura een pesterig sms'je: of het nu eens afgelopen kon zijn met het bongo'en, en trok zich om halfelf terug in haar slaapkamer. Haar vaste telefoon ging, en ze schoot bijna in de lach – wanneer had die voor het laatst gerinkeld? Het kon alleen haar moeder zijn.

'Kind, was je vanmiddag bij ons?'

'Ja. Jullie waren er niet.'

'We waren naar Robert,' zei haar moeder. Ze aarzelde. 'Naar zijn graf,' zei ze toen, 'in Utrecht. Het was heerlijk daar, je vader heeft er op de plaid liggen slapen.'

'Echt waar, mam?' Monica kon ineens wel huilen; niet om haar slapende vader op de begraafplaats in Utrecht, niet om haar moeder, maar om zichzelf en Robert, die ze zo miste.

'Ja, echt. De steen staat er nu, heb jij hem al gezien? Hij is mooi geworden, Monica.' De steen – helemaal vergeten. Drie keer was Monica bij het graf geweest, alle drie de keren stond er zo'n lullig geel plastic paaltje dat je ook bij bloemisten in de plantenbakken zag staan, met een paar nummers erop. Twee keer had ze over de steen gebeld met de kunstenaar die hem zou maken, het kreng was al betaald, en nu stond hij er dus, eindelijk.

'Ik ga snel kijken, mam,' mompelde ze. Hoorde ze nou beneden weer die vleugel? 'Wat is het warm, hè?' gooide ze het over een andere boeg.

'Morgen krijgen we onweer, zeiden ze op tv,' antwoordde haar moeder.

'Mam...'

'Ja?'

'Laat maar.' Ze had naar Nico willen vragen. Ze had haar oudste broer een jaar geleden voor het laatst gezien. Ze hadden ruzie gehad. Hij had Robert een loser genoemd. Zij had Nico een draai om zijn oren gegeven, een schitterende klap. Hij had excuses geëist, nou, mooi niet. Een jaloerse lul, Nico.

'Nou, kind,' zei haar moeder, 'ik hoop dat we je snel weer zien. De groetjes van papa.' Ze hing op.

Monica beet op haar lip. Ze kon ontzettend kwaad zijn op haar moeder, maar altijd was ze er te laat mee. Waarom had het mens niet aangevoeld dat er iets aan de hand was? Ze stond op, en wankelde.

Ook dat nog, de wijn.

Beneden hoorde ze nou toch echt de piano. 'Kalm blijven,' zei ze tegen zichzelf. Ze toetste het nummer van haar ouders in, maar halverwege hield ze ermee op. Ze wist toch zeker dat ze Nico's stem op haar moeders antwoordapparaat had gehoord. Waarom belde hij haar niet? Omdat ze hém niet belde – dat was het antwoord. Ze stampte woedend op de vloer.

Stilte.

Ze begon haar kleren voor de volgende dag klaar te leggen: een blauw flodderjurkje van Kookai, een stringetje, een bh van Aubade, twee zomers oud maar leuk, met oranje bloemetjes die in de diepe hals van het jurkje leuk omhoog piepten, een spijkerjack voor eroverheen, want een beetje gekleed moest ze wel zijn. Ze aarzelde het langst over haar schoenen, en koos toen de platte Prada'tjes die ze vorig jaar in Milaan had gekocht. Beneden begon de baby te huilen. Ze stuurde Laura een sms'je.

'Gaat het?'

'Joh, geweldig!'

'Weer zo lekker?'

'Ja. Jaloers?'

'Geen piano AUB!'

'Roger. Sorry.'

'Dacht dat-ie bongo speelde.'

Geen antwoord.

In de binnentuin klonk gelach van mensen die het gezellig hadden. Ze sms'te Heleen dat ze een kutavond had, en Heleen sms'te meteen terug dat zij ook een kutavond had, en of Monica geen zin had om langs te komen. Even overwoog ze het, maar ze vond het al te laat. En ze was aangeschoten. Ze ging in bed liggen met haar laptop en stuurde een hitsig mailtje naar Willem – die op zondagavond meestal werkte. Ook nu dus, want hij stuurde vrijwel meteen een mailtje terug, tamelijk nietszeggend, maar wel aardig. Ze replyde dat ze wilde neuken, maar daar reageerde hij niet op.

Ze was dronken.

Nee, aangeschoten.

Ze dacht aan Laura. Beneden was het weer stil. Ze kon zich precies voorstellen hoe ze erbij lagen, de geliefden in het bed dat een ravage was. Haar glimmende, bezwete borsten en harde tepels, zijn lul, plakkend en slap, de ademhaling van twee mensen die samen de nacht afwachtten, hand in hand, want meer aanraking konden de lichamen niet verdragen nu de liefde voorbij was en de nacht te warm en te klam om tegen elkaar aan te liggen. Ze kon, als ze wilde, de geur van het bed ruiken – de verspilde sappen, het zweet, de opwinding. Ze werd er nat van.

Een van haar favoriete minnaars was een Fransman geweest die Gérard heette. Als ze een snel en makkelijk orgasme wilde, dacht ze aan hem, al kon ze zich zijn gezicht inmiddels – hij was van ver voor haar huwelijk met Ben – al nauwelijks meer herinneren. Hij had haar het spel geleerd, de hogere seks; in toiletten van dure restaurants, op de motorkap van zijn Renault Alpine in de lagunes langs de Middellandse Zee, in liften van hotels, in badkamers – zij net klaar met haar make-up, helemaal gekleed voor een chic avondje uit, hij achter haar. Zij leunend met haar handen op de rand van de wastafel, kont naar achteren, hij die haar rok op haar rug sloeg, en haar slipje op haar knieën trok, en haar genadeloos penetreerde – een ander woord was er niet voor. Altijd en overal, dat was Gérard, maar de hartstocht had hem uitgewist; ze zou hem nu niet meer herkennen, tenzij ze zijn handen, dwingende grijpers, op haar heupen zou voelen, of zijn mond, machtig en nat, in haar hals. Ze hadden buiten zichzelf geleefd, in een universum dat alleen uit lust bestond – eng en gevaarlijk.

Ze kwam klaar.

Maar ze was niet tevreden en stond na een tijdje op. In de keuken maakte ze een beker Goede Nachtrust-thee. Ze zette de tv aan en keek even naar MTV. De thee smaakte haar niet, maar ze werd er wel rustig van. Ze dacht dat ze beneden een deur hoorde, en voetstappen op de trap. Laura die de bongospeler uitzwaaide.

Ze stond op en liep naar het raam om te kijken of het zo was. Nee dus. Ze streelde haar buik. Er knetterde een pizzakoerier door de straat. De klep van de kist achter op de brommer waar de pizza's in stonden, hing open en danste wild op en neer. Toen het geluid verstomde hoorde ze iemand aan haar deur kloppen. Prompt sloeg haar hart over.

Het was niet Laura die een kopje suiker kwam lenen, maar de pianospelende bongospeler. 'Hi, I am Xavier,' zei hij en hij lachte een rij witte tanden bloot. Zijn korte broek had hij verruild voor een lange, linnen broek met in plaats van een riem een vrolijk rood touwtje met een strik erin die eruitzag alsof hij losgetrokken wilde worden. Verder droeg hij een wit hemd.

'Hi, Xavier,' zei Monica – ze concentreerde zich op zijn ogen, die donker als kool waren, maar lui en zelfverzekerd stonden.

Hij aarzelde.

Monica keek hem aan. Het was een mooie jongen, Laura had gelijk. Hij had een grote mond, met niet te dikke lippen, een ranke neus met vleugels die lichtjes trilden, een hals waarin dikke aderen klopten, een borst met blond, krullend jongenshaar. Ze glimlachte. Ze voelde zich een beetje week, omdat ze daar zin in had, waarom niet – ze leefde maar één keer, ze kon overal aan toegeven. Ze dacht aan Gérard, en een tintelende siddering trok over haar rug – had ze Laura wel eens over Gérard verteld?

'I am a present,' zei Xavier, en hij boog iets naar voren, alsof hij haar wilde kussen. Met één hand leunde hij nonchalant tegen de deurpost. Monica bewoog iets naar achteren, waardoor de kus mislukte. Xavier liet zich niet uit het veld slaan, hij raakte even, met zijn andere hand, haar gezicht aan, alsof hij haar keurend in haar wang wilde knijpen, maar dat deed hij dan weer niet – hij streelde haar met twee stugge vingertoppen, de vingers van een pianist.

In het trappenhuis hing de lucht van veel te rijpe meloenen. Shit, dat was de vuilniszak die ze nog buiten moest zetten – zou ze hem dat vragen? Ze giechelde. 'Come in,' zei ze. 'Xavier.' Ze proefde de naam in haar mond, liet hem even op haar tong liggen, rolde hem rond.

Ze ging hem voor naar de woonkamer. Terwijl hij de deur sloot, hoorde ze een sms'je op haar mobieltje binnenkomen. Ze wist dat het een bericht van Laura was, maar haastte zich toch om het te lezen. 'ENJOY!' luidde de tekst. 'Maar maak niet te veel herrie. Haha!' Ze grijnsde, deed haar telefoon uit, knoopte haar kimono los en draaide zich om naar Xavier.

Blauwe schoenen

'Daar gaan we,' zei Nico. De laatste tijd praatte hij hardop tegen zichzelf. Dat kwam ervan als je vierenveertig was, voortdurend op je leesbril ging zitten en van je vrouw af was. Hij sloeg de deur van zijn flatje achter zich dicht en liep naar beneden. Zijn auto stond aan de overkant. Veel te mooi en veel te groot voor deze armzalige straat.

Het was heet, zo heet dat het hem even duizelde. Dat was de kater. Gisteravond te veel gedronken. Pathetisch. Alleen drinken. Beetje over internet surfen en een fles wodka leegdrinken. De sites waar je op terechtkwam werden steeds smeriger. En dat terwijl hij eigenlijk wilde werken.

Hij stapte in, startte de auto.

De airco begon te loeien, maar het duurde lang voor het echt koel was. De radio had moeite boven het geblaas uit te komen, hij zette hem harder. Een discussie over een ontsnapte tbs'er die een Amsterdamse bejaarde had vermoord op een bootje. Nico reed achteruit en draaide. Terwijl hij de straat uit reed, werd hij getroffen door een liedje van een Belgische zangeres: *Dans me naar het altaar nu en dans me daar heel zacht. Dans me door mijn tranen heen en dans me onverwacht.* Hij dacht aan Joke – de vrouw die hij zo had laten zitten.

Hij voelde zich kut.

Waar kwam die uitdrukking vandaan? Naar ook – om zo'n belabberd gevoel aan zoiets moois te koppelen. Moest-ie eens iemand uit laten zoeken, zat een stuk in. Hij draaide de buurt uit, de Haarlemmerweg op, richting Amsterdam. Maar goed ook, want het was bijzonder druk, de andere kant op. Gezinnen en verliefde stelletjes, op weg naar het strand. De radio meldde dat het wel eens de heetste dag sinds tientallen jaren kon worden vandaag. In Gilze-Rijen was het al 35 graden. Fucking Gilze, dacht Nico; hij kende dat oord toevallig, omdat er een grote concurrent van hem zat met wie hij een paar jaar geleden intensief over een fusie had vergaderd. Uiteindelijk afgeketst, gelukkig maar, anders zou hij nog steeds naar Gilze moeten.

Hij reed door Amsterdam.

De Haarlemmer Houttuinen, voor het station langs, de Prins Hendrikkade, rechtsaf naar de Stopera, linksaf de Wibautstraat in, richting Ring en het Gooi. Hij had zijn werk in Amsterdam, maar hield er niet echt van. Hij dacht aan Monica, zijn zus; die was dol op Amsterdam. Hij moest haar eens bellen. Niet zo kinderachtig doen. Ze had het moeilijk. Hij scrolde met zijn rechterhand door het telefoonboek van zijn telefoon aan het dashboard. Hij had haar nummer niet. Uit boosheid gewist, ooit. Hij toetste het nummer van zijn moeder in en kreeg het antwoordapparaat.

Vreemd, op een zondagmiddag.

Ouders moesten thuis zijn.

'Mam, met mij. Alles goed bij jullie? Bel me vanavond even. Gewoon thuis.' Dat klonk gek. Gewoon thuis. Hij verbrak snel de verbinding. De Wibautstraat trilde in de warmte. Hij haalde diep adem en liet de autoradio langs de voorkeurstations floepen: *Langs de Lijn*, popmuziek, nog meer popmuziek, Bach – een cantate natuurlijk. Dat er mensen waren die bij dit

48

weer naar cantates luisterden. *Was Gott tut, das ist wohlgetan.*

Ja ja, dacht Nico, en hij dacht aan zijn broertje, dood, en aan zijn vrouw en kinderen, springlevend. 'Doe zelf iets goeds,' zei hij grimmig en hij deed de radio uit. Eigenlijk haatte hij muziek.

Joke was niet blij toen ze hem zag. Maar hij was de vader van hun kinderen en ze kon moeilijk zeggen dat hij op moest hoepelen waar ze bij waren. Dus liep hij achter haar aan naar de tuin en ging hij zitten, onder de Pepsi-parasol, in een witte, plastic stoel met groen-geel gestreepte kussens, god, wat haatte hij die stoelen!

'Heb je cadeautjes, pap?' vroeg Bruno. Het mannetje had de bolle toet die zijn moeder in het fotoalbum van haar jeugd ook had.

'Bruno!' zei Joke streng.

'Dat heeft hij beloofd,' riep Bruno terug. 'Toch, pap?'

Nico boog zich naar zijn zoontje toe. Hij wilde zeggen dat hij altijd meer beloofde dan hij waar kon maken, dat hij zo nu eenmaal in elkaar zat, maar het jongetje deinsde achteruit en Nico vermande zich. 'Papa is de cadeautjes vergeten, de volgende keer, oké?' mompelde hij.

'Papa heeft het druk, schat,' zei Joke, 'maar hij vindt je heus erg lief, hoor.'

Bruno hobbelde snikkend weg. Vanaf de schommel keek Juliette hem na. Ze was twee jaar ouder dan Bruno, en had een frons op haar voorhoofd die Nico kende van zijn eigen spiegelbeeld. Ja, hij was duidelijk weer thuis.

*

Hun huwelijk was stukgelopen op sleur. Nico had dat altijd onzin gevonden: sleur, bullshit. Het hele leven was sleur. Je kon overal wel over zeuren. Toen had hij Sylvia ontmoet, en Sylvia had alles wat Joke niet had. Die vaststelling alleen al was net zo plat als het idee sleur, maar goed, zo ver kon je dus afglijden. Sylvia was jonger dan hij, een vrouw van de wereld; ze liet zich niets welgevallen, niets aanleunen, ze nam met nee geen genoegen.

Hij veranderde.

'Wat is er toch, Nico?' vroeg Joke steeds vaker als hij een hele avond niets tegen haar zei. 'Je moet gaan sporten,' vervolgde ze dan, 'of neem een hobby. Je hebt geen hobby. Je ontspant je niet.'

Maar dat was nu juist wat hij wel deed. Iedere keer als hij in Sylvia klaarkwam. En iedere keer als hij het erf af reed en aan het einde, bij de groene brievenbus, rechts afsloeg – de wereld in, de vrijheid tegemoet. Het was allemaal zo klassiek als kantoorhumor.

'Ga je vreemd?' had Joke op een avond gevraagd. Ze lagen in bed. Zij lag te lezen, hij lag te lezen. Ze lazen wat af. Ze keek niet eens op van haar boek toen ze het vroeg. Haar leesbril glinsterde op haar neus.

'Sodemieter op,' had Nico geantwoord. Verontwaardigd. Dat ze dat van hem kon denken.

Later schoof hij tegen haar aan. Ze lag al op haar zij. Joke was altijd de eerste die met lezen ophield. Hij vouwde zich om haar warme lichaam en wreef met zijn onderlichaam tegen haar billen.

'Doe het licht maar uit, schat,' mompelde Joke.

Hij deed het.

Daar lag hij dan, in het donker.

'Slaap lekker, schat,' zei hij.

Hij had het gevoel dat hij in een tekening van Peter van Straaten lag, heel beklemmend. Ze hadden alle stadia van een verhouding doorlopen en nu waren ze op dat punt waar een half woord volstond. Maar halve woorden waren geen woorden. Nico sprak er de huisarts op aan en die verwees hem door naar een psychiater. De man had grote oren, maar ook bij hem sprak Nico halve woorden, of in ieder geval halve waarheden. De verzekering betaalde.

De zaken gingen voorspoedig. De bladen die hij uitgaf deden het goed, de winst had hij in een internetpoot gestoken die de grote uitgeversconcerns voor miljoenen zouden willen kopen als hij hem goed van de grond kreeg. Of het zover zou komen was een tweede; hij had al eerder ideeën ontwikkeld waar volgens hem goud in zat, maar die uiteindelijk niets dan verlies hadden opgeleverd. Maar hij lag er niet wakker van.

Sylvia was de uitzondering op al zijn regels. Zij was geen meisje van de zaak met wie hij wat rotzooide. Zij was nooit hetzelfde, maar altijd anders. Dat kwam ook doordat hij haar niet vaak zag. Ze werkte in de luchtvaart, de ene keer zat ze in Tel Aviv, dan in Amsterdam, dan weer in Houston. Ze had een kleine verdieping in Amsterdam waar ze elkaar troffen. Een van zijn regels was dat hij altijd thuis sliep. Hij wilde Joke niet bedriegen. Al bedroog hij haar wel. Sylvia belde hem als ze tijd had, en zin, hij belde haar als hij ineens bij haar wilde zijn. Ze improviseerden. 'Zolang het geen vaste prik is, is het goed,' zei Sylvia wel eens. Daarna was ze ineens een week onbereikbaar.

'Wat denkt u er zelf van?' vroeg de psychiater toen Nico hem had verteld van de halve woorden die hij en Joke wisselden. Nico had eraan toegevoegd dat hij bang was voor de stilte.

Hij keek naar de oren van de psychiater. De man had zijn spreekkamer aan de achterkant van een villa. Verderop lag een drukke spoorlijn. Een trein rommelde voorbij. Nico was opgestaan en had de psychiater alleen gelaten. De man zei niets. In de gang kwam Nico de echtgenote van de psychiater tegen.

Ze had een klein, begrijpend glimlachje op dunne, droge lippen: een vrouw die alles doorzag. Hij verliet snel het huis. Niemand kwam achter hem aan.

So much for psychiatry.

Sylvia liet hem praten. Stelde hem de gekste vragen. Ze wilde alles van hem weten. 'Je bestaat uit woorden, schat,' zei ze, 'kom, voor de draad ermee.' Hij vertelde haar over zichzelf alsof hij zichzelf voor het eerst zag. Fietsend langs de IJssel waar hij was opgegroeid. Studerend in Nijmegen. Reizend door Europa voor de reisgidsen die hij maakte. Ze moest om hem lachen. Ze boog zich over zijn naakte lichaam en nam zijn lul in haar mond. Als hij maar bleef praten.

'Het gaat niet goed met ons,' zei Joke op een dag.

'Nee,' zei Nico, 'het gaat helemaal niet goed met ons.' Dit was zowel een antwoord als een vaststelling en voor Nico's doen een grote openhartigheid.

Het was een vrijdagavond, ze lagen onderuit op de bank, Nico met de weekbladen, Joke met een van haar dikke boeken. Ze was in afwachting van haar favoriete televisieserie die iedere vrijdagavond later leek te beginnen. Nico was moe, maar redelijk tevreden. Hij had die middag bij Sylvia in bed oesters gegeten. Daarna had hij nog vergaderd, en te veel bitterballen gehad. Zijn maag speelde op in de stilte die viel.

Het ging niet goed.

Ze hadden het gezegd.

Nico verwachtte dat Joke een plan van aanpak had, ze was praktisch ingesteld. Hij verwachtte dat ze wist waarom hun huwelijk was stilgevallen, ze was vrouw en moeder – als iemand het wist, was zij het. Maar ze zei niets. En hoe langer ze zweeg, lezend in haar veel te dikke boek, hoe wanhopiger Nico werd. Kennelijk moest hij zeggen wat eraan schortte en hoe ze verder moesten. Maar er kwam geen woord uit zijn mond, niet eens een half woord – het leek wel alsof hij iemand anders was. En net toen hij iets wilde gaan zeggen, deed Joke de tv aan en begon haar serie. Nico stond op. Hij moest ineens ontzettend naar de wc, wat een kutleven.

Een week later vroeg Sylvia of hij iets voor haar wilde doen. Ze had nieuwe schoenen gekocht, en die moesten naar haar schoenmaker, want ze liet in haar nieuwe schoenen altijd een speciaal binnenzooltje zetten. De schoenmaker zat bij Nico's kantoor om de hoek.

'Geef maar mee,' zei hij.

'Als je zegt dat ze van mij zijn, weet-ie wat-ie moet doen,' zei Sylvia terwijl ze hem de schoenendoos aanreikte. Ze was naakt op een gek vissershoedje na. Nico opende het deksel om te zien wat voor schoenen het waren.

Ze waren blauw, diep flonkerend blauw, bijna paars – de kleur van de monochrome schilderijen van Yves Klein die Nico op een van de eerste trips die hij naar Parijs had gemaakt in Centre Pompidou zo vaak uren had bekeken, niet omdat er iets op te zien was, maar omdat het kijken ernaar een verdwijnen erin was, een bijna mystieke ervaring. Een van de weinige keren dat hij een echt gesprek met zijn broer, Robert, had gehad, was het daarover gegaan. Robert verdween in zijn muziek en zijn drugs. Eigenlijk begreep Nico hem wel. Al was hij dan drie jaar dood. De eikel.

Hij keek Sylvia aan.

Ze glimlachte.

Hij pakte voorzichtig een schoen uit de doos. Het was een soort muil met een hak en een riempje dat om de enkel heen moet. Er zat een klein, maar zorgvuldig gesmeed gouden sluitinkje aan. Klein had ook in goud gewerkt, herinnerde Nico zich, een grimmig soort goud, zanderig. De sluiting was een klein kattenkopje.

'Doe ze eens aan,' zei hij, gebiedend ineens – zonder dat hij er erg in had. Alsof de schoenen het hem influisterden.

'Doe ze eens aan,' herhaalde Sylvia. Ook zij voelde dat er iets kantelde in hun relatie, of beter: op het punt van kantelen stond. Er was gevaar in geslopen. Ze aarzelde.

Hij zei niets.

In de verte klonk het geluid van een ouderwetse grasmaaier. Een paar panden naast Sylvia woonde een oud echtpaar – de man deed niets liever dan zijn gras maaien. Mevrouw keek dan toe van onder een parasol, puzzelboekje op schoot. Het geluid deed Nico aan zijn jeugd denken. Geluk bestond. Nog verder weg klonk het rinkelen van een tram. Tussen Sylvia's borsten liep een druppeltje zweet. Ze had kleine borsten, die een beetje hingen, en donkere, grote tepels – erg gevoelig als hij erin beet.

Ze pakte de schoen uit zijn hand en haakte hem aan de bijbehorende voet. Ze steunde met een hand tegen de muur, en deed de andere schoen aan. Ze deed het zo casual mogelijk, slordig, onaantrekkelijk. Alsof ze probeerde het momentum te keren. Ze keek hem niet aan.

'Loop eens een stukje,' zei hij.

Ze deed een paar passen.

'Schouders recht, kont naar achteren,' zei hij.

Ze deed het.

Ze had de mooiste billen die hij ooit had gezien. De schoenen deden er nog een schepje bovenop. Hij kreeg een erectie, en opende zijn broek. Het was maar een paar stappen naar haar koele rug – hij legde er een hand op.

'Niet met je broek om je enkels,' protesteerde Sylvia. Stijl was alles voor haar.

Hij duwde haar voorover, tot ze met haar handen de grond raakte. Hij moest op zijn tenen gaan staan om goed bij haar binnen te komen. Dat was het nadeel van die schoenen, ze tilden haar net iets te hoog op. Hij ramde haar zo hard hij kon, en ze stootte haar hoofd tegen de muur. Ze probeerde hem weg te duwen, maar hij ging door tot hij hijgend tegen haar aan hing.

'Klootzak,' zei ze, en tien minuten later stond hij op straat met zijn ogen te knipperen, de schoenen in hun doos onder zijn arm.

Vanaf dat moment liep alles mis.

Hij was met de auto en moest de halve stad door om bij kantoor te komen. De grachten stonden vol, er was geen doorkomen aan. Hij werd gebeld: zijn afspraak van twee uur zat al een tijdje te wachten. Vervolgens bleek zijn gereserveerde parkeerplaats bezet door een Duitse Mercedes die weliswaar gewielklemd was, maar daar schoot hij niets mee op. Toen hij eindelijk een plekje had gevonden, was het kwart voor drie. Hij besloot eerst naar kantoor te gaan en aan het einde van de middag de schoenen weg te brengen. Daar moest hij dan flink voor omlopen, maar goed – zo was het nu eenmaal. Hij haastte zich naar kantoor, waar hij om vijf voor drie aankwam, drie minuten nadat zijn afspraak boos was vertrokken. Hij raakte prompt verzeild in een productieprobleem van zijn belangrijkste maandblad, was tot vijf uur druk aan het telefoneren, haastte zich toen met de schoenen onder zijn arm naar de schoenmaker, die dicht en op vakantie bleek, waarna hij de lange omweg naar zijn parkeerplaats liep en daar ontdekte dat zijn auto was weggesleept. Toen hij eindelijk thuiskwam die avond, na ook nog langdurig in de file te hebben gestaan, vergat hij de schoenen op de achterbank.

De volgende dag was hij jarig. Vierenveertig. Joke was al op voor de kinderen. Slingers ophangen. Ja, de huiselijke details. Ze ging ook met de kinderen naar de bakker. Dan kon papa lekker uitslapen. Er kwam een taart met vierenveertig kaarsjes. Bruno had het hem al verklapt. Dochter Juliette had de hele week voor papa zitten knutselen en schilderen en plakken. Hij moest zijn beste beentje voorzetten, had Joke hem bezworen. Het was ook een feest voor de kinderen die trots waren op hun vader.

'Van wie zijn die schoenen?' Joke stond in de deuropening van de badkamer, Nico lag in bed. De dag zat erop. Hij had een mountainbike gekregen die met slingers versierd in de woonkamer stond. Zijn ouders waren geweest. De kinderen hadden genoten. Zijn moeder had er slecht uitgezien. Verdriet om haar lievelingszoon die dood was, boos op haar dochter die niet eens gebeld had om te feliciteren.

'Welke schoenen?'

'Die in de auto liggen.'

'In de auto,' hoorde Nico zichzelf herhalen. Het bloed steeg naar zijn gezicht. Ineens zweette hij overal. Sylvia's schoenen, hij had ze op de achterbank laten liggen. Joke was vanochtend met de kinderen naar de bakker geweest. Vierenveertig kaarsjes stonden er op de verjaardagstaart. Hij had ze niet eens in één keer uit kunnen blazen. Tot grote hilariteit van Bruno en Juliette.

'In de auto, ja!' schreeuwde Joke nu. Ze kwam de slaapkamer in. 'Moet ik ze voor je ophalen?'

'Ooh, die schoenen,' deed Nico. Hij kwam overeind in de kussens. Hij wist het weer helemaal. Die schoenen. Die waren van een meisje op kantoor dat hij een lift had gegeven. Hij opende zijn mond.

'Als je gaat zeggen dat je die schoenen voor mij hebt gekocht, dat het een cadeautje is, vermoord ik je,' siste Joke. Ze stond aan het voeteneind van het bed. Haar borsten gingen boos op en neer in haar onderjurk. 'En ik zie aan je gezicht dat je een smoes hebt verzonnen. Ik wil hem niet horen.' Dit was een nieuwe Joke. Of eigenlijk de Joke die hij was vergeten. Joke op wie hij verliefd was geworden toen ze samen na afloop van een studentenfeest over een verlaten kermis hadden gezworven. Joke die vroeger schreeuwde als ze klaarkwam. Joke die van woede huilde als ze op het wad een dode zeehond vond. Joke die vijftien jaar geleden een verhalenbundel had gepubliceerd die niemand wilde lezen, en die sindsdien compromisloos zweeg.

'Jezus, Jook,' kreunde Nico.

'Het is wel mijn maat, maar het zijn niet mijn schoenen,' beet ze hem toe. 'Zulke schoenen draag ik niet. Of fantaseer je over zulke schoenen? Wie is dat wijf dat ze draagt? Voor wie zijn ze?' Ze balde haar vuisten. Op de achtergrond, in de badkamer, zoemde de elektrische tandenborstel die ze vergeten had uit te doen.

Dit was het begin geweest.

Twee maanden later gingen ze uit elkaar. Verheffend was het niet. Kinderachtig was het ook niet. 'Ik moet mezelf en de kinderen beschermen,' zei Joke, en ze huilde er niet bij, haar gezicht was strak en wit en vastbesloten. 'Jij hoeft niemand te beschermen. Jij hebt alleen jezelf.'

Was dat zo?

De schoenen van Sylvia bleken na dat desastreuze weekend verdwenen.

'Hé, schat,' mompelde Sylvia – ze lagen in bed – 'ik belde vanochtend met de schoenmaker. Wat is er met mijn schoenen gebeurd? Ben je ze vergeten?'

Hij loog.

Hij was er niet aan toegekomen, hij had ze op kantoor neergezet. Hij zou ze morgen even bij de schoenmaker afgeven.

Het was de angst voor kinderloosheid die sommige mensen tot een kinderachtig leven dreef, had hij eens ergens gelezen. Hij was de vader van twee kinderen. Hij loog als een schooljongen. Overmorgen zou hij weer moeten liegen. En uiteindelijk zou hij met de waarheid op de proppen moeten komen. Onontkoombaar. De tijd tot de volgende keer dat de vraag zou worden gesteld was de vrijheid die hij had. Tussen de eerste keer dat de vraag werd gesteld waar het leugenachtige antwoord op volgde en de tweede keer, als de leugen nog kon worden bijgesteld, maar toch nog een leugen bleef, lag zijn leven. Hij zag het liggen, een kort lijntje.

'Mmm,' deed Sylvia, onder de strelingen van zijn hand, die nu over haar venusheuvel gleed, maar of het van genot was of van twijfel aan zijn antwoord – Nico wist het niet. Sylvia's telefoon ging en ze nam op, iets wat ze opwindend vond onder het vrijen. Maar ze liet de telefoon vallen toen hij een vinger diep in haar kont stak, vloekte en gaf hem een klap.

Pas toen hij bij Joke vertrok, ging hij over haar nadenken en zag hij Sylvia in een helder licht. Zij was bijvoorbeeld niet de juiste vrouw voor hem. Hij was al te ver gevorderd in zijn leven om opnieuw te beginnen, laat staan zich te schikken in het leven van een vrouw die niet van zins was háár leven om het zijne te laten draaien. Alsof hij dát nodig had.

Ja, dat had hij.

Alsof Joke dat gedaan had.

Nee, dat had zij niet.

Maar de cirkels van hun levens hadden perfect in elkaar gegrepen. Het was één cirkel geworden. Dat kon je romantisch noemen. Maar je kon het ook handig noemen. Of zelfs: de loop der dingen. Zo ging het nu eenmaal. Het was de stelligheid waarmee het raderwerk in elkaar had gegrepen die Nico miste toen hij alleen was. Hij realiseerde zich dat hij weliswaar af en toe heftig naar Sylvia verlangde, maar ook dat hij niet de energie had de kloof te overbruggen die er tussen hen lag, alleen met geweld – en daar schrok hij zelf van, nog los van het feit dat Sylvia er niet van hield en hem na die ene vinger wekenlang niet had willen zien. 'Ik weet het niet, Nico, ik denk dat we op elkaar zijn uitgekeken, denk je niet?' Zo opende ze uiteindelijk hun laatste gesprek.

*

'Ben je nog steeds met dat wijf?' vroeg Joke.

'Het is geen wijf, en nee, ik ben niet met haar. Nooit echt geweest ook.'

'Ooh.'

Nico had het heet. Hij had het zwembad opgepompt voor Bruno. Met de fietspomp, want de pomp die bij het zwembad hoorde was kapot. Hij vroeg zich af of hij binnen een korte broek uit de kast zou halen, de meeste van zijn spullen waren hier nog. Maar hij was bang dat Joke het verkeerd zou begrijpen, en ook bang dat hij het zelf verkeerd zou begrijpen – handelingen van vroeger waren zo weer handelingen van nu. Voor je het wist stond hij ook de barbecue weer aan te maken en lag hij vanavond weer naast Joke naar de twee aquarelletjes aan het voeteneinde in de slaapkamer te kijken: een ondergaand zonnetje aan zee en een Toscaans landschap, hoe kwamen ze er eigenlijk aan?

'Blijf je eten?'

Klonk het nou verwachtingsvol?

Hij aarzelde.

'Of heb je plannen?'

Hij had zeker geen plannen. Het enige wat hij kon was naar huis gaan, nou ja, naar het flatje in Geuzenveld waar zijn vieze overhemden lagen. In de portiek hingen Marokkaanse jongens rond die hem Mister Big noemden, waarschijnlijk vanwege zijn x5.

'Het is ook goed voor de kids,' zei ze nu. 'Zie je niet dat Bruno bang voor je is? Ze hebben je nodig.' Ze keek hem aan, en het viel hem op dat ze haar wenkbrauwen had geëpileerd, veel strakker en dunner dan anders. 'Af en toe,' voegde ze eraan toe.

Hij bleef eten, niets bijzonders: pasta, een salade, een glaasje wijn. Daarna had Joke de kinderen verbazingwekkend snel in bed, en kwam ze met een nieuwe fles wijn. Het had toch wel wat, om op een zomeravond in je eigen tuin te zitten, vond Nico, al wemelde het van de muggen.

Ze dronken de fles leeg en het viel hem op dat Joke sneller dronk dan hij van haar gewend was. Ze kletsten intussen over van alles en nog wat, altijd rakelings langs de grote onderwerpen heen, alsof dat de manier was om ze te bezweren.

'Mijn ouders hebben niet gebeld,' realiseerde hij zich toen hij op zijn horloge keek. Het was kwart voor twaalf.

'Zouden ze bellen dan?' vroeg Joke. 'Hierheen? Dacht je dat je ging blijven dan?' Ze keek hem neutraal aan, een tikje spottend. Het was duidelijk wie de baas was.

'Kennelijk,' mompelde hij.

'Kennelijk,' herhaalde Joke. Er klonk een zweem van teleurstelling in haar stem door. Alsof zijn voornemen een streep door haar plannen was.

'Hebben wij het nummer van Monica?' vroeg Nico.

'Vast wel,' zei Joke, 'hoezo?'

'Die moet ik bellen,' antwoordde Nico.

'Hebben jullie weer contact?'

'Nee. Daarom wil ik haar bellen,' zei Nico, 'maar het kan wachten. Ik doe het morgen wel.'

'Ooh,' zei Joke. Ze schonk de glazen bij. Ze wilde doorgaan op het onderwerp, maar ook weer niet. Nico wachtte af. Ze liet het rusten. Joke was niet zo dol op zijn zus sinds ze gescheiden was van Ben. Alleenstaande vrouwen waren eng, gevaarlijk.

'Ik mis haar soms,' flapte Nico eruit. Hij had te veel gedronken, realiseerde hij zich. De wodka van gisteren, de wijn van
vanavond. Misschien moest hij toch maar eens gaan. Hij
durfde Joke niet aan te kijken.

'Misschien moet je blijven slapen,' zei zijn vrouw, 'je hebt
te veel gedronken. Je moet niet meer rijden.'

Hij knikte.

'Kom,' zei ze, 'ik heb een verrassing voor je.' Ze stond op en
stak hem haar hand toe. Ze loenste een beetje, van de wijn. Hij
wilde haar hand vastpakken, maar ze hielp hem niet met overeind komen. Ze glimlachte. 'Kom,' zei ze nog een keer.

Hij liep achter haar aan – godbetere, zijn eigen huis in. Ze
wiegde licht met haar heupen, niet nadrukkelijk, niet zwaar,
nee, heel subtiel, dat ontging hem dan toch weer niet. Ze gaf
hem de kans niet zich te bedenken, want in een vloeiende
beweging ging het door de openstaande schuifdeuren, de
woonkamer, de gang, de trap op. In de slaapkamer waren de
aquarellen aan het voeteneinde van het echtelijke bed verdwenen.

'Kleed je uit,' zei Joke.

Het was een precair moment, een interessant moment, een
duizelingwekkend moment, niet in de laatste plaats omdat
Nico te veel had gedronken en zich begeerd voelde.

'Ik kom zo,' zei Joke, 'schiet op.' Ze glipte de badkamer in.

Nico trok zijn broek uit. Hij viel bijna, maar wist overeind
te blijven. Hij trok zijn onderbroek en zijn T-shirt uit en ging
op het bed liggen, ruggelings. Aan het plafond was niets ver-
anderd, en ook de geluiden die uit de badkamer kwamen,
waren van alle tijden: de ruisende kraan van de wastafel, de
wc, de handdoek op het rekje, het klepperen van het kastje
naast de spiegel.

De deur van de badkamer ging open – daar was ze.

Hij wist dat hij moest kijken, en hij wilde ook kijken, sterker nog: hij keek. Maar hij zag niet meteen wat er aan de hand was: het duurde even voor de Joke van nu uit de Joke van vroeger tevoorschijn stapte. Ze was onder andere een stuk groter, en ze stond rechter. Ze was ook naakt, maar dat zei hem verder niet zoveel, behalve dat ze naast haar wenkbrauwen ook haar venusheuvel zorgvuldig had bijgewerkt. Ze kwam langzaam op het bed af, een serene, ietwat spookachtige glimlach om haar lippen. Pas op het allerlaatste moment zag Nico wat het verschil maakte, wat haar zo omhoog stuwde en groots en machtig maakte, en hem zo klein, hulpeloos en pathetisch.

Ze droeg de blauwe schoenen van Sylvia.

Wachten op onweer

'Wat sta je te kijken?' vraagt Yolanda. Ze is bezig met het eten, pasta met zalm. De kinderen zijn in de tuin. Over twee dagen gaan ze drie weken op vakantie. Voor het weer hoeven ze niet weg te gaan. Het is snikheet, een hittegolf die volgens de radio nog wel een paar dagen aanhoudt. Ronald staat voor het raam en kijkt door een kier in de lamellen naar buiten. Hij is net thuis, en heeft zijn colbert aan zijn pink over zijn schouder hangen. Yolanda plukt de vette plakken vis uit de verpakking en snijdt ze aan stukken.

'Ik geloof dat er iemand dood is,' zegt Ronald.

Het water kookt. Yolanda laat de tagliatelle in de bubbels zakken. Haar rug is bezweet, haar jurk plakt. Ze heeft zin om onder de douche te gaan. Dan realiseert ze zich wat Ronald heeft gezegd. 'Iemand dood? Wie dan?' Ze denkt aan haar ouders die niets mankeren. Mama sprak ze gisteren nog. Papa was in de tuin het gras aan het maaien. Ze kon het geluid er zo bij denken.

'Geen idee. Iemand aan de overkant.' Ronald draait zich om. Hij heeft zijn roze stropdas om. Ze houdt niet van zijn roze stropdas. Hoe vaak heeft ze hem dat nou al niet gezegd? Een roze stropdas maakt slap. En iedere keer doet hij hem weer om. Misschien moet ze hem gewoon weggooien.

Ze loopt naar hem toe. Ze is toch wel benieuwd. De dood is nog niet eerder in hun straat geweest. De straat is er ook nog niet zo lang trouwens. Een jaar of vijf pas. En er wonen eigenlijk alleen jonge gezinnen in, gezinnen zoals zij – twee kinderen en een bakfiets om ze mee naar school te brengen, twee banen en in het weekend allemaal klussen in de tuin en barbecueën. Alle mannen in Dockers, alle vrouwen in H&M'etjes, lekker makkelijk.

'Je ruikt naar vis,' zegt Ronald als ze naast hem staat.

'Ik ben pasta met zalm aan het maken.'

'Lekker,' zegt Ronald, zonder veel overtuiging. Pasta met dit, pasta met dat, hij vindt het allemaal kindereten. Maar het is al beter dan patat met appelmoes en hotdogs of pannenkoeken, zo eerlijk is hij ook wel. 'Kijk,' zegt hij, en hij schuift de lamellen weer een stukje opzij.

Yolanda aarzelt, want ze moet dicht bij haar man gaan staan om naar buiten te kunnen kijken en ze weet dat zijn hand dan op haar billen terecht zal komen. De laatste tijd kan ze dat absoluut niet hebben. Aan de ene kant kinderachtig, hij bedoelt er niets mee, het is gewoon een reflex – kont in de buurt, hand erop, en het is ook best aardig, ze heeft een mooie kont tenslotte, ze is er trots op, maar aan de andere kant: hij kan toch ook wel een beetje begrip voor haar hebben? Het leven draait toch niet om haar kont?

Haar nieuwsgierigheid wint.

Ze kijkt naar buiten, en in plaats van dat Ronald zijn hand op haar billen legt, slaat hij een arm om haar schouder heen. Dat is al beter. Ze ruikt zijn zweet, oud en vers door elkaar heen, oud onder zijn armen, vers in zijn hals. Dan ziet ze de lijkwagen – vijf huizen verderop, aan de overkant. Het is een grote, fonkelend zwarte Amerikaan, de gordijntjes achterin zijn dicht. Ze kan niet zien of er een kist in staat. 'Wie is er dood?' vraagt ze.

'Geen idee,' zegt Ronald. Zijn hand knijpt geruststellend in haar schouder.

Ze kijken samen even naar de lange, zwarte wagen. Hij detoneert zo verschrikkelijk in de straat dat het pijn doet aan de ogen. De warmte speelt ook mee. Aan de einde van de middag is het op straat niet te doen – de hitte trilt tussen de huizen, iedereen heeft de gordijnen, lamellen en luxaflex potdicht. Het leven speelt zich af aan de andere kant van de huizen, in de tuintjes die allemaal aan het water grenzen, smalle grachten die uitkomen op een royale plas met een opgespoten eiland in het midden.

'Het is geen dag om dood te gaan,' zegt Ronald. Hij doet zijn stropdas af en knoopt zijn overhemd open. 'Ik ga mijn korte broek aandoen.' Hij laat de lamellen los en de dood is uit het zicht verdwenen.

Yolanda loopt terug naar de keuken. Ze is vergeten de kookwekker voor de pasta te zetten. Uit de koelkast pakt ze bosui, bieslook en de room voor de saus, uit de pannenla een koekenpan waar ze een druppel olijfolie in doet. Ze hakt de bosui en schuift het van de snijplank af, in de pan. Ze vraagt zich af wie er dood is in de straat. Ze kan niemand bedenken. Een knetterend onweer, stortbuien die als grijze gordijnen uit de hemel vallen – daar verlangt ze ineens naar. Maar er zit geen onweer in de lucht, nog niet.

'Gaan we eten, mam?' Dat is Robin. Hij is acht. Hij heeft altijd honger, maar hij lust niks, nou ja, pasta dus, en Pringles en alles van McDonald's. Wat dat betreft is Sabine makkelijker. Die eet alles. Robin is in zijn blauwe zwembroek, en kletsnat. Er vormt zich een plas water aan zijn voeten.

'Je moet een handdoek pakken als je binnenkomt,' zegt Yolanda, terwijl ze de pan lager zet en de room bij de bosuitjes doet. 'En we gaan zo eten, je kunt buiten de tafel dekken.'

'Wat eten we?'

'Pasta met zalm.'

'Hè, bah,' zegt Robin, en weg is hij.

Daar doe je het dan voor – denkt Yolanda. Ze doet de zalm-snippers in de saus, roert even, en vist dan met een vork een sliert tagliatelle uit de pan. Ze gooit hem tegen de muur – als hij valt is de pasta niet gaar, als hij blijft plakken wel. Het kan ook andersom zijn, ze vergeet altijd hoe het ook alweer zit, en bij wie ze het heeft gelezen. Was het Nigella Lawson of Jamie Oliver? Ze leest trouwens liever kookboeken dan dat ze kookt. De sliert blijft even aan het tegelwerk hangen en valt dan op het aanrecht. Ze steekt hem in haar mond. Er zitten een paar broodkruimels aan, maar hij is mooi al dente, net niet gaar genoeg dus voor de kinderen. Ze geeft de pasta nog een mi-nuut en giet hem dan af. Terwijl hij afkoelt, roert ze in de saus, die is ook goed. Ronald komt binnen. Hij heeft zijn korte broek en een verschoten т-shirt van De Dijk aan. Hij opent de koelkast voor zijn biertje. 'Glaasje wijn, schat?'

'Je kunt buiten de tafel dekken,' zegt ze, 'en de kinderen moe-ten uit het badje.' Ze wonen dan wel aan het water; je kunt er niet in zwemmen. Net als alle andere buren hebben ze daarom een groot opblaasbad in de tuin staan. Iedereen heeft hetzelfde bad, van het tuincentrum. Deprimerend eigenlijk. Net als de stoelen en tafels en bankjes en plantenbakken en schuttingen. Allemaal van hetzelfde tuincentrum. Ronald trekt zijn biertje open, neemt een slok, en trekt de bestekla open om lepels en vorken te pakken. In het passeren glijdt zijn hand even over Yo-landa's billen. Ze geeft hem een tik, en hij lacht. Ze roert de saus door de pasta en drukt hem de pan in handen. 'Ik neem de bor-den wel mee,' zegt ze en terwijl hij naar de tuin loopt, gaat zij naar het raam aan de straatkant. Ze begrijpt niet goed waarom en ziet haar vingers trillen als ze de lamellen een stukje opzij houdt. Twee mannen in grijze jassen halen een blankhouten kist uit de lijkauto en dragen hem een huis binnen.

De telefoon gaat.

Yolanda schrikt. Ze laat de lamellen los, ze rinkelen zachtjes, als kleerhangers in een winkel, en haast zich naar haar mobieltje dat op het aanrecht ligt. Ze herkent het nummer dat in haar display staat. Ze aarzelt, vermant zich – stel je niet zo aan – en neemt dan op.

'Heb je het al gehoord?' De hese stem van Babette. 'De man van Elsbeth heeft zelfmoord gepleegd.'

Yolanda kent geen Elsbeth.

'Die blonde van hier schuin tegenover, met die tweeling,' gaat Babette verder. Yolanda voelt een koude rilling over haar rug gaan. Ze kent die vrouw natuurlijk, al weet ze niet dat ze Elsbeth heet. Ze heeft slechts af en toe wat vluchtige woorden met haar gewisseld, over het weer, de tweeling, nog heel jong, twee jaar, de buurt, dat werk. Elsbeths man moet ze ook kennen, maar ze kan zich geen gezicht voor de geest halen.

'Die lange gozer, weet je wel, met die Audi. Een knappe man,' vult Babette in. 'Jacques of zo. Hij heeft zich verhangen.'

Yolanda kent geen Jacques, ze heeft geen oog voor auto's en ze wil eigenlijk niets meer met Babette te maken hebben, hoewel ze een tijdje hoopte dat ze goede vriendinnen konden worden.

'Mam, eten!' Daar is Robin weer. 'Papa heeft honger, maar we hebben geen borden.'

'Ik bel je later terug,' zegt Yolanda tegen Babette, en ze hangt op. Ze gaat Babette helemaal niet terugbellen. Ze pakt de borden en loopt achter haar zoon aan naar de tuin. Als ze het felle zonlicht in stapt, wordt ze ineens duizelig. Ze ziet haar gezin onder de rode parasol zitten – ze kijken verwachtingsvol naar haar. Ze voelt haar benen trillen, en grijpt zich vast aan de keukendeur. De borden glijden uit haar hand en vallen stuk op de grond. Bij de buren klinkt gelach.

2

Ronald ligt al in bed. Yolanda staat voor de spiegel in de badkamer haar nachtcrème op te doen. Ze is moe. Naast het bed staan de reistassen half gepakt open voor de vakantie. Drie weken Frankrijk, ze ziet ertegen op, maar ze weet niet precies waarom.

'Kom je nog?' roept Ronald.

Ze poetst haar tanden. Ze doet er langer over dan normaal. Met tandenpoetsen kun je twee kanten op. Je kunt al doende aan iets anders denken. Maar je kunt je ook helemaal op het poetsen concentreren, en nergens anders mee bezig zijn. Ze poetst vol overgave, zorgvuldig en precies. Af en toe schieten toch de zwarte lijkwagen en de blankhouten kist voorbij die ze aan de overkant van de straat naar binnen gedragen zag worden.

'Wat is er, schat?' vraagt Ronald als ze eindelijk in bed stapt. 'Pieker je over die man?'

Ze knikt. Het bed zou eigenlijk verschoond moeten worden, maar zo vlak voor de vakantie heeft dat geen zin meer. Het ruikt alsof ze er al weken in liggen. De ramen staan open, de gordijnen zijn dicht. Er staat geen zucht wind. Buiten klinken stemmen, gedempt gelach, zacht glasgerinkel. Soms is het net alsof ze op een camping wonen; tot twee uur zitten de mensen in hun tuin, om zeven uur hollen de eerste kinderen alweer gillend rond. Het is gewoon te heet. De lakens plakken aan haar lijf. 'Wie pleegt er nou zelfmoord, Ronald? Twee kleine kinderen, een mooi huis, een leuke vrouw.'

'Misschien was ze niet zo leuk voor hem,' antwoordt Ronald, 'misschien had hij schulden, de zaak geflest, weet jij veel.'

'Welke zaak?'

'Geen idee, ik heb nooit een woord met die man gewisseld. Ik weet niet eens hoe hij heet.'

'Jacques of zo.'

'Jacques of zo,' herhaalt Ronald. Hij bedoelt het niet zo, maar het klinkt treurig.

Yolanda vraagt zich af of ze het zich zo aantrekt omdat ze misschien denkt dat het haar ook had kunnen overkomen – thuiskomen en je man ineens in het trapgat zien hangen. 'We moeten hier weg,' flapt ze uit.

'We gaan overmorgen op vakantie.'

'Dat bedoel ik niet.'

'Dat weet ik. Maar, schatje, we wonen hier net. En we kunnen hier niet weg. Waar wil je heen? Het is hier geweldig voor de kinderen. En als we verkopen, maken we verlies.'

Ze hebben deze discussie al vaker gehad sinds het drie maanden geleden met Babette en Luuk uit de hand liep. En een andere discussie hebben ze sindsdien ook voortdurend: 'Waarom hebben we geen seks meer?'

'Dat weet je best. Zodra je erover begint, wil ik al niet meer.'

'Als ik er niet over begin, wil je dan wel?'

'Misschien. Soms.'

'Ik merk er niks van.'

'Niet alle vrouwen zijn als Babette.'

Drie maanden geleden: een etentje bij Luuk en Babette. Ze hebben een jongetje dat bij Robin op school zit, dezelfde leeftijd, maar een andere klas, leuke mensen. Ze wonen drie huizen verderop. Hij werkt in Den Haag, op een ministerie, zij drie dagen in de week bij een modezaak. Het zijn hun soort mensen, ze lezen wel eens boek, ze gaan regelmatig uit, ze houden van lekker eten, gaan altijd naar Frankrijk op vakantie. Ze zitten allebei vol praatjes, je kunt met ze lachen. Ze zien er goed uit, Babette donkerblond, een goed figuur, Luuk breed en blond, stoer. Ronald en Yolanda voelen zich bij hen op hun gemak, en het is wederzijds. Ze zien elkaar bijna ieder weekend. Hapje eten, glaasje, kletsen – soms een filmpje. Niks aan de hand, tot die ene zaterdagavond waarop Babette ineens 'Wij zijn swingers' zei, waarbij ze Yolanda indringend aankeek.

Yolanda zei bijna dat ze ook van dansen hield, maar net op tijd begreep ze wat Babette bedoelde, en meteen daarna bloosde ze als een boei. Ze probeerde oogcontact met Ronald te maken, maar die deed net een greep in de schaal met zoutjes. Pas later kwam ze erachter dat hij het al wist, dat Luuk het er met hem over had gehad. Ze had natuurlijk gewoon luchtig 'Ooh, leuk, wij niet' moeten zeggen en een ander onderwerp aan moeten snijden, maar ook dat bedacht ze zich pas later. En misschien had ze ook minder moeten drinken die avond, en ze had zeker niet moeten blowen, maar ja, Luuk en Babette rookten nu eenmaal graag een jointje. En zo kon het gebeuren dat ze een uur later met een zwoegende Luuk tussen haar benen op hun enorme bed lag, Ronald naast haar die met Babette tekeerging. Het was alsof ze in een film zat, en ze vond het verschrikkelijk, en al helemaal dat ze nog klaarkwam ook. Daarna had ze in hun badkamer alles ondergekotst.

Een paar dagen later stonden Luuk en Babette met een flesje wijn op de stoep om erover te praten. Ze hadden zich vergist, ze waren te ver gegaan, ze hadden het idee dat Ronald en Yolanda er wel in voor waren, het was uit de hand gelopen, zand erover en kom, even goede vrienden, het was maar seks, niks aan de hand, et cetera. Yolanda begreep wat ze bedoelden, en ze zou het ook best wel willen vergeten, maar het punt was: ze had het meegemaakt en ze kon het niet vergeten; de beelden bleven maar in haar hoofd rondspoken. Niet dat ze preuts was, of bang voor haar eigen fantasieën – ze wilde het gewoon niet delen met anderen, in ieder geval niet met Luuk en Babette, vooral niet met Babette, eigenlijk – de gulzigheid waarmee die zich op Ronald had gestort vond ze gewoon smerig.

Punt.

Uit.

Luuk en Babette deden alsof ze het wel snapten, maar dropen uiteindelijk af, en daarna verwaterde de vriendschap snel, al bleven ze elkaar natuurlijk regelmatig zien, op straat, in de supermarkt, bij school. Het lukte Yolanda dan wel te groeten, of een klein praatje te maken, maar meer kon ze niet opbrengen. Als ze te lang naar Babettes dikke mond keek, zag ze haar Ronald erin verdwijnen. Ze hield Robin een beetje weg bij Patrick, het zoontje van Luuk en Babette, en Robin maakte gelukkig eindelijk zelf ook vriendjes, in zijn eigen klas. Ronald voelde zich schuldig – hij had Luuk doen geloven dat Yolanda er wel voor zou voelen, mannen onder elkaar, opscheppen, altijd hetzelfde –, maar al snel werd hij boos en mokkend: ze moest zich eroverheen zetten, ze moest het niet groter maken dan het was. 'Jij hebt jezelf niet bezig gezien met dat wijf,' zei ze dan.

'Je bent gewoon jaloers!'

Was dat het?

Misschien. Nee. Een beetje, toch? Nee. Waar moest ze jaloers op zijn? Dat Babette kon seksen als een pornoster? Walgelijk vond ze het – iedere keer als ze eraan dacht. Het was onverdraaglijk, eigenlijk, al deed ze haar best zich eroverheen te zetten. Wat haar het meest stak was de gretigheid waarmee Ronald erop in was gegaan. Even had ze in haar man een man gezien die ze zou kunnen haten, en dat nam ze Babette kwalijk.

'Hè, toe, schat, je moet het vergeten,' fluistert Ronald in haar oor. Hij is tegen haar aan gekropen. Ze verstijft, maar blijft liggen. Hij raakt haar verder ook niet aan.

'Jaja,' mompelt ze.

'Hebben we zin in de vakantie?' vraagt hij. 'Moet je nog veel doen?'

'Valt mee,' zegt ze, en ze denkt aan de koelkast die leeg moet, de kinderspullen die nog ingepakt moet worden, de badhanddoeken die nog even in de wasmachine moeten, de slaapzakken die nog gelucht moeten. 'Heb jij de tent en de spullen klaar? De auto schoon?' Ronald gaat over het kampeergedeelte en de auto. Niet alleen thuis leven ze op een camping, ook op vakantie gaan ze naar de camping. Alles om het de kinderen maar naar de zin te maken. Waar is de tijd gebleven dat ze met z'n tweetjes dagen achter elkaar op het strand lagen?

'Bijna,' zegt hij. 'Ik heb er zin in. Een beetje afstand. Je zult zien, als we terugkomen, ziet alles er anders uit. Dan begint het leven opnieuw.' Hij kust haar op haar oor. Ach, hij is ook best lief, houdt ze zichzelf voor. Ze voelt iets hards tegen haar bil opkruipen, en laat het maar gebeuren.

'Ik hoop het,' zegt ze.

'Morgen heb ik een halve dag,' gaat hij verder, 'dan kunnen we 's middags rustig inpakken, de auto schoonmaken, alles klaarmaken.' Hij zoent haar in haar nek.

Niet doen, wil ze tegen hem zeggen. Maar ze houdt zich in en denkt aan het begin van hun relatie, toen Ronald haar met aandacht en cadeautjes overlaadde; nooit eerder had ze een man ontmoet die zo goed kon luisteren. Toen de kinderen kwamen, eerst Robin, drie jaar later Sabine, heeft hij zich ongelooflijk ingezet – een ideale vader, zorgzaam, enthousiast, een meester in het verschonen van luiers, 'een lot uit de loterij', zoals haar zus Annemarieke zei.

'Nu niet, schat,' zegt ze tegen hem als hij haar opnieuw in haar nek kust – hij weet dat het een gevoelig plekje van haar is. Ze accepteert zijn erectie tegen haar billen, dat is al heel wat.

'Oké,' zucht hij, en hij draait zich van haar af.

Ze heeft onmiddellijk met hem te doen, maar ze is ook blij dat hij haar begrijpt en ineens ziet ze niet meer tegen de vakantie op. Ze komen er wel, ze redden het wel. Even verbeeldt ze zich dat ze buiten in de verte vaag het gerommel van een naderend onweer hoort, maar ze weet dat ze zich vergist.

3

'Hebben we alles?' vraagt Ronald. 'Alles uit? Het gas? De koelkast open? De deuren op slot?' Hij kijkt Yolanda aan. 'Je hebt je gordel nog niet om.'

Ze doet haar gordel om. 'Rij nou maar,' zegt ze. Ronald is altijd zenuwachtig als ze op reis gaan. Hij drinkt te veel koffie voor ze vertrekken, en eet niets. Ze heeft boven in de tas tussen haar benen een broodje ham voor hem liggen. Als ze straks een halfuur rijden, ontspant hij en krijgt hij honger.

'Oké, jongens, we gaan op vakantie,' zegt Ronald op de toon van een reisleider. Hij draait zich om naar Robin en Sabine die half slapend op de achterbank zitten, Sabine in haar zitje, Robin op een kussen. Yolanda heeft een dun dekentje over ze heen gelegd, de kunst is om ze zo lang mogelijk rustig te houden. Ze reageren gelukkig niet op hun vader.

'Hup,' zegt ze tegen Ronald, 'gas.'

Ze rijden weg. Het is tien over zes, het gaat alweer een heel warme dag worden – en gisteren heeft ze op het internet het weer in de Dordogne gecheckt; daar is het nog heter. Het zou van haar wel wat minder mogen. Een paar fikse buien, een lekker donderend onweer, ze verlangt ernaar, maar op de weerkaart van Frankrijk was geen bliksemschicht te zien, alleen maar stralende zonnetjes. Als ze drie weken in de brandende zon staan, wordt het afzien. Sabine heeft nu al last van de warmte. Ze is een kind met heel gevoelige darmen.

Tot Breda is het rustig in de auto. Het is al druk op de weg, maar ze schieten lekker op. Ronald eet zijn broodje, Yolanda staart wat voor zich uit. Ze heeft slecht geslapen en probeert nergens aan te denken. De laatste tijd slaapt ze wel vaker slecht – ze droomt veel, ze ligt wakker. Het is de warmte, en het rumoer in de tuinen om hen heen, houdt ze zich voor. Dat gaat de komende weken niet veranderen, de herrie blijft. Ze hebben eens twee weken aan de Tarn gestaan: prachtige plek onder de bomen, maar naast hen een Duits gezin met twee verschrikkelijk drukke jongetjes. Die ouders deden daar niets tegen, en die jongens holden tot 's avonds laat met plastic zwaarden en stokken achter elkaar aan om de tent. Het was om gek van te worden.

'Hoe gaat het eigenlijk met Annemarieke?' vraagt Ronald ineens. Dat is een vraag die hij stelt als hij geen andere vragen heeft.

'Goed, geloof ik,' antwoordt Yolanda zacht. Annemarieke is haar jongere zus die het de laatste tijd moeilijk heeft. Jan-Fred is bij haar weg, tijdelijk, beweert ze, om tot zichzelf te komen, maar er is natuurlijk ook een andere vrouw in het spel. Het is altijd hetzelfde. Je leest erover, alle films die je ziet gaan erover, de bladen staan er vol mee; hoe je overspel moet plegen, hoe je het moet ontdekken, wat je ertegen moet doen, hoe het je huwelijk een impuls kan geven, maar als het dichtbij komt, is het altijd een drama en kan geen vrouw ertegen, zelfs Annemarieke niet, en dat is iemand die alles altijd geweldig voor elkaar heeft.

'Is Jan-Fred al bij d'r terug, of zit-ie nog steeds op dat flatje over zijn leven na te denken?' Ronald heeft het nooit goed kunnen vinden met zijn zwager. Hij is een beetje bang voor hem. Jan-Fred is een man van de wereld. Hij draagt goede pakken, hij rijdt in een auto waar Ronald graag in zou willen rijden. Hij verdient veel. Hij is charmant, ook tegen Yolanda.

'Mam, mogen we wat lekkers?' vraagt Sabine ineens. Ze zijn inmiddels al in België, Antwerpen nadert.

'Straks stoppen we en gaan we wat eten,' zegt Yolanda, 'we hebben nog niet ontbeten.' Ze moeten zo lang mogelijk niet snoepen. Hoe meer suiker ze binnenkrijgen, hoe vervelender ze straks worden.

'Maar ik wil nu iets lekkers,' jengelt Sabine.

'Later, schat, we zitten nog uren in de auto. Stop je zo, Ronald?'

'We rijden net zo lekker,' zegt hij, om zich meteen te bedenken. 'Ja, natuurlijk. We stoppen over een halfuur. Even Antwerpen voorbij.'

'Zal ik K3 opzetten?' vraagt Yolanda aan Sabine.

'Hè, getver, nee,' roept Robin, 'K3 is voor meisjes.'

'Ik ben ook een meisje,' roept Sabine en ze geeft Robin een klap. Robin slaat terug en Sabine begint te huilen.

'Kom op, jongens,' roept Ronald, 'Robin, jij zet je koptelefoon op. Ga maar naar Paul van Loon luisteren.' Ronald heeft gisteren nog een goedkoop discmannetje voor Robin gekocht.

'Hij doet het niet,' roept Robin boos.

'We moeten nu stoppen, Ronald,' zegt Yolanda. In de verte ziet ze de borden van een Shell-station. Ronald neemt de afslag en parkeert achter het benzinestation bij de enige lege picknickbank. Als Yolanda haar deur opent, slaat de warmte haar tegemoet. Het is negen uur. Ze tilt haar boodschappentas naar buiten en helpt daarna de kinderen uit hun riemen. Sabine piept dat ze moet poepen. Yolanda stuurt Ronald met haar naar het benzinestation, rol wc-papier mee, en begint aan de picknicktafel broodjes te smeren en gekookte eieren te pellen. Uit de koelbox achter in de auto haalt ze voor Robin een halve liter melk – hij is gek op melk. Hij zit aan tafel te klooien met de discman. 'Hier, een broodje,' zegt ze hem. Ze geeft hem een broodje kaas en pakt de discman van hem af.

Ze drukt op de knopjes, hij reageert nergens op. Er zitten geen batterijen in. Hebben ze batterijen bij zich?

Ronald en Sabine komen terug. Ze zijn de rol wc-papier vergeten. 'Ze is aan de schijterij,' zegt Ronald. Hij zet Sabine op de bank en schenkt een kop koffie in uit de thermosfles. 'Wat een lekker weer, hè,' zegt hij. Sabine zet haar tanden in een droge volkorenkoek. Yolanda staat op.

'Wat ga je doen?'

'Batterijen kopen. Er zitten geen batterijen in die walkman.' Ze loopt weg zonder op Ronalds commentaar te wachten. De parkeerplaats staat vol Nederlanders. Ze heeft de pest in dat ze een korte broek aan heeft. In de winkel koopt ze batterijen, en ze gaat plassen. In het hokje naast haar hoort ze iemand telefoneren. 'Jezus, meid, ik was zo geil.' Ze haast zich weg.

'We rijden over Valenciennes en niet over Gent en Lille,' zegt Ronald als ze over de ring van Antwerpen rijden, 'dat gaat sneller, en het is weer eens wat anders.' Dat is het zeker, want vlak voorbij Mons komen ze in een file terecht. Het is halfelf als ze aansluiten, en halftwee als ze eindelijk weer rijden. Ondanks de airco die op volle toeren blaast, wordt het steeds warmer in de auto. De etenswaren beginnen te stinken. Twee keer moet Yolanda met Sabine de auto uit om haar aan de andere kant van de vangrail te laten poepen. Er is ook daar geen sprankje schaduw, en het wemelt er van de muggen. Robin houdt zich met zijn walkman redelijk gedeisd. Ronald vloekt af en toe, het zweet gutst van zijn hoofd, Yolanda wordt misselijk van de dieseldampen van de vrachtwagen van Willi Betz die al die uren voor hen staat te ronken. Ze doen spelletjes – Ik zie ik zie wat jij niet ziet, Ik ga op vakantie en neem mee – en wachten. Uiteindelijk gaat de boel rijden, en natuurlijk komen ze er niet achter wat de file veroorzaakte.

Om vijf uur zijn ze bij Parijs. Daar neemt Ronald weer een

fijne beslissing. In plaats van in westelijke richting de Péri-phérique te nemen, nemen ze hem in oostelijke richting – dat heeft de ANWB geadviseerd. Ze komen terecht in stapvoets rijdend verkeer en doen er tweeënhalf uur over om voorbij Parijs te komen. Yolanda stelt voor om de stad in te rijden en een hotelletje te nemen.

'No way,' zegt Ronald, 'eerst uit de drukte.' Ze hebben vlak voor Parijs gewisseld. Yolanda rijdt, Ronald leest de kinderen voor uit *Pluk van de Petteflet*. Hij is achterin gaan zitten, en maakt er een hele show van. Yolanda glimlacht af en toe be-wonderend. Ze heeft toch best een leuke man. Als ze vlak bij de *péage* zijn, nemen ze de afslag naar Dourdan. Ze hebben geluk, en vinden meteen een hotel, midden in het centrum, een ouderwets Frans hotel. Ze hebben nog één kamer vrij, een grote kamer, met drie bedden. Voor Sabine kan er een ledikant worden bijgezet. Er is geen airco, maar met de luiken en de gordijnen dicht, valt het best mee. De zon staat niet op de ramen. Ze eten op het terras van een kleine pizzeria, in een smal straatje vlak bij de kerk en het marktplein. De kinderen krijgen een grote sorbet toe en daarna is het aan Yolanda om ze in bed te stoppen. Ronald slentert naar het plein voor een afzakkertje.

De kinderen zijn moe, Yolanda heeft ze zo in slaap. Dat is wel eens anders geweest. Een jaar geleden nog maar kon Robin er uren over doen om in slaap te vallen in een vreemd bed. Nu slaapt hij bijna meteen. Sabine is altijd een makke-lijke slaper geweest. Even voorlezen, en weg is ze. Yolanda overweegt even zelf ook maar te gaan slapen, ze is moe, maar het is nog geen eens tien uur, en Ronald zit op haar te wach-ten. Ze sluipt de slaapkamer uit. Dat doet haar altijd aan haar eigen kindertijd denken. Het heeft iets stiekems, iets ondeu-gends, en dan staat ze weer buiten. Ze loopt terug naar het marktplein, waar Ronald op een terras de krant zit te lezen.

'Slapen ze?' vraagt hij. 'Wat wil je drinken?'

'Een roseetje,' zegt ze.

Ronald bestelt een fles, en twee glazen. Ze drinken en kijken naar de flanerende jeugd van Dourdan. Ze zijn te moe om veel tegen elkaar te zeggen. Maar Yolanda voelt zich goed – ze is blij dat ze in een andere wereld is. Ze drinkt iets te veel, maar dat kan haar voor de verandering eens niets schelen. Het wordt langzaam donker, maar de warmte blijft. Op de trappen van de kerk aan de overkant van het plein zitten vrijende stelletjes. Het is er een komen en gaan van scooters. De sfeer is uitgelaten, opgewonden, zaterdagavond. Ineens heeft ze zin. Ze pakt Ronalds hand. 'Kom,' zegt ze, 'we gaan.'

Hij kijkt haar verbaasd aan. Haar stem is hees.

Ze lopen terug naar het hotel. Ronald lijkt te snappen wat er aan de hand is. Hij is net zo zenuwachtig als zij. Het is alsof ze weer twintig zijn. Ze zoenen voorzichtig in de gang naar de kamer. De kinderen slapen. Ze hebben nog nooit gevreeën met de kinderen in de kamer. Ze kleden zich snel uit, en gaan op het bed liggen. Het piept en kraakt. 'Kom,' fluistert Yolanda. Ze kan nauwelijks wachten. Hij komt op haar liggen, en ze helpt hem in haar. Hij durft niet te bewegen.

'Wat doen jullie, mam?' klinkt slaperig het stemmetje van Robin.

'Niets, schat,' zegt ze, 'slaap maar lekker verder.'

Ze wachten roerloos of hij nog iets zal zeggen, maar hij slaapt verder. Ze zoenen elkaar, en giechelen. Dan maken ze het snel af.

4

'Dit is het dus,' zegt Ronald met een zucht. Het is niet duidelijk wat hij bedoelt.

'Dit is het, schat, hier blijven we lekker drie weken staan,' antwoordt Yolanda. Als puntje bij paaltje komt, is zij toch degene die de moed erin moet houden. Hij heeft de camping op het internet gevonden, hij was er enthousiast over, hij heeft haar overtuigd, maar nu ze er staan, maakt hij zich zorgen dat zij het niet leuk zal vinden.

Ze zitten voor de tent. Ze zijn hier nu twee dagen. Ze hebben een schitterende plek, vlak bij een uitgestrekt meer, en in de schaduw van een reusachtige kastanjeboom. De kinderen kunnen voor hun neus zwemmen. Het is bovendien niet druk op de camping, om niet te zeggen: rustig. Er klopt niets van wat de website beloofde: er is geen speeltuin, geen restaurant, geen supermarkt, geen entertainmentteam dat twee keer in de week langskomt. Het enige wat er is, is een groot meer, en een kleine snackbar waar de gasten 's ochtends stokbrood kunnen kopen en de rest van de dag patat en pannenkoeken. Pas aan het einde van de middag wordt het druk aan de waterkant – uit de wijde omtrek arriveren dan Fransen, bewoners van de streek.

Toch zijn Ronald en Yolanda niet de enige Nederlanders op de camping. Vlak bij de snackbar staan twee grote tenten van twee Nederlandse gezinnen die zes kinderen bij zich hebben. Voor Robin en Sabine is het ideaal, ze kunnen zomaar vriendjes maken. Ronald vindt het ook prettig als hij af en toe een praatje kan maken. Yolanda had ze liever niet in haar buurt gehad – ze heeft op de een of andere moeite met alles wat haar aan thuis doet denken, alsof ze niet op vakantie is, maar op de vlucht. Ze probeert de snackbar te mijden.

'Wat is er, schat?' vraagt Ronald.

'Met mij niks,' zegt Yolanda snel, 'ik dacht dat er met jou iets was.' Het is tien uur 's ochtends. Ze zitten aan de koffie. De kinderen zijn verderop aan het spelen. Het wordt opnieuw een hete dag. Het meer ligt als een ansichtkaart te schitteren. Op de heuvels aan de overkant grazen koeien, bruine stippen.

'Ik ga een krantje halen, straks,' zegt Ronald, 'in het dorp. Moet ik ook wat boodschappen doen?'

Yolanda nipt van haar koffie. Ze begrijpt het niet, maar ze is doodmoe. 'Neem iets lekkers mee,' zegt ze. Ze zou een complete boodschappenlijst op kunnen ratelen, ze hebben van alles nodig, maar het ontbreekt haar aan de energie. Liever vandaag weer pannenkoeken en frites en bier en een ijsje dan nadenken over wat ze vanavond zou kunnen koken. 'En fruit,' zegt ze, 'perziken, meloen, vitaminen.'

'Wat is er, schat?' herhaalt Ronald. 'Of moet je ongesteld worden?' Hij krabt aan zijn knie, een muggenbeet. Dat is een nadeel hier, veel muggen.

Yolanda zegt maar niets. Ze vindt het zo'n stomme vraag, maar ze weet dat hij het goed bedoelt. Het huwelijk hangt van goede bedoelingen aan elkaar. Zo is het leven. Je moet je best doen, dan kom je er wel. Waar je komt, is onduidelijk. Ze is trouwens net ongesteld geweest, dus dat is het niet. Het ergert haar zelf ook dat ze niet weet wat er aan de hand is. Sinds ze weer met Ronald heeft gevreeën heeft ze weer van die gruwelijke Babette gedroomd, nogal smerig ook: Ronald en Babette in actie. Oké, dat is één keer gebeurd, onder haar eigen ogen, terwijl Babettes eigen Luuk op háár lag, maar waarom kan ze het niet vergeten? Waarom is ze zo kinderachtig? Bijna begint ze er nu over, maar ze houdt zich in. Met een rilling schiet haar ineens te binnen dat ze vannacht ook van de blankhouten doodskist heeft gedroomd die een paar dagen geleden nog maar bij haar in de straat een huis werd binnengedragen. De man van Elsbeth met de tweeling had zelfmoord gepleegd. Als hij dat niet had gedaan, had Yolanda Elsbeths naam niet eens gekend. Nu wel, en ze vindt Elsbeth een mooie naam. Ze krijgt er bijna tranen van in haar ogen.

'Jongens, wie gaat er mee boodschappen doen?' Ronald is opgestaan. Hij draait zich naar Yolanda om. 'Heb je lekker een paar uur voor jezelf,' voegt hij eraan toe. Het is niet duidelijk of hij het oprecht meent, of dat hij kwaad op haar is. De kinderen reageren natuurlijk zoals te verwachten: ze willen allebei mee. Even later zijn ze weg en is Yolanda alleen met de lege koffiemokken op de kampeertafel. Na een tijdje maakt ze een pan water warm en gaat ze op een badhanddoek voor de tent haar benen scheren. Ze gebruikt Ronalds scheerschuim. Als ze klaar is, slaat ze de handdoek als een sarong om haar middel en wandelt ze naar het waslokaal om te douchen.

Het is weldadig koel in het lokaal. Op een van de wastafels staat een geopende toilettas. Er steekt een tandenborstel uit. Iemand staat zich te douchen achter een gesloten deurtje, verder is er niemand. Yolanda neemt de douche ernaast. Ze begint met lauw water, maar al snel draait ze de rode kraan helemaal dicht en laat ze het koude water over haar lichaam stromen. Het wordt steeds kouder, haar tepels richten zich op en ze krijgt kippenvel. De stralen zijn hard. Als ze haar hoofd er recht onder houdt, is het alsof ze dwars door haar schedel willen; het doet gewoon pijn. Maar ze blijft staan tot ze helemaal is verkleumd. Ze bibbert als ze de douche uitdoet.

Het is doodstil in het lokaal. Ze slaat de handdoek om zich heen en opent de deur. Bij de wastafel met de toilettas staat een vrouw die alleen een blauw bikinibroekje draagt. Ze heeft kort blond haar, en haar nek en schouders zijn rood verbrand. Ze heeft een tube crème in haar hand. Ze staart geschrokken in de spiegel. De hand met de tube hangt stil in de lucht. Even kijken de vrouwen elkaar via de spiegel in de ogen, en dan ziet Yolanda dat de vrouw maar één borst heeft, een grote ook nog die een beetje glimt. Op de plek van de andere zit een rood litteken. 'Sorry,' zegt ze. Het klinkt laf in het stille lokaal.

'Kanker,' zegt de vrouw. Ze draait zich niet om, en heeft haar blik neergeslagen – zodat Yolanda in de spiegel nog even

naar het litteken kan kijken. Ze kan haar ogen er niet van af-
houden. Ze schaamt zich.

'Hij is er nog geen jaar af,' vervolgt de vrouw. Ze heeft een
Gronings accent. 'En het is net alsof hij er nog zit.' Ze streelt
het litteken, en kijkt ineens via de spiegel recht in Yolanda's
ogen. 'Je weet dat het kan gebeuren, maar als het dan gebeurt,
weet je niet wat je overkomt.' Ze lacht schril. 'Maar het leven
gaat door.' Ze knijpt een dot crème uit de tube en smeert haar
borst in. 'Ik hoop dat je niet erg geschrokken bent,' zegt ze
nog.

'Geeft niet,' zegt Yolanda en ze loopt het waslokaal uit.

Eén stap buiten en de hitte slaat weldadig tegen haar koude
lichaam. Ze slentert rustig terug naar hun tent. Het is alsof
de warmte haar langzaam opneemt. De wereld sluit zich om
haar heen. Ze heeft zin om Ronald te bellen en te zeggen dat
ze gelukkig is. Bij de tent zoekt ze in haar tas naar haar mobieltje. Ze heeft zes berichten van Annemarieke. 'Bel me
ASAP!' Haar hart slaat over, en ze belt haar zus. 'Waar ben je?'
vraagt die als ze opneemt.

'In Frankrijk, op vakantie,' zegt Yolanda. 'Ik had mijn telefoon niet aanstaan.'

'Papa heeft een beroerte gehad,' gaat Annemarieke verder.
Ze klinkt boos, en beschuldigend, alsof het niet gebeurd was
als haar zus niet op vakantie was gegaan. Yolanda staart naar
haar enkels. Ze is een paar haartjes vergeten. 'Hij ligt op de intensive care.'

'Jezus,' zegt Yolanda. Ze heeft haar moeder nog gebeld, vlak
voor ze vertrokken. Alles was goed. Papa was het gras aan het
maaien.

'Het zag er even heel kritiek uit,' vervolgt Annemarieke, 'hij
was bijna dood.'

'En nu?'

'Hij ligt op de intensive care.'

'Moeten we terugkomen?' vraagt Yolanda.

'Dat weet ik niet,' antwoordt Annemarieke. 'Hij is stabiel nu, bij bewustzijn gelukkig. Hij heeft een dag in coma gelegen.'

'Hoe is mama?' Yolanda probeert na te denken. Het lukt niet. Daarnet was ze nog gelukkig. Ze voelt zich schuldig. Ze is nog steeds gelukkig. Ze wil Ronald bellen, haar kinderen om zich heen. Zwemmen, ballen, zonnebaden, een glaasje voor de tent, aan niets anders denken dan de koude douche van daarnet.

'Mama is in het ziekenhuis, met Jan-Fred.'

'Met Jan-Fred?'

'Hij is terug. Alles opgebiecht, en we gaan verder. Ik heb geen zin om te scheiden. Het kost alleen maar geld. En waar ging het nou om? Een beetje neuken met een ander wijf. Ik zit er niet mee. Als ik nog eens een leuke tuinman tegenkom, ga ik ook vreemd. Dat hebben we zo afgesproken.'

'Ooh,' zegt Yolanda. Ze ziet een colonne rode mieren over de kampeertafel trekken. Ze vervoeren een paar broodkruimels. 'Ik zal met Ronald overleggen wat we doen.'

'Joh, als je terugkomt, kun je niets doen, hoor. Hij ligt aan allerlei machines. Als hij onverhoeds verslechtert, kan ik je bellen. Maar hou dan wel je telefoon aan.' Annemarieke is weer koel als altijd. Yolanda denkt aan haar koude douche. Ondanks de hitte die nu snel in intensiteit toeneemt, is ze vanbinnen nog steeds koud. Boven de heuvels aan de overkant van het meer hangen dreigende, donkere wolken. Ze bewegen niet, maar zijn de voorbode van onweer. Yolanda staat even op het punt haar zus over de partnerruil met Babette en Luuk te vertellen, maar het lijkt wel alsof het drama uit haar systeem is weggespoeld.

'Wat is er?' vraagt Annemarieke.

'Niets,' zegt Yolanda, 'ik ben blij dat Jan-Fred weer terug is.'

'Ja, een geluk bij een ongeluk,' lacht Annemarieke. 'Nou, schat, overleg met Ronald, kijk of je in de buurt een vliegveld hebt, zodat je eventueel snel hiernaartoe kunt komen. Ik spreek Jan-Fred straks. Een vriendje van hem werkt in het ziekenhuis. Ik bel je later. Hou je taai.'

De zussen hangen op. Yolanda toetst het nummer van Ronald in en hoort zijn telefoon in de tent overgaan. Ze schiet in de lach. Ze pakt haar handdoek op en loopt naar de rand van het meer. Ze gaat in het gras liggen en kijkt naar de lucht. Ze denkt aan haar vader. Ze denkt aan zichzelf. Ze heeft ontzettend zin in drie weken niets doen. Niets is bijna als de dood zelf, maar ze voelt zich ontzettend levend. Ze wacht op het onweer.

Twee dagen voor kerst

Het was twee dagen voor kerst, het einde van de middag, en Gerda had boodschappen gedaan. Nu stond ze in de file naar de nieuwbouwwijk waar ze woonde. Op de achterbank zat Tamara in haar stoeltje op een speen te zuigen. Het regende pijpenstelen. De ruitenwissertjes van de oude Panda flapperden dapper heen en weer. Waarom regende het altijd met kerst? Gerda zuchtte. Voor haar stond een bestelbus. IN DROMEN KUN JE NIET WONEN stond er met krullende letters op de achterkant. Een meubelfirma. Iemand in de buurt die nog voor kerst het nieuwe bankstel binnenkreeg.

Ineens kwam haar over de lege rijbaan links van haar een auto tegemoet die ze kende. Een zwarte Hyundai Tucson. Koen. Nee. Koen was nog op de zaak. Die kon hooguit achter haar in de file staan. Maar het was Koen; in een flits zag ze hem zitten, rechtop, de armen gestrekt naar het stuur. 'Kijk, papa,' hoorde ze zichzelf tegen Tamara zeggen, en ze tilde haar hand van het stuur om te zwaaien, een pure reflex. In dezelfde seconde zag ze dat Koen niet alleen was, er zat een blonde vrouw naast hem. Ze vergiste zich niet. Een blonde vrouw in iets roods. Ze had haar gezicht naar Koen gekeerd, ze had haar mond opengesperd. In de achteruitkijkspiegel zag

Gerda de Tucson de rotonde op draaien en rechts afslaan, naar de snelweg. Op de achterruit zat de sticker van Corsica Ferries. Daar waren ze van de zomer geweest.

Haar hart sloeg over.

De bus voor haar schoof een stukje op, en Gerda liet een gat vallen om snel uit de file te draaien en achter Koen aan te gaan. Het plan had bezit van haar genomen voor ze er erg in had. Maar ze lette niet goed op, en botste met de rechterkant van de Panda tegen de bestelbus op, niet hard, maar toch, ze hoorde van alles kraken. Shit! Achter haar begon Tamara te huilen, en auto's toeterden. De bestuurder van de bus stapte uit, een lange slungel. Hij kwam zonder haast door de regen haar kant op, maar eerst stond hij nog een tijdje stil bij zijn achterbumper. Gerda draaide zich om en zocht tussen de boodschappen naar de speen van Tamara. Toen ze hem had, stopte ze hem eerst in haar eigen mond en toen in die van haar dochter. Ze stapte uit. 'Goed gedaan, mevrouwtje,' zei de slungel.

Ze zag het in een oogopslag. De bestelbus mankeerde niets, en haar koplamp lag eruit. Auto's die achter haar hadden gestaan, wurmden zich over de andere weghelft langs hen heen. 'Wat nu?' hoorde ze zichzelf boven de herrie uit roepen. De slungel zat op zijn hurken bij zijn achterbumper en liet zijn vingers over de lak glijden. Het deed Gerda met een schok aan seks denken, zo sensueel zag het eruit. Onmiddellijk daarna zag ze de vrouw naast Koen weer. Die rode mond. Het zou toch niet waar zijn dat...? Ze durfde het niet te denken. Ze moest hem bellen. Nu.

'Een kras,' hoorde ze de jongen zeggen.

Ze hurkte met tegenzin naast hem neer. Hij had gelijk. Er zat een krasje op zijn bumper. Maar die kras kon er al maanden zitten. Ze probeerde een verband te leggen met haar eigen schade en hoorde Tamara weer huilen. Bellen, ze moest Koen bellen.

'Zullen we de papieren er maar even bij pakken?' stelde de slungel voor. Hij keek haar aan. Zijn gezicht was heel dichtbij. De regen droop over zijn wangen. Hij had aardige, blauwe ogen, en lange wimpers. Gerda vergat even waar ze was.

De jongen keek naar haar koplamp die kapot was. 'Dat ziet er beroerd uit,' zei hij, 'maar ja, wat ging je nou ook doen, hè? Jouw fout. Weet je wat. We laten de papieren zitten.'

Ze kon hem wel zoenen. In plaats daarvan veerde ze overeind. 'Dankjewel,' zei ze.

'Volgende keer niet meer inhalen,' zei de slungel over zijn schouder, terwijl hij wegliep om in te stappen. Gerda wilde hem achterna om uit te leggen dat ze hem niet in ging halen, maar dat ze achter haar man aan wilde die met een vreemde vrouw naast zich voorbij was gekomen, maar dat sloeg nergens op. Ze stapte in haar auto en trok voorzichtig op. Haar rechterhand grabbelde in haar handtas, op zoek naar haar mobieltje. Ze rook dat Tamara het in haar broek had gedaan. De ramen van de Panda besloegen. Ze kwam weer stil te staan, en toetste het nummer van Koen in. Haar hart bonkte ritmisch mee met de tringel die overging. Maar Koen nam niet op. Ze kreeg zijn voicemail.

*

Het eerste wat ze thuis deed, was Tamara een schone luier geven. De kleine zat onder, en ze had ook nog eens overal uitslag. Gerda had moeite haar gedachten erbij te houden, maar ze was een goeie moeder; ze kon twee dingen tegelijk: aan Koen denken en lief zijn voor Tamara. Ze waste de billetjes, poederde de uitslag, prietpraatte tot de kleine tot bedaren was gekomen, deed haar een nieuwe luier om, trok haar een schoon broekje aan, en hup – klaar was het alweer. Tamara glunderde opgelucht, en Gerda vergat even dat ze zich zorgen om Koen maakte, en tilde haar dochter op om haar te knuffelen. Er ging toch niets boven je eigen kind.

Met Tamara op haar arm liep ze naar de trap. Bij het passeren van de slaapkamer zag ze dat het bed beslapen was. Ze wist toch zeker dat ze het vanochtend had opgemaakt, maar de sprei vertoonde duidelijk de kuilen van een lichaam. 'Het moet toch niet gekker worden,' mompelde ze tegen zichzelf terwijl ze de slaapkamer even snel inspecteerde. Er was verder niets bijzonders. Hun trouwfoto stond gewoon rechtop op de televisie. Ze keek er even naar. Ze waren nog maar vier jaar getrouwd, maar het leek al een eeuwigheid. Wat waren ze jong, Koen met het vlinderstrikje dat scheef zat. Waar was hij?

Beneden zette ze Tamara in de box. Vrijwel onmiddellijk begon ze weer te huilen. 'Mama gaat zo eten maken,' zei ze, 'eerst de boodschappen uit de auto halen en papa bellen.' Ze had ineens zo'n haast dat ze al hollend bijna tegen de glazen keukendeur liep. Al dat glas ook in huis, het was soms net alsof ze in een aquarium woonden. En het ergste was nog dat de buren ook zo'n glazen doos hadden. Soms zaten ze gewoon naar elkaar te zwaaien. Best aardige mensen, maar niet echt Gerda's stijl: iets te openhartig, iets te makkelijk, iets te snel met de rosé en de gezelligheid, Suzan bovendien altijd in veel te open jurkjes, altijd maar met haar tieten schuddend, Toni het type toffe gozer.

Ze pakte haar mobiel en toetste Koens nummer weer in. Geen gehoor. Woedend gooide ze de telefoon op de grond, en dat was nou ook weer niet handig. Kapot. Ze tilde de boodschappen uit de auto en bracht ze naar de keuken. Zou Koen haar bedriegen? Ze had zich eigenlijk nog nooit afgevraagd of hij dat ooit zou kunnen. Maar waarom niet? De laatste tijd zeurde hij steeds vaker over seks, en een paar weken geleden wilde hij zelfs een pornootje met haar kijken. Ze hadden er vreselijk ruzie over gemaakt. Aan de andere kant: Koen was nou ook weer niet het type dat dan meteen maar een vriendin zou nemen. Hoe zou hij er trouwens eentje moeten vinden? Ze kon zich er geen voorstelling van maken. Daar werd ze nog onrustiger van.

Ze deed de lichtjes van de kerstboom aan, en zag ze weerspiegeld in haar eigen ruiten en die van de buren. Als die hun boom, een veel grotere natuurlijk, aandeden en ze lieten allebei de gordijnen open, was het net alsof ze samen een grote oliebollenkraam vormden.

De huistelefoon ging.

Ze schrok gruwelijk.

Het was haar moeder, die vaak rond etenstijd belde. 'Hoi, mam,' zei ze. 'Hoe is het? Wat hebben jullie gedaan?' Haar vader was sinds kort gepensioneerd.

'We zijn vandaag eens lekker thuisgebleven,' begon haar moeder. Ze had de gewoonte zeer uitgebreid verslag te doen van haar dagen.

'Mam, ik bel je straks terug,' sneed Gerda haar de pas af, 'ik sta te koken. Tamara moet eten.'

Haar moeder wilde iets zeggen, maar op de achtergrond bromde haar vader. Die luisterde vaak mee op een ander toestel. 'Oké, schat,' zei haar moeder teleurgesteld, 'dan bellen we later wel. Kusje voor Tamara.' En ze hing op. Gerda ook, maar ze had niet in de gaten dat ze de hoorn net naast de haak legde. Ze kreunde. Ze kon zich levendig voorstellen hoe haar ouders nu kibbelden. Papa die zei dat mama haar dochter met rust moest laten, mama die tegenwierp dat Gerda het toch altijd zo gezellig vond als ze belde, enzovoorts. Koen? Waar was hij? Wat was er aan de hand? Ze holde ineens de trap op en stormde zijn werkkamer binnen. Zijn computer stond aan. Ze ging erachter zitten, en scrolde door zijn mail. Haar vingers trilden, de muis werd nat. Maar ze vond niets, omdat ze niet wist waar ze naar zocht. Veel spam van Viagra, berichten van de zaak, een mailtje van ene Anja. Ze haalde diep adem en klikte het open. Het bleek de secretaresse van Jan-Willem, de baas van Koen; ze vroeg of hij voor oud en nieuw nog tijd had om met sales te praten. Groetjes. Gerda trok een bureaula open. Beneden begon Tamara te gillen.

Ze rommelde door paperassen, visitekaartjes, folders. Wat een rommel maakte haar man ervan. Toen zag ze ineens rechts van zijn computer, naast een grote foto van Tamara, zijn mobiele telefoon liggen. Nu werd het wel heel gek. Ze pakte het toestel en zag dat ze zelf twee keer had gebeld. Ze ging door het telefoonboek. Niets bijzonders. Ze bekeek wie hij het laatst gebeld had. Gerda. 9.13. Dat was vanochtend geweest. Hij had gevraagd of ze scheerzeep voor hem mee wilde nemen als ze boodschappen ging doen. Had ze gedaan natuurlijk, en mesjes ook voor de zekerheid, en voor haarzelf ook, want ze had zich voorgenomen haar benen weer eens mooi glad te maken en voor kerst een mooi nieuw setje ondergoed te kopen. Verdomme, waar deed ze het allemaal voor? Ze holde de trap af, en struikelde op de laatste trede. Ze viel zo'n beetje de woonkamer binnen.

*

Oké, wat moest ze doen? De politie bellen? Misschien was er iets gebeurd. Hoe kon het trouwens dat zijn telefoon thuis lag? Toen hij haar belde, was zij thuis, en hij onderweg naar de zaak. Hij was dus eerder thuisgekomen. Dat gebeurde nooit. Misschien voelde hij zich niet lekker. Of wilde hij haar verrassen, zo vlak voor kerst. Nee, dat laatste niet, want hij had het beredruk. Wat dan? Een ander? In hun eigen huis? Ze had Tamara te eten gegeven, in bad gestopt en in slaap gezongen. Nu dronk ze een glaasje wijn, de gordijnen dicht. Ze had geen licht aangedaan.

Ze keek naar de feestelijke kerstboom, de lampjes, de glinsterende ballen, de piek die nog van haar oma was geweest. Waar was Koen? Ze had het gevoel dat haar leven op het punt stond in te storten. Je las wel eens over mannen die even een pakje sigaretten gingen halen en daarna nooit meer thuiskwamen. Nee, dat was het niet. Zo was Koen niet, en bovendien had er een vrouw bij hem in de auto gezeten. Ze wist toch zeker dat hij het was? Ja. Honderd procent. Als ze haar ogen dichtdeed, zag ze hem voorbijrijden, de vrouw naast hem, het blonde gezicht naar hem toegekeerd, de mond open. Was het Suzan, de buurvrouw? Ze keek door de gordijnen. Bij de buren was het donker. Niemand thuis. Toch vreemd. Ze waren er bijna altijd, en zeker om deze tijd. Ze schonk nog maar een glaasje wijn in en zette gedachteloos met de afstandsbediening de cd-speler aan. Elvis zong kerstliedjes – grapje van Koen, die cd had hij voor de lol gekocht. Gerda begon het nu toch wel erg moeilijk te krijgen. Ze liep heen en weer door de kamer. Ze had het dan weer koud, en dan weer warm. Af en toe flitsten beelden van een naakte Koen door haar hoofd, en ze zag vrouwenvingers door zijn borsthaar kroelen, dan weer zag ze hem in een autowrak zitten, het witte gezicht opflitsend in blauw zwaailicht.

En toen hoorde ze ineens zijn auto.

De opluchting deed haar denken aan de blijdschap die ze vroeger als kind voelde als haar ouders thuiskwamen na een avondje uit. Maar meteen daarna werd ze kwaad. Ze dronk snel haar glas leeg, en ging op de bank zitten, de benen strak gekruist. Ze hoorde zijn voetstappen, de keukendeur, zijn stem. 'Ger, waar ben je?' Ze probeerde alvast iets te concluderen, zodat ze zich ergens op voor kon bereiden, maar hij klonk zoals hij altijd klonk als hij thuiskwam. Ze gaf geen antwoord. Hij stapte de woonkamer binnen. Ze zag meteen dat er iets aan de hand was.

'Waar ben je geweest? Wie zat er naast je? Ik heb jullie zien rijden.' Ze beet het hem toe.

Koen keek haar aan. 'Hoho,' zei hij rustig.

'Wat nou "hoho"? Koen! Met wie was je? Wat hebben jullie gedaan?' Ze voelde paniek door haar lichaam razen.

'Schatje toch,' zei Koen, 'ik was met Suzan. Die moest ineens dringend naar het ziekenhuis. Ze heeft een miskraam gehad.'

Gerda geloofde het niet. Maar als het een leugen was, was het wel een heel absurde. Ze aarzelde. 'Waarom had je je telefoon niet bij je?'

'Vergeten, schat, ik was vroeg thuis en zat boven wat te werken. Ineens stond ze bloedend aan de deur. We moesten meteen weg. Wil je het bloed in de auto zien?'

'Ik wist niet eens dat ze zwanger was,' kon ze nog net uitbrengen.

'Vier maanden. Ze kon Toni niet bereiken. Ik heb jou een paar keer vanuit het ziekenhuis gebeld. Ook naar de huistelefoon. Maar die was in gesprek. Ligt de hoorn ernaast of zo?'

Gerda hapte naar adem. Alles klopte. Ze had zich in haar man vergist, en in zichzelf. Tranen sprongen in haar ogen, en met trage uithalen begon ze te huilen.